UNBREAKABLE

CAROL RAYYAN

ACKNOWLEDGMENTS

A big thanks again to my wonderful friend and editor Noah Ross; We finally did it! It has been a pleasure working with you to complete this trilogy. Thank you for helping me make my dream come true.

To all of my family and friends; thank you so much for putting up with my relentless brainstorming and need for your opinions. Your patience and support helped make this possible.

And of course, to my incredible husband Isa; you made sure I pushed through to complete this series and I am so grateful to you for all of your constant love and support. I love you to pieces!

1. SEARCHING
-TRISTAN-

"Damn it! Take them," I said, rematerializing the keys from my palm and throwing them at the guards. I ran outside, but Selena was nowhere to be found.

"Where did she go?" Lexi asked breathlessly as she came running to me. Her blonde hair was a mess, her pink streak almost hidden, her brown eyes showing worry.

"I don't know!" I growled, "She teleported, God knows where." I ran down the street as if she would actually be there, helplessness urging me to keep moving. Lexi followed silently, trying to keep her panic in check. We searched the whole block, but she was long gone. My heart was consumed by fear; fear that Selena would get hurt, fear that she would hurt herself, fear that I failed her.

Selena, where are you? I sent silently, hoping she would respond. There was only silence. I tried to listen in case she had a thought about me... some way that I could mentally hear where she went, but there was nothing. If she had so much as thought my name I would have been able to hear her. Clearly, I wasn't on her mind at all.

"What the hell just happened?" Lexi finally asked.

"There's something wrong. She was acting... different." I didn't know how to explain it. I kept replaying the events that just took place, but I couldn't understand it. The mischief in her eyes as she pressed her body against mine, daring me to give in to the temptation. How quickly she became enraged when I didn't, and the way she rushed out of the room as if someone were calling to her.

"Come on, let's go back to the room and figure this out," Lexi said, bringing me back to the empty street.

I ran my hand through my hair and let out a growl of frustration. We jogged back to the hotel with tension pressing heavily on our shoulders. Lexi went to retrieve the keys, and I heard her apologize for the inconvenience. If you ask me, the only inconvenience was letting Selena get away. Now that she could teleport, who knew where she could be?

We walked back to the room in silence, and I pictured Selena's excitement as she rediscovered her powers and revealed just how powerful she truly was. She wanted me to join her, to finally be with her. I wish I could have given in; it would have been so easy, but Selena wasn't herself. And that scared me.

The door closing behind us snapped me out of my thoughts. Lexi sat on the couch in the living room. It shivered and transformed into an arm chair, and I paced in front of it.

"Okay, so explain how Selena was acting different." Lexi crossed her legs. I let out a sigh.

"She came at me, like a lioness." I cringed at the word. I couldn't explain this right. Lexi's facial expression confirmed that. It was a mask of confusion.

"Huh?" She asked.

"She," I started, but I really didn't want to talk to Lexi about this. I knew what she would say and how she would lecture me, but I also knew she needed to know how Selena changed. "She pressed herself against me and was trying to seduce me," I finished.

Lexi raised her eyebrow, "I don't see the problem here. It's about damn time one of you made the first move."

I ignored her insinuation. "Lexi, you don't understand. She wasn't being shy, cautious Selena. She was bold and fearless and when I denied her, she made the doors slam out of anger. I was actually scared."

"Well, she did just get her powers back. She was probably feeding off the high of that."

"I don't know. It's not that she had the guts to say something, it was how she said it. She was on the prowl, it was…" I let the sentence hang as I tried to find the right word.

"Hot?" Lexi supplied.

"No!" I yelled out of frustration, "It was wrong. It's not who she is and you know it."

"Are you sure? Maybe she's just tired of holding back," Lexi stood and placed her hands on her hips. "I know you guys like each other. Hell, Tristan, I know you love the girl. I just don't understand why you deny it. And that boundaries crap? What the hell is that?"

I knew she would lecture me. I tried to keep my anger in check, but couldn't.

"Lexi, enough!"

Lexi blinked and stepped back from my outburst.

"This is not the time for discussing relationships. We need to focus on finding Selena. Keep our priorities in check, damnit." I let out a slow long breath to calm my nerves. Lexi stayed silent, her lower lip protruding slightly.

"Fine," she finally said, sitting back down. She stared at the carpet, lips puckered deep in thought.

"It's just... Selena is missing," I pleaded. "We need to figure out what's wrong with her."

Lexi let out a sigh. "You're right. I'm sorry." She looked up at me. "Okay. I just don't understand how she could change so drastically. And did you see her power? I almost vomited from envy. I knew she showed a lot of potential before but... that thunderstorm was insane!"

I was immensely relieved that she followed the change of subject, though this topic was just as uncomfortable. Remembering how Selena created her own personal thunder-storm in the palm of her hands, sent shivers down my spine.

"It was also terrifying. That much power for one person, and one person who is now missing and not herself, is very bad." My stomach turned at the thought. "And you saw how she was when she tried to leave. She jerked away from you, she would never do that to you," I pointed out.

Lexi nodded in contemplation.

"Okay, I'll give you that. But how do you know she is missing? Maybe she's just exploring her powers. She'll probably be back soon." Lexi tried to comfort me, but it didn't work. "Or, can't you just teleport to her?" She added as an afterthought.

"Not without knowing where she went. Selena's teleporting is unlimited. As long as she wants to be somewhere, or if she wants to be with someone, she can teleport without having to know where it is. I need to know exactly where I'm going, or it won't work," I explained, feeling frustrated at my lack of power. "Lexi, I'm pretty sure she can read minds too."

"Yeah, I thought that might be how she was able to hear your telepathic comment to me."

"I honestly don't think there is a limit to her powers at all."

"Do you think, when Jeremiah removed the bond, he also removed all blockages of power, increasing it even more than it would have been if it developed naturally?" Lexi asked.

"I suppose that could be possible, yeah." There were too many possibilities, too many options to consider and nowhere to start.

"I think we need to pay Jeremiah a visit. Get some answers. What do you think?" Lexi asked.

"That's a good idea actually."

"Well, don't act so surprised. I have good ideas quite often." I scoffed, and we headed back to the courts.

The court building was much busier now than it had been earlier. Lexi and I had to wait fifteen minutes before we could even see a clerk. Unfortunately for us, it was the same punk who gave me a hard time that morning.

"You're back I see," the clerk said with an attitude I wanted to punch out of him.

"Clearly," I answered sarcastically. "We need to see Elder Lacour again."

"Yes, well he has left for the day."

"Already? We were just here."

"Yes, and I said he left, not that he was never here. It doesn't take quite as long to leave a building as you may imagine," he snarled. I clenched my jaw to prevent myself from doing or saying anything inappropriate.

"Do you know when he will be back?" Lexi asked.

"No," was all the kid said.

I walked away from the counter, Lexi in tow.

"What now?" She asked, a look of concentration on her face. She was obviously trying to answer her own question.

"Now, we wait until Jeremiah comes back."

"Yeah, but he might not come back for days. Who knows what the Elders' schedules are."

I let out a sigh of frustration and ran my hand through my hair. I wanted to tear it all out!

Just then I saw Victoria walking across the lobby. Her grey-streaked black hair flipped behind one ear. We met at the Bloomston festival when we were trying to find an Elder to remove the binding from Selena. I jogged toward her, not sure if Lexi was following or not, but I didn't care.

"Excuse me?" I stepped in front of Victoria, blocking her path. She startled slightly at my presence.

"Yes, I remember you, young man. What can I do for you?" She asked politely.

"Well, I wanted to thank you again for recommending Elder Lacour. He was able to help with our particular situation," I started. Victoria's eyes brightened at the news, and a small smile played on her lips. "However, there was some sort of side effect. It seems all her inhibitions have been removed."

Victoria's eyebrows pulled together, "I have never heard of that happening before. Have you asked Jeremiah about it?"

"Well, we came here to, but he's already left."

"That is an inconvenience. He has been talking for the past few weeks about his expertise on the subject, which is why I thought to recommend you to him. I'm afraid he would be the best one to see."

"Alright, thank you." That's not what I wanted to hear. I couldn't put all my hopes on Jeremiah.

"I'm sorry I couldn't be of more help," she said, her eyes crinkling as she smiled. I smiled back and she walked away.

"This is so frustrating!" Lexi grunted. I nodded in agreement.

"You're right," I said. "We don't know when Jeremiah will return, so there's no point wasting our time here. Let's go to the library and see if we can find any information there."

"Okay. It's as good a place to start as any."

The library was deserted. I almost thought it was closed and the door had been left unlocked accidentally, until I saw Mrs. Ledsmith. Her grey hair was pulled back in a bun as usual, with her glasses perched on her nose like a real-life mother goose.

"Tristan! How nice to see you again. Who's that with you?" She asked cheerfully.

"It's me, Lexi."

"Oh, Alexis! My you have grown. I haven't seen you in years." She reached over and gave Lexi a hug. "How is everything?" Mrs. Ledsmith asked, eyes boring into mine.

"Well, not as good as I'd like," I answered.

"Anything related to spell binding?" She asked, lowering her voice despite the lack of people around us.

"Somewhat. Darien had someone bind Selena's powers, but we managed to reverse the process. Only problem is Selena changed after the ritual."

"Changed how?" Concern filled Mrs. Ledsmith's tone.

"She became fierce and fearless," Lexi answered a little too enthusiastically.

"Hmm, there is a spell that comes to mind, but I don't see how it could be related to an unbinding." Mrs. Ledsmith started walking, and Lexi and I followed automatically. The book shelves were around ten feet high, and stocked fully with thousands of volumes. Sunlight soaked through the windows, giving the library a bright, warm and cozy feeling.

Mrs. Ledsmith led us to the back of the library to a black door that had a chain-linked gate locked in front of it. She waved her hand, and the gate clinked open. She then cast a silent spell to unlock the black door, and it too swung open, revealing a dim, dusty room full of boxed books.

"This is where we store any books that contain spells that are meant to harm others, or have a negative, evil effect on another witch. I trust you will not tell anyone about this room." The librarian looked over the rim of her glasses at us. We nodded in agreement. "Very well then." She moved through the boxes with ease, knowing exactly what she was looking for and where to find it.

She sifted through one of the boxes and straightened abruptly, pausing a moment before diving into the box again.

"I don't understand," she said under her breath.

"What's wrong?" I asked.

"It should be here," Mrs. Ledsmith said, burying her arms even deeper into the depths of the box. "I just saw it here."

"Can I help?" Lexi asked, standing next to the librarian. "What's the name of the book?"

"Chants of the Abyss," Mrs. Ledsmith said, and took a step back from the box. "But I doubt you'll find it. I'm afraid it's missing."

"Or stolen," I added.

"No, that can't be…" Mrs. Ledsmith let the sentence hang.

"Why not?" Lexi asked.

"This area is protected and closed to the public. No one would be able to even attempt to come in here without my knowing of it."

"Then the book should be here," Lexi said, and rummaged through the boxes.

Mrs. Ledsmith stood off to the side, eyes staring unseeingly, deep in thought.

"Excuse me," she said, and hurried out of the room.

"What's that all about?" Lexi asked. She lifted a box, placed it on the floor and sat cross-legged in front of it.

"It's an unnerving thought that someone could break into your sanctuary," I said and started looking through a box of my own.

"I'm sorry," Mrs. Ledsmith said, walking back into the room. "Something isn't right." She raised her hands, palms facing outward and closed her eyes.

A shadow flashed across the room making me step back instinctually, electricity sparking at my fingertips ready to attack.

"Calm yourself, Tristan," Mrs. Ledsmith said, eyes still closed. "It is just an imprint." Lexi stood as the shadow shimmered and lightened into a translucent image of a person. Whoever it was had no defining features, a watercolor of their true selves. "The witch's image has been shrouded," Mrs. Ledsmith said, as if reading my thoughts.

"What's an imprint?" Lexi asked, stance rigid in anticipation.

"It shows events that have come to pass, so we can see what happened here."

The figure searched through the room, strode a few steps toward the back corner and looked through the shelf. After a moment the figure searched through some of the boxes, before settling on one final box. The box with the Chants from the Abyss book contained within. The image flickered a few times before vanishing.

"Who was that?" Lexi asked, frustration in her tone.

"Could it have been Darien?" I asked. Mrs. Ledsmith shrugged in response.

"What do we do now?" Lexi asked.

"I'll go see if I can place an order for another copy. Perhaps it would be best if you came back another day."

"Are you sure that was the right book?" Lexi asked. "There are a ton here that could have the information we need."

"I appreciate your optimism, Alexis, however I know my library inside and out. I know that book is the one we need."Mrs. Ledsmith hustled out of the room.

My disappointment grew. I didn't know why I thought it would be easier to find the answer. I looked around the room one more time, scanning the books. Most of them had black covers, and seemed to be whispering, tempting us to open them. Lexi and I shared a glance before leaving the room.

"Good news is I should have another copy by tomorrow," Mrs. Ledsmith said as we approached her desk. "I'll make sure to call you the moment it comes in."

I nodded and Lexi and I left the librarian at her desk chair, slouched in thought.

"What now?" Lexi asked as we stepped into the sunlight.

"Now we wait."

2. BEHIND ENEMY LINES
-SELENA-

I teleported away from Tristan and Lexi and materialized in a forest clearing. Rich green grass grew beneath my feet. Tall, full trees encircled the area, and the sun shone down, warming my skin. I knew I was still in the Hidden City because of the perfect temperature and fresh, clean air.

Selena, where are you? I heard Tristan in my head. I snarled and ignored him.

I looked around, trying to find the person who had called me before, when a figure came out from behind a tree. As he came closer I recognized his face.

"Darien," I said.

"Hello, beautiful."

A smile crept across my face... that quickly turned into a sneer.

The wind blew around me, and I redirected it toward him, pushing him back.

"Selena, I just want to talk," he yelled through the gust. I didn't want to talk. I promised myself I would make Darien pay for taking my powers and I had every intention of following through. The wind blew harder, throwing Darien off his feet.

He stood and retaliated, waving his arms; a branch broke off one of the trees and came straight at me. I moved out of the way easily. I stood my ground; clouds rolled in, covering the bright sun, darkening the forest. Lightning cracked and I smiled. A small burst of lightning shot through a branch and struck Darien's arm. He howled in pain and grabbed his shoulder.

His eyes were wide with fear and disbelief. I suppressed a laugh. I lifted my hand so it was pointing at Darien and then I made a fist, concentrating on clenching it as tightly as possible. Darien's arms pressed to his sides, and blood rushed to his face. I reveled in literally squeezing the life out of him.

"Am I big and bad enough for you now?" I asked, smiling. I was certain he would never doubt my strength again.

"Jeremiah," he gasped, wheezing through the name. I hesitated, suddenly unsure of what I was doing. Yes, Darien harassed me, haunted my mind, sent rabid bats, but was that worth killing him? No. Then again, he did make me almost jump to my death, but I could no longer find the rage to kill him for it. I quickly released my grip and watched Darien fall to the ground gasping for air. Jeremiah walked out of the wooded area and smiled at me.

"Good choice, Selena," he praised. I smiled, wanting his approval. "We have much work to do, and killing Darien isn't on our list. I think it would be best if you apologized so we could move on," he said calmly.

I nodded eagerly. "Darien, I'm very sorry."

Darien glared at me, and then shot an angry glance at Jeremiah.

"You should have stopped her sooner," Darien chided, grabbing his ribs in pain. Jeremiah shrugged his shoulders.

"I was curious to see what she could do," he explained. Darien wheezed into an upright position, sitting on the ground. His dark eyes bore into mine and I found myself curiously drawn to him. What was it that had repulsed me before? I couldn't seem to remember. All I could focus on were his deep brown eyes, his lightly tanned complexion and his full lips.

"How did she get here so fast?" Darien asked after he caught his breath.

"Please don't talk about me like I'm not here. And I got here by teleporting."

"Ah, it's as I suspected," Jeremiah said. "Her powers are unmatched. Even when compared to the other one," Jeremiah said, talking only to Darien. I looked between the two, confused. Jeremiah went to Darien, and touched his shoulder, ribs and sides healing them immediately. It didn't even look like it took a toll on his energy the way healing usually does.

"Selena, dear," Jeremiah started. I rushed to his side. I looked up to Jeremiah like a father. I wanted to please him and make him proud. He basically brought me back to life. "We must work on our plan. Let's go." I nodded and followed obediently.

Darien walked beside me and I caught myself checking him out from the corner of my eye. His arm swung slowly by his body and I was tempted to hold his hand, to feel his skin on mine. Before I could reach out, Jeremiah spoke.

"It is nice to act upon our feelings, Selena, but wait. Soon you will have all that you desire and more." He said, looking from me to Darien. Darien nodded his head, I wasn't sure what Jeremiah meant though. Had he read my thoughts? I wanted clarification so I probed his mind.

I was hit with a mental wall. I let out a small gasp. Jeremiah looked over at me, his knowing eyes gazing into mine.

"You will soon learn that there are places you are allowed to go and others that are forbidden." He kept walking, and I stopped trying to read his thoughts.

We walked through the woods until we reached a one-story concrete building. There were a few windows set far apart with bars across them, and there didn't seem to be a front door. I followed Jeremiah to the side of the building where he swept his hand across the smooth concrete surface, making a door materialize with the action. I smiled in awe at him.

Walking inside, I found that it was one large room with white walls and concrete floors. Along the walls were papers sticking randomly to most of the surface. There were black tables set up around the room with stacks of papers on each, and about ten people poring over them, making notes.

"Welcome to our headquarters, Selena," Darien said. I smiled and looked around. At the sound of my name, everyone stopped working abruptly and stared at me. I raised my chin, met everyone's stare and relished in the attention.

"What is everyone doing?" I asked Darien after they got back to work.

"Research," he answered vaguely.

"What are they researching?" I pressed. Darien stood still and stared me down. It didn't faze me the way he thought it would. I stared back, just as confident and fearless.

"Later," he answered when he realized he couldn't intimidate me to stop inquiring. I shrugged.

"So what now?" I felt restless, I needed to do something.

"Damn it, Selena. You're like a child. Irritating and badgering. Go sit in a corner or bother Jeremiah. I don't have time for you."

I clenched my teeth in an attempt to calm myself but it didn't work. Papers flew off the walls and every table, creating a whirlwind of chaos. The lights flickered and I sneered. I was vaguely aware of everyone staring at me, most of them pressed their bodies up against the wall in an attempt to stay out of my way.

I opened my palms and fire sprang to life from my hands. The flames sprang forth from my palms towards Darien, who was trying to duck and dodge away from the inferno. Some of the papers caught fire, starting a searing blaze.

"Selena, stop!" Darien pleaded, covering his head with his arms. I kept throwing them until someone touched my arms. I looked up to see Jeremiah, and a rush of calmness poured into me. The fire dissipated and I let down my arms, bringing the wind down as well. Everyone in the room straightened up and hesitantly started moving to pick up their papers.

Jeremiah swept his hand across the room and it went back to normal. It would seem he had the same ability as Lexi to undo the effects of a spell. Jeremiah chuckled. I looked at his face with confusion.

"What a marvel! You're powers are fantastic." Then to Darien he said, "We have a lot of training to do with her. She needs to learn to control her powers, and her temper for that matter. I think it would be best if you worked with her."

Darien snarled. "No. I have more important things to attend to."

"Yes, I'm sure," Jeremiah started unconvinced, "But it would seem you have a knack for angering her. It would be the best test if she can control herself around you."

Darien clenched his jaw, and it reminded me of Tristan.

"Fine," He agreed. "Come on, Selena."

I looked at Jeremiah for permission.

"Go, practice. I want you to be the best you can be." Jeremiah smiled. I nodded and followed Darien.

We went outside behind the building. We walked through the woods until we came upon a clearing full of tents.

"This is where we sleep," Darien explained sounding bored. He kept walking until he reached a large blue tent that was pointed at the top and draping onto four poles, and then held the flap open for me. I walked in and was surprised to see that it had a bedroom, bathroom and sitting area. Darien swept his hand across the room moving the couches and tables to the side to make room in the sitting area. And probably clear anything that I could destroy or use as a weapon away from me.

"Sit down," he ordered.

I stayed standing.

He huffed and ran a hand through his hair. He paced impatiently and then turned, getting right into my face.

"Sit down so we can begin," he said through clenched teeth.

"What exactly are we going to do?"

"You need to learn to control your emotions so that you will be able to control your powers. If your magic flares up every time you get mad, you won't be able to fully control them. You want to be able to call them up at will."

"Like this?" I asked, flicking my wrist and levitating one of the couches. "I have control, Darien. You just bring out the devil in me." I smiled wickedly. A look of fear and attraction crossed his face.

"Alright. If you think you have control over your powers, then show me you won't react to this."

He looked at my feet and I felt something swipe my legs forcing me to fall. I knew Darien was instigating, trying to prove I didn't have control.

He was right.

My hands shook, my body shook. I just didn't have any control over my rage lately. I levitated the couch again and threw it at him. He barely moved out of the way in time.

"Control my ass," he sneered as the couch crashed to the ground.

"Well, tell me what to do then," I said defeated. I didn't have the slightest idea how to reel in my anger.

"For starters, you can breathe," he instructed. I took a deep breath and did feel better. "Then you have to stop and think instead of just reacting. You need to assess the situation and act appropriately. Otherwise a lot of people you didn't mean to hurt could wind up injured or dead."

I knew this should have bothered me. I never wanted innocent people to get hurt. Today though, I couldn't care less. It would be their fault for getting in my way. Why did Darien care if anyone got hurt anyway? I shrugged.

"Whatever," I said.

Darien growled out of frustration.

"Just breathe, Darien," I said sarcastically. Darien stood tall and again I felt myself losing my balance and falling.

I stood up quickly, ready to throw a spell at him, but then I stopped and thought like he told me to.

Then I punched him.

In the face.

Darien grabbed at his nose, and I saw blood trickle down out of it. I smiled in satisfaction.

"At least I didn't use magic."

"It's the same concept!" He yelled, rushing to the bathroom.

Selena, be nice. I heard Jeremiah in my head as Darien washed up. The familiar sound was comforting, and a feeling of longing washed over me again. When Darien came out of the bathroom, his nose had stopped bleeding, but it was crooked. I had broken it. Instead of feeling smug, I felt guilt. I couldn't seem to figure out my emotions. One minute I wanted to kill Darien, the next I wanted to kiss him.

I walked to him and raised my hand. Darien flinched reflexively.

"I won't hurt you," I whispered. I slowly raised my hand to his nose and imagined that it was straight and healed. With a snap and a grunt from Darien, it was back to normal.

"Thanks?" He said, making it sound like a question. No doubt he was as confused with my mood swings as I was.

I sat down on the floor. "Okay, let's get this done."

Darien's eyebrows rose in confusion, but he sat down across from me.

For the next few hours I practiced keeping my cool. Darien would throw spells at me or mean remarks, and I had to teach myself not to react violently, at least not right away. The hard part was getting myself to stop, think and rationalize the situation. After that, I pretty much had it down. No matter what Darien did or said to get a rise out of me, I stayed calm and took it. I didn't forget though, and I was still able to retaliate at will.

"Are you done now?" I asked after Darien tested my temper yet again.

"I guess," he said.

"Good." I waved my hand, flinging him onto the one couch I hadn't thrown across the room. Darien's eyes widened with surprise. Once he landed safely on the cushions he flicked his own hand at me and I flew toward him. I was expecting to land hard on his body, but before I did, my descent slowed, and I landed softly on top of him.

"Like that?" He asked smiling.

"Very smooth," I responded. Feeling his body beneath me, I tensed. My attraction to Darien became impossible to resist and I found myself lowering my face to his. When our faces were inches apart, Darien grabbed the back of my head and pushed it down so our lips met. There was no softness, just passion. It was like an inexplicable hunger. Our kisses became fierce. One of Darien's hands was tangled in my hair, the other trailing down my body keeping us close together.

An image of Tristan came to mind and then just as quickly it was gone. I stopped kissing Darien abruptly. We lay there, my body on top of Darien's, both breathing heavily. My head was foggy and I felt very confused.

Why had I been kissing Darien? Why did I stop? I couldn't seem to focus long enough on any one question before another one popped in my head.

"Selena?" Darien asked speculatively.

"Yes?" I answered, my mind still a jumbled mess. What had I just been thinking about? There was an ache in my chest I couldn't explain. I felt like I was forgetting something important. Like I was missing a part of me.

"Come here," Darien whispered, pulling me down so I rested on his chest. The feeling was familiar, but I couldn't place it. It didn't get rid of the ache.

3. WHY SO CRYPTIC?

-TRISTAN-

It was 9 am, after three cups of coffee -- the caffeine a mistake I had realized in hind sight since our nerves were already stretched to their limits-- when Mrs. Ledsmith finally called. Lexi and I were out the door minutes later.

We rushed through the main doors to find Mrs. Ledsmith waiting for us in the lobby. Her shoulders bunched as she gave a tight-lipped smile.

"It's here," she said with minimal relief. We followed her to the back room, where the dark magic books were kept hidden. Mrs. Ledsmith turned and held up a black leather-bound book, flipping through the pages in silence. When she found what she was looking for, she handed the book to me.

I took it and read the page. Lexi stood next to me to read as well.

The heading was, `Implant Awakening`, and below it read;

`Enables the spell caster to control the subject and implant thoughts or ideas in their minds that they normally would not have.`

Following was a list of ingredients, which included candles to call the elements.

"What was the Herkimer diamond for then?" I asked after I noticed its absence from the ingredients list.

"I believe it was for this," Mrs. Ledsmith took the book and flipped through a few more pages and pointed to a spell that could awaken one's inner feelings and remove any fears or conscience so they can act upon them.

This spell required the candles... and a Herkimer diamond. The very stone Jeremiah had given us a riddle to find. The riddle that led Selena, Lexi, Genevieve, Lachlan and myself to go grave-digging and almost die fighting shadow men. Below the ingredients was an incantation in Latin. As I read the words, there were a few that struck me as familiar.

"Son of a bitch," Lexi whispered. "He merged the unbind-ing spell with these two spells."

"How is that possible?" I asked through clenched teeth.

"Jeremiah must be skilled in spell-fusion," Mrs. Ledsmith said, earning blank stares from Lexi and I. "It's a very rare gift."

"I thought spell-fusing died thousands of years ago," I said.

"Apparently not," Mrs. Ledsmith said, coming to look over my shoulder. "You can clearly see that he wove these three spells together."

"Wait," Lexi said. "What's the big deal? What can Jeremiah do with spell-fusion?"

"The question isn't what he *can* do, but rather what he *can't* do," Mrs. Ledsmith said. "Think of the endless possibilities merging spells could provide."

"We really have no idea what we're up against, do we?" I asked, almost under my breath.

Lexi shook her head. "I wish I spoke Latin," she said. "All I know is that bastard definitely said these words."

"How did I miss that?" I growled, translating the incantation in my head. They pretty much explained what the spell was doing. I remembered hearing Jeremiah say something about awakening in Latin, but Selena's pain was distracting. I was even more consumed when I heard her thought about trying not to scream so she wouldn't scare me. The memory made my heart ache. It also made me realize why I shouldn't love Selena. "Damn it, Lexi, I failed," I said disgusted with myself.

"We both failed."

"No, you can't speak Latin; you wouldn't have known anyway."

"Tristan, you only know the basics. Don't flatter yourself by thinking you're fluent. And don't be so hard on yourself, okay?" Lexi placed her hand on my shoulder for comfort. She was right; I did only know the basics, but it should have been enough for me to hear his intentions. I moved away from Lexi and started pacing.

"What does this mean?" I thought aloud.

"What does what mean?" Lexi asked.

"Was Jeremiah the Elder who bound Selena? Is he in alliance with Darien?" I processed, my gut sinking as the thoughts kept coming.

"It would make the most sense. And he is now controlling some of her thoughts and actions, which is why she brushed me off so easily and probably why she wanted to leave so abruptly.

But it was her own feelings she was acting on when she came on to you," Lexi answered.

"But why would he unbind Selena's powers. Why not keep her bound, so she could die?" I asked, a memory fluttering through my mind. I pushed it aside.

"Why kill something when you can use it yourself?" Mrs. Ledsmith, who had been quietly observing our brainstorming, spoke up. "If she is as powerful as the prophecy says, it would be a shame to kill her. If he has control over all her power on his side, he will be indestructible."

"Damn it!" I yelled, throwing the book across the room. "How could I not see through his façade?" I pushed a stack of books off the table and they landed on the floor with a thud. I took a deep breath and sent an apologetic glance to Mrs. Ledsmith, who nodded. She waved her hand over the spilled books and they righted themselves.

"So it's very possible that Selena is with Darien or Jeremiah?" Lexi asked.

"I think so. I wish I had her ability to teleport to a person. This would be so much easier."

"Does the book say anything about how to break the spell?"

I admired Lexi for keeping her cool and thinking clearly. I walked across the room and picked up the book. I found the page and read through it. There was nothing there on how to break the spell. I looked to Mrs. Ledsmith.

"I'm afraid I don't know that answer, but when I ordered the Chants from the Abyss, I noticed the author had also written a second book. I ordered it as well, in the off chance it could offer further information. It hasn't arrived yet, but you are welcome to sift through these until it does if you like." Mrs. Ledsmith said.

I nodded, "Thank you. That would be helpful." We had nowhere else to look at this point, and couldn't know for sure that this second book could even help.

"Let me know when you're finished so I can lock up." Mrs. Ledsmith smiled and left Lexi and I to search.

We had been searching through the boxes for hours and I was about ready to lose my mind. Each book I sifted through had tons of dark magic. I couldn't believe people capable of doing these things to each other. I completely understood why these books would be kept away from the general public, but it was still unsettling that they existed at all.

"It doesn't make sense that the counter curse wouldn't be listed under the original spell," I said through clenched teeth. I had searched that book dozens of times, hoping that I would find something new.

"I know," Lexi said, sounding distant as she studied a book of her own. "There is something interesting here though," she finished.

"A way to break the spell?" I asked, not daring to get my hopes up as I walked toward Lexi. She shook her head no, and my heart sank.

"I found a locator spell though. It seems simple enough."

I looked over her shoulder to read the ritual. All we needed was a personal item of Selena's, two white candles, a pendulum and a map of the area we wanted to search.

"Perfect. It might be the fastest way to find Selena. Make a note of the incantation. We'll do the ritual once we get back to the hotel."

Lexi nodded and started typing the spell into her cell phone. I paced the room thinking of any place I failed to look. A thought occurred to me then, and I wanted to kick myself for not thinking of it sooner. "Lexi, can you cast a detection spell to find the counter curse we're looking for?"

Lexi looked up from her cell phone and thought for a moment before answering.

"I'm not sure. It won't hurt to try though." She put her phone and the book down and stood up. Closing her eyes, Lexi took a deep breath and concentrated. She held out her hands and started feeling for any sign that the book we were looking for was in that room. "I think I sense something. Hang on," she said.

"Oh!" I heard Mrs. Ledsmith cry from just outside the doorway. I ran out of the room just in time to see the small, black book in her hands shake and shoot out right into Lexi's hand.

She let out a sigh of satisfaction and opened her eyes.

"Well!" Mrs. Ledsmith said in exasperation. "I was about to come and tell you the second book arrived, but it seems you've found it yourselves."

I couldn't help but smile. The anticipation of finally seeing the counter curse was almost too much to bear. Lexi flipped through the pages, just as anxious as I was.

"Here it is," she said in a whisper, as if scared to believe it could be right there in front of us. We read the scrawl together and my heart sank.

"What does that mean?" I asked, frustration building inside me. Lexi shook her head and read the words out loud.

"'With truth comes freedom.' Maybe if we tell her Jeremiah is controlling her it will snap her out of it?" She asked hopefully.

I shook my head, "It can't be that easy. This has to be some deeper truth, or…something." I clenched my jaw, and willed my brain to solve this riddle, but I came up blank. I took the book from Lexi and read the page, hoping to find something else. I flipped through the adjacent pages but nothing else was relevant. That one sentence was all we had to go on.

"Why don't we call it a day, grab some food and try to figure it out tonight?" Lexi said, stretching and walking toward the door. "At least we can try to find Selena in the meantime." I nodded and followed her out. Mrs. Ledsmith locked the door behind us.

I tried not to focus on the confusing counter curse. It was only going to drive me crazy. Instead I was looking forward to trying the locator spell so I could at least have the peace of mind of knowing where Selena was.

"What is that?" Lexi asked squinting as we approached the car. I looked in the direction Lexi indicated but saw nothing.

"What?" I asked, becoming highly alert for any threat. Lexi walked to the back door of the car and opened it. Lying on the seat was the ring Selena's mother had left her and the necklace I bought her.

"Why didn't she put them back on?" Lexi asked confused as she lifted the items and placed them in her palm.

I thought about it a moment then sighed. "Jeremiah's spell must repel protective charms," I answered, finally realizing why he had her take them off in the first place. "I think if Selena wears them, then it will protect her at least in part from Jeremiah's influence."

"Even her mother's ring? It's not protective is it?" She played with the ring trying to figure it out.

"In a way, it is. It was infused with a comforting spell, remember?" I answered. "When it helped her deal with Crystal and Yuri's deaths by showing her how bad they were and how many more witches they would have killed if they were still alive, it protected her frame of mind. Protected her conscience."

"Oh. So what if we get her to put them on now? Will that break the spell?"

"I doubt it. It might hinder it though." I shook my head and got in the driver's seat. Lexi sat in the passenger side, placing the jewelry in her pocket.

"So, food and then hotel?" Lexi asked, buckling her seatbelt.

I nodded, "Yes, then we're going to get Selena back."

We grabbed some sandwiches and ate quickly as we headed back to the hotel, though, having no appetite, I had to force mine down.

Things felt so different without Selena, and I felt a surge of emotion just thinking of her. I was angry at Jeremiah and Darien for taking her, angry at myself for not seeing it sooner, and angry that I just didn't give in to her when she wanted me. My longing for her was growing and I would live to regret not telling her my feelings. Damn my stupid boundaries rule.

"I'm going to get two white candles," Lexi said. "Pass me the map, would you?" Lexi pointed to the worn, folded map sitting on the side table. I passed it to her, and she kept talking. "I also need a pendulum. You don't have one, do you?" She spread the map flat on the table.

"No, sorry," I answered, "What if she's not in the Hidden City anymore?" I asked as an afterthought.

"Then the spell will tell us. At least we have somewhere to start. And we can go through as many maps as we need to in order to find her, okay?" Lexi placed her hand on my arm in an attempt to comfort me. Surprisingly it helped...well a little anyway. She bounded out the door in a flash, and I sat down in front of the map to wait for her.

I traced the circles we'd drawn around the cemeteries on the map with my finger, and remembered how brave Selena had been to jump in grave after grave those nights. She was so strong and determined, even with her powers bound and her energy draining. I thought of my mother then, and remembered how she looked in her final days. The binding spell had literally sucked the life out of her.

I just couldn't bear to tell Selena when she was trying to meditate her way out of the binding. I wish I had known a way to save my mother, but I would lose her again if it meant we would save Selena.

The door snapped open, breaking my train of thought as Lexi jumped in with two white candles and a quartz stone hanging from a silver chain.

"No sense in wasting any time. Are you ready to find her?" Lexi asked, reviewing the spell on her phone.

"Absolutely."

She placed each candle at either side of the map and as she lit them, said and incantation in Latin. Then she took Selena's ring and placed it in the center of the map.

"This is a token of Selena's, guide us to where she hides."

Then she sat in front of the map and gently swung the pendulum so it moved in a clockwise motion. As it swirled, Lexi spoke another incantation, this time in a language I didn't recognize. Suddenly the pendulum started spinning erratically, a gust of wind swept through the room almost extinguishing the candles, and almost blowing the map off the table. I quickly placed my hand on the paper to keep it in place. The pendulum flew from Lexi's fingers and landed on the top part of the map, drawn to it like a magnet. The wind vanished, the candles resumed their slow burning and calm was restored. The pendulum had landed on Caeruleus Caligo Sylva.

Lexi squinted, trying to read the unfamiliar words. "What does that mean?" she asked.

"The Blue Mist Forest. Let's go," I said, standing abruptly, holding my hand out to Lexi so we could teleport.

"Wait," Lexi started, as she stood next to me. "We don't even have a plan. She won't be alone. Jeremiah will most likely be there, and Darien and God knows who else. We have to be smart. Not to mention we still don't know how to break Jeremiah's spell."

I ran my hand through my hair and let out a sigh of frustration. I didn't care about a plan; I just wanted Selena back,

31

the old Selena back safe and sound. But Lexi was right. I reluctantly sat down on the couch and placed my head in my hands.

"Okay, here's the plan," I started after a few moments of silence. "I will call Lachlan and Genevieve, run all this by them and see what they think about the counter curse. Then when we have the details set, I will teleport us just outside the forest and we will sneak in and figure out how many people there are and what our course of action will be then."

"Now you're thinking." Lexi smiled. I took out my cell and dialed the number.

"Selena did what?" Lachlan asked in disbelief. He and Genevieve had come over right after I called, always willing to help. Lachlan's short, curly red hair and freckles complimented his Scottish heritage. Genevieve's green eyes widened in surprise at the news. They sat side by side on the couch as I paced in front of them and Lexi sat on the chair to their right.

"She is with Darien and Jeremiah, but it's not her fault," I explained. "Jeremiah cast a spell on her that allows him to control her mind." My heart sank as the words rolled off my tongue.

"Alright, so how do we break the spell?" Genevieve asked, flicking her platinum hair over her shoulder.

"Well," Lexi started, but the disappointment was evident in her tone. "We found…something. I guess you could call it a counter curse but we're not sure what it means."

Lachlan and Genevieve exchanged confused glances and then looked back at me.

"All we found was a sentence: 'With truth comes freedom'" I cringed, angry at those four stupid words that were supposed to help bring Selena back.

"Is there anythin' else?" Lachlan asked eagerly.

"No. That's it," Lexi said. "Which is why we are confused. You guys have any ideas?" She asked hopefully. Lachlan and Genevieve sat quietly, thinking it through.

"Well, what is the one truth that Selena needs to know?" Genevieve finally asked, breaking the heavy silence.

We all sat in silence.

"I do have a theory," Lexi said.

"Well?" I pressed.

"You're not going to like it."

I stared at Lexi, waiting for her to continue.

"Maybe the way you feel about her?" Lexi answered, staring me down. I clenched my jaw.

"Not this again!" I threw my hands up in the air. "That has nothing to do with anything. I am here to protect her, that's all."

Lexi scoffed, "You are so full of shit. You want to hear how I know? Alright. Take a seat and grab a notepad, 'cause I have a lot of proof coming your way," she said, crossing her arms over her chest. I looked at Genevieve and Lachlan, now at the edge of the couch, looking like they were interested in hearing Lexi's proof. I turned to Lexi quizzically. When she realized I wasn't going to sit, she continued. "How about the fact that you dated Stefania?"

"What does that have to do with anything?" I asked, anger finding its way into my voice.

"Uh, she looks exactly like Selena! Well she did when her hair was longer; think about it. She used to have long black hair, blue eyes; she was the only girl you ever dated, and she looked like Selena! Right, guys?"

Genevieve nodded and Lachlan shrugged.

"No, she didn't," I protested, but then I thought about it. There were some resemblances, but I wasn't about to admit that to Lexi.

"What about the necklace you bought her? I know you didn't buy that on this trip," Lexi drilled.

"It was for her protection, that's all," I argued, thinking of the amethyst necklace I had given Selena after Darien made her sleep walk and almost jump off the roof of our hotel. I shook off the memory. "Look, you pushed me to be with her. You literally shoved me to lay with her that one day. That was you, not me." Though to be fair, when Selena had learned that her powers were bound until her death, all I wanted to do was comfort her.

"Unbelievable!" Lexi threw her hands up. "I see the way you look at her; there is no denying that. And don't you dare tell me that you didn't enjoy staying in bed with her. She was fast asleep and you still didn't move, so don't try that macho, I don't have any feelings garbage. Just man up to it." She glared at me, and I looked away. I felt embarrassed arguing about this with Lachlan and Genevieve staring at us. Lexi did have an awful lot of evidence, though. I hadn't been hiding my feelings as well as I thought.

I thought back to how it felt to have her sleep in my arms. The feel of her body, the peaceful look she had on her face as she slept, the feeling of her soft hair through my fingers. Lexi was right. I enjoyed it, probably too much. I couldn't even bring myself to leave when Selena gave me the opportunity.

"Lexi, whether I like her or not isn't the point right now."

She stood up and walked toward me, stopping only inches away.

"Look, I already know. You and Selena are the most stubborn people I've ever met. Why do you think I sent that guy away at the club? You remember? What was his name? Something goofy... oh yeah, Chad. I did it because I knew you were into each other. You can thank me for that now by the way." She barely stopped for a breath. "I want to hear it. Just admit to me that you love her," she pressed. She was so irritating. I wanted to swat her like a fly. I cringed at the memory of Chad though, so I had to give her that one.

"No."

"Ugh! Just-" She grabbed my arm and her body tensed. Her eyes became unfocused, and she was no longer staring at me, but through me. "Lexi?" I asked, but she didn't respond.

"What's happening?" Genevieve asked, getting to her feet.

After a moment Lexi took in a deep, jagged breath as if she was just coming up from the water. Her eyes focused back on my face.

"Oh. My. God," she whispered and sat back down.

"What is it?" I asked concerned.

"I saw. I saw the truth. Tristan, when I touched you and blatantly lied to my face," she started. "I was able to see that you were lying. I saw how you really feel about Selena. Or maybe I should say I felt it. It was like I was seeing and feeling from your perspective, from inside your head."

The thought made me uneasy.

"I didn't know you guys kissed," she continued, and I was embarrassed with how much she knew. "How can you deny your feelings after that? I can't believe how full of shit you really are! I can't believe Selena didn't tell me, that ass. And I can't believe I just discovered a new power." She sat smiling, and almost hypnotically nodding her head, probably replaying what she saw in my mind. I already hated this new power of hers.

She let out a long sigh of satisfaction. "Finally," she cried. "I am going to enjoy this one." She savored the feeling for a moment. I wasn't sure if she was more satisfied that she knew how I felt about Selena or that she got a new power.

"You're a precisionist," Genevieve said to Lexi.

"Nice," she beamed.

I sighed out of frustration. "Listen. That has...there's nothing...how can...no." I didn't see the relevance of my feelings for Selena, or revealing them.

Lachlan shook his head, "Why are you still trying to deny it?"

"There has to be some deeper, more important truth that Selena needs to know," I argued.

"Alright, let's say there was something else, what would be the one thing Selena needed to know?" Genevieve asked again, thankfully veering away from my feelings. But none of us could think of anything, which caused Lexi to stare me down again.

I stared at the ceiling. "That can't be the only thing she needs to know. This isn't some stupid little fairytale where a kiss can save the girl. Give me a break!" I quickened my pacing. Genevieve raised her eyebrow and crossed her arms over her chest, Lachlan leaned back onto the couch and Lexi averted her gaze from mine.

I continued pacing and then found myself sitting on the edge of the couch-which extended to accommodate me-and staring at the wall in front of me. It's not that I didn't want to tell Selena how I felt; I just couldn't accept that how I felt was the truth she needed to know. I wracked my brain trying to think of something, anything, but I just didn't know the answer to this one.

"What about the prophecy?" Genevieve asked.

"You think that's the truth Selena needs to know?" Lachlan asked.

"No one knows where it is," Lexi answered. "Even the copy is gone."

"No," I answered. Last thing I wanted to do was reject an idea that took the focus off me, but I just didn't think that was the answer. "Selena already knows about the prophecy, and although none of us know the details of what it says, it's not the jarring, shocking truth I imagine she would need to learn."

"You might be right," Lachlan said. "We should just go to the forest and try to get her back; That way we will actually be productive rather than sitting here doin' nothin'."

Finally, something I could wrap my head around. I nodded and stood up.

"But it's too late now," Lexi added. "We should get some rest tonight and go there tomorrow. We need to be alert and well rested since we have no idea what we will be facing."

"Tomorrow? That's too long! She could be in danger or…" I stammered.

"She's fine," Lexi said. "Jeremiah went through the trouble of unbinding her powers, he's not about to kill her."

I sat back on the couch. "It's too risky," I said

"Well it's not a good idea to go there now when we're all high-strung and unrested. I promise she'll be fine." Lexi said.

I shook my head but didn't argue. I stood and paced again. To Genevieve and Lachlan I said, "You two share a bed here and I will share the other with Lexi. We leave first thing tomorrow."

"Tomorrow night. We need the cover of darkness," Lexi said.

I exploded "Are you crazy? Do you know how many things can happen in that time? We've already been away from her too long. Who knows what's happening?"

"Please Tristan, it's the smart way."

I punched the wall and ignored the pain that shot through my knuckles. Genevieve and Lachlan were startled by my outburst.

"We'll get her back," Genevieve said. "But we have to be smart and cautious."

I nodded, but not out of agreement. I just knew that it wasn't worth arguing when everyone was against my idea.

I barely slept, but the rest itself was helpful. I really wanted it to be Selena sleeping next to me instead of Lexi.

I woke to an excruciatingly long morning, followed by an excruciatingly long afternoon and then an excruciatingly long evening. It took all my effort not to teleport immediately. I wanted Selena back, I needed her back, and it had to be now.

The only things keeping me in check were my friends, who were struggling to convince me to stay the whole day.

Finally the evening sky darkened enough and I could be productive. I walked into the living room where Genevieve and Lachlan were standing ready to go.

"Do we know if she's still even there?" I asked anxiously.

"I recast the spell half an hour ago. She's still there," Lexi said. Resolve settling in her demeanor.

I looked at the map and tapped the area just outside the forest.

"We are going to start here and scout the area." I grabbed a couple of my favorite throwing knives and safely tucked them away in my jeans. "We will get any other reinforcements we need once we find out exactly what we're dealing with."

Everyone nodded in agreement and we left the hotel. As soon as we returned the keys and walked outside, I took Lachlan's arm. "Ready?" I asked him.

"Aye." I teleported us outside a wall of large oak and maple trees. We quickly scanned the area and found it deserted. Lachlan headed for cover, and I teleported back.

"Place seems empty so far," I informed the girls. I took Genevieve's arm next, and we landed beside Lachlan, and a moment later I returned with Lexi in tow.

"So, do we just start from here?" Lexi asked, craning her neck to see the tops of the large trees in front of her. I shrugged my shoulders.

"No better place I guess. We need to keep low and keep quiet," I instructed. We crept into the Caeruleus Caligo Sylva.

There was a mist in the forest that hovered over our ankles, and it slowly rose as the night went on, giving off a faint blue glow, earning its name. The dark sky overhead made it almost impossible to see.

Genevieve cursed under her breath in front of me as she tripped on a fallen tree branch.

Can I provide a little light? She asked telepathically.

Yes, but keep it dim. We don't want anyone to see us, I responded. Genevieve pointed her index and middle finger toward the ground and moved them in a circular motion. A silver stream manifested from them and fell to the ground lighting a path before us. It was bright enough that we could see where we were stepping but not so bright that anyone else would see it. I smiled at her in appreciation, cast a spell of my own to prevent anyone from seeing us, and we headed along the path.

We walked for what seemed like hours, but no one complained or even made a noise. It was completely quiet in the forest, not a bird was chirping or an animal scurrying, nothing. That's when I heard the whispers.

I stopped abruptly, earning three confused glances.

Did you hear that? I sent silently to my companions. All three of them stood completely still, listening. When I heard the whispers again, Lachlan's eyes widened, and he nodded quickly to me before instinctually retreating behind a large tree. The rest of us took cover as well, not wanting to take a chance of being caught even with my spell in place. But when the whispers got closer, we saw no one. The mist had risen to waist level, carrying the whispers with it.

After a minute the whispers faded until we were immersed in silence again. Lexi came out from behind her tree of cover and squinted at the area before us. She walked slowly, deliberately, as if she could see something the rest of us could not. She tentatively held out her hand and placed it flat against the air in front of her.

What are you doing? I asked Lexi.

Just wait. There's something here, she thought. Suddenly, from where her palm rested against what seemed like nothing, a bright golden light shimmered, spreading from her fingers outward. What once was an empty forest was now a small clearing, about a hundred feet ahead of us. In the clearing were scattered tents and behind the tents was a flat building that looked like a warehouse. "Truth will out," Lexi whispered. I was grateful for her new truth revealing powers…though I wasn't a fan when she used them against me.

"It was a cover spell," Genevieve informed us whispering. Her eyes widened in bewilderment. "If Tristan hadn't cast his cloaking spell, they could have seen us even if we couldn't see them. We could've walked right through them!"

"What now?" Lexi asked, taking cover behind a tree again. I counted the tents and wondered how many people were in each of them. We were likely in over our heads.

"We need to scout the area and see how many people are here," Lachlan answered. "We should split up. Let's walk the perimeter and meet right back here." Lachlan and Genevieve went around the south side while Lexi and I scouted the other way.

We crept silently around the clearing, automatically taking cover behind trees anytime we thought we heard a noise. By the time we reached the warehouse, we had counted ten people just out by the tents, plus another ten standing guard around the camp. No idea how many would be inside the building, but I had a feeling it was a lot more. As we reached the side of the warehouse, the door swung open and two people walked out. Lexi and I took quick cover and watched from behind the tree.

My pulse quickened when I saw that it was Selena, then I saw she was holding hands with Darien. I took a deep breath to steady myself. Darien stood in front of Selena, pressed her against the wall of the building and kissed her. I looked away, and turned back in time to see that she was kissing him back. She raised her arms and wrapped them around Darien's neck as his hands freely roamed her body. My hands began to shake, my breathing grew heavier. Lexi grabbed my arm before I could do something stupid and forced me to look at her.

I stared into her brown eyes and she silently sent, *It's not her; it's Jeremiah.* But I wasn't so sure.

Just then Selena's head snapped up and searched the trees like an eagle looking for its prey. Remembering that Selena could hear our thoughts, I cleared my mind, making it completely blank. I assumed Lexi was doing the same thing because after a few moments, Selena returned her attention to Darien. She took his hand and led him off to the tented area.

I tried not to think of what they would do in there. Hands still shaking, blood pumping so hard I could hear it surging through my body; we walked the rest of the perimeter and met back up with Lachlan and Genevieve.

"We counted fifteen witches outside," Genevieve said. "No way of telling if anyone is in the building though."

"We counted ten standing guard and ten outside the tents. Well twelve actually with Selena and Darien," I said through clenched teeth. Lachlan nodded his head.

"Aye, we saw them as well," he said, looking at his feet.

"So there are thirty-seven witches to get through, that we know of," Lexi said. "What do we do? There are only four of us." She fidgeted with her fingers, looking around for any threats.

"We wait for them to sleep, and then we get Selena," I answered. That earned me a dumbfounded look from Lexi.

"Hello? Did you not see her all cozy with Darien? What makes you think we will be able to get her away?" She had no fear of hurting my feelings.

"I don't know. Maybe I can try that telling her my feelings thing," I answered sheepishly, trying not to make eye contact with Lachlan or Genevieve.

"Ugh, you are being so stupid right now." Lexi's patience was wearing thin. "You are like a love-struck teenager, all hormones and no brain. Getting Selena to listen will be the hard part. Once she sees us, her first reaction will be to attack. Once she does that everyone awake or asleep will know we're here. We need something better."

"Lexi's right," Genevieve agreed. "We need a better plan. Maybe we should come back with more witches. I'm sure the Elders would be interested in knowing what is going on here."

"We don't have time to build an army," I hissed.

"Please, try to be smart about this," Genevieve pleaded, no doubt worried I would lead them to their deaths.

I clenched my jaw, "Alright, what do you propose we do? Something a bit more time-conscious than creating an army, please."

"We cast a sleeping spell," Lachlan, who had been quiet for the past few minutes, finally spoke up. I looked at him, waiting for more information.

When he didn't continue, I prodded, "I can't cast a sleeping spell, well at least not on forty people. How can that work?"

"I can," he answered. "I will be able to put this whole camp to sleep, and keep them that way no matter the noise, but I can only hold it for fifteen minutes. Everyone will be in a deep sleep except Selena. Will that give you enough time to go to her and tell her what you need to?"

"I hope so," I answered, my anxiety rose with the thought of having to open up to Selena. I wasn't sure if I would be able to do it.

"You can do this," Lexi said as if reading my thoughts. "You have to at least try. It could save her."

As the reality of Lexi's words sank in, my resolve grew. I could and would do this. I had to. For Selena.

"Alright, time to put this camp to sleep. Are you ready?" Lachlan asked.

"Absolutely."

4. FINALLY
-SELENA-

I followed Darien to the tent and sat on the bed.

"Tomorrow will be a busy day," he said, laying on the bed beside me.

"What's first on the agenda?" I asked. Darien took a moment to respond.

"What was I saying?" Darien asked through a large yawn.

"You were starting to tell me about tomorrow's plan," I reminded him, feeling unreasonably impatient.

"Oh…right." Darien's eyes drifted closed. I nudged him to wake up, but he was passed out.

"Hello?" I called in his ear, but he didn't so much as twitch. What the hell was his problem? I tried pushing him again, and when he still didn't wake, I pushed him right off the bed. He landed on the floor with a loud *thud* but still didn't wake. I laughed.

Selena? I heard a familiar voice inside my head, but I couldn't place who it was.

"Who is that?" I asked out loud. I could feel his proximity to me. My skin tingled with anticipation, but I had no idea who it tingled for.

I need to speak to you. Can you please come outside? I weighed my options. I had no idea who this person was or what they wanted, so I carefully left the tent, making sure no one was hiding in the shadows. Once I was outside however, I saw I had nothing to worry about. No one was around. I stood tall, taking in my surroundings, looking for the voice.

"Show yourself," I ordered into the dark night. Then in a flash, a man stood before me. His green eyes so familiar, but I had never met him before. He raked a hand through his shaggy hair and he looked me straight in the eye. He swallowed hard once before speaking out loud.

"Selena, I know you probably don't want to see me right now, but there's something you need to know." He swallowed again and took a deep breath. But before he could speak, a tendril of recognition seeped through my mind. I knew him. I couldn't remember his name, but I remember him hurting me. The details were fuzzy, but all I knew was that he betrayed me somehow.

Rage soared through me and I no longer wanted to hear what he had to say. I swept my arm out in front of me and the man went flying. He landed hard on the ground and I almost smiled.

Jeremiah is awake! I heard someone tell the man telepathically.

"And why wouldn't he be awake?" I asked the night, and those lurking in its shadows. "Come out and face me!" I called as I pressed my hands together. It took some effort but the action forced my attackers out of hiding. There were four of them in total. I knew them; Lexi with her stupid angelic face, Genevieve with her blazing determination and platinum hair, Lachlan with his red curls and freckles, but the last man, him I could not place.

"Please just listen," Lexi pleaded. "We're trying to help you." But I wasn't interested.

"There's nothing to help with. Go home," I yelled. Just then Jeremiah stepped behind me and placed a hand on my shoulder. Suddenly my anger became fury, my face contorted into a snarl and I called on the wind to force these people away. The wind blew fierce, and with a sweep of my hand, it rushed forward, knocking all four of them down.

Lexi stood up first, creating a sphere shield around her and the others. I rolled my eyes out of frustration. I created lightning and sent it crackling down from the sky, but it didn't even put a dent in their damn bubble.

"You can't stay in there forever," Jeremiah said. "You should leave or suffer the consequences." His eyes glinted with anger. I felt so proud.

"What do you want with Selena?" Lexi asked. Jeremiah tilted his head back and laughed.

Suddenly the force field was gone, and Lexi was right between Jeremiah and me.

I took advantage of the lack of protection and an electric current sprang forth from my hands toward Lexi, sending her to the ground with a thud and jerking for a moment before lying motionless. With the shield out of the way I was able to attack the others. Lachlan and Genevieve immediately took cover, but the last man stood his ground, as if unconvinced I would hurt him again.

"Selena, please," he said, arms raised in surrender.

I flicked my wrist and the man dropped to his knees, gasping for air. He fell back on the ground, reaching around his neck to loosen my invisible grasp.

"Stop!" Genevieve yelled, jumping in front of me, shooting icicles at me. Lachlan was right behind her with fire balls. Fire and ice, how nice. I deflected them, which allowed the man to catch his breath. I frowned at him, swept my hand outward and Genevieve with it, ready to attack the man again.

"What do you plan to do with her?" I suddenly heard Lexi from behind me. I hadn't even realized she'd come to. Before I could react she grabbed Jeremiah's arm and quickly took mine. Just then a slew of images transferred from her mind to mine. They rushed so fast at first I couldn't understand what I was seeing, but then they started to slow. I saw memories but they weren't mine, it was as if I was seeing through someone else's eyes. I'm standing in front of a house, and as I pass one of the windows I see my reflection, but it isn't mine; it's Jeremiah's. Only he's younger.

It's night time and he creeps to the front door. He's inside now, cutting a gas line. He pours liquid on the floor. He lights a match and throws it in the kitchen. A blaze of fire erupts, engulfing the kitchen in flames. Smoke creeps up and the fire alarm blares. I hear voices from upstairs, but I can't make out what they're saying. He needs to take out the mother first. She will be the biggest threat. He creeps around the stair case, waiting for her.

A young girl flies down the stairs and out the door. He runs up the stairs to go after the mother. He will go after the girl later. A woman stands at the top of the stairs glaring at him. He wants to kill her. She sweeps her hands, sending him flying, but he recovers fast, grabbing her leg as she reaches the bottom of the stairs. He is determined to kill her. She burns, right there in front of him, and once he knows she won't get up, he runs out just as the house explodes.

The scene changes from memories to thoughts, but they are so jumbled it's hard to tell what they are. I saw a ritual, something written in a book, moon phases, ingredients, the words 'raising the witch' and then a girl who looked an awful lot like me. Suddenly I was jerked out of the vision and I was gasping for air.

"Get off me, you Poxy!" Jeremiah flung Lexi away. All that had happened in a matter of seconds, but it felt like a lifetime.

"It was you?" I asked, voice hoarse.

"What are you blabbering about?" He yelled.

"You killed my parents. All these years I thought it was an accident!" My resolve hardened, something inside me broke free like pressurized water breaking through a dam, and I flew at Jeremiah. I didn't know I could fly until that very moment when I lifted him into the air and flew him into the ground. I landed on top of him and he wheezed as my weight compressed his lungs. His eyes widened in shock and then he placed his hand on my shoulder, staring into my eyes. I felt a thought probe into my mind, but it didn't get very far. I suddenly saw Jeremiah's aura, something I had never seen before for some reason. It was black with a small haze of brown – a murky mix that kept changing, and swirling, giving me the feeling of fury and darkness.

"What are you doing?" I asked through clenched teeth feeling violated. Jeremiah's expression changed to rage and he pushed me off him with so much force I landed on my back a few feet away.

I stood quickly, electricity sparked at my fingertips as I watched Jeremiah with hatred. How had I ever looked up to this man? I sent out the sparks like bullets, straight at him, but he blocked them one at a time.

"What the hell is going on here?" I heard a man ask. I turned to see that Darien was standing outside the tent, watching me attack Jeremiah. I expected to feel the usual longing, but only rage came. Rage as I remembered kissing him, and letting him touch me. Why did I do that? I sent a whirlwind toward him and it knocked him down. Then I heard more voices, confused tones as they all started to gather around.

"We need to get out of here!" Genevieve yelled. Lexi pulled me by the arm, leading me away from Jeremiah and Darien, and I let her. My mind was a jumble of memories and thoughts. Thoughts that weren't my own. Were they? I tried to piece it all together, but it was too much. My brain was on overload.

"Come on," I heard that familiar voice, only now I knew who it belonged to. Tristan. I looked up into his yellow-specked green eyes, and saw something there I had never seen before: Vulnerability. I didn't understand how I could have forgotten him, when seeing him now made me feel so alive.

"Come with me, Selena. I'll keep you safe," he said.

My heart raced and I took his hand as we ran. People were coming out from their tents and the building, shouting after us. I looked over my shoulder and saw Jeremiah standing next to Darien. Their eyes blazed with fury. Before I could see anything else, I was sucked, pulled and twisted, landing in front of the hotel.

"I'll be back," Tristan told me, holding my arm a little longer than necessary.

"Wait, I can teleport, I can help you," I offered.

"No, you need to stay here. Stay safe. I'll be back with everyone in a flash." He smiled at me and lightly brushed his fingertips along my jaw. A moment later he was gone. Three moments later he was back with Lexi, Genevieve and Lachlan safely. We hustled through the hotel and to our room.

Once I saw that everyone was alright, I fell onto the couch. Then jumped back up as it started shivering. I sat on the armchair instead. There was so much to process and I didn't even know half of what was going on. I had so many questions, and my mind was fuzzy making it difficult to make sense of anything.

"What happened back there?" Genevieve asked. Lexi shrugged her shoulders.

"I don't know, I just thought about the counter curse, about truth and figured maybe if Selena knew the truth about Jeremiah's plans it would snap her out of it."

"Wait, what? Snap me out of what?"

"Jeremiah cast a spell on you," Lexi explained. "When he broke the binding spell he placed one of his own, one where he could control you and your thoughts."

"No, that's not possible," I started, but then I thought about my actions, my inexplicable attraction to Darien, my anger toward Tristan and Lexi, even forgetting who Tristan was. "Is it?" I asked. I then understood what Jeremiah had been trying to do when I had him pinned on the ground. He had tried to control me. I felt sick.

"His aura..." I said.

"What about it?" Tristan asked.

"I never saw it before, but when he tried to control me when we were fighting I saw it. Why wasn't I able to see him for what he really was?"

"Some witches can hide it," Lexi answered. "Not just reel it in, but make it disappear altogether."

"I can't believe this happened," I said, shaking my head.

Tristan nodded. "Yeah, it was hard to watch." He clenched his jaw and turned away, obviously remembering something I wasn't aware of. Then I remembered how I basically threw myself at him, and my face flushed with embarrassment. I couldn't believe I did that! And I had read his mind...the thought triggered an idea. I tapped into his thoughts now to see if he was thinking of the same moment I was. I gasped when I realized he wasn't; he was seeing me and Darien together. The image made my stomach flip in disgust and embarrassment. Feeling what he felt at that moment, the rage, disappointment and pain made me retreat quickly back into my own mind, but not before Tristan shot me a look.

"So what was it that I saw back there?" I asked Lexi, wanting to get my mind away from Tristan's.

Lexi looked confused. "Which part exactly?"

"When you grabbed my arm, what was that?"

"Oh! Okay, so I discovered a new power! I can tell if someone is lying just by touching them. Or maybe I should say that I can see the truth. So I figured if you could see what I saw then it would break the spell."

"What?" I was so confused, I couldn't put anything together.

"Oh jeez, your brain got fried, didn't it?" Lexi started again, "Okay, quick recap. You got put under Jeremiah's spell and you were acting all weird and edgy, though I kind of liked that side of you..."She rambled on without taking a breath, telling me everything I had missed. "...I think that about sums it up." She looked to the other three to confirm she didn't miss anything important. I took a few moments and processed it. In the end I felt guilty and embarrassed.

"I'm so sorry. I never meant to hurt you guys, or be rude or make you have to come rescue me. I guess I'm not as strong as I thought." I looked down at my hands, my head was hurting and I felt terrible. What I had done to Tristan and Lexi forced its way to the forefront of my mind, and I almost cried. I faced them, trying to find the words, and only came up with; "I'm so sorry I almost tried to kill you... God how do I even begin to apologize for that? I didn't know who you were, Tristan."

"What do you mean?" He asked.

"I didn't remember you, only that you hurt me. That's why I tried..." I let the sentence hang.

"Jeremiah controlled your mind, remember?" Lexi said. "He must have made you forget Tristan so you could get close to-"

"It wasn't you," Tristan said softly.

"That is hardly an excuse!" I snapped.

"Babe, it's okay, we're okay," Lexi said.

"Thanks to Genevieve," I whispered.

"There's nothing to apologize for, okay?" Tristan pressed. I nodded, not because I believed they forgave me, or because I forgave myself I just knew there was no use arguing about my guilt. I changed the subject.

"So why did I see Jeremiah kill my parents, and, well, try to kill me really?"

"Well when I asked what his plan was with you it must have taken us back to his original plan where he tried to kill you as a child," Lexi explained. "Though it seems he's changed course. At the end we were looking at parts of his plan that he hadn't enacted yet. Since those were just ideas and not memories the images were choppy and hazy. Tristan, I did see that he was going to try some kind of ritual, and Stefania was there."

"What does she have to do with anything?" Tristan asked, deep in thought.

"Who's Stefania?" The confusion was creeping up again.

"She's Tristan's ex," Lexi blurted. "His only ex actually; the guy never dates. The relationship didn't even last that long." Tristan shot her a glare that could have frozen fire. "She was the girl you saw in the vision with the dark hair and blue eyes," she continued, unaffected by Tristan's reaction.

"Oh," I said, remembering seeing a girl that looked like me.

"Really, Lexi, you need a filter," Genevieve said shaking her head.

"What did I say?" She chirped innocently.

"You seem to be able to completely control your powers now," Tristan said in an attempt to change the subject.

"Yeah, Darien taught me at the camp," I said before I thought the words through.

Tristan flinched, "Oh, okay."

"I think I need to lie down." I stood, heading for the room.

"It's late. We should all get some rest." Lachlan stood, and Genevieve followed as they headed for the door.

"Thank you for your help. Again." Tristan hugged them in turn and they left, waving good bye.

"Here let me help you." Tristan gently held my elbow, guiding me to the bed. I took my jeans off and pulled back the covers. "You left these behind. I thought you might like them back now." He held out my mother's ring and the necklace he bought me. My heart swelled as I took my mother's ring and placed it on my finger. It tingled gently against my skin. Tristan clasped the necklace around my neck, the stone warming my chest where it rested.

"Thank you," I whispered, hugging him tightly. I couldn't care less about what he thought or his rules. He already saw me throw myself at him, what worse was there? I was surprised when he wrapped his arms around me and held me tighter against his body.

"I'm sorry," he said, pulling away to look me in the eye. "I never should have let you leave. I will regret that for the rest of my life, especially after seeing what Jeremiah made you do…and with Darien." He clenched his jaw, no doubt reliving the scene he saw in the woods. I was smart enough to stay out of his head this time. I didn't want to relive that with him.

"I'm sorry too. For all the pain and trouble I put you through. You know I would never willingly do that, right?" I searched his eyes for forgiveness.

He smiled, placed his hand under my chin and lifted my face. He kissed my forehead gently, and I felt that familiar longing, that feeling of wanting Tristan, but not being able to have him. I looked down before he could read the disappoint-tment in my face. He shifted uncomfortably.

"Good night," I whispered, crawling in bed, all but hiding underneath the covers.

"Good night," he said as he walked out to the living room.

I was exhausted but I couldn't sleep. I kept replaying the image of my mother's death over and over, and my blood boiled with anger. I would kill Jeremiah for what he did to my family. I would kill him for what he did to me. But before he died, I would make sure he suffered with the burning pain of a thousand suns.

"What are you doing out here?" I heard Lexi ask Tristan.

"What do you mean?" He asked, oblivious to Lexi's thought process.

"You just got the girl back. Stole her right out from under the bad guy's nose, and you're here in the living room with me? Don't you think you should be getting it on or something? Are you really that clueless?"

"Are you really that desperate?" He countered. "She just found out her parents were murdered. Just found out she was forced to kiss and do who knows what else with her enemy, and you think I should be in there making out? What's wrong with you?"

That sounded like a good idea to me, but I pushed the thought aside.

Lexi's tone softened. "What are you so scared of?"

"You know better than anyone how I feel. I just want to give her some time. There's nothing wrong with that."

"Alright. I give up…for now." I could hear a smile in Lexi's response.

They stepped in the room, trying not to wake me. Lexi deliberately got in the other bed; clearly she hadn't given up completely. Tristan surprisingly didn't put up a fight, but he stood at the doorway of the room, and I could sense he was thinking. Just when I thought he would go sleep on the couch, he lifted the covers on my bed and got in. I was happy and confused at the same time, but I decided not to over think it.

After a few minutes, I could hear Lexi's deep breathing and I knew she was fast asleep. I was still wide awake, I just couldn't relax. I rolled over onto my side so that I was facing Tristan. He was shirtless, lying on his back, one arm bent behind his head propping it up, and he was looking at me.

"Do you mind that I'm here?" He whispered.

I smiled, "Why would you ask that when you already know the answer?" I knew he did, there was no reason to pretend.

"Do you want to talk about anything that happened?" His gaze bore into mine, and I stopped breathing for a minute. "Selena?" Tristan asked after a long quiet moment.

"Huh?" I finally breathed. "Oh, um, kind of. But I don't want to at the same time. I can't explain it."

"No rush. Just know that you can talk to me about anything, anytime. Okay?"

I nodded my head, "Thanks." I inched my body a little closer to his, wanting to feel his warmth. His jaw clenched as I got close enough that our bodies just touched.

I looked up at him and bit my lower lip in contemplation.

"What are you thinking about?" He lifted my face.

"Just wondering how close I can get before you get uncomfortable," I answered honestly. He chuckled, and lowered himself so his body was parallel to mine.

"Funny, I usually hear your thoughts when they're about me," he whispered, reminding me of our telepathic connection. If I so much as thought his name he would know what I was thinking.

"I remembered to block it from you this time."

Tristan smiled.

We lay like that for a few minutes, both of us on our sides facing each other. My emotions were raw from the day's events and being so close to Tristan without being able to be with him saddened me more than it should have.

"What are you thinking now?" He pressed. I smiled sadly and rolled out of bed. Tristan's brows knitted together in confusion, but I just walked out of the room. I needed some space. A few seconds after I got to the living room he was there standing behind me.

"What's wrong?" He asked.

"Nothing, I just feel so confused." I turned to face him.

"What about?"

"I just don't know what to do with everything I'm feeling."

"About your parents?"

"Well that's definitely affecting how I feel, yeah, but there's something else bothering me too."

"Darien?" Tristan asked, a hint of disappointment in his tone.

"No," I scoffed.

"I have to ask," Tristan said and took a deep breath. "Did you... did you two...?" He let the sentence hang.

"We only kissed."

He nodded. "Do you miss him?"

I shook my head, "I don't even know why it happened. It wasn't what I wanted."

"Trust me, it's not what I wanted either," Tristan ran a hand through his hair. "I'm sorry you had to go through that."

"It's fine, my feelings have nothing to do with Darien." I looked down at the plush carpet.

"What's the problem, then?"

I looked up at him and took in his gorgeous features, his muscular body, the low waistband of his sweat pants.

"He isn't the one I want."

"Oh," he whispered. "Selena..."

"Please save me the boundaries speech you are about to give me."

Tristan laughed. "I've given up on trying to follow the rules."

He gently placed his hand on the side of my face and lowered his own. Our lips met gently, softly, I could feel every emotion running between us. Our kisses became more passionate, hungry, quenching our desire like rain after a drought. His lips moved with mine and it felt so right.

He lifted me up, and I wrapped my legs around his waist and my arms around his neck. His strong arms wrapped around my back and held me tighter to him. I ran my hand through his hair, feeling its soft strands between my fingers. He laid me gently on the couch, lying on top of me, and he let his hands roam the length of my body, caressing my bare legs. My hands travelled down his back, feeling his smooth skin and every tight muscle underneath.

Tristan moved his hand back up my leg and under my shirt. His warm fingers moved at my waist, at my stomach, warming my skin everywhere he touched. This was nothing like the last few times we kissed; there were no reservations, no fear holding either of us back.

"Tristan?" I whispered, breaking our kiss.

"Yeah?" His voice was ragged as he kissed my neck.

"What were you going to tell me in the forest?"

He raised his head, and looked at me. He swallowed hard once before saying, "I love you."

My heart stopped for just a moment before resuming its erratic beat.

"I love you too," I admitted. He brought his lips back to mine.

5. QUIET

"How did they find me?" I asked, sipping my coffee the next morning.

"Who?" Lexi looked to me for clarification.

"Well my parents bound my powers when I was a kid so no one would find me, right? So how did Jeremiah find me?" I had been wracking my brain about my parent's death most of the night, trying to make sense of it. Well, after I managed to get Tristan out of my system.

"You know how he found you. You saw his memories, remember?" Lexi rubbed my arm comfortingly. I thought about the images I saw, but I couldn't tell what Lexi was talking about.

"You remember when you saw yourself running down the stairs?" She asked, keeping eye contact, making sure I was paying attention. I nodded yes. "Do you remember how you looked?" I sat quietly thinking for a moment, and then it came to me.

"I was glowing," I lowered my gaze to my mother's ring, snug on my finger. The ring that should be on my mother's hand now, had I not gotten her killed.

"Hey, listen, it's not your fault," Tristan chimed in, as if reading my thoughts. "Your aura is amazing, it's who you are. Even with your powers bound, it was there. It's Jeremiah you should blame."

I wasn't quite agreeing where the blame should be placed, but I didn't feel like arguing about it just then.

"I thought Darien was the mastermind behind all this," I said. "If Jeremiah killed my parents, Darien was only, what? Thirteen? No way could he have orchestrated that."

"It wasn't Darien. Never has been," Tristan said with certainty. "He is just a puppet, a front man to protect Jeremiah. I figured he was working for someone, I just didn't know who until recently."

"What made you think that?" I met Tristan's gaze waiting for him to explain. He exchanged a glance with Lexi and then he turned away.

Lexi huffed, "For crying out loud. Just tell her already."

"Tell me what?" My curiosity piqued. I resisted the urge to read their thoughts.

Tristan shook his head at Lexi, and then looked at me. "Darien is my brother, my twin brother to be specific."

"What?" My mind reeled. How could Tristan, this beautiful kind man, be related to the spawn of Satan, Darien? "No way you guys are brothers. You look nothing alike. You act nothing alike for that matter."

"Well we are obviously not identical twins. It happens." Tristan ran his hand through his dark, stylishly messy hair, and then I saw the small similarities in their habits like clenching their jaw when they're tense. Tristan continued, "Look, we were never really close as kids. My mother's powers got bound for a second time, and we didn't have any way of knowing how to save her like we did with you. We were only thirteen when she died, and Darien blamed the Elders for her death, while I blamed my mother. I came and protected you, he went and I guess found Jeremiah somewhere along the way… or maybe Jeremiah found him. He must've been very convincing to get Darien to work with an Elder."

"So you didn't see Darien after that?"

"Our paths crossed a few times. Not often though. We didn't agree on much, and certainly weren't close."

"You didn't think to tell me this sooner? Don't you think this is important?" I asked angrily. Then I thought of how I kissed Darien and then I kissed Tristan – brothers! I mentally groaned.

"I was kind of ashamed, I guess," Tristan admitted. "And please don't think about kissing Darien. I have been trying to forget that part."

"I wasn't-" I broke off. Damn connection! I had forgotten to block my thoughts.

"It's also because they are twins that Darien was able to get past Tristan's protective spell on you. Remember the bugs?" Lexi added, leading the conversation back on course. I cringed from the memory and Tristan shot her another frustrated look, obviously not happy to have this weakness on display.

"Well, this is fantastic," I mumbled. I thought back to my coffee date with Darien when he told me he had no brothers or sisters, and how final his statement was. I guess he didn't consider himself related to Tristan either. That triggered another memory.

"When I went out with Darien," I started and shot Tristan a 'cool it' look. "He texted someone after he dropped me off. Do you think that was Jeremiah?" I asked.

Tristan shrugged, "Probably. Who knows who he has connections with though?"

I thought about that, and then thought about Tristan and Darien as young boys, growing up together. "Can I ask why your mother's powers were bound?"

Tristan worked his jaw, "She had a bad habit of tampering with people's free will. Apparently she didn't learn her lesson the first time her powers were bound. I suppose that's where Darien gets his rebellion from."

"I'm sorry," I whispered. I felt terrible, especially knowing how it felt to be bound. At least I understood why Tristan was so certain about the details of a binding spell. Tristan just shrugged.

"It was a long time ago. No need to dwell on it."

"What's to stop Jeremiah from binding my powers again?" I asked uncertainly, the thought popping up in my scattered brain. I was scared of the answer; I never wanted to feel that way again.

"Binding a witch takes a physical toll on the Elder who casts the spell. It's not something that can be done often. Jeremiah will need to wait at least a few months before he will be able to bind anyone again. Unless there's another Elder involved who can perform the ritual, I don't think you will have anything to worry about for a while. Besides when you were there it seemed he wanted to use your powers for himself. He wouldn't risk binding them again and losing your powers."

"I hope you're right." My fear was only slightly abated. Just thinking there was a chance of that happening again was unsettling. "Darien seems determined," I added.

"Well, speaking of Darien, would you happen to know what his plans are?" Lexi asked, changing the subject. "You came right out of their camp."

"Yeah, I uh…" I let the sentence hang as I thought back to my first moments when Jeremiah confided in me, but my thoughts came up blank. "I did, but I can't seem to recall them now. That's so weird! I remember him telling me what we were going to do, but I can't remember anything he actually said." I wracked my memory for the conversation.

"Smart son of a bitch," Tristan mumbled.

"What?" I asked.

"He wiped your memories. I have no idea how or when, but he must have known or at least suspected you were going to come back to us. Did he make you say anything, any type of spell after he told you the plan?"

"Not that I can remember," I admitted.

"He probably cast a precaution spell," Lexi added. "So that as long as you were with him you would remember, but once you left, so did your memories."

"Huh, that is brilliant," I conceded. "Inconvenient for us, but brilliant."

"Don't worry, we'll figure it out soon enough." Tristan sat next to me and placed his hand on my thigh. Lexi did a double take, and then studied us. Her eyes narrowed, slowly roaming over each of us.

"What have you guys been up to?" She scrutinized.

"Nothing," I said a little too quickly. Lexi's eyes narrowed and a knowing look flashed across her face.

My face flushed in response.

"Wait, really?" Her eyes widened. "What does this mean? Are you guys like...together officially?" She asked with such certainty I could only assume it was a part of her new power.

Tristan and I exchanged a glance and smiled.

"Finally. I can now happily move on with my life." Lexi dropped in the arm chair smiling. I rolled my eyes; this was so high school.

"Anyways, moving along. What do we do now?" I asked. Tristan and Lexi exchanged glances, but they both stayed quiet. "So, basically that means we have no plan. Is that right?" I pushed.

"Yep, pretty much," Lexi admitted.

"Should we tell the Charge about the camp?" I asked.

"I already did," Lexi said. "Last night, but the Charge didn't find anything. If the camp were there, they would have found it, even cloaked, so it looks like they moved."

"How will we find Darien again?" I asked.

"Don't worry, he won't stay hidden for long," Tristan said.

"Do you have anything personal of his by any chance?" Lexi asked Tristan.

"No, why?"

"I thought we could cast a locator spell. No matter, I'll figure something out." She sat in contemplation.

"Can you cast a locator spell on an object?" I asked. "Like, say, the prophecy?"

Lexi thought about it for a moment. "I don't think it works like that – at least not the spell I know. You need something that belongs to the person, remember? What would belong to an object?"

"Besides," Tristan added, "the Charge would've already cast some sort of finding spell when the Journal went missing."

"What Journal?" I asked.

"You know, the one where all the prophecies are published," Lexi said.

"What are you guys talking about? You told me there was a page framed in the library that copies were made from."

"Why would a library check out a one page document, Selena? It doesn't make any sense," Tristan asked, eyebrows knitting together as he studied me.

"That's exactly what I thought, but you're the ones that told me that!" I practically yelled.

"Stop," Lexi said. "Don't you see what's happening here?"

"I can honestly say I don't," I answered.

"This is an effect of the ritual. Tristan and I knew of the prophecy, so the spell affects our minds where the prophecy is concerned." When she got a blank stare from me she continued. "Look, it's the exact same way Jeremiah made you forget what you learned in his camp, or when he bound us so we couldn't speak of the riddle he'd given us. My grandfather told me about this," Lexi became more animated as she spoke. "He told me how the story we remembered would change the more time passed. He thought it would get closer to the truth, and that we would remember it more accurately as the spell wore off."

"So, the prophecy was in a journal?" I asked, trying to piece it all together.

"Yes," Tristan answered, sounding more confident of his answer. "The prophecy, along with all the other prophecies from that year, went into a yearly publication called the Prophetic Journal."

"But that's what's missing? The whole book?"

"I think so?" Lexi said, but it sounded more like a question. "It'll come to me."

"I'm starting to get a headache," Tristan said. We sat in silence for a minute before Tristan spoke again. "Come on, Selena, we should train. We never did get to use your full powers. Training would be much easier for you now."

"Yeah, um, do I really need to train? I mean in case you forgot, my powers are pretty bad ass. Don't think I'll need to throw a punch anytime soon."

"Hmm," Tristan nodded. Within a second he was behind me, arm wrapped snugly around my neck in a choke hold. Any more pressure and he would have cut off my air. I flicked my fingers in an attempt to magic him off me, but it did little to move him. I sent a whirlwind toward him and it knocked him down, but he took me down with him, forcing me to fall off the couch and land with my back on him. His arm was still around my neck.

"If I was applying full pressure, you would have passed out by now. Do you still think you don't need physical training?"

I rolled my eyes. "Fine," I said through clenched teeth. I really didn't want to get back into our vigorous training, but I couldn't deny that it wasn't easy to get out of his hold. Tristan let go and I stood up feeling a little embarrassed at my lack of fighting skills.

"I mean, did you forget everything I taught you?" He asked, brushing his pants off.

"I…well…no," I said with attitude, "I just didn't think to use it when I could use magic instead."

"You're hopeless."

"Well thank you very much," I snarled.

Tristan chuckled. "I think we should train outside. It would be a nice change of scenery."

"Whatever you say, coach."

"Well, while you two go on your karate kid mission, I will call Genevieve and Lachlan and try to think up a plan," Lexi said.

"That's a good idea. You do that," Tristan said.

"I wasn't asking your permission. Jeez, you have like an alpha male complex or something?" Lexi teased.

I shook my head at them. I decided to go change into appropriate workout clothes while they finished their argument.

"Woof, woof," I heard Tristan sarcastically remark as I closed the door. I threw my hair up in a high ponytail, threw on a tank and shorts along with my runners. When I felt it would be safe to go back out to the sitting area, I quietly opened the door, listening for any last minute quips. It was thankfully quiet.

"Ready?" Tristan asked.

"Yup."

"Follow me."

We left the hotel through the back entrance that led to a grass field interspersed with trees and flowers. After a few quiet moments, Tristan took my hand and intertwined his fingers with mine. His hands were soft and warm and gave me a sense of comfort I hadn't known I needed.

We walked through the canopy of trees, and the temperature dropped a few degrees. I had a sudden longing to be closer to Tristan, like holding his hand wasn't enough. I stopped short and Tristan turned to face me. He looked around, trying to figure out why I stopped, and when he couldn't, he looked back at me.

"What's up?" He asked slowly, as if questioning my sanity.

I had no idea what I was thinking or why, but before I knew it my arms were wrapped around Tristan's neck, and I pulled him down and stood on my toes, kissing him. He hesitated for a moment, like I caught him off guard, which I'm sure I did. I caught myself off guard.

It wasn't long before he kissed me back though. He wrapped his arms around my waist and held me closer. A few moments later he broke the kiss.

He smiled, "Maybe making out here isn't the best idea right now."

"Yeah, you're right...race ya!" I didn't wait for his response; I just booked it. I ran as fast as I could, which isn't saying much, since Tristan was right on my heels within a blink and was passing me seconds after that.

You'd think since I got my powers that I would be faster, but I guess that's where Tristan excelled. He got a few feet ahead of me before he came to a sudden halt and turned to face me. I couldn't stop in time.

I crashed right into him.

He made an *oomph* noise, and we both went down laughing. He stood first, brushing twigs and leaves from his jeans. He took an exaggerated amount of time before he offered to help me up. After I stood, I pushed him playfully, but he didn't budge.

"Come on, 6'2" remember?" He said moving his hand up and down his body to show it off. Then he made the same gesture toward me, "5'5"? You can't do any damage here," he teased.

"Oh, really?" I asked, hiking up my eyebrow.

"Really," he answered smugly. I shrugged my shoulders and started walking. I got a few steps ahead of him, and then I looked over my shoulder, giving Tristan my most seductive smile. His lips turned up in a half smile in response.

I flicked my fingers and he fell backwards, and landed right on his butt. I laughed loudly and then sauntered off.

"You have guts, Arturro!" He yelled my last name as he charged me. I contemplated letting him hit me, kind of wanting the contact, but then, seeing his face, I quickly changed my mind. I dared to go invisible.

I wasn't sure if it worked as I hadn't tried to disappear since before my powers were re-bound. So I side-stepped just in case. Tristan plowed through thin air and then stopped quickly. He pivoted in a circle searching for me.

"Selena?" He said playfully, but there was a hint of panic in his tone. I quietly crept behind him, and jumped on his shoulders and pinched his nipple. He grunted in surprise-and hopefully pain-and gently flung me off his back. As I landed, I made myself re-appear. "That is seriously creepy," Tristan said catching his breath.

I laughed. "You were saying something about damage?"

"Yeah, yeah, I take it back," he said rubbing his chest. I laughed at his pain. He had it coming.

We walked quietly hand in hand after that, our pent-up energy having been released.

"So I've been curious about something, but I don't want to pry," I said after a long moment.

"What's up?" Tristan encouraged.

"Well, what was it like growing up with Darien?"

Tristan's lips tightened as he thought.

"It was...hard, annoying, like it is with any sibling," he finally answered.

"Did you guys ever get along? Or were you fighting from birth?"

He let out a sigh, "Since birth actually. My mom told me we couldn't even sleep in the same crib without crying, or kicking or something. Then growing up Darien used to steal my toys, so I played with his old ones. When he saw that I was happy with those, he wanted them back.

"It was kind of the same thing in school, with friends and girls. We both got good grades, but it was always a competition as to whose were better. I don't know, maybe it was all just typical brother stuff, but with Darien everything was much more intense. We never had good days. It was all just so exhausting. Then my mom died, and like I told you before, we just went our separate ways."

"What was your mom like? She must have been an amazing woman," I inquired.

"I don't know that I would go so far as to call her amazing," he said. Then when he caught my shocked expression he added,

"Don't get me wrong, I loved my mother. I love her still, it's just that she did some stuff that I'm not proud of. That's why her powers were bound."

"You told me that your mother had boundary issues with abusing people's will? What exactly did she do?" I asked cautiously. I didn't want to upset Tristan.

"Honestly? That's all the Elders would tell me. I asked around a lot, but no one really had any information. I really don't know what she did; I just knew it was bad." He dropped his gaze to the ground.

"Why did Darien blame the Elders while you blamed your mother?"

"Darien felt that the Elders were wrong to bind her powers, that it was an excessive form of punishment. I don't agree with the form of punishment myself, but I felt my mother should have known better. Everyone knows the consequences for what she did. She should have thought about what that would do to us."

"I'm sorry," I said quietly. He just shrugged in response. "Where was your dad through all this?"

He sighed. "I don't know that either. I never knew who my father was; my mom was the only one who raised us. I didn't have any other family, or anywhere to go when she died, and I'd heard stories about you." He smiled then. "When I was asked to protect you, I jumped at the chance."

"How did that happen?"

"How did I come to be your protector?" He asked. I nodded. "Shortly before my mother died, she had Darien and I in a school here where they focused on determining what our magical abilities were. They helped us enhance them as they developed to apply toward career paths based on which powers we possessed. My abilities and characteristics were prominent in protection and teachers started to notice. One of the teachers asked if I would be willing to use them to help you. I obviously accepted, and when I left I found out that Darien had been approached as well."

"Wait, Darien was asked to protect me?" I almost laughed at the irony.

Tristan nodded and cleared his throat. "The teachers actually asked him first."

"Really?" I could hardly picture Darien showing protective tendencies that would rival Tristan's.

"I know, I was surprised too. He declined the offer though. Didn't want to do anything to help the Elders or our city."

"Wow." The thought crossed my mind of how much different things would've been to have Darien as a protector. Would he have replaced Lexi? Or Tristan? An alternate future threatened to consume my thoughts.

"I think he regretted not helping you. Our mother's stories haunted me so I can imagine the impact it had on him. I suspect by the time he realized his mistake it was too late." Tristan paused a moment before continuing. "Then he got kicked out of that school and lost any chance to change his mind."

"Why did he get kicked out?"

Tristan sighed, "He was always just so angry, all the time. I remember one day in class this jerk, Troy called our mother a name. I can't remember exactly what he said, but he basically called her a child murderer, said that was why she was sentenced to death. Darien defended her, but then some of Troy's friends backed him up, laughing at us, chanting insults. I wanted to hurt them all, but I kept myself in check. Darien on the other hand wasn't very level-headed. He levitated one of the desks and threw it at Troy and his friends."

"Really?" I would've liked to see that.

"No one got hurt," Tristan added quickly. "But by then the damage was done. The hard part for me to deal with was that the school we were at was like a boarding school – you get kicked out of there you go back home. Since we no longer had a home, it meant getting kicked out onto the street." Tristan shook his head. "I begged the board to let him stay, but they had a strict policy and a thirteen year old didn't exactly have any leverage. Plus Darien didn't help his case when he started swearing at the teachers and claiming he didn't need them or that school anyway."

"I'm sorry," I whispered, seeing the anguish of the memory in Tristan's eyes.

"Anyway, I found out later that he went to another school, but it's not the kind of school you want your kids in. It had a very bad reputation since they only allowed troubled kids in there. Then I left the school and met Lexi for the first time when we came to your house."

That threw me off. "What? When did you come to my house?"

"Shortly before your parents died. Mrs. Laurel, the teacher who noticed our talents, brought us to meet your parents. She wanted to make sure they approved of us to watch over you.

"We were supposed to be your friends, just to be close to you and keep you safe. Then your parents died, and the plan changed a bit. Lexi obviously became part of your life, while I kept watch from a distance. I still remember the first time I saw you." He smiled, and my heart swelled.

"You do?" I asked, my face flushing a bit bashfully.

"Sure. Take a peek." He tapped his head, giving me the go ahead to read his thoughts. I wondered if he knew I had done this a few times before.

He chuckled. "I have an affinity for you, remember? I know when you're looking," he said, hearing my thoughts this time. I quickly looked away. "I'm giving you permission now," he added teasingly. I stopped walking and faced him, allowing my mind to connect with his as I saw his thoughts.

I saw myself, looking down from my bedroom window in my parents' house. It was night and there was a faint glow from my bedside lamp shining beside me, lighting up my features. I was looking straight at him. I felt through his emotions that there were no romantic tendencies, but I wouldn't expect there to be. We were both so young. He was feeling a strong desire to protect me though, and that made me smile. He hadn't changed much.

I got out of his head and started thinking. If he had seen me staring at him, shouldn't I remember seeing him too? I bit my lip in contemplation, searching through my memories for the right one.

"What are you thinking?" Tristan asked. I looked up to see that he was studying my face.

"I just can't remember seeing you that-" Then the memory hit me and I suddenly saw it. I saw the older woman walking with a very small Lexi and Tristan in tow. I hadn't known who they were then, and I remembered being curious about them. I hadn't even realized that I had seen Lexi before I met her playing at the park outside one of my foster homes.

I saw a young Tristan gazing up, and I remembered seeing his green eyes and dark hair and being curious as to how he saw me in my window and why he was looking at me that way.

"I wonder if that's how I knew." I asked under my breath,

"Knew what? You kind of switched thoughts mid-sentence," Tristan inquired.

"I had a dream about you after I saw you that night in the club. In my dream I knew exactly how your eyes looked, and the color of your hair, even without having seen them before. At least I thought I hadn't seen them before. Now I know I did," I finished in a whisper as I put my thoughts together. "Huh," I added shrugging my shoulders.

"We've walked far enough," Tristan said, standing in a clearing. "This is as good a spot to train as any."

"I've been thinking," I said.

Tristan waited for me to continue.

"Do you think you can teach me to block pain?"

Tristan frowned. "I'm not sure I could do that."

"Why not?"

"Because couldn't stand the thought of you being hurt, never mind hurt you to teach you to block it."

"I get that, but I need to learn this. After Crystal and Yuri I realized that I'm not as mentally strong as I'd like. I just need you to teach me how to do it. You can skip the hurting me part."

Tristan hesitated. "Are you sure about this?"

"Oh yeah. Bring it, coach."

I finished showering and changed into jeans and a tank. I felt confident that I was mentally trained as well as physically. He taught me meditation, and I felt well-rounded. Tristan couldn't hurt me, which was just fine, I wasn't eager for that either. But he did teach me how to control my thoughts. How important mind over matter was.

Selena, I heard a man's voice in my head as I walked out toward the living room. I groaned internally. This guy was starting to freak me out. He had sent me warnings and messages before, but I had no idea who he was, or why he was helping us. I had grown to fear his voice though, since he always gave me bad news.

"What?" I asked, with irritation in my voice. "What now?"

Tristan and Lexi looked up at me skeptically. I held my finger up to tell them to wait.

It would be a good time to gather your belongings and go to the cottage.

"Why?"

For your safety. Have I steered you wrong yet?

"No," I admitted.

Go then. I let out a growl.

"What is it?" Lexi asked.

"Time to tell Genevieve and Lachlan they're getting roommates," I said. "Pack your things, we have to go."

"Another warning?" Tristan asked, getting to his feet.

"Yep." I pursed my lips and headed back to the room with Tristan and Lexi in tow. Tristan sent Genevieve and Lachlan a telepathic message as we quickly packed. We returned the keys to the clerks and teleported to Genevieve and Lachlan's cottage.

6. THE MORE THE MERRIER

"Is everything alright?" Genevieve asked as she let us into her home. It looked like an exact replica of the half-way house we had been in, in Arizona...or wherever it was. It was pretty neat that witches could do that.

"Yeah," I answered. "Just decided it would be safer here, better protection from Darien and Jeremiah." I didn't think it would be wise to tell them I was hearing voices, telling me to run. "I hope this isn't an inconvenience."

"No, not at all. I love company," Genevieve said, beaming.

"Thank you," I said, walking into the living room.

"You can have the same rooms as before," Genevieve offered.

"Thanks," Lexi said. She and I went upstairs and to the room on the right, while Tristan headed to the room across the hall. I felt a twinge of disappointment.

"You know what?" Lexi spoke up, "You two should share a room...get to know each other better," she teased.

Tristan looked at me, eyebrow raised. I laughed, but shrugged. Lexi rolled her eyes and took her bag to the other room, while Tristan walked into mine smiling.

His cell phone rang then, startling me. I had forgotten about them since we could communicate telepathically.

Tristan's eyebrows pulled in confusion as he read the caller I.D. He answered the phone.

"Yes, this is Tristan…no we checked out this morning… what?" There was a long pause while the person on the other end spoke.

"Unbelievable… yes… thank you very much for checking up on us. I'm sorry that happened… Bye." He hung up.

"What was that about?" I asked concerned.

Tristan ran a hand through his hair and sat on the bed. "That was the hotel. There was a disturbance there," he started. "They wanted to make sure we had checked out and see if we were alright."

"What kind of disturbance?" I asked, chills running through my body with fear.

"Some kind of explosion went off in our room…everything was destroyed. I guess Darien and Jeremiah aren't too pleased you're gone."

"Man, that room bill will be enormous," I joked.

"Who is this man who keeps saving us?" Tristan asked, deep in thought.

"I don't know, but if I ever find out, I'll owe him big time."

"I knew Darien and Jeremiah would come after you, but I didn't think they would risk hurting you after everything they went through to get your powers back."

"If I won't join them, they'll have to kill me."

We filled the others in on what happened at the hotel, and they sat stunned.

"You said you don't own any guns, right?" I asked, remembering Genevieve telling me as much at the half-way house.

She nodded her head, "Guns don't work for witches."

"Why?" I remembered Tristan explaining this to me before, but I still couldn't wrap my head around it.

Genevieve shrugged. "They just don't work right. Sometimes they'll fire, sometimes they'll even fire straight, most times they don't work at all. Physics is different where large groups of witches concentrate. The magic in the air changes it." She shrugged again. "Best anyone has been able to explain it anyway."

"We don't have a lot of need for most human inventions," Tristan offered, "so no one really cares to study them."

"You're such an advanced society and you can't be bothered to learn why some of the most effective human technology doesn't work here?"

"Okay," Lachlan said, "picture this. Humans persecuted and condemned witches in the past, right? They did it mostly with superior numbers. Witches typically don't have a need for guns, but humans would in a human-witch conflict. The fact that guns don't work keeps us safe. If we studied that and found out a way to make guns that work, it doesn't really help us, but that research, that theoretical technology could be quite detrimental to us in human hands."

Reluctantly I nodded. "That makes sense, I guess." I still

didn't like the answer. "Wait a minute," I said, turning back to Genevieve. "You said they don't work near large concentrations of witches because of the magic in the air. What about in an anti-magic room? They should work there, right?" No one answered for a moment, though they shared curious glances. Eventually Tristan shrugged.

"Maybe," he said.

"Maybe," the others agreed.

"Well, I'm getting one, but until then, what other options do we have for more protection?"

"Strength in numbers?" Lachlan said. "I know some people we can trust."

"Who?" Genevieve asked.

"Do we really need anyone else involved in this right now?" Lexi added.

To Genevieve, Lachlan said, "Fay and John," Then he turned to Lexi "and we can use all the help we can get."

Tristan's forehead scrunched in concentration.

"Do I know them?" He asked after a moment of straining.

"You met John once or twice. Good guy, maybe you'll remember when you see him," Lachlan said hesitantly.

"And you're sure they can be trusted?" Tristan pushed.

"Aye. They saved my neck a few times already," Lachlan ensured.

"The more the merrier," I put in, hoping I would feel less afraid with more people around. Lachlan nodded his head and went to the kitchen.

"Do you know them?" I asked Genevieve.

"Yeah. They are trustworthy, though Fay can be a bit hot-headed, especially about John."

"Have they been together long?" I asked.

"No, they're not together. That's the problem."

I nodded, remembering the feeling, and how frustrating it was to try to be seen.

"Are they protectors too? That's why they can't feel more for each other?" I asked, remembering what Lexi told me before.

"What?" Genevieve said, "No, only Tristan and Lexi are protectors and they can feel however they want. Why would you think they couldn't?"

I turned to Lexi who was averting my gaze, "You lied to me?" I asked.

"You wouldn't believe me any other way. I kept telling you I wasn't interested, but you didn't buy it so I added a little lie. I was telling the truth though, I wasn't then, nor am I now interested," Lexi stammered.

"Interested in what?" Tristan asked. We all grew silent.

"Damn it, Lexi!" I said, but she just laughed. Understanding dawned on Tristan's face, and I swear I think he almost blushed.

"You were asking about me? How sweet," Tristan teased. I gently punched him in the shoulder.

"Shut up," I snapped.

"Alright, gave 'em a call," Lachlan said, walking into the room and bringing the business tone back with him. "They'll be here soon."

"So, what exactly is going to happen when they get here?" I asked.

"Well, for starters we can use an extra couple o' heads. Easier to think up a plan. Then we'll see," Lachlan answered.

"Well now is as good a time as any for lunch," Genevieve said walking toward the kitchen.

"Let me help," I offered, following her.

We ate sandwiches and drank iced tea, making it truly feel like summertime. I was helping Genevieve clean up when a knock on the door made me jump almost out of my skin. Tristan watched me carefully, as Lachlan went to answer the door. I closed my eyes and took a deep breath to calm my nerves. I wasn't usually so on edge, but I kept feeling that Darien or Jeremiah would pop up and take me back.

I walked into the living room followed by Lexi and Genevieve. Lachlan came in then, followed by two people. The man was only a little shorter than Tristan. He had sandy brown hair and blue eyes. His skin was lightly tanned and his teeth were gleaming white, though one of his front teeth slightly overlapped its neighbor giving him a boyish look. He had the same muscular build as Tristan and Lachlan; built but lean. The woman was around my height, but had a smaller build. Her auburn hair fell to her shoulders and her brown eyes studied each of us. She wore a black, sleeveless turtle-neck, black slacks, and even her nails were painted black.

"Everyone, this is John and Fay. John and Fay, this is everyone," Lachlan introduced casually.

Fay stood still, arms hanging tightly at her sides as she said hello to the room. Her aura was a dim golden brown, and I could feel a sense of reluctance, like she wasn't entirely happy to be there. John was loose and comfortable, shaking hands with everyone. He stopped when he got to Tristan, eyeing him familiarly.

"Do I know you?" He asked Tristan.

"Not sure. Lachlan says we've met a few times, but I can't seem to recall when."

"Huh," John said, and moved on. He gave Genevieve a hug and turned to Lexi who smiled. He shook her hand and held it a moment longer than he had with Tristan.

John came to me next, and I shook his hand. His grip was warm and strong.

"I'm Selena," I introduced. He beamed.

"It is such an honor to meet you." He pulled me into a light hug. "Sorry, got excited." He smiled. I laughed. Tristan stepped beside me and placed his arm around my waist, making me smile. Fay studied us and then turned her attention to the group.

"So how do you know Lachlan?" I asked.

"Oh, we go way back...we went to school together," John said smiling. Tristan turned speculative.

"I don't remember you from school," he said.

"Oh, that's probably because I ended up moving away for a few years, but as soon as I came back it was as if I never left. He's a great friend."

Lachlan almost looked embarrassed. "You're the one who saved my ass."

"What's the story there?" Lexi asked, getting comfortable on the couch.

"Oh, that's a great story," John said, sitting in the arm chair.

"I don't think you need to tell this one," Lachlan said, getting uncomfortable.

"I have to hear this," I said, sitting next to Lexi.

Lachlan sighed as John began to speak. "Okay, so this was like, five years ago, before Lachlan and Genevieve got together."

"A ton of relationships get destroyed by stories that start that way," Tristan said sitting down, and Genevieve followed suit, while Lachlan paced.

"So we're at a casino in Vegas," John said, and Genevieve groaned. "And Lachlan was down to betting his shirt, he was flat broke." He chuckled.

"Yes, and John gave me money, thus saving me. The end," Lachlan said quickly.

"Right," I said sarcastically.

"You brought this up, it's only fair we hear it out," Genevieve said, a small smile forming on her lips.

"Anyways," John continued. "I finally convince Lachlan to leave the black jack table so he wouldn't end up in debt. As we're about to leave the casino, a woman approaches us, and she was...wow... legs that went for days and-" John stopped himself. "Anyways, this woman starts flirting with Lachlan here, and starts nibbling-" Again, John stopped himself and cleared his throat. "So, turns out this girl has a boyfriend. He barrels up to us, all pissed, and we back off, not wanting any trouble. The guy doesn't want to let this go, so Lachlan bets this human to leave us alone-"

"And a thousand bucks," Lachlan added.

"Right," John laughed.

"Hey, I needed the cash," Lachlan said.

"Anyways," John continued. "Lachlan bets our safety and a thousand bucks that he can make a chair levitate. The guy obviously agrees, thinking he can win this easily. So Lachlan makes a show of it and wiggles his fingers at a specific chair. Naturally, it lifts off the floor about a foot. The guy thinks he's being played and rushes to the chair to see if there are any strings or whatever attached to it. He finds nothing and gets pissed. He challenges Lachlan to do it again, only to a chair of his choosing. Lachlan agreed, and again he made the chair levitate."

I looked at Lachlan pacing.

"Obviously, the human is pissed, knowing he's getting played but unable to prove it. He tells Lachlan he's going to get cash, and we see him walk outside of the casino. We followed distantly, not wanting the guy to feel threatened, but making sure he wasn't going to take off. What we didn't notice was that he had called his friends for back up.

"We followed him to a deserted section of the hotel by an ATM. Again we gave him his space, not hovering over him. He walked back to us, and was quickly flanked by four guys. Lachlan and I aren't really worried at this point because we have spells, and they don't. Unfortunately, I didn't see the guys that came up behind us until they knocked Lachlan out, and were about to come after me.

"I had to act quickly. I cast a fire spell at the group of guys around us. I didn't burn them, but they were obviously freaked out and ran away. I threw Lachlan over my shoulder and took him back to the room. When he came to, all he asked was 'Did you get the money?'" John laughed.

"Aye, and that's why I will never try to mess with humans again…it's not worth the grief," Lachlan huffed, still pacing. "All that and we didn't even get paid."

"I was hoping that was going to be a much more embarrassing story," Lexi said.

"Oh, I have a bunch of those," John replied. "I just didn't want to get Lachlan into too much trouble."

"Thank God," Lachlan said under his breath. "I was sure you were going to tell the one-" He cleared his throat, catching himself and looking sheepish.

Lexi smiled and stood. "Why don't I give you guys a tour?" She said, gently taking John's arm as he stood.

"Is this a physical tour?" Fay asked, eyeing Lexi's hand. Lexi just shrugged indifferently, but she removed her hand from John. Well this was going to be interesting.

"Calm down, Fay," John said."Jeez you're high strung today." He started walking alongside Lexi.

Fay's body tensed at the remark. Either John was completely oblivious to how Fay felt about him or he didn't care. The three of them headed out of the room with Lexi chatting lightly.

7. SCHEMING

The rest of the morning passed slowly and uneventfully. After Lexi gave Fay and John a tour of the house, everyone gathered in the living room to brainstorm.

"What if we went back to their camp and spied on them?" I heard John ask. "Try to get some information that way?" My mind snapped to attention. I was scared for these people. I worried that I wouldn't be able to keep them all safe.

"The Charge already scoped the area out and found nothing," Lexi said.

"What's the end goal here?" I asked. "Are we going to hunt and kill Darien and Jeremiah?"

"Yes," Lachlan and John said in unison.

"We'd be seriously outnumbered," I said.

"From what I've heard, we can't be outnumbered with you," John said. I felt my face pale. "You could take them all out by yourself." He smiled.

"Well," I started, trying to organize my thoughts. "Assuming we found their new camp, they could have stronger spells, and more witches. We have no idea what we'd be getting ourselves into."

"We didn't know that when we went to get you either,"

Lexi said. "All we can do is try, unless you have another idea?" I felt guilty that my friends had to put themselves in such danger just so I wouldn't be hunted anymore.

"I think we should check the site again," Tristan said. "Lexi," he held his arm out. "Would you do me the honor of accompanying me?" he smiled. Lexi jumped up.

"Hell yeah!"

"Wait!" I protested. "Where are you going?"

"I'm taking Lexi to the camp to see if there's anything the Charge may have missed; some clue as to where they may have gone."

Lexi beamed.

"Alone?" I gasped. "What if someone's there?" I started to pace.

"Selena, relax," Tristan said. "We just need to see if there's any chance we can track them, otherwise all of our planning is for nothing."

"Fine," I huffed, and plopped myself down on the couch, arms crossed over my chest. "For the record I think this is a terrible idea."

Tristan chuckled, kissed the top of my head and teleported with Lexi.

"Well, I could eat," John commented. "Need some brain food."

"We have some extra sandwiches." Genevieve went to the kitchen, always the good host.

"I'll help. I know what he likes," Fay offered, getting to her feet so fast she was almost a blur. I wondered why she was trying so hard when John clearly didn't care. Then again, I probably came across the same way with Tristan.

"Thanks," he replied, and went to talk to Lachlan.

"Damn it," Tristan said, appearing back into the room with Lexi.

"Nothing there?" I asked.

"Nope," Lexi said, popping the p at the end of the word. "Didn't even have the courtesy to leave any personal belongings behind for me to scry with." She let out a sigh, held her hands out and sealed the house. The gesture unnerved me. A reminder that we weren't safe.

I left them and went to my room, trying to clear my head so I would know how to deal with this. I lay back on the bed, and stared at the ceiling thinking. I knew we had to go after Darien and Jeremiah, but I was scared. I didn't want anyone getting hurt.

I hadn't been in the room for two minutes before there was a knock on the door.

I got off the bed and opened the door. Lexi stood there, smiling. She looked around behind her once before coming in the room.

"Everything okay?" I asked, closing the door behind her. She sat at the edge of the bed and looked up at me.

"Yeah, I just wanted to make sure you were okay. You looked a little stressed."

I sighed. "Yeah, I just don't know what to do, that's all. I just need some time to think and I'll be fine."

"You sure?"

I nodded.

"Okay, well let me know if I can help in anyway." Lexi

stood and walked toward the door.

"Hey, Lex?"

"Hmm?" she turned to face me.

"I may be reading the situation wrong, but I hope you weren't planning on…" I stopped, worried I was over-thinking things.

"On what?"

I took a deep breath. "On pursuing John." Lexi opened her mouth to respond but I kept talking. "I mean, I just noticed a few things, looks, stuff like that, and I don't think it's a good idea."

"I mean," Lexi started, "I do think he's kind of cute. Don't you think he's nice?"

"I don't know Lexi, I just met the guy. And so did you. It's not about him being nice or not. It's just a bad time."

"Well I know, I just thought he was cute, that's all." She gave me a knowing look then dropped her gaze to her hands and my guilt welled up. I know she was wondering how I could tell her not to pursue a guy when I pursued Tristan. I had to explain this better to her.

"He is, and he does seem nice." I let out a sigh, "That's not what I'm worried about. Fay's got a thing for him, so you might be getting more drama than you're bargaining for, and we just can't afford that kind of distraction right now."

"Yeah, you're right," Lexi said on a sigh. "I think I just needed something to get excited about." Lexi lowered her voice to a whisper. "Why do you think he hasn't given Fay a shot yet?"

I wasn't sure how to respond. I didn't know what John was all about or how he felt about Fay. What if something happened between them before and they decided not to pursue it, but they both really wanted to?

"I don't know, but be careful. We need everyone focused right now, not fighting over a guy you know?"

Lexi nodded, "I get it. I'll be good. Swear." She crossed two fingers over her chest and held them up. "Scout's honor."

"You were never in the scouts."

Lexi laughed, "It's the same principle. Who cares?"

I shook my head and smiled. Lexi smiled and threw her arms around me. "Thanks BFF."

I laughed and hugged her back. It was actually nice not having to think about anything serious. It was a nice break from my mental ranting. "Okay, I'll leave you alone now. Let me know if you need anything, okay?"

"I will. Thanks."

Lexi stood and walked to the door, closing it behind her. I sat back down on the bed and thought about Tristan. I wanted him to come to the room, but I didn't want everyone to know. I liked to talk to him, talk out my thoughts and worries.

There was another knock on my door and I went to answer it, assuming Lexi had forgotten to ask me something else.

"You called?" Tristan asked, standing in the doorway.

"Nope," I smiled

"Yeah, you did." Tristan tapped his temple.

"Oh crap! How do I keep forgetting about that connection?"

Tristan laughed. "Can I come in?" I held the door wider, and he swept past me. I closed the door and turned to face him.

"Tristan-"

He pressed his finger against my lips to silence me.

"Don't say anything." He lowered his face to mine and

kissed me softly.

Passion flooded through me, consuming my entire being. I grabbed the back of his head, pulling him closer to me, kissing him harder. Tristan's eyes widened in surprise, but he recovered quickly. We fell onto the bed, never breaking our kiss. Before I knew it, my shirt was off and Tristan's fingers were working the button on my jeans. I ran my hands under his shirt, feeling his smooth, warm skin, and pulled it off over his head.

Tristan unbuttoned my jeans and shimmied them down, and he pressed his warm body on mine. Our hands were everywhere, and we gasped for air in between kisses. Tristan kissed my neck, my collar bone, my chest, and down to my navel. The lower he got, the more anxious I became. I pulled him up and rolled on top of him. He trailed his hand through my hair and down my back, as his lips moved with mine.

It was when he started fumbling with my bra that I sat back, still straddled on his lap.

"What's wrong?" He asked, studying my face.

"We can't do this. Not here and not now. It's too weird. We're in Genevieve's house, everyone is around us, and we're in the middle of a war here. I'm sorry, I just can't do it."

"It's okay, this is enough for me, I can't get enough of kissing you." He pulled my face down and pressed his lips against mine. Without the pressure hovering over me, it was much more enjoyable. After a while I moved so I was lying beside him. I rested my head on his bare chest and listened to his heart beating.

Tristan softly kissed my fingertips, and all thoughts of talking about my worries disappeared.

8. DREAMS

My sleep started out blissful and then changed. I was running through the forest, running away from someone or something. I turned to look behind me, to see what I was so afraid of, but I saw nothing. All I could hear were the heavy footfalls and crunching leaves as my pursuer ran over them.

I looked back again, still running, but having no idea what from. Then I saw them. Crystal and Yuri chased me with angry snarls on their faces. I ran faster, pushed harder.

"Here, Selena! Come here!" I heard him and my heart leapt. I veered to the right, following his beautiful voice. "I will keep you safe," he reassured.

I sprinted with renewed vigor, and after a few moments I saw him, his neat brown hair brushed to the side, his brown eyes welcoming me. I ran straight into his outstretched arms, forgetting my pursuers. He was all I could think of.

He lowered his face and pressed his lips against mine. My heart raced, "Oh, Darien," I whispered.

I bolted upright in bed.

"Selena? You okay?" Tristan asked groggily, turning to face

me in bed.

"Yeah, just a weird dream," I answered, feeling guilty.

"Yuri and Crystal again?" I didn't correct him. It wasn't uncommon for me to still have nightmares about the two witches who tortured me. There was no way I would tell Tristan I was dreaming about kissing his brother! Why wasn't I disgusted like I usually was with Darien? Why did I still feel his kiss? And why did I want more? God, I hoped it was just some remnant of Jeremiah's spell. Maybe it was just a dream and I shouldn't read into it too much. I just didn't like the feeling in my stomach.

Tristan pulled me back to bed and wrapped his arms around me. It felt wonderful, but Darien kept popping back into my head.

"It was just a dream," Tristan reassured. Had he known what I was really dreaming about? I desperately pushed the thought away and finally I was able to fall back asleep.

This time the dream was different. It didn't feel like a dream; it felt like I was still awake or in between levels of consciousness.

I was in some kind of jail cell; it was dark and the smell of human waste made me want to retch. Breathing through my sleeve didn't help, so I lowered my arm when I heard him rasp.

"Selena." The voice was familiar, and my stomach dropped in response.

I looked around, but saw no one. "We don't have much time," the voice continued.

"Who's there?" I asked, looking around again. Then from the corner of the cell, out of the darkness an old man slowly crept forward. His clothes were ragged and torn, his hair and beard grew into each other, and spilled down the man's frail body.

"I'm afraid there's no time for small talk. I need you to get me out of here," the old man pleaded.

"What? Who are you?" I asked feeling extremely confused.

"I was the one who sent you all those warnings. You must help me. He will kill me when he has no more use for me, and that time is coming near. I can help you find the prophecy. I know what Jeremiah's plans are ahead of time. Please just get me out!"

I had no idea what to think, but this man's urgency was overwhelming.

"Where are you?" I asked the old man.

"Underground, beneath the court house. I'll show you." He reached his bony hand out, and I reflexively pulled away. "Please, there's no time!"

He grabbed my arm before I could react, and a slew of images fluttered through my mind. I was flying through the front doors of the courthouse, through a long hallway that led to another less used hallway. Through a hidden door in the wall that lead to a spiral staircase, that led down, down, down into the darkness. Then through another door that led through a damp, dark, tunnel that led to three flights of stone steps leading even farther down. Through a hatch in the ground, down the rails on the side, and down the hallway to a small cell, where an old man stood.

I gasped as the man released my arm. What was this? Why was he kept prisoner here? There was a sense of familiarity, as if I had been there before, or seen it in a dream before, but I couldn't place it. I had a million questions, but I didn't get to ask a single one.

Tristan shook me awake. My eyes fluttered open, and in the deep recesses of my mind I heard the man's voice echo. "Help me!"

"Selena, what's wrong?" Tristan stood beside the bed, already dressed. The sun streamed through the windows comfortingly. What had I just been dreaming about?

"What time is it?" I asked.

"Just after nine. What's wrong?" He asked again.

"What do you mean?" I sat up, threw the covers off me and stood next to Tristan.

"You were talking in your sleep, and you looked scared," he explained.

I shrugged my shoulders, "Must have been a weird dream."

"Crystal and Yuri, again?" He asked, with a weird hint in his tone. Something flittered through my memory. "'Cause you looked pretty scared when you woke up from that one last night too."

Then it came back to me, my dream about Darien. My face flushed, I didn't want to have any feelings for Darien other than hatred. I kept telling myself it was just a dream. You can't control them, and sometimes they feel real and make you feel things you normally wouldn't. It would wear off soon, I was sure of it. No big deal and no need to dwell on it.

Feeling satisfied with my analysis, I easily pushed my Darien dream aside, needing to forget it. I shrugged my shoulders and went to the bathroom, leaving Tristan standing by the bed. What had I just been dreaming about though? I washed up, got dressed and headed down the stairs, but I still couldn't recall my dream.

Down in the kitchen, everyone was already awake and eating, or had already eaten breakfast. I helped myself to a muffin and poured myself some coffee, then sat down at the table across from Fay and John. Genevieve was busy tidying the kitchen, while Lachlan placed his plate in the sink and headed toward the living room to join Tristan and Lexi.

"You guys sleep okay last night?" I asked John and Fay.

"Yep, like a baby," John joked. Fay rolled her eyes.

"How did you sleep?" Fay asked, analyzing my appearance. I knew what she was seeing, dark rings around my eyes, my hair pulled back into a ponytail, no make-up. I'm sure I was a sight.

"I slept okay for the most part, just had some weird dreams. I feel like I'm forgetting some though." I concentrated, trying to search through my mind for that damn dream.

"What did you dream?" John asked.

"One was..." I stopped, and then decided to tell them half of it, "Crystal and Yuri were chasing me through the woods. But I can't remember the other one."

"Crystal and Yuri?" John looked disgusted. "That would give anyone nightmares. Lexi told me how you handled them. It was very impressive."

"Thanks," I said, feeling self-conscious.

"It'll come to you. Just don't try so hard," Fay said, taking her plate to the sink and washing it before Genevieve could get to it. I did the same after I finished my muffin and headed to the living room.

Lexi was laughing at Lachlan, who had spread himself over

one of the couches.

"What?" He asked. "I ate too much; I need to digest."

Lexi kept laughing, "You are such an old man." The others giggled along, but something tickled my memory. Just as I thought I might have something, it slipped away again. Frustrated, I sat down beside Tristan.

After a moment of silence, John spoke up, "Man, whoever took the prophecy knew what they were doing." Again, something tickled my memory. "It might have helped us figure out what to do next."

"Does anyone know what the prophecy is by heart?" Fay asked.

"I only know parts of it. Only what my mother told me," Tristan answered.

"That's the spell," Lexi filled the others in on the reason why they couldn't remember much about the prophecy or how it vanished. "I only know bits and pieces too." The rest nodded their head in agreement. Lexi reached for an old magazine that sat on the table and started to flip through it.

"It would be best to find the full thing," Genevieve added. "Who knows what it really says? There could be a lot of stuff in there that could help us."

"What's up, Selena?" Lexi asked.

"Huh?" I responded.

"You look constipated. You okay?" she retorted.

I laughed, "I'm just trying to remember my dream. I can't help but think it has something to do with the prophecy."

I gasped. Suddenly the entirety of my dream came rushing back.

"I think I know someone who can help us find the prophecy," I started, but then stopped myself. It was just a dream, wasn't it? Or was it real? What if it's a trap?

"Selena, what are you thinking so hard about?" Lexi asked.

"I remember my dream. I'm just not sure…" I let the sentence hang as I thought it through.

"I swear that dream is going to give her an aneurism," John joked.

"What did you dream? It'll help if you talk it out," Tristan suggested.

I recanted the details of the dream.

"It was probably just a dream," Genevieve said sympathetically.

"No, that sounds real and I say we get him out," Lachlan pushed. We turned to look at him. "Look, he's real. I've heard of witches with his abilities. He's a strong telepath if he was able to send a vision to Selena when she was awake. This guy's a psychic, and a strong one at that. A strong enough psychic can create and send her the dream for that matter. And he says he can tell us where the prophecy is and he will know what Jeremiah is doing ahead of time. We could use him on our side."

We sat in silence, taking in the information.

"But how do we know he can be trusted?" Genevieve asked.

"What have we got to lose?" Lachlan asked. Tristan gave him a knowing glare, but he continued. "I mean why send you these warnings to begin with?"

"Maybe to get us to trust him so we'll want to help him, and then after we get him out he'll-" Genevieve started, but Lachlan cut her off.

"He'll what? Run and not help us?" Lachlan said. "I doubt he'll get us killed. If he hadn't warned them, Tristan, Lexi and Selena would probably be dead by now."

"If we died, we wouldn't be able to help him escape," Tristan said. "Once he's out and he doesn't need us anymore, all bets are off."

"The question is: do we want to take the chance?" Fay asked. "Even if his intentions are pure, we could get hurt or killed just trying to help him escape, and there's no way to know for sure if he will or can help us once he's free."

"Where else do we start?" Lexi asked. "If we don't save this guy and take a chance that he can help us find the Wayward or the prophecy, how do we find it on our own?"

"I don't know," Tristan said. "No one knows where it is, but we could check the library, see if we can find anything."

"He did sound like he was running out of time," I said. "He said Jeremiah would kill him when he had no more use of him. Think what would happen if Jeremiah found out he'd been helping us. I mean we have often been one step ahead of him so far."

"That's a big piece of information you forgot to mention," Fay added hotly.

"What? Why?" I asked.

"With that, we know that he's directly working with Jeremiah and that he's against them," she explained.

"That's assuming he's telling the truth," Tristan joined in.

"Look, we don't have time to lose," I said. "Why don't some of us go to the library and see what they can find while the rest of us prepare to get the guy out. That way if there is a lead from the library we can follow that but if not, then we didn't waste any time."

Tristan let out a sigh, "Genevieve and I will investigate the disappearance of the prophecy. Find out what articles they have on it at the library and you guys figure everything else out. We should be back in an hour or so." He brushed a piece of my hair behind my ear, "You should stay here where you're well-guarded." He looked around at the group of withes he was leaving me with, and then walked toward Genevieve. He was about to teleport when Lexi abruptly stood.

"Wait! I put the security spells on the house. Hang on a sec." She waved her hand across the room and took a deep breath. "You can go now. And you're welcome, by the way, that could have really hurt." She sent a sarcastic glance toward Tristan who made a face back. I remembered how much that did hurt when I tried teleporting out of a protected house a while ago. In a flash Tristan and Genevieve were gone.

"John and Fay," I said. "I think now is as good a time as any to let us know what your abilities are."

Lachlan and Lexi looked at one another and then settled on John and Fay.

"I can control air and manifest fire, among many other things," John announced with a smile.

"I can manifest and control water as well as telekinesis, telepathy, and what I like to call 'the boom'." There was a sparkle in Fay's eyes I had never seen before. I was a little scared.

"What's 'the boom'?" Lexi asked.

"You just might see," Fay answered.

"Now that's settled," Lachlan said changing the subject. "You know where he's being held?" He grabbed a pen and paper.

"Yeah, let me think," I drew out the way through the courthouse and hallways, all the way down to the cell.

"Do you know what kind of protection there is?" Fay asked. I shook my head no.

"That can be a problem," John said. "There can be any number of barrier spells, guards, or enchantments around him."

"I might be able to find out," Lexi said. "I need to make a call." She left the room.

"So what if I teleport us to him," I said. "Tristan and Genevieve will stay here and wait for the all clear. If we can get in and out easily, Tristan may not even have to come."

"That could work," Lachlan said.

"I had to leave a message," Lexi said coming back into the room.

"For who?" I asked.

"An old friend. What could work?"

"To try and teleport us to him," I said.

"Well, if you can teleport there, and this guy is a psychic, then why did he show you exactly how to get to his cell?" Lexi asked sitting back down on the floor. It was a good question. I didn't know the answer.

"Maybe he thought it would be easier if Selena knew exactly where she was teleporting to," Lachlan analyzed.

"Well, I say when Tristan and Gen come back, we follow through with that plan," John jokingly wiggled his eyebrows at

Lexi who rolled her eyes.

Fay glared at the two for a moment, "So I guess there's nothing left to do now but wait," she said as she headed to the kitchen.

9. LOG BOOK
-TRISTAN-

The musty smell of books was welcoming and I quickly searched for Mrs. Ledsmith. The library was uncharacteristically deserted.

"Hello?" I called, but no one answered.

"That's weird. I don't remember a single time that I came here and Mrs. Ledsmith was away," Genevieve said, looking around cautiously. She was right; I couldn't remember a time either. It felt wrong. The help desk was also empty.

"Alright, let's see what we can find." I said, and headed to the history and news section. Large books of old articles filled the shelves, the old newspaper clippings spilling from the covers.

"How do we narrow this down?" Genevieve asked. "Do we know what year the prophecy went missing?"

I shook my head. "Maybe we can just generalize it." I stood and faced the shelf. "Show us anything pertaining to the missing prophecy." I demanded. Three books flew from the shelves, landing on the table next to us and opening to specific pages. Genevieve and I sat at the table and started reading.

"This doesn't say much," Genevieve said after a few silent

moments. "Just that a page in the prophetic journal was erased and that the page was blank in all the journals that were published. It says that those who had read it couldn't seem to recall the details to rewrite it. That must be from the spell Lexi was talking about."

"Does it say what year?"

"It just says it was shortly after it was published." She checked the pages before and after the article. "Nothing else."

"This one says pretty much the same thing. Let's see the last one." I moved the third book so it was facing me and Genevieve and we read it together.

"What?" I asked under my breath as I read the article. "This could be the lead we need."

"There's no way to know where to find this," Genevieve said. I did another search on this new information, but came up blank.

"I think this is all we're going to get," I said, sweeping my hands over the books and watching them return to place.

"Let's go," Genevieve said.

The library was still empty, and I felt very unsettled by the isolation. We passed the front desk, but Mrs. Ledsmith hadn't yet returned.

"Hey wait," I said. I sat behind the desk and rummaged through the drawers. Finally I found the large brown log book.

"You're not supposed to touch that," Genevieve said. "Only Mrs. Ledsmith can have access to those witches' names, and she can't release them."

"Well, it's a good thing she's not here right now," I said, looking around to be sure. If she came out though, I'd be in big trouble.

I reached into the drawer to remove the tome but as soon as my fingers got within an inch of the book I was shocked. I pulled my hand back reflexively; damn that hurt.

Genevieve chuckled. "Told ya."

"You have a better idea?" I asked.

"Move over."

I obliged and Genevieve hovered over the drawer.

"Maybe we should call Lexi," I said after a few minutes. "This is her area of expertise."

"Just give me a minute." A soft rattling behind us made me spin around, but there was nothing there.

"Hurry up," I hissed.

"Got it!" Genevieve said, and handed me the book.

"How?"

Genevieve smiled and shrugged. I didn't have enough time to press it just then. I quickly rummaged through the pages. It was full of witches names, dates and books signed out. Next to the book title was a column for the number of days allotted before it magically returned itself.

"I wish we knew when it went missing." Genevieve said, reading over my shoulder. I thought back to the last time the copy was here.

"All I know is I came here to find the copy just before Selena's 25th birthday, to make sure I had all the information and proof for her, but when Mrs. Ledsmith went to get it, she found it missing." Then it dawned on me and I wanted to smack myself in the forehead.

"I just remembered Mrs. Ledsmith checked the records

when she couldn't find the prophecy, and she said there was no recent listing in here of it being checked out."

"Well we might as well check again," she comforted.

"So if the prophecy disappeared shortly after it was published in 1988 we're looking around the late 80's, early 90's," I said.

I flipped to the front of the book and saw that it was dated back to 2010.

"Is there another book?" Genevieve asked. I searched through the rest of the drawers, but found nothing. I let out a growl of frustration.

"Relax," Genevieve said. "We'll find something."

"I need this book," I waved the tome in my hand around, "to have the information starting from around 1988. How are we going to get that?"

The book flew from my hand, landing on the desk.

"These books are jumping around a lot today," Genevieve said, just as the cover flipped open. The first page, which had been dated 2010 shimmered and expanded, making the book three times as thick. I squinted to read the new first page.

It started at 1988.

A smile spread across my face. Oh, yeah.

I looked around again to make sure we were still alone. I skimmed through, when something caught my eye. I squinted on the first page, and scrawled in ink in the book title column was *Prophetic Journal 1988.* In the Author column were only three names, though I'm sure there were dozens who contributed to the journal. *Damien Brooks, Artemis Siff, Jeffry Wright.* I looked at the date. It was checked out July 15, 1988. I checked the name of the witch who borrowed it, but the ink was slightly smudged.

"Here use this," Genevieve said, holding a small magnifying glass I'd seen Mrs. Ledsmith use on numerous occasions. I took the object and held it over the page. The small print expanded, but I still couldn't make out the name.

"There are no days allotted to whoever checked this out." I clenched my jaw. I skimmed through the list, page after page, trying to find the next person who checked it out.

I had reached 1992 and still no record of anyone checking out the prophecy. Finally I saw something.

"Right here it shows Prophetic Journal 1988 2nd Edition. So that's when the copy was checked out." I checked the name and smiled. Honoria Arturro.

"Do you think she checked it out because she was starting to suspect Selena?" Gen asked.

"That would make sense. It shows she had it for three days." I kept searching each page. The second edition had been checked out and returned numerous times by various witches, but the original was never listed again.

"Hey look!" Genevieve pointed to a line in the book. It was the prophecy copy checked out in 1993 by Jordana Gabriel. "That's your mother's name, isn't it?"

I nodded. A lump formed in my throat as I remembered her. I thought back to the days when she used to tell me about the prophecy, about the girl it foretold. It was almost like a bed time story, and by the time I turned thirteen I was ready to protect the girl who would save us all.

I flipped to the back of the book. The last time the copy was checked out was April 2013. It was checked out by a witch I didn't know, and he had it for only three days.

"That was over a year ago. Mrs. Ledsmith said she had it here just days before I tried to check it out myself," I analyzed.

"Then someone stole it without checking it out."

"How did no one notice it missing?" I questioned.

"Maybe the spell to erase the original spilled over to the copy as well?" Genevieve answered.

I stood up and started to pace.

"We need to find Mrs. Ledsmith." Genevieve started searching through each row of the library, but the place was completely empty.

"Wait. There's one place we didn't look." I rushed toward the back of the library, to the room that was closed off to the public, and knocked on the metal gate enclosing it. "Mrs. Ledsmith, if you're in there please open the door. It's Tristan and I really need to talk to you."

There was a flutter of noise from the other side as the doors opened and a frazzled looking Mrs. Ledsmith came out.

"Heavens! I'm terribly sorry; I had no idea anyone was in here. How are you, Tristan dear? And Genevieve, look at you, as beautiful as ever." She pushed her glasses up on her nose.

We'd been in the library for over half an hour. What had she been up to all that time?

"Hello, Mrs. Ledsmith." Genevieve smiled.

I tried to look in the room behind her to see what she had been doing, but she closed and locked both doors before I could get a peek in.

"I'm confused actually," I started. "We wanted to ask you about the prophecy. When we couldn't find you, we..." I paused.

I really didn't want to get in trouble for this, but I had to let her know what we knew. "We searched the log book ourselves."

"Now Tristan, that's not for public use," Mrs. Ledsmith chided. "You're lucky I was back here and didn't catch you." A knowing glint shimmered in her eyes.

"Yes, lucky." I smiled. "The last witch checked the second edition out over a year ago. Was there no activity since then?" I asked.

"Tristan, those log books are kept up well. If there is no record of it being taken out since then, then there was no more activity."

"If those books are so up to date, how come you don't know where the copy is now?" I argued.

Mrs. Ledsmith's face flushed red. "I told you last time that no one had checked it out recently. I don't know where it is, or how it was taken from here without my knowledge, but I am trying to find out! Don't you think I am humiliated and angry enough that someone could have taken something from this library, from *my* library under *my* watch?" Her anger flared.

I let out a sigh. "I'm sorry, Mrs. Ledsmith, I'm just so frustrated. I don't understand where it went and we need it."

"Well if I ever figure out who took it, you'll be the first to know." Her anger seemed to subside slightly.

Mrs. Ledsmith sighed and walked toward the front of the library. Genevieve and I followed.

"All I know is the prophecy disappeared a couple weeks after it was published leaving only a blank page in every copy of the publication, in every printing proof. Artemis, the witch who wrote that particular prophecy was nowhere to be found. It couldn't even be republished." She shook her head sadly and continued. "A year or two after the disappearance, Elder Lacour donated his copy to the prophecy board on behalf of his missing friend, saying that it is the last remaining true copy."

"Wait... What?" I couldn't even form the question I desperately needed to ask.

"How did Elder Lacour get the copy?" Genevieve asked.

"Elder Lacour and Artemis were friends. When he donated his copy they added the new prophecy as an addendum to the 1988 edition. The copy didn't help convince witches that the prophecy was legitimate, until that too went missing.

"Apparently someone performed a ritual to make people forget the prophecy existed, only it didn't work entirely. Eventually some people started remembering and asked about the prophecy, but the others who forgot doubted the prophecy ever existed.

We reached her desk and she plopped down into the chair. I guess Lexi's grandfather was right.

"Do you remember what was in the original?" Genevieve asked.

Mrs. Ledsmith shook her head sadly, "It's been twenty-six years and I only read it once. All I remember is what was in the copy. I wish I could remember what the original said. I'm sorry I can't be of more help."

"Can you order another copy of the second edition?" Genevieve asked.

"I did, many times, but each time the publishing company would lose the record that I ordered it. There's some magic around that book that I can't seem to bypass. I even tried to go to the Prophetic Journal's head office, but it's like their eyes glaze over when I ask for it."

"What did the copy say?" I asked, wanting a refresher.

"It said that there was a girl with black hair and eyes as blue as the ocean. She would have powers no one other witch would have. On her twenty-fifth year, she would be awakened. It had a date, but I can't remember it. She would be the one to conquer the dark ones, and keep us all in the light. Something along those lines."

I remembered it somewhat like that as well, but my mother used to elaborate more. Maybe she had been creative with it, feeling it wasn't long enough for a story.

"This was helpful actually. Thank you." Genevieve smiled kindly.

"I'm sorry I was so angry," I started. "I just don't know where to go from here." I ran a hand through my hair.

Mrs. Ledsmith gave me a tired smile. "I wish I could help you, Tristan."

10. RESCUE MISSION
-SELENA-

It was over an hour before Tristan and Genevieve popped back into the living room.

"What'd ya find?" Lachlan asked as he came in from the kitchen. We all sat in our usual seats, waiting for the information.

Genevieve filled us in on the information they had learned.

"There's something else," Tristan said. We found a third article and it said that there was rumor that a copy of the prophecy was saved. It was believed to have been written in blood by the author in order to salvage it. It would be huge if we could find the original instead of the copy."

"Are the rumors true?" I asked.

"No idea, but it's the only lead we have," Genevieve said.

"Well what does the copy say again?" I asked.

Tristan recapped the copy of the prophecy.

"That still doesn't prove it's me," I said.

Tristan sighed, "I think it does, and I think that the original would probably have more specific details about you."

"Yes, I think the prophecy is a lot longer than we thought,"

Genevieve added. "I think there are more information and predictions that Jeremiah didn't want anyone else to know."

"So why not go straight to the source? Where is this Artemis guy?" Lexi asked.

"I don't know. Mrs. Ledsmith said he disappeared a few days after the prophecy was written," Tristan answered.

I groaned.

"What?" The group asked in unison. I would have laughed at the moment had I not just had a great epiphany.

"I feel so stupid. I don't know why I didn't figure this out sooner," I started, speaking more to myself than the others. I looked up to see Lexi staring curiously at me. "Jeremiah worked with a psychic to get the prophecy. He didn't want anyone to know what it really said, so he cast a spell to erase the prophecy from the journal but he had to get rid of the source. The psychic he worked with just happened to be unreachable. We just happen to have a strong psychic locked away in a cell in the courthouse where Jeremiah works. Is anyone else putting the pieces together?"

"I told ya!" Lachlan boomed, getting to his feet. "Let's get him out of there!"

"So wait," Fay said. "You're saying that the old man who sent you some dream is Artemis Siff, the guy who made the prophecy?"

"Yes. It makes sense, doesn't it?" I said excitedly. "Let's go."

"Wait," Tristan said. "You're telling me this guy has been locked away for twenty-something years and never told anyone else where he was?"

"Maybe he did," Genevieve said.

"Maybe he did, but they didn't make it out," Fay added.

"Look," I said. "I know this looks suspicious, but I really feel that he can help us. I don't know why he's still locked up, or what his story is, but we need to get him out."

Fay looked skeptical, Genevieve looked nervous, Lexi, John, and Lachlan looked excited, and Tristan looked at me.

"I don't know about this," Tristan said still studying me.

"I do," I said trying to reassure him.

"Great. Let's go," Lachlan said

"Wait," Tristan said. Lachlan and I let out frustrated sighs. "What's the plan?"

Oh yeah. I had forgotten to fill them in.

"I will teleport the group there, and hopefully back, but if we're in a place where we can't teleport or we need help, we'll call you and Genevieve in."

"I guess that's as good a plan as any," Genevieve reluctantly agreed. "You have cell phones and everything you need?"

"Yeah we're all set, just been waiting for you guys to return," I said as Lexi, John, Fay, and Lachlan gathered around me.

"Wait," Tristan interjected yet again.

"For the love of all that is holy, what is it now?" Lachlan asked, exasperated.

"I'm sorry. I still don't like the idea of Selena going without me," he said to Lachlan, and then he turned to face me. "I don't have a doubt in my mind that you can take care of yourself, I just..." He looked away, then back at me, "I just don't like you doing this without me," he finished, holding my gaze with his

117

piercing green eyes. It took me a moment to find my words.

"I'll be fine, and with any luck, I'll see you in about thirty seconds." I kissed him lightly. He nodded, but his jaw was clenched.

"I have an idea that will help," Lexi said, coming to stand next to me and Tristan. "Selena, where are you going?" She grabbed my hand and placed hers on Tristan who gasped. After a few moments she said, "There, now Tristan knows where you're going and can come after you if he needs to." She beamed.

"I should go instead of her," Tristan said gallantly.

Lexi rolled her eyes at him, and to me she said, "The alarm is still off."

"Okay here goes nothing," I said before Tristan could get a chance to take over. With everyone gathered around me, I closed my eyes and imagined the old man and his cell, imagined myself just outside of it. I felt the pull, but then nothing. It was as if I was floating in nothingness. I opened my eyes, but I only saw darkness, like I was in a room with no windows and all the lights were off.

Then I felt it. My body slammed hard against some unseen object and it hurt. It felt like I was being sucked backwards, and then I landed hard on my back, the wind knocked out of me.

"What the hell happened?" I heard someone ask. I opened my eyes and saw Tristan hovering over me. I was back in the living room.

"Where is everyone?" I whispered, trying to catch my breath.

"We're all here," Lexi answered, coming to stand above me.

"You're okay?" I asked.

"Yeah, we never left. Only you did," she explained.

"What?" I tried to sit up but my body hurt. "I thought you turned off the security spell."

"I did," Lexi said. "What happened?"

"I started teleporting, and then it felt like I was floating in nothingness, until I smacked into what felt like a Mac truck and was sucked back here." I moaned in pain. Genevieve knelt beside me and assessed the damage.

"See? I should've gone," Tristan said. I ignored him.

"Huh, there is actually some major bruising starting. I can take care of that though." Genevieve looked at me for permission.

"Won't it drain you?" Genevieve assessed me again.

"I should be alright," she said.

I nodded my head once, because it hurt to nod more than that. She placed her hands around my sides and back, healing the pain.

"Thanks, Gen," I said. She smiled at me, and went to rest on the couch. Within minutes I was feeling amazingly better, and it looked like Geni was too.

"Remember those barrier spells we were talking about?" John asked.

"Yeah," I said, getting to my feet.

"I think you found one." He smiled.

Damn.

"How come it was just me?" I asked.

"It's part of the spell, like my security spell," Lexi answered. "Whoever tries to teleport in will get hurt. You were the only one technically teleporting, so you got hurt, but it seems their spell is more advanced. They didn't even let you bring anyone else. Like just the intent to go there blocked us."

"Now we know why the old man gave you such specific directions." Fay chuckled.

"Damn," I said. "I knew it was too easy just to teleport there and back. Okay so I guess we're walking."

"Well we can teleport to the courthouse, just not inside I don't think," Tristan said.

"No, no more teleporting for me. At least for a little while; I'm scarred." I shuttered dramatically. Tristan scoffed and put his arm around my shoulder, directing me to the couch.

"Walking it is," John said.

"Couldn't we drive?" Lexi asked.

"We can fit four of us in our car," Genevieve offered. "But there isn't room for everyone."

"The rest of us can go in our car," John said.

That seemed to settle the transportation.

We reviewed the route the psychic showed me, and one by one, Lexi cast her truth spell on the others to show what I had seen. We decided it would be best to leave at night so we could go unnoticed. It was one thing to leave in the daytime if we were to teleport in and out unseen. But to go now, where everyone could see us - it would look very strange if we were lurking around hallways and came up with a withered old man out of nowhere.

A chirping noise sounded. "Be right back," Lexi said and bounded out of the room, putting her phone to her ear.

Genevieve and Lachlan were discussing strategy with John

and Fay, but Tristan sat quietly.

"You look tense," I said to Tristan.

"I can't say I really like this, but I'll be fine."

"It'll all work out," I said, placing my hand on his forearm. Tristan looked down at me, and studied my face, then nodded.

"I bought you something," he said.

"Really?" I smiled, excited to see what it was.

Tristan smiled back and handed me a small, black case, with a latch in the middle. I opened it and inside sat a small gun, surrounded by a foam frame. I lifted the little revolver, silver and sleek and a perfect fit in the palm of my hand.

"I love it!" I threw my arms around Tristan's neck.

"Careful with that thing," he said, pulling my hands from around him, and taking the little gun from me. "It's loaded."

"When did you have time to get that?"

"Genevieve and I made a stop, somewhere off the beaten path." He lifted the gun. "The safety is here," he pointed to a small button on the side of the pistol that slid back and forth."

"You're wonderful, thank you." I took the gun and placed it in the case and gave Tristan another hug.

He kissed my cheek. "I just want you to be safe."

"With you, I always am."

"That was Amy," Lexi said, coming back into the room.

"Who's Amy?" I asked.

"She's an old school friend of mine, but more importantly she's an ex-employee of the courthouse."

Tristan raised an eyebrow in appreciation. "What did she have to say?" he asked.

"I asked her about the security system. Now, keep in mind

she hasn't worked there in over a year so things could have changed. She told me that they place a barrier spell around the entire building as soon as they close. Then, once the last clerk leaves, motion detectors are set. So we need to get in before the barrier spell is placed and out before the last employee leaves."

Tristan shook his head. "What happens if we don't make it in time?"

"I'm hoping I can figure it out," Lexi said.

Lachlan checked his watch as Tristan opened his mouth to respond.

"Court house closes in a little over an hour," Lachlan said, cutting off Tristan's protest. "We need to leave now."

So much for leaving at night.

We did another quick review of the path to the psychic's cell, and once we were comfortable, we gathered our things, ready to head out. I held my new gun, hesitant on where to hide it. I had this fear of it going off in my pocket. I made sure the safety was on and tucked it in the front of my pants, still a little unnerved though.

Lexi re-sealed the living room, and then we all headed out toward the courthouse.

"What if this guy is not Artemis? What if he's someone else?" Genevieve asked as we walked to the cars.

"That's a possibility," Lexi answered. "It just makes the most sense for him to be Artemis." We walked a few more steps in silence.

"Like Occam's Razor," Tristan said.

"Who's what-now?" I asked

Tristan chuckled. "It's a principle in science and philosophy that the simplest explanation tends to be the correct one."

My jaw dropped. "Who *are* you?"

Tristan smiled, "I'm not just a pretty face," he joked.

I shook my head, smiling, then I suddenly felt exposed, like we were being watched.

"This is a terrible plan," I said. Tristan, who had been walking quietly beside me turned to face me. "Think about it, we are being pretty obvious. There are seven of us walking like thieves. If we all drive to the courthouse together, it will look weird. We should split up in twos or threes, and walk there from different directions. When we get to the courthouse we should keep our groups separate until we end up inside."

"You're right," Tristan said.

"So, no driving?" Lexi asked almost in a whine.

"I'll go with Lexi," John offered, brightening Lexi's mood.

"I'll join them," Fay added, eyeing the couple suspiciously. Lexi turned away, but I saw her roll her eyes.

"Geni and I will pair up," Lachlan said.

"That leaves me and Tristan," I said. With that we all went our separate ways.

Tristan and I walked straight, keeping an eye on our surroundings. "You sure you don't want to change your mind and teleport? It's kind of a hike from here," Tristan said.

"Yeah I'm sure. Wait, what do you mean by hike? How long will it take us by foot?" I asked. It should have been something I looked into since I was forcing the whole group to endure it.

"About an hour," Tristan answered, eyes straight ahead. "We'd get there in time, but it would be tight."

CAROL RAYYAN

"An hour?" My jaw dropped. "Balls." No wonder Lexi wanted to drive. I suddenly felt very guilty for my selfish reason to not teleport.

"Balls?" Tristan asked, looking at me from the corner of his eye.

"Yeah, it's my version of crap."

Tristan shook his head and chuckled. "You can be so strange sometimes."

"Shut up." I nudged him playfully

Tristan smiled and put an arm around me, towing me to the courthouse. I started to get nervous. I didn't know what to expect and I hoped that we would be able to get the old man out easily, and that he wouldn't kill us somehow afterwards.

Tristan sensed my tension and squeezed my shoulder reassuringly.

I thought about the hour hike and sighed. This was silly. I was being selfish and we were wasting time because of it.

"We need to teleport. We shouldn't be wasting time just because I'm nervous."

"You sure?" Tristan asked, but I could see that he agreed with me. It amazed me what my friends would let me get away with, even when they knew it wasn't the best plan. I shook my head disapprovingly. Tristan misunderstood the motion. "You don't have to do anything you don't want to," he offered.

"No, it's not that. I was just thinking how you are all such enablers; allowing me to be weak. I'm very disappointed." I let out a dramatic sigh.

Tristan raised his eyebrow at me. I laughed quietly, and then I focused my thoughts.

124

Guys? I asked mentally, expanding my mental voice towards the others. *Can you hear me?* I added uncertainly.

I heard a collective mental *Yes.*

We're going to teleport. We shouldn't be wasting any more time than necessary, I sent.

Thank God. I heard Lexi think, and I laughed to myself.

We'll be right there. I heard Lachlan say. Thankfully they hadn't gotten too far around the wood.

They reached us a few minutes later, and we gathered together.

"Glad you came to your senses." Lexi smiled at me, but there was sarcasm in her voice. I shot her a glare.

"Ready?" I asked. They all nodded. "Okay," I said more to myself than them. I was trying to mentally prepare myself so I wouldn't psych myself out. I reminded myself that I was teleporting behind the courthouse, no need for any spell to block me or hurt me there.

I took a deep breath and imagined us all at our destination. The familiar pull and twist started, and I held my breath hoping that I wouldn't smack into a wall again. The movement stopped and I took a chance at opening my eyes.

My heart rate returned to normal when I realized I had gotten the whole group safely to the back of the courthouse.

Tristan kissed my forehead and then gave me a thumbs-up. I almost started laughing at his boyish behavior. We split up into the groups we had been in before and entered the courthouse separately and with two minute intervals in between each group's entrance.

I walked in with Tristan, but didn't see where the others had gone. I headed for the bathroom, where I figured I could stay hidden until closing time. Tristan grabbed my arm, and gently pulled me toward the counter. His eyes scanned the white stone surface in front of the clerks and paused as he reached one in particular.

Tristan groaned when he saw the scrawny young man sitting behind the counter.

"Let's go to someone else," I said when Tristan started walking toward the boy. "This kid was rude."

"I know, but I need to see him specifically."

"Elder Lacour isn't here," the boy said on a sigh when we reached the counter. His eyes were downcast, as if he were busy with the papers in front of him. "You may want to learn to call in and make an appointment. It would save you time in the future."

Tristan clenched his jaw, but smiled. "We were actually here to make an appointment."

Just go with it Tristan told me telepathically. *Distract him.*

The boy looked up, his eyebrows pulling together, unconvinced. I read the boy's name tag.

"Josh," I started, and leaned over the counter, inching closer to him. I ran my finger across the back of his hand, sending an alluring sense of emotion through the boy, although I couldn't be sure if it worked.

"Can you look in that little book of yours and let us know when Elder Lacour will be available next?" I batted my eyelashes, unsure if this kid could even be fazed. He stared at me, open-mouthed, and nodded his head.

Nice.

Tristan studied me for a moment, but I avoided his gaze. No

need to tell him where I learned that spell. Josh picked up the appointment book and fumbled with it, sending it landing on the floor with a *plop*. As Josh crawled under the counter to retrieve the book, Tristan discreetly reached over the ledge of the counter and palmed something so quickly I couldn't tell what it was. Josh came up with the book in hand and opened it.

"Looks like Elder Lacour is booked for..." he flipped several pages, confusion spreading over his face. "For two months." He looked up at me apologetically.

"That won't do," I said, leaning back from the counter. "Thanks anyways."

"Uh, miss?" Josh called after me. I turned to face him. "Please, let me know if there's anything else I can help you with."

I smiled, and Tristan groaned again.

"Punk," he said under his breath as we walked away. "What exactly did you do?"

I smiled and shrugged.

"What did you do?" I asked.

Tristan smiled and shrugged. He led me to an empty hallway.

"Call the others and have them meet us back here."Tristan said, and leaned against the wall. I obliged and we waited.

It was only a matter of minutes before the others joined us.

"What do we do now?" Lexi said.

"Stand together," Tristan answered.

"This is a bit conspicuous, don't you think?" Lexi hissed.

Tristan ignored her, closed his eyes and made the hand motions for a spell I'd seen him do before: A cloaking spell.

Now we wait Tristan said.

It felt as if we were waiting forever before the lights flickered off and on.

"The courthouse will be closing in five minutes," a voice said, echoing throughout the building. "Please make your way to the exits."

I crept to the end of the hallway and peered into the lobby. There weren't many clients left, and within minutes the room was emptied of visitors.

We waited a few more minutes, and I watched. A few clerks remained organizing papers in front of them. Slowly they tapered off, some leaving the building; two picked up a stack of papers and went to a back room behind the circular counter.

The lights snapped off, and overnight lights –small pot lights set sporadically in the ceiling- switched on, casting a dim glow. The area was deserted.

"There are two clerks in the back," I told the others as I walked back to them. "Motion detectors should still be off."

"How many others are still here, though?" Tristan asked. "This is risky."

Fay let out an exasperated breath.

"Hang on," she said as she closed her eyes. "There are the two clerks in the back offices there," she said, pointing to the area I had seen the clerks go into. "There are five more on the second floor, but I don't sense anyone else nearby." Fay smiled proudly.

"Well, now that we're in here, once the security is set…" Genevieve said. "How will we get out?"

I took a breath and opened my mouth to respond, and shut it. I had no idea.

"I guess we'll find out." Lachlan shrugged.

"Let's just get this over with," I suggested, feeling unnerved by the idea of getting trapped inside.

Genevieve swirled her hand, and a small silver light shimmered from her fingertips and floated on the floor before us, illuminating the way much better than the overnight lights.

"Cool," I said admiringly. Genevieve beamed proudly.

Tristan turned to look at me puzzled, then said, "Oh yeah, I forgot you hadn't seen her do that before." He smiled. I pulled the memory he was thinking of out of his head. Seeing the forest and Genevieve's handy work, I nodded.

"Hmm," I said.

"We seriously need to create boundaries for your mind reading. I'm feeling violated," Tristan complained. I shrugged, only feeling a little guilty. It was awfully convenient for *me*.

"Now you know how I feel," I shot back.

"Can we focus, please?" Fay interrupted, obviously irritated.

"Sorry." I said, looking around.

Voices from the main lobby forced our silence. I couldn't make out the conversation but there were two distinctive voices. I crept along the wall and peered into the lobby. The two clerks who had been in the back room headed out of the front doors, swiping a key card on their way out.

The main glass door slammed behind them with a bang and a blue light shimmered across the outside of the surface.

"Shit," Tristan said. "Nobody move."

"What?" I asked, freezing in place, scared to even breathe the word.

"The sensors just got triggered," Tristan whispered.

"But there are still people in the building," Genevieve said.

"How do you know?" Lachlan asked at the same time.

"The light," Tristan pointed to the corner of the ceiling with his eyes. Moving my eyes only I found the spot Tristan had been staring at, and a blue light was shining back at me.

Damn.

"There are people upstairs," Lexi said. "But this floor is empty, so maybe only the main floor alarm activated."

"How does the system know we're not employees?" I asked.

"Usually government buildings have a spell on their employees," Fay said. "Like humans would use a microchip."

"Lexi," John said. "Can you override it?"

Lexi's eyes widened. "I have no idea." She stood still, deep in thought. "I could try to sense where the detectors are and how the sensors work." She paused a moment. "This could go very wrong," she said. She spread out her fingers and closed her eyes.

We all stood completely still and waited.

"Lexi?" I asked, after she had been quiet for a minute too long.

"Okay," Lexi said. "There are light sensors, like that blue one in the ceiling, that point to specific areas in the wall. It's a zigzag pattern. That, we may be able to work around but-"

"But?" Tristan hissed.

"But there are sensors in the floor that detect our weight. If we move, the alarm will go off."

My eyes roamed over each member, all standing perfectly still, all tense with worry.

"What do we do?" I asked.

"Can you disarm it?" Lachlan asked Lexi.

"I can try, but I have no idea what I'm doing. This is out of my league."

"I knew this was dangerous," Tristan said. "Why didn't your psychic show you this?" he asked me, his temper simmering just below the surface.

"I don't know," I answered honestly. How were we going to get past this?

"Just, quiet." Lexi said. She closed her eyes again and slowly inched her hands up from her sides as if feeling velvet on invisible walls around her. The blue light in the ceiling flickered, and I dared hope we'd get out of this. The sensor light fizzled and shut off.

"Yes!" I cheered.

"Don't mo-" Lexi started as I took a step toward her. "Move." She finished as alarms blared around us.

Crap. Crap. Crap.

"Damn it, Selena," Lexi said. Forcing her eyes shut, she put every ounce of effort into her new task. Lexi placed her hands palm down on the floor, crouching to put her weight into her hands. "Come on, come on…" She whispered under her breath.

The rest of us stood tensely, hoping that Lexi would be able to silence the alarms before it was too late.

"Tell me what to do!" I yelled, pressing my hands on the floor, copying Lexi's pose. She shook her head.

"I…I don't know!" she stammered.

I closed my eyes, forcing my power into the floor, willing the alarms to shut down, but I had no idea what I was doing.Lexi abruptly pushed herself up, and stumbled in her haste. John stepped forward to steady her, and Lexi leaned back against his hands for support.

"Lexi…?" I asked. I heard running, and shuffling of feet approaching.

"Lexi?" I hissed again, worried.

"Run!" She motioned urgently for us to take cover.

11. DESCENT

We hustled to hide, running down the hallway and trying to open every door we came across.

"In here!" Tristan said. He held one of the office doors open and we clamored inside. Tristan quietly shut the door behind us and we curled in the shadows. The room only had a desk and chair in the center with some picture frames on the floor leaning against a wall. The surface of the desk was empty, making me assume this office hadn't been used in a while.

What the Hell, Selena? Fay said telepathically.

I'm so sorry. I messed up! I answered. *I thought Lexi disarmed the sensors!*

That's an understatement, Fay snapped.

I thought you said you could disarm the alarm! Tristan said, directing his accusation toward Lexi.

No, I said I would try, and I was close. I broke through the light sensors, but I didn't get a chance to finish the job. She glared at me.

In the distance we heard the security guards rush around in the building. I crept toward the door to see what was going on outside the room.

Where are you going? Tristan asked at my heels.

I looked through the bottom of the window in the door, and saw five men searching the hallway and lobby.

They were stealthy, yet coordinated. I was sure they were communicating through telepathy themselves.

Tristan, I started, *is the cloaking spell still in place?*

He nodded. I joined the others and we all crouched down, waiting for the coast to clear.

I saw the shadow of one of the guards through the glass; it stretched and grew as the figure got closer. I expanded my telepathy to eavesdrop on their tactics, and opened the link so my friends could hear.

Building's clear, one of them said.

Perimeter's clear, said another.

Probably some kids playing a prank. Scout your zones one more time and meet in the lobby.

The guard paused in front of our door. I waved my hand for my group to get back. We pressed ourselves against the walls, keeping low to the floor.

Soft footsteps hit the tile as he came to the door and turned the knob. We held our breath and stayed perfectly still. The guard peered in, sweeping a spell-made light in the doorway. He squinted as his eyes roamed over us. It seemed that he couldn't see us, but could see something.

Tristan, I said. *Reinforce the spell!*

He worked quickly, but the guard had come into the room, slowly creeping toward our corner.

I can't completely cover us, Tristan said. My heart was beating in my throat as the guard approached.

Tell me how to do it! I said to Tristan.

We don't have enough time. Tristan had shifted his position, ready to pounce on the guard.

Wait, I said. I stood very slowly, only inches away from the guard. He instinctively took a step back but I knew he had no idea what he was seeing.

A spell came to mind, but I had no way of knowing if it would work. I had read it in one of Tristan's old text books, but only tried it out once... unsuccessfully.

I knew the guard was seconds away from telling the others that something was wrong, so I had to try.

Tapping into his mind I inserted an image of a stack of boxes where we had been crouched.

The man shook his head.

It's just boxes, I mentally whispered to the guard. I had to be on a low enough frequency that he wouldn't detect my voice, just think it was his own thought.

He squinted again, and I held my breath.

Just boxes, the man thought. I let out a mental sigh of relief.

He glanced around the room one last time, and retreated back to his post.

My heart still raced until the guard left the room, closing the door behind him.

Coast is clear. Let's reseal the building and clear out. A guard said.

The guards finally left and all the lights in the building went out with them. The overnight lights flickered on again. Fay cast her sensing spell again and nodded in satisfaction.

I shook my head. "I'm so sorry guys, that was way too

135

close."

"Far as I'm concerned," Lachlan said, "You redeemed yourself when you did… whatever you did to get the guard to leave."

"True," Lexi added. "If Tristan had jumped him, the others definitely would've known something was wrong."

"What do we do about the sensors now?" I asked Lexi. "How do we get out of here without the guards coming back?"

"She almost disarmed it," John said placing his hand on her shoulder. "Maybe if she has more time, she can finish the job?" Lexi half smiled.

"I'll try," Lexi said.

"Please," Fay started, shooting a glare at John's hand. I groaned mentally. No good could come of this. "She almost got us caught!"

"That was my fault," I said.

"No, she's right. I couldn't disarm the alarm in time," Lexi said, averting her gaze. "Maybe this wasn't such a good idea."

Fay's tensioned decreased a notch.

It wasn't Lexi's fault at all in my opinion, but I knew she wouldn't listen to me. I looked around the room.

"I got it!" I said, startling the others.

"Lower your voice, will you?" Tristan hissed.

"Sorry, but okay, listen," I started. "Lexi can disarm the wall sensors like last time. I think I can handle the floor."

"How?" Genevieve asked.

"Tristan," I said, ignoring Genevieve's question. "Can you teach me to replicate an object like you did with the bed in your house?"

"Yeah," he answered, eyeing me.

"Good, Lexi work on the wall sensors and let me know when they're taken care of."

We each took a few minutes to work on our tasks. Tristan explained how I needed to see the object and then envision it appearing where I needed it to be.

"Okay, I took care of the wall sensors," Lexi said.

"How are we doing this?" Genevieve asked again.

"Well the floor sensors are activated if we move, or step and shift our weight to another area, right?" I looked to Lexi.

"Yeah, I think so."

"So if we remove our weight from where we are, will the sensors go off?" I asked her.

"It will when we land on another part of the floor."

"Exactly," I said. "So let's not take another step on the floor."

"What are you talking about?" Fay asked, irritation in her tone.

"This." I swept my hand over the floor and a path of tiles spread out in front of us hovering inches over the original floor. I took a step onto the path and waited. No alarms sounded. I let out a sigh of relief.

"Ready?" I asked the others. One at a time they stepped onto the path and we moved toward the door. I cracked the door open and peered outside, but it was empty.

"Fay," I said. She nodded, knowing what I was asking.

"Still clear," she said after a moment. "Even the people who were on the second floor are gone."

"Not like we have to get out before them at this point," Lexi said.

I nodded. "Let's go," I opened the door and the path splayed outward before us like a puzzle putting itself together.

"Okay so I saw a hallway that looked like this one, but I can't be sure if it is *exactly* this one or not."

"No, it's another hallway," Lachlan answered, leading the way. I was grateful that Lexi had shown them what I had seen – I would have gotten us lost if they relied on my directions alone.

Lachlan led us around the corner to a long hallway. This one definitely looked right. We quietly but quickly walked through it and then turned right onto another hallway. My dream was starting to come to life and it sent shivers down my spine.

You okay? Tristan sent mentally. I nodded once.

This hallway was obviously less travelled; there were streaks on the floor, and dust had collected along the trim and corners of the walls. The floor was a dull grey under Genevieve's light and it reminded me of an old, unfinished basement floor.

"Stop," I whispered. Everyone obeyed immediately. I turned to the right side of the hall and saw the secret door I had seen in my dream. If I hadn't known it was there, I never would have found it. The wall before me was smooth, and I hoped I was in the right spot. Even if I was, I had no idea how to open the door.

The psychic's vision just showed the door open. But how? Why wouldn't he show me the answer to this one? I stood there pondering a way to get through this obstacle.

"What's the problem?" Fay asked impatiently.

"This is where the secret door is supposed to be, but I don't know how to open it," I admitted to my utter dismay. Fay let out a huff.

"Didn't the psychic show you how?" Genevieve asked kindly. I shook my head.

"Maybe you already know how to do it?" Lachlan offered. "He wouldn't have let you come all this way just to get stuck at the beginning. You must know how to do this already."

I thought about his words and wondered if he were right. Where would I know how to do this? Would it really have killed the old man to show me anyways? I shrugged my shoulders and pressed my hands along the crease where I imagined the door would open. I tried to see if there was any secret latch or knob like the table that encased the crystal, but there was none.

I sighed. This was wasting time we didn't have. I slammed my fist against the wall angrily, the loud bang echoed down the halls.

"Can you *not* be an idiot please?" Lexi hissed. "Just because the building seems empty doesn't mean there isn't someone around that can hear this," she added.

"The building is empty. I already checked, remember?" Fay asked through clenched teeth.

Lexi smiled sarcastically. "Mistakes happen, and we should always be prepared," she shot back.

"You would know." Fay clenched her jaw tighter, and I saw her fists curled into little balls at her sides. Lexi opened her mouth to reply.

"Lexi, cool it," I said, hoping to defuse the tension. "And Fay, stop blaming Lexi. I'm sorry, it was stupid. I just can't figure this out."

I knew why Fay was going after Lexi, and knew I was right to tell Lexi to wait to pursue her romance. Not that it did any good. It seemed Fay could sense the sexual tension between Lexi and John. Her irritation and short temper were going to make this harder than it already was.

"Well, Jeremiah obviously went through great lengths to keep this hidden," Genevieve said. "I'm sure the answer won't be that easy."

Jeremiah.

The name triggered the memory of another hidden door: One to the operations building at the camp. When we had gone to the building, there was no sign of a door at all, but he just waved his hand and one appeared. Maybe the answer was easier than I thought.

I swallowed hard and stepped in front of the wall, where the door should be. I swept my hand and willed the door to open. It slid silently into the wall beside it, like a fancy patio door.

"Yes," I whispered.

"See? No problem," Genevieve complimented.

After our brief triumph we all stood in front of the dark doorway and looked down onto the spiral stairway. It was dark, and we couldn't see the bottom of it. I knew from the vision that it was steep and went down a long way.

"I doubt any court house employee knows about this to put any floor sensors down there," I said. "Lexi, can you check just to be sure, though? We don't know what traps Jeremiah may have in store for us."

Lexi took a moment, eyes closed, feeling the area past the door.

"Seems sensor free," she finally said.

I led the way.

They all followed tightly behind me. Only Tristan was by my side each descending step. Our footsteps scuffled faintly along the dark, stone steps, but that was the only noise we made. We didn't dare speak, afraid that there may be someone down here that could hear us; someone who could not be detected by a spell.

It felt like we had been descending for hours, though it was only minutes. The darkness seeped all around us, giving off a horror movie vibe. It honestly could have been a scene right out of *Dracula*, and I half expected arms to come out of the walls carrying torches. Thankfully, that didn't happen. Genevieve's light helped show the way, but the shadows it made on the stone walls were unnerving.

Finally, my calves and thighs burning from the repetitive motion, we reached the landing. There was nowhere to go but straight, and that's where the next door stood. This one was not locked. I was surprised that Jeremiah hadn't had more protection; he was hiding a person for crying out loud. Then again, maybe he was confident that no one would ever know this place existed. He had been hiding the man for quite some time; assuming we were right that it was Artemis in that cell.

Although we had no hindrances so far, I was still wary opening the large, intimidating, metal door. It was maybe ten feet high and four feet wide. The handle wasn't a mere knob, but a metal ring, something else that could have come from *Dracula*. I braced myself and opened the door. It took a lot of effort, but Tristan came to lend me some strength.

Once the door was open, I gasped. The moldy stench violated my senses. I heard the others instinctively step back, and

I saw Lexi cover her nose. Again, I led the way through the rank, damp, dark tunnel. The wet floors reflected Gen's light, and made our footsteps slosh noisily. I hoped there was no one down here to hear this. My paranoia of witches hiding to ambush us grew. I stopped short.

Fay, can you please cast another spell to make sure we're still alone? I sent silently, though I made sure everyone could hear, so they would know why I stopped.

Fay nodded and closed her eyes. After a moment she smiled reassuringly, but then her face fell into a grimace.

My heart raced faster. Was someone here? Where could they be? Would we have enough time to get ourselves out? A million questions fluttered through my mind until Fay mentally spoke to us.

I'm not sensing anyone, she said. Okay, that was good.

So, why the face? Lexi asked. Fay all but cringed at her.

I'm not sensing anyone, she emphasized. Lexi made a face.

Yeah we got that, I still fail to see—

I can't even sense the psychic! Fay interrupted, mentally yelling at Lexi. Oh, that was interesting.

Maybe it's because he's still too far away? I asked, thinking of how much farther into the ground we still had to go. Fay shook her head.

*I think he's being blocked, that way no one would ever be able to sense him, even by accident, s*he explained.

Then Jeremiah could be blocking others as well, others who are supposed to guard Artemis, Tristan added, running his hand agitatedly through his hair.

Alright, let's not panic. Let's just proceed with caution, I instructed. The others looked uneasy but agreed. I wondered if this was another bad plan that they were just allowing me to enforce. I really hoped not.

We started walking again, as quietly as possible, and I tried desperately not to breathe through my nose. You'd think extremely close proximity to a corpse would have made me immune to bad smells, but it didn't.

The tunnel ended abruptly above stone steps that dragged us farther into the earth. I wondered how deep we had gotten, but then the sense of claustrophobia started to hit me, and I had to push the thought aside. I took a deep breath through my mouth to reassure my lungs that I was still able to breathe easily.

We headed down the stairs, and the smell receded. Slowly, stealthily, we made our way down the wet stone steps, straining to listen, to make sure there was no one waiting for us at the bottom. I leaned forward trying to keep my ears open, but unfortunately, my eyes weren't as focused. I stepped down, but I overshot it. My foot landed right on the edge of the step in front of me, and I slipped on the slick stone.

My feet flew out from underneath me, and I fell backward. Tristan reached out instinctively to catch me. I almost took him down with me, but his strength righted my falling body. My heart raced and beat in my throat. The steps were so steep, if Tristan hadn't caught me I would have slid the whole way down. I cringed at the thought of what that would have felt like.

I shot Tristan an appreciative look, and he nodded, though his mouth was pressed in a hard line. I knew he was willing me to be more careful. I shook it off and continued down the steps. We descended the three flights. When we reached the bottom, I was already searching the ground and found the hatch I knew was there. Again it wasn't locked, and again I wondered how easily this had been going.

I lifted the hatch door, and it creaked as I opened it wide enough for us all to fit through. I looked into the dark hole in the ground and swallowed. There was no way to see the bottom.

Before I got my feet on the rungs at the side, Tristan grabbed my wrist. I looked up to see him gazing at me intensely, his jaw clenching and unclenching.

What? I asked mentally.

We don't know what's down there, he said.

I do. I've seen it.

You don't know that the vision was accurate. There could be people waiting down there to capture you. You know how important you are.

Wait, wait, I started. *Number one, the psychic has been right so far, and there hasn't been anything to worry about. Two, we came all this way, and you're having doubts and fears now? It's a little late, don't you think?* I almost mentally yelled.

I admit that my timing is horrible, but this has been way too easy so far. Don't you think that's weird? He asked, mirroring my thoughts.

I had no argument for that. I also couldn't tell him anything he wanted to hear.

We were going to do this; we were almost there. There was no way to stop now. I shook my head roughly and glared at him.

Come on, was all I sent, and then I descended down the rails on the side.

At least let me go first, Tristan pleaded, but I ignored him. If

I'm supposed to be super powerful, why was everyone so scared for me?

It wasn't far to the bottom, and I reached it quickly. As the others followed, I looked around to make sure Tristan wasn't right, and that there were no bad guys lurking in the shadows. Far as I could tell we were still alone.

The anxiety built the easier this got. The others reached the bottom one at a time, with Tristan in front. He glared at me as he passed to lead the way. I let him. There was only one way to go from here.

We walked through the final hallway, and I could smell the human waste as it permeated the air. This smell was actually worse than the moldy hallway, and I almost gagged. The others were disturbed as well, only breathing trough their mouths. To be honest, that made me even more paranoid; I didn't want anything finding its way into my system through my mouth. When I tried to breathe through my nose again though, I regretted it.

"She comes! She comes!" I heard in a sing-song tone, followed by a chuckle.

I stopped abruptly, nerves stretched to the max, before I recognized the voice. The others stopped at the sound of the voice as well with Tristan mentally cursing and giving me a knowing look.

It's just him, I said, hoping to calm the others. I stared at Tristan for a moment before huffing lightly and moving ahead.

We walked a few more feet and there, on the left-hand side was the cell.

"Don't come any closer," the old man said, though I noticed

he wasn't whispering. I wasn't sure if that was a good thing or not. Either he knew we were alone, and no one would hear us, or he was counting on someone coming after us and had no need to hide it.

We all stopped where we stood, and I had a sense of déjà vu. I don't think I had ever had a dream come true, and this one was very unsettling.

"Who are you?" Tristan asked.

"Who are you?" the old man mimicked, creeping from the shadows. The others saw him for the first time, and I heard their quiet gasps. He looked exactly as he had in my dream, old, frail, and in desperate need of a shave and like... four showers. His aura flickered weakly, but when the man shook his head as if to clear it, it shone, a white brilliant light. "My name is Artemis, though I believe you already knew that. We don't have time to waste," the old man said "You must be on guard."

My body tensed at Artemis's words. Be on guard for what?

Artemis's old eyes snapped to my face. "Once you open this door, they will come. You must be prepared," he croaked.

"I knew this was a trap!" Tristan growled.

"This is no trap, but as you said, this was too easy," Artemis said. "The reason will be evident to you in the very near future." I wondered if there was anything he didn't know. He flashed a weak smile at me.

"I know much, but I don't know all," he said.

"Who's coming?" Lachlan asked, ignoring Artemis's seemingly random comment. He had been so quiet this whole time, I had almost forgotten he was here.

"The skotadi."

12. FIGHT FOR SIGHT

"Skotadi?" Genevieve asked nervously, "Are they like shadow men?" she finished, probably remembering our last encounter at the cemetery.

"Skotadi are much worse," Artemis started. "Jeremiah could never risk anyone knowing about me, so he created the skotadi. To answer one of the many questions you've been asking, it has been very easy because Jeremiah knows no one knows I, or even this place, exist. Yet, in the off chance he was wrong, he put the skotadi in place to guard me."

"What are skotadi?" I asked in a whisper, afraid of the answer.

"They are soldiers, created for the sole purpose of guarding a person of value," Artemis started. "Well, technically, one is created and then replicated. The only way to kill them, is to destroy the real soldier. Otherwise, the replicas will keep rematerializing. Once you unlock my cell, they will appear."

Tristan looked unconvinced. I could tell he was still wondering if this was a trap. He shot a glance in my direction and I saw the confirmation of my thoughts in the tight set of his mouth. Knowing that he heard what I was thinking about him, I turned away.

"Alright, let's do this," I said, taking a step forward, but Tristan grabbed my wrist again.

"Wait," he said. Then he looked to Artemis.

"Yes, you're wondering why I haven't gotten myself out, aren't you?" Artemis asked. Tristan stood taller, but said nothing. "For starters, only Selena has the ability to unlock this cell. I have been waiting her entire life for her to get her powers and get me out. This door is rigged so that not only will the skotadi appear, but the door itself will explode." Artemis paused, seeing our shocked expressions, then continued. "I have seen many scenarios where I try to contact another witch, or even the Elders, but they always fail, dying in the explosion and killing me in the process. Only Selena is powerful enough to override the trap, so it will be very easy for her. This is part of her destiny."

This all sounded like *The Sword in the Stone* to me.

"Secondly," Artemis continued, "even if I had the ability to unlock my cell without blowing myself to pieces, do you really think, in my... delicate condition," He gestured to his frail body, "That I would be able to fight off skotadi?"

Tristan's shoulders relaxed a little, but his eyes were still intense caution. He didn't like that I was being put at any kind of risk or danger to free this man.

"Get out of my head," he hissed to me. I cringed back reflexively.

"I assure you, young Tristan, that I mean you no harm," Artemis said. "I promise you that this rescue will not go unrewarded. I have much knowledge you will need. I give you my word; I will answer any and every question you have. But first, please, get me out of here," he hissed.

I pulled my hand away from Tristan and focused on unlocking the door. I held my breath, fear coursing through me that I could blow us all up if I failed. Genevieve and Lachlan instinctively took a step back. I felt the desire to do the same, but Artemis would know this would succeed... right?

Just then a vision fluttered before my eyes and came into focus. I saw what I had to do; how to bypass the trap. The room came back into focus and Artemis gave me an encouraging look.

I took a chance. As soon as I opened the door, there was a loud explosion. I instantly cast the spell he had shown me and the explosion was sucked into itself before it could expand. Only a small flame remained, flickering and hovering in the air. Artemis was right; it was relatively easy... nerve wracking but easy. Artemis was right about the other part too. The skotadi were coming.

The room shook, and we all took a protective stance.

"Everyone behind me!" Lexi shouted. We obeyed automatically. I remembered what she had been able to do against the brakti before and was hopeful it would work on the skotadi as well.

Lexi sprung the sphere shield and covered us all under its protective bubble. Then the skotadi appeared close enough to touch us. There were too many, maybe fifteen or so. If it was possible, the skotadi were even uglier than shadow men. They were... skeletons, only the bones were an inky black, giving the illusion they were made from tar. They wore metal helmets, and vests as if they had been real soldiers called forth from the pits of

Hell. Their jaws snapped at us as they appeared, and they looked completely identical; I had no idea which one we had to kill.

Their hollow eye sockets endless darkness. An oblivion of black evil. I stepped back instinctively. They stopped just outside the force field. With our combined powers, Lexi made the sphere shield lethal and pushed it outward forcing it upon the closest skotadi.

An inhuman shriek – which sounded like a combination of tires squealing and a thousand cats getting skinned – filled the small room as the skotadi was consumed by her power. The others backed away, out of the shield's reach, as their fallen comrade was reborn before our eyes.

Damn, I really hoped we could have gotten that right on the first try.

Fay tensed beside me, and I turned to see that she was focusing all her energy. The pressure of the room changed, sucking in the air and holding it tight.

"Not in here!" John yelled.

She relaxed and the power exploded outward, knocking the skotadi away.

"Boom," she said with a smile.

It was impressive, but unfortunately it had little effect on these creatures.

"You can't do that underground. We could have a cave in," John said. I wasn't so sure, it looked like it did no more than a strong gust of wind would have. I centered myself and created a ball of energy, focusing to make sure that I built it big enough and strong enough. At the point where I thought it would burst, I released it.

They gave another inhuman shriek and I was tempted to cover my ears. It was bad enough with just one, but with a group of them it was almost too much to bear. They shriveled and withered as they burned from the inside out. I got a morbid satisfaction from this. They were not human, not people, and I had no reason to feel any kind of guilt or remorse.

This was fun.

Until they all returned, and I realized I hadn't killed the original soldier. I searched, finding one that had been off to the side, but as the rest of the skotadi reappeared, I lost it in the shuffle.

The others joined in shooting spells at the skotadi from behind the protection of Lexi's sphere shield. Lachlan and John shooting fire from their fingers, Fay sent electric currents, Genevieve ice stars, Lexi her mysterious blue light. I opened my hands, felt the magic coursing through my fingers as a bright orange light shot forth disintegrating any nearby skotadi.

It worked great, until the skotadi changed course. They shot their own spells at us; white lightning bolts shot from their core, but our safety bubble repelled them. One of the skotadi flew over the shield, landing right behind Lexi, and before I could scream, it shot an electric current in her back. She fell writhing to the floor. The force field vanished.

I cried as I ran toward her. Tristan wrapped his arm around my torso and flung me back.

"She'll be fine. You have to focus," he yelled. I looked around and saw that Genevieve and Lachlan were fighting side by side; Genevieve blocked a spell, sparks flying as it was deflected, and Lachlan lifted and flung his attacker away with a swipe of his hand. John was beside Fay fighting, but once he saw Lexi fall he ran to her side. Fay's anger boiled and she flicked her wrists, sending a spell that killed a skotadi.

It re-appeared immediately. Tristan began using hand-to-hand combat, his fists crunching against the slimy bone, and I felt hideously overwhelmed.

Tristan yelled out in pain. "Don't touch them!" he backed away, cradling his fist. "It's like they're made of acid." The flesh on his knuckles bubbled and blistered. We all stepped back, keeping distance and only using spells to fight. I tried to reach Tristan, but there were too many skotadi coming after us.

Everywhere I looked, my friends were fighting, and it looked like they were losing. There were too many of these things, about twice as many as us, and they could die several times. We only had to die once.

Two skotadi rushed toward me, electric sparks preceding them like a lighted path. I twisted out of the way of one, but was too slow to move out of the way of the second. Sharp, burning pain spread throughout my arm where the spell hit me. A yell escaped my lips.

"Selena?" Tristan called, trying to move away from the skotadi he fought.

"I'm fine," I yelled through gritted teeth.

John helped Lexi to her feet, and I was relieved to see that, although she was in some pain, she was fine. John rejoined the fight, creating fire balls and shooting them like bullets at the skotadi. Lexi tried to recreate her sphere shield, though she seemed to be in too much pain to focus.

I tried to raise my arms and send a spell out to kill the

skotadi, but I could barely move my right shoulder. I could only imagine how much pain Lexi was in.

The skotadi Tristan fought cornered him and I couldn't get away from the two coming at me to help. I closed my eyes and imagined the skotadi flying away from me, hoping that my mental will would be strong enough to work, but feeling like I needed to move my hands for enough power. I opened my eyes and saw the two skotadi fly away from me, just as Lachlan killed one of the skotadi cornering Tristan, allowing him to fend for himself.

The skotadi shot their current spells, Genevieve dodging one by merely inches. We were injured and outnumbered. I knew I needed to do something and fast.

I swallowed my fear and looked around. I saw Artemis standing to the side smiling reassuringly. I wished I could know what he knew, but I didn't have the time to search his mind. I took his smile as a good sign, boosting my confidence.

It was now or never. I had to save my friends.

"Get out!" I yelled to the others.

"What?" Tristan asked as Artemis hobbled toward the door smiling.

"I have an idea, but I need you all to leave."

"Like Hell," Tristan grunted, still casting spells at the skotadi.

"I don't think that's a good idea either," Genevieve said. Lachlan and John glanced at me a moment but said nothing as they resumed casting fireballs at the skotadi.

"Yes," Artemis said. "Come, come along now."

No one seemed to be listening to me or Artemis. They

continued facing off with the skotadi, but they were losing ground. We were all going to die.

"Damn it!" I yelled. "Listen to me!" I spun and glared at Lachlan, "You, take Artemis; John, you take Lexi. Genevieve and Tristan get the hell out now and close the door behind you."

"You're out of your mind if you think I'm leaving," Tristan yelled back. I gritted my teeth.

"Go!" I yelled and created a whirlwind so fierce it whipped Genevieve's hair around her face. I spun the wind to push the skotadi to one side and my friends out the door and slammed it shut as they stumbled and tripped into the tunnel. I created a glass wall to barricade them in the hall and blocked out Tristan slamming his fist against it screaming my name.

I jumped into the now vacant cell before the skotadi could reach me and slammed the door shut, hoping against all hope that I was right. The skotadi converged on the cell, their black slimy bones stabbing through the spaces in the bars. I backed away from the door, my back hitting the wall.

I stared at the flame flickering just outside the cell, the flame containing the explosion meant to kill anyone who tried to break Artemis out. Kill anyone, but not Artemis. I hoped.

I crouched in the corner, waved my hand and released the explosion. A bright light blinded me, and I covered my head with my arms. The resounding blast echoed through the small room carrying the screeches of the skotadi, and I covered my ears instinctively. The rooms shook, debris whipped through my hair and face, and I kept my eyes squeezed shut until all fell silent. I stayed there a moment, waiting for the room to settle and the ringing in my ears to subside.

I could barely make out my friends screaming through the door, calling my name, asking if I was alright. I stood, taking in the dust and ruin around the cell, but where I stood was untouched.

For a few seconds it was quiet. All the skotadi had disappeared.

I stood there warily, looking around, but there was no need. This battle was over. I stepped from the cell and removed the glass barrier.

"Selena!" Lexi called, relief flooding her features.

"Are you alright?" Genevieve asked. I nodded.

Tristan's face changed from relief to fury. I averted his glare.

"Come, we haven't time to lose!" The old man said, and he started hobbling as fast as he could down the hallway. The ground shook, sending dirt through the cracks in the ceiling. The power of the explosion must have been too strong in this confined space. We wobbled as we tried to regain our balance. I now understood what John had been warning Fay about.

Oops.

"Let's go!" Lachlan called. He ran ahead, scooped up Artemis, and headed for the rungs.

Leaving was much faster than coming, now that we knew no one was waiting to stop us. We climbed out of the hatch and I closed it behind us. When Jeremiah came back, I didn't want him to know Artemis was missing right away.

We ran up the three flights of stairs as fast as we could, and I was grateful Tristan had trained me as hard as he had before, but my muscles still protested. We ran down the smelly hallway, through the heavy metal door, and then we were faced with the spiral staircase. I willed my muscles to move, but about a quarter of the way up I was dragging and panting, my lungs feeling like they were going to explode.

"Come on, Selena," Tristan called from in front of me. The others were already closer to the top. Tristan came back, grabbed my hand, and pulled me forward.

I pushed my body beyond the point I thought it could go. My thighs burned with the effort, my calves felt tight, I hated this. Then a thought came to me, and I shot forward.

"What-?" Tristan asked, but I pulled him with me, flying the rest of the way up the stairs.

I landed when I reached the others, and we raced down the last two hallways, making sure to close the secret door behind us. After having to run up steep stairs, running on a flat surface was almost too easy. We ran over the tile path, the squares barely attaching themselves in time for us to run along them. We reached the front door, but it was locked.

"Selena," Tristan called, running toward me. I pulled at the door handles, rattling the door, but it wouldn't budge. I must have pulled too hard; the shaking of the doors triggered the outside barrier alarm sending it blaring in a frenzy.

"Move!" Tristan said, swinging his hand over the magnetic lock. He pushed the front doors open.

"That was nuts!" Fay said. I didn't wait for anyone to respond; we had to leave before the guards came back. I grabbed them and teleported us back to the cottage landing behind the house. We rushed inside and fell on the closest furniture to us, catching our breath.

The only one of us not panting from exhaustion was Artemis who had been carried the entire way. I had a new appreciation for Lachlan, having had to run up so many flights of stairs with a man on his back, albeit a frail, skinny man. But still.

"How did you get the door open?" I asked Tristan, breathless.

He waved the access card with Josh's name on it.

I smiled and shook my head.

"Are you okay?" Tristan asked, looking at my scorched arm.

I nodded, but it reminded me that Lexi was in much worse shape.

"Lexi, let me take a look at your back," I said after a few moments of gasping for air. Lexi came and turned her back to me. I pulled her scorched shirt up, and she winced. I clenched my teeth to keep from making any sound to alarm her.

Lexi's back was red, blistered and raw. On the outer edge of the massive wound, her skin was scorched black. I gulped my sob down, trying to be strong for her. I was confident that I could heal her; I just couldn't stand to see her hurt.

I placed my hands gently on her back, hoping to find a spot that wouldn't hurt her. She jerked when I touched her though, so I guess I didn't succeed. I imagined her skin healing, mending, and rebuilding itself. I took a deep breath and concentrated.

Lexi let out a small gasp, and it was a sound I knew well, having been healed a million times in the past few weeks. This was a good sound. I looked down and saw that her back was now smooth, clear and healed. I smiled to myself, proud that I could help Lexi when she needed it.

"That's so much better. Thank you," Lexi chirped. She turned and flung her arms around me in a hug. I squeezed her back, glad that she was alright, even though the pain in my arm was protesting.

"Tristan," I said, "give me your hand."

"It's fine, take care of your arm first."

I gave him a look, grabbed his hand and healed his blistered knuckles.

"You're so stubborn," he said, studying his hand. "Can you please take care of yourself now?"

"I can help, if you like," Genevieve said.

"Thank you, but I'd hate to drain your energy. I'm well enough to do it."

Genevieve nodded, casting her eyes down to the floor. I placed my hand on her shoulder, and then set to work on my arm.

"What do we do about him?" Tristan asked, watching Artemis cautiously.

"I say we let him take a nice shower," I answered, dropping my hand from my now healed wound. "And then we give him some food and a bed."

"We don't know if he can be trusted," Tristan whispered.

"Trust. What is trust?"Artemis chuckled."Tristan, I've been trying to figure out a way to ease your worries, but I can't seem to. If I told you what you wanted to hear you would assume that because of my abilities, I would know whatever you wanted to hear, but wouldn't mean it. If I say nothing, you will be cautious and paranoid at my silence. All I can say is that we got out safely, and I am eternally grateful to you all for that. Whatever you decide to do with me now is entirely up to you. I only offer my assistance in return for yours. Any answers you seek, I will give, perhaps information about your mother?"

Tristan tensed and shut down. I wondered why Artemis would say that, he must have known the outcome. Yet there was a glimmer in Tristan's eye, one that he was trying, unsuccessfully, to hide.

"Look, it's late. We can have Lexi seal his room if it makes you feel better," I offered. "But please, let us feed the man." I didn't wait for a response. I went to the kitchen and fished out some leftovers.

Artemis sat at the table slowly, and I found some leftover pasta, garlic bread and a muffin and placed it in front of him, hoping it would be enough to fill him.

"This is plenty," he responded to my thoughts, eyeing his plate. "Thank you." He ate quickly, and I brought him water to chase it down.

"Would you like more?" I asked, sad he must have been starved most of his life.

Artemis smiled, but declined.

I showed him to the bathroom, gave him a towel, scissors, a razor and some clothes Lachlan was nice enough to lend, even though they would be too big. I knew I wouldn't be able to ask Tristan for any. I couldn't imagine why he was being so hostile.

"I hope I'm not being invasive but, I can see that you're in pain, and I was wondering if you might allow me to help...heal you?" I asked feeling very self-conscious.

"I am an old man, I have come to terms with aging, but if you could ease my back, I would be extremely grateful."

I smiled and nodded. Standing behind him I wished I had let him shower first, then I regretted my thoughts knowing he probably heard them.

"Sorry," I mumbled and placed my hands on his back. It was weird; I was able to know exactly where he hurt. I concentrated on fixing it, and I heard him release a breath after a moment. He stood up straight, took two long, fast strides.

"Thank you," he said. I nodded and closed the door.

Heading downstairs to the others, I wondered what exactly we would do with Artemis. Could he give us the answers we sought? Did he still remember the full prophecy? I was so lost in thought, I almost ran into Tristan.

"Sorry," I said, not meeting his gaze.

"We need to talk," he said, gently pulling my arm and leading me back upstairs.

"What's up?" I asked tiredly as Tristan closed the door to our room behind us.

"You need to be more cautious. We have been taking way too many risks lately, and I don't like it. I don't want you getting hurt. You said we were enablers, well I'm saying 'no' to your risky, crazy ideas."

"I don't understand. It's over, why does it matter now?" I argued.

"Because I know you. You are impulsive; you don't always think things through, but you need to start. Our species needs you." He paused, and I sensed he needed me too. "So you can't keep being so reckless and selfish." He clenched his jaw, but his gaze never left my face.

"Selfish? You think I'm selfish?" I asked incredulously.

Tristan sighed, "Don't get mad. It's just that you are only thinking one track. You need to realize the bigger picture."

I was confused, so I automatically searched Tristan's mind for the real meaning behind his words to understand them more. Before I got in, Tristan snapped.

"Enough!" He growled. I flinched. "I know I gave you permission to search my head earlier, but this is too much. You have to give me some privacy!"

"It's a habit. I don't mean to! And you don't give me any privacy. Any thought I have of you, you can hear," I countered.

"Yeah, and I'm sorry about that. *Believe* me," he enunciated. "But I can't control that. It just happens."

"What's that supposed to mean?" I asked, anger heating my face.

"Which part?" He snapped.

"That whole 'believe me' part! Are my stupid, naïve, adoring thoughts about you that bad?" Sarcasm seeped in my voice.

Tristan laughed humorously. "You know that's not all you think about."

When I stayed quiet, waiting for more, he gave it to me. "You think I like knowing that you dreamed about my brother? Just because you think my name in the same thought I have to know about that!"

My face drained. Oh God, this was humiliating. I couldn't control my dreams. I didn't know why I was having them or why I felt the way I felt. So how could I respond to Tristan now? What was I supposed to say? I didn't want to hurt him, but it seemed now that it was too late. I felt horrible but still angry. It

161

wasn't my fault. How could he blame me for that?

I bit my lip and held back the tears that were threatening to expose me for the weak girl I was. I rushed passed him and threw the door open. I guess I was going to sleep in Lexi's room tonight. I closed Lexi's room door behind me and sat on the edge of her bed.

The thought of sleeping away from Tristan was uncomfortable. I had gotten used to his warmth and safety. My heart hurt with longing at the thought, but we both needed our space. The stress of the past few weeks was affecting our relationship now.

My mind reeled. Maybe this just wasn't meant to be. Maybe Tristan had been right about keeping boundaries so we wouldn't get involved. Maybe this relationship was taking precedence over something much more important, like the prophecy.

Tomorrow I would get my answers from Artemis. Tonight I would try to get some rest and keep thoughts of Tristan away. I curled up into Lexi's queen-sized bed and tried to relax. I forced myself to think of positive things like successfully breaking Artemis out, and all of us being safe and together.

Without my permission, my mind wandered back to Tristan. I hoped that he would come in the room after me, hold me and tell me he was sorry, and take me to sleep next to him where I belonged.

After an hour or so I managed to fall asleep. Tristan never came.

13. TOO MUCH INFORMATION

The next morning was kind of rough. I was so tired, my body hurt, and I was absolutely dreading facing Tristan. I lay on my back awake, staring at the ceiling, wondering how long I could hide in Lexi's room.

Next to me Lexi rolled over and her eyes slowly fluttered open. After a few minutes, she looked at me.

"So, what happened?" She asked quietly. "Why have you decided to grace my bed with your presence?"

"I sort of got in a fight with Tristan and I didn't want to sleep there," I answered.

"I figured as much. You freaked me out, you know? I came into my room, expecting it to be empty, but there, on my bed, is a Selena-sized lump. I almost attacked it before I realized it was you. So what's the long version of the story? What did you fight about?"

"He was mad and called me selfish and reckless. And he said I was in his head too much."

"It's not your fault if he's thinking about you."

"No, I…read his thoughts. Often," I answered hesitantly, wondering what Lexi would think of me.

"Right, I remember him telling me that was one of your abilities. Cool." She was quiet a moment and then, "Have you read my thoughts?"

"No. I don't know why, but it's just Tristan. I'm just so curious about him I guess. Anyways, he can hear my thoughts when I think about him, so he has no right to get mad."

"Well, he can't control that the way you can. I know you have the ability to do it, and it's tempting, but it's not fair to others. You need to control your powers and keep boundaries. He deserves privacy. I get that. I'm surprised you don't."

I clenched my jaw feeling guilty. "I do understand it. I mean it drives me crazy when he knows what I'm thinking, but..." But, what? How did I finish that statement? But I'm too curious? No, Tristan and Lexi were right; I needed to start minding my own business.

"About the recklessness," she continued, oblivious to my thoughts. "He's kind of right about that one too, but I like your risky behavior personally. Just don't tell him I said that. Then again that explosion thing was a little intense." She paused, lips puckering in thought, before she continued. "But you're not some thrill seeker, you do what you have to. You know he gets mad only because he cares about you so much, right?"

Lexi was killing me. Somehow I became the bad guy. I groaned and threw my pillow over my face. I debated telling Lexi the rest of the fight, about my Darien dream and decided against it. I knew what she would say. She would defend Tristan again saying he had a right to be mad if I was crushing on his brother - even if I had no control over my dreams.

I rolled out of bed and went to wash up, not wanting to talk about Tristan anymore.

By the time I got to the kitchen, everyone was awake and gathered around the table. I mumbled a good morning to the room and got myself a mug of coffee.

"We should move to the living room," Genevieve said. "There's more room there."

"What's going on?" I asked, making sure to avoid Tristan's gaze.

"Artemis is going to give us some answers," Lachlan said eagerly.

"Answers, yes, answers," Artemis mumbled. "I have a lot of information for you, so we best start early." I did a double take at the man sitting at the head of the table. Somehow I hadn't noticed him when I first came in the room.

His hair was cut short and brushed neatly, his face cleanly shaven. He was actually a very handsome man, his new appearance showing that he was probably twenty years younger than I had originally thought. He stood quickly and easily, now that his back was healed, and he led the way to the living room.

I followed the man with my eyes, realizing I could no longer refer to him as 'the old man.'

Everyone silently followed Artemis. He sat down in the arm chair and watched us as we got comfortable.

Lexi took her place on the floor in front of the coffee table, John beside her. Fay sat on the love seat, and Tristan sat next to her. Lachlan, Genevieve and I sat on the couch. I cradled my mug of coffee, staring into its warm brown liquid so I wouldn't have to see Tristan's angry expression.

"Before I answer any specific questions, there is something

you all need to know," Artemis said, capturing our attention immediately. We all exchanged worried glances. "Nothing to be afraid of," he continued, "You just need to know Jeremiah's story to understand why he's doing what he's doing. After I show you his tale, you can then ask me any questions you have."

"Show us his tale?" John asked curiously. Artemis nodded, and then he was in my mind. I heard the others gasp quietly and knew he was in theirs as well. The image he showed us was like a narrated movie. I heard the story, and as it was told, the picture unfolded before my eyes, as if I were there...

ENGLAND 1863

Evelyn Lacour was a beautiful young woman. Her hair was the color of autumn, her eyes the color of emeralds. She crossed the street, holding the hands of her ten year old son Jeremiah, and her seven year old daughter Lily. Lily looked like her mother with the same hair and eyes.

She pulled them along and stopped in front of a tailor shop. She opened the door and the kids ran inside.

"Daddy!" Lily called, running toward her father. Benjamin Lacour's blue eyes crinkled as he smiled and knelt down for her convenience.

"Hello Lily pad," he said, holding her tight.

Evelyn kissed her husband on the cheek. "How's work today, dear?" She asked kindly.

Benjamin looked fondly at his wife. "Good, considering we've only been here a month. Being one of the two tailor shops in town doesn't hurt." Evelyn handed him the package he had been waiting for.

"This is for Mrs. Flannigan's infection," Evelyn informed him.

"Hopefully the business will pick up enough that we won't have to sell your remedies under the table to pay our bills." He smiled, took the package and hid it in the desk drawer.

"Come, let's get the children home." Benjamin lifted Jeremiah, who had been watching the exchange quietly. "How's it going, old boy? Are you taking care of your mother?"

"Yes, father," Jeremiah answered proudly. Benjamin locked up and they headed home.

A few months passed, and still the tailoring business hadn't picked up enough to cover all of the Lacour's expenses. Evelyn worked round the clock making remedies, vials and antidotes for the locals.

It was a normal day, Evelyn walked with the kids to the tailor shop to drop off the remedies for the next day. As Benjamin was locking up, a woman approached them, followed by a group of around twenty people.

"There she is!" The woman cried.

"What seems to be the problem?" Evelyn asked calmly.

"You poisoned her, you did! My daughter! You cast some kind of spell on her and she's taken ill!" The woman cried. The crowd behind her roared, yelling curses and obscenities.

"She's a witch!" one of the crowd yelled, creating an uproar from the others.

"Kill her!" Another yelled.

"She must be burned at the stake!" Cried another.

"No please, there must be some mistake. I would never hurt anyone, I make medicine," Evelyn pleaded.

"Lies!" The crowd yelled, closing in around the small family. Benjamin stepped protectively in front of his wife.

"My wife is a good and kind woman and would never harm a soul. Leave us be or I shall call the constable," he threatened.

"The constable?" One woman laughed. "Call him! He will take care of the likes of you!" The crowd crept closer, forcing the small family up against the walls of the shop. Evelyn bent down and pulled Jeremiah to her. She looked him straight in the eye.

"Jeremiah, listen to me very carefully. I want you to take Lily back to the house and hide in the crawl space."

"Yes, mother," Jeremiah whispered.

"Good, that's a good boy. Now I want you and Lily to stay there until I come for you. Do you understand?" She held back a sob. Jeremiah nodded. "Good, now go! Run quickly before anyone takes notice."

Jeremiah took Lily's hand and pulled her away from the crowd, too distracted to notice the two small children running away. They ran across the street and into the woods.

"You're hurting my arm, Miah!" Lily cried as they reached the middle of the woods.

"I'm sorry, but we're almost there." Jeremiah dragged his crying sister all the way into the house and beneath the floor boards in the closet.

There they sat and waited. Lily was still crying and rubbing her arm.

"What's happening?" She asked, tears streaming down her

face.

"I don't know. Mama wants us to hide here until she comes for us," Jeremiah said, and after a few quiet minutes added, "Do you remember why we had to move here from our last home in France?"

Lilly nodded.

"I think the same thing is happening."

Jeremiah and Lily hid in the tiny space for what seemed like hours. Finally, the closet door opened above them and the boards were removed. The children squinted from the sudden light.

Evelyn was there, her hair disheveled, and parts of her dress were torn. "Come children quickly," she urged. "We must leave immediately."

Jeremiah looked up at his mother's tear streaked face.

"Where's Daddy?" He asked. Evelyn held back another sob.

"He'll meet us there," Evelyn answered hesitantly, but Jeremiah knew she was lying.

"What happened to Daddy?" He pushed. Evelyn grabbed her children and pulled them roughly from the closet.

"I will explain later, just please hurry! We haven't time to lose. They're coming."

"Who's coming, Mama?" Lily asked. Evelyn ignored her and rushed the children into the woods. The sound of the crowd grew louder as they approached, running through the woods after Evelyn.

"Turn this way! Quickly!" Evelyn ordered, and the children ran faster to keep up with her. "Hide in here." She motioned to a small hole in the ground, deep enough for all three of them to hide in and cover with a few branches. She dropped Jeremiah in first and was about to put Lily in when they caught up to her.

"There she is!" A man shouted, and the crowd converged on her and Lily.

"Please!" Evelyn cried. "Please leave my daughter. She's just a child!"

"A child witch!" A woman cried. They took Evelyn and Lily. No one seemed to notice Jeremiah's absence or thought to look for him. Jeremiah hid in the hole quietly until he was sure they were gone. He climbed out carefully and silently followed the path the crowd took.

They carried his mother and little sister to the town square where a makeshift stake was being assembled and tied them both to it.

"This is barbaric, what's the meaning of this?" Jeremiah heard a woman ask another local.

"Witches to be burned," the man answered shortly.

"Witches, here?" The woman started, and then as she thought more she added, "Without a trial?" The man shrugged his shoulders. No one else spoke up.

"Mama, I'm scared!" Lily cried as they tied her in front of her mother.

"I'm so sorry, Lily. So very sorry," Evelyn cried. To the crowd she begged, "Let my baby go! Please she is just an innocent child, please?!" Her throat was raw from screaming but no one paid attention.

"You didn't care when you poisoned my daughter!" The first woman who approached carried a torch. People from the town threw branches, twigs and logs at Evelyn's and Lily's feet. Without hesitation, the woman threw the torch onto the twigs and they caught fire slowly at first. The flames lazily spread over some of the twigs until it erupted and engulfed them.

Evelyn and Lily cried out, their flesh blistering and burning as they begged to be released. To no avail. Evelyn focused her attention to the sky, and it opened up, releasing large drops of water.

"It's true! She uses her magic!" One man yelled, as the rain poured down, starting to ease the flames. Another charged Evelyn, swinging a piece of plywood and knocking her unconscious. The rain stopped, and the fire roared.

Jeremiah watched in horror as his mother and sister were killed before his eyes. He focused his energy and willed the flames to recede but it didn't work. He was too weak. Why hadn't his mother used magic sooner? Jeremiah was angry and confused. Why didn't his mother save herself or Lily?

"We mustn't forget this one," a man called very close to Jeremiah. The boy was about to flee when he saw another man drag his father's lifeless body across the street. There was blood all down his father's shirt. The man dragged Benjamin to the fire and threw the body atop the flames.

The townspeople cheered.

"This is not right," the kind woman said quietly, but still she did not speak up. A few people close to her looked around, seeming uncomfortable. It was too late, now. Jeremiah cried, hot silent tears, and then he ran.

He ran hard and fast and did not stop until he felt his lungs would burst. He ate scraps from the garbage and slept in the dark alleys. Time passed, but still all Jeremiah could think about was avenging his family. All he could see were their dead bodies in front of him. He vowed that one day he would be strong enough. One day he would find a way to get revenge. They would pay, all the stupid, evil, weak, humans would pay.

The vision fast-forwarded; the next few months of Jeremiah's life rushed in a silent blur, then it stopped.

Jeremiah walked by a dark hovel, the door slightly ajar, seemingly vacant. The temptation of a warm place to stay the night outweighed his fear of being caught trespassing. He quietly crept inside, and made it half way through the room when someone grabbed him by his collar.

"Whaddya think yerdoin' in me 'ome?" The man yelled. Realizing he was holding a young boy, he lowered his voice. "Where's yer family, boy?" The older man asked. He was wrinkled, and had bad teeth. Jeremiah tried to squirm from the man's grasp. "Hmm, ya 'ave the glow of a witch," the man said, watching Jeremiah. The boy squirmed harder, his little heart racing with fear.

"Calm down boy, I can 'elpya. Where is yer family?"

"Dead," Jeremiah said with a steady tone.

"Ah…" He looked grimly into Jeremiah's eyes. "'Umans?"

Jeremiah stopped squirming, the fight leaving his body. He looked away silently, biting his lip with fury. The old man studied the boy in front of him, eyes assessing his potential, and nodded.

"I know a man might be interested in a whelp like ya." The old man paused, "'Ave ya ever 'eard of the 'idden City?"

Jeremiah shook his head. The older man nodded. "Alright

then, I'll take ya."

We all sat in silence, absorbing what we had just been shown.

"So, why didn't Evelyn fight back sooner?" Fay asked.

Artemis shrugged, "I'm not sure. Personally I think she was scared. Maybe she thought she'd be able to get out of that situation and when she realized she couldn't, she tried using her magic, but it was too late. That's why Jeremiah has an obsession for power; he thought his mother had been weak."

"So what happened after that?" Tristan asked. My heart pounded at the sound of his voice, but I kept my eyes averted.

"Well, the man in the alley, he was a witch too, so he brought Jeremiah to the Hidden City," Artemis said. "Jeremiah went to school, learned about his abilities and their limitations. He grew up here, all the while wondering how to seek revenge, and decided he wanted to create an army of witches to kill the humans. Once he delved deeper into his plan though, he realized he could get more than revenge.

"It's completely illogical of course, but is hatred or revenge ever rational?" He asked rhetorically. "We crossed paths almost thirty years ago and he discovered what I could do. A year after I met him he asked me how he could get his revenge, how he could become strong enough to beat his enemies, and that's how the prophecy came to be." Artemis sat quietly a moment, deep in thought. Finally he spoke again but it was as if he were talking to himself.

"Regret, regret," he whispered. "Yes. I would regret the day I joined him, regret the day I wanted the power he promised. But

I didn't know, you see? I didn't. I have this great ability and yet I can't know everything. I did not understand the extent of Jeremiah's yearning for power, didn't know. Didn't know it would drive him to do such violent and terrible things."

"I knew we couldn't trust him," Tristan said, getting to his feet.

"You don't understand!" Artemis said. "It's been long years since I craved power. Being held captive for most of your life will do that!" He slammed his fist on the arm of the chair. "All I can think of is getting my own revenge. All I can do to help myself is help you!"

We all stayed silent as Artemis composed himself. I didn't know how to take this information. Artemis was Jeremiah's ally. I understood why he'd helped us, and yet felt uneasy about trusting him. Finally he continued.

"He didn't hide me right away. It wasn't until someone published the prophecy that Jeremiah felt exposed. He was sure I was responsible. After that he captured me and locked me away. I couldn't see it, didn't see it. I suppose I couldn't because it was meant for me to be locked up for so long. I couldn't thwart fate it seemed."

"I don't understand," I spoke up. "Why is he still so mad at humans? I mean the ones who actually killed his family have been dead for a hundred and fifty years or so. What's the point?"

"Like I said, hatred is not rational," Artemis answered. "He has been carrying this anger with him so long it is ingrained in his essence. He doesn't know how to exist without his plot for vengeance. It is what has been driving him, giving him his determination."

"What do his followers get out of this?" I asked.

"Jeremiah has promised them power, promised that when he performs his ritual and takes his revenge, they will be in charge with him."

"People can be so power hungry," Genevieve said sadly.

"What kind of ritual?" I asked.

"I'm afraid I'm hazy on the details at present. The prophecy would help jog my memory."

"Don't you remember the prophecy?" Lachlan asked.

Artemis shook his head.

"A spell was cast to affect the memory of any who had known of the prophecy, as you know. I had a feeling I would need it one day though. I created a copy, written in my blood, protecting its contents from the trickery of the spell Jeremiah cast."

"So the rumor was true," Genevieve said.

Artemis nodded.

"Where is it?" Tristan asked.

"Perhaps we should eat. The coffee was lovely, but I could use some substance."

Artemis rose and went to the kitchen mumbling something about cockroaches. We reluctantly followed. I knew none of us wanted to eat, we just wanted answers.

Genevieve whipped up eggs, bacon and pancakes as quickly as she could. We all ate in haste, rushing to get to the heart of the matter, the main reason for breaking Artemis out. We all finished eating except for Artemis who took his time. We waited politely for a while, and then decided to clean the dishes and table around him, hoping he would get the hint. I'm sure he knew, but it did nothing to hurry him.

Finally he rose from the table, patting his stomach with satisfaction. It pleased me that he was finally full.

Sensing he couldn't delay any further, he settled himself back into the arm chair in the living room. The rest of us assumed the spots we had been in before breakfast and sat awaiting his next words.

"I hid it, yes I had to keep it away from him," Artemis said, almost to himself.

"Where is it?" Tristan asked again.

"Hmm?" Artemis said, looking up into Tristan's eyes. "Oh yes, I hid it where no one would find it." He paused a moment, and shook his head. Clarity found its way into his eyes. "It's hidden in my old home."

"Let's go then," I said.

"It's not that simple," Artemis said. "They sold my house after... after no one returned home."

"Okay, so we'll just go knock on the door and tell whoever lives there what's going on," John said.

Artemis sighed. "Jeremiah lives there."

"What?" Lexi asked before I could.

"The skills of a prophet are very rare," Artemis said. "Yes, very rare indeed. You'd be surprised how much people are willing to pay to know their future, and Jeremiah was always a very jealous sort."

"So, how do we get in then?" Lachlan asked.

"The old fashioned way," Artemis said.

14. BLOOD IS THICKER THAN WATER

"This is not a good idea," Tristan said, sidling along the outside of the house. I could see why Jeremiah would covet such a home. The house must have been at least five thousand square feet. The exterior walls were white with black roofing, the numerous windows sparkling clear. I could only imagine what the inside looked like.

The front yard had plush bushes trimmed neatly but in a way that looked decorative, and it was enclosed by a gated fence, which was thankfully only secured by a latch.

I crept at Tristan's heels, taking comfort in his proximity, even if he was only talking to me out of necessity.

"It'll be fine," I said. "We'll be in and out in no time."

Perimeter is all clear, Lachlan sent.

I don't see anyone either, Lexi added.

The four of us decided to go, leaving Artemis with John, Fay, and Genevieve back home in case anything went wrong. Though part of me wished I'd stayed back instead. Being here with Tristan when we were barely being civil sucked.

Doesn't look like anyone's home, I said.

That doesn't mean he doesn't have security in place,

Artemis said.

"I am so over security systems right now," I whispered to Tristan. His lips twitched almost in a smile.

Once you get inside, I will tell you where to go, Artemis said.

Tristan sighed but crouched in front of the polished black front door.

Lexi, get ready, Tristan said as he snapped the handle off the door, which swung noiselessly open.

I don't sense any alarms, Lexi said. We all paused, unsure of what to do next.

Be quick, Artemis said. *You haven't much time. Go up the stairs to the last room on the left. Hurry!*

I peeked through the open door, ignoring Artemis for the moment. Slowly, still crouched, I eased the door open wider, and stood up straight. The feeling of abandonment stretched from the empty foyer. Tristan paused as well, just a step behind me.

I lit the path before us, the silver light spread from my fingers, shimmering and brightening up the room. I hesitantly took a step inside, my shoes squeaking against the white marble floor where a detailed mosaic had been artfully rendered. I could feel there was no one here, and based on Tristan's calm demeanor, I knew he didn't sense any urgency either. I took a moment to take in my surroundings.

Before me a curved staircase wound its way up the right wall, a crystal chandelier hung from the ceiling that was so high I had to crane my neck to see where it reached.

Not my home, I heard Artemis whimper.

Are we in the wrong place? I sent back urgently.

No, no, right place. So many changes. I could hear the

sadness in Artemis' thoughts. *Not my home.*

"Let's get this over with," Tristan said, heading for the staircase.

An engraved wooden door stood off to the side, catching my eye. I hesitated, wanting to follow Tristan, but my curiosity took over. I quietly reached for the brass doorknob and slowly turned it. The door opened to a study. I brightened my light spell, and saw a large, mahogany desk sitting at an angle in the corner of the room. Book shelves wrapped around the room, filled to the top with various books.

"Selena," Tristan hissed. "We have to go."

"Go on ahead," I snapped. "I may find something we could use."

"Jeremiah wouldn't keep anything important here," Tristan snapped back.

I ignored him, sitting behind the desk and opening the drawers. Tristan practically growled but didn't leave.

I searched through the two drawers on the side, but they only had files and documents related to Elder business. I pulled the handle of s small drawer that sat just below the desktop, but it didn't budge. I then noticed a small keyhole in the front panel.

"This one's locked," I said, excitement in my tone. Maybe there's something here after all.

Tristan stood in the doorway, one foot in the study, the other ready to get to the task at hand.

"You have one more second, Selena," Tristan said.

I swept my hand over the key hole and heard a small click. I quickly pulled the drawer open, ready to find Jeremiah's secrets, but inside lay a few pens, one really cool quill, and a photograph.

I picked up the picture, black and white, the sides yellowed and one edge burned. A family stared back at me; a woman in a dress with billowing skirts and a high collar, a man in a suit, and two small children standing in front of them. The girl so young, wide innocent eyes staring at the camera, a doll hanging from her small hand at her side, and the boy standing rod straight, eyes forward, no expression on his young face. Jeremiah.

It figured that he wouldn't have anything of use in a drawer so easily unlocked with magic. Oh well.

Enough of this! I heard Artemis scream in my mind. *Go! Now.*

I heard a noise from outside, Tristan's curse and the drawer slamming shut as I pushed myself back from the desk and ran back to the foyer.

I nearly tripped on the bottom step, trying to run up them. Lachlan and Lexi still stood guard outside, while Tristan and I maneuvered our way up the stairs.

We reached the last room on the left and faced a closed wooden door. I took a deep breath and turned the knob. With a creak, my heart raced and the door opened to a musty room with a wrought-iron bed frame and a worn mattress. Clearly this was the spare, spare room; the one you only gave to a guest when there was just no other place aside from the couch to sleep on. And clearly, Jeremiah hadn't had many friends over.

In the closet, on the floor to the right, Artemis said. *There's a loose floorboard.*

Tristan walked to the closet, a one door walk-in by the look of it. I stood right behind him as he swung the door open, took one stride and waved his hand over the right side of the floor.

The loose board popped up, revealing a small space beneath with a withered piece of paper folded in a square within it.

Take the paper and leave! Artemis yelled urgently in our heads.

Someone's coming, Lexi said right after. *Should we take them out?*

I heard voices approaching the house.

"Why do we have to come here?" a man said. "This place creeps me out for some reason."

"We won't be long. Jeremiah needs his things," said a second man.

No, we need to try to leave unnoticed. We don't want anyone knowing we were here, I said.

I heard footsteps enter the house, then pause abruptly. "Didn't he say he hadn't been home for weeks?" another voice said. Well there goes that plan.

"Let's go," I whispered. Tristan pocketed the paper and we looked around. "We just need to get outside, and then we can teleport."

"Jeremiah won't be happy his door is busted open," one of the men said.

"Quiet! They may still be here," whispered the other.

"Are we sure there was a barrier spell to begin with?" Tristan asked.

"That's what Artemis said, and there's no reason to take a chance now. Out the window," I whispered. I unlocked the window latch and pulled the pane up. It was stiff and I grunted, only managing to open it a few inches.

Tristan shooed me with his hands and I moved out of the

way. He pushed the window and it popped up with a loud crack.

"Upstairs!" One of the men said.

"Shit!" Tristan lifted me and practically pushed me out the window. I landed on the roof below and watched as Tristan got one leg out on the ledge, before he was pulled back in.

Guys we have trouble! I sent to Lexi and Lachlan and jumped up to reach the ledge and crawl back into the window. Tristan punched one man in the face before another tackled him. The third man saw me and cast a spell shooting a red beam of light at me. I'd never seen that before, but I didn't want to find out what it did. I blocked the spell and cast one of my own, sending the man flying head first into the wall. He sprawled on the ground unconscious.

Tristan grappled with the man on the floor and the second man came toward me, sparks shooting from his fingers.

"Selena!" Lexi called and I heard her heavy steps clomping up the stairs.

"In here," I called back. I charged the man, and slammed the butt of my palm into his nose. He grunted, stepping back and reaching for his bloody nose.

Lexi barged into the room with Lachlan at her heels, just as Tristan rolled over the man who had tackled him and hovered over him while punching him in the face. Lexi jumped behind the man I was about to hit again, and grabbed his head snapping his neck.

"Damn, Lexi," I said.

Tristan threw one final punch and stood, leaving the man bloodied and unconscious.

"You get it?" Lachlan asked.

Tristan nodded, catching his breath.

"Let's go then."

I ran for the door, but Tristan grabbed my arm.

"What?" I asked.

"There may be more downstairs, or outside even," he said. "Let's go out the window, just in case."

I rolled my eyes but agreed.

We jumped onto the roof below, then onto the ground, finding ourselves on the side of the house. I heard voices carried by the quiet night, coming from the front. I waved my friends to silence and crept to the side of the house. I was able to make out two figures peering in the front door.

"Perhaps we didn't teleport in time," a tall, lanky man said.

"No, they're still here." The voice made the hair on the back of my neck stand. As the man looked toward the second floor window, the soft light from the moon fell across his face. Jeremiah.

There are only two of them, I said. *We can end this right now.*

Determination flashed through Tristan's eyes and I knew we were on the same page for once. I looked at Lexi and Lachlan and they gave me a nod.

Ready?

No! Artemis screamed inside our heads with such conviction I thought he was there with us. I rubbed my ear reflexively as if that would help quite the voice. *One of you will die and he will still get away.* Tristan tensed, and took a step forward. I reached for him instinctively, but his movement caught Jeremiah's attention.

He turned slowly, eyes meeting mine and roaming over me once before looking over at the others. He cocked his head, and frowned as though I were a disappointing child. My rage flared and it took every ounce of self-restraint not to kill him right then. The thin man followed Jeremiah's gaze and studied us, his face turning into a grimace.

Lexi began a sphere shield as the thin man stepped in front of Jeremiah. Lachlan hurled a fireball but the thin man deflected it without even moving.

Stop, I said to the group. The thin man began gesturing with his arms, the pressure in the air around us building. *We're leaving. Now.*

The thin man began to glow, illuminating Jeremiah's face contorting into a smirk, and thrust his arms forward. My friends rushed to grab hold of my arms and I started teleporting as a wide sphere of grey light shot toward us.

My eyes never left Jeremiah's until the walls of Genevieve's house materialized around us.

"May I see it?" Artemis asked as he got comfortable. Tristan hesitated a moment before passing the parchment to him. Artemis practically pet the paper before unfolding it and staring at its contents, the dried blood seeped through the back of the paper. "Hello old friend," he said. Something in his tone saddened me.

"We should study that now," Tristan said.

"Would you mind terribly if I read it to you?" Artemis asked. "I missed it so."

"I… guess," Tristan answered, assessing the man.

Artemis sat upright. He spoke slowly but clearly, and we all hung on his every word.

"One year from now she will be born in the valley of the sun. She will have hair as black as ebony, and eyes as blue as sapphire. An orphan she'll be, but she will not be alone. Two protectors watch over her; the girl will be like a sister, the boy a lover, but he is part of the Gemini and rivals his brother. On the twenty-first of June, in her twenty-fifth year, they will battle, awakening her to the magic of our world. This will allow her to accept the power that has begun growing within her.

"Her glow will surround her; such power has never before been seen. Not one single witch will be able to match it.

"There will be another who will come close, though she isn't the one, she will still be needed.

"In the black book that is kept hidden, is written the spell that must be performed on the correct day.

"The two needed to perform this spell are two halves of one whole. Darkness resides in each, though one will be consumed by it, the other will choose the light.

"The Gemini will love her, and fight for her. One will even sacrifice his life for her, following the light, the other will gain strength from the darkness.

"One of the Gemini will assist in this task, but it will be for his own gain.

"The power sought will be found, but satisfaction will not.

"Revenge can be achieved if darkness is chosen, but remember, there cannot be darkness without the light."

The room became eerily quiet. We waited for more, for what

would happen. Artemis sighed, lowering the paper to his lap.

"That's it?" I asked, somewhat disappointed.

"Was that not enough?" He asked.

"Not really. How do we know the prophecy was about me?" I asked irritated.

"Normally, I would agree that the prophecy is too vague to use as a credible indicator of whom it speaks. However, since you found the source, me, I can assure you that you are the one I see - the girl of the sun." He smiled. "You are not the only one in this prophecy so don't be fooled, you can take comfort in recognizing your friends in there as another indication you are the one."

I wanted to feel good, feel relieved that I didn't have to doubt myself anymore, but I couldn't. My focus kept shifting, there was so much to process, and I suddenly had more questions.

"So, my whole purpose, the whole point to all of this is just to stop Jeremiah from getting his vengeance?" My voice was too loud in the shadow of Artemis's quiet tale.

"There is more information there that you should consider, and that you can use to help you," Artemis said. "I have told you what I could, but yes, in the end that is your purpose. Though you should be relieved - I know you did not want to have to lead anyone. All you have to do is fight, and the others will follow. Decide what you will, and the outcome will be what you want."

I *wanted* to bang my head against the wall. All this fuss, all the torture, and stress and anxiety and life-threatening crap that happened was for this? I knew I would have to do something along those lines, but I guess I just thought there would be more.

I was pissed off.

"Remember the lives you can save, not only human lives, but witches. You chose the light once. Will you do so again?" Artemis asked.

"What is it with all the choices? I choose for this to be over, so I can get on with my life," I argued.

"Yes, but with whom would you want to spend the rest of that life?" Artemis asked, leaning his back against the chair.

"What?" I asked confused. I noticed Tristan shifting in my peripheral vision, but again I didn't want to look in his direction.

"It's all up to you. The prophecy will come to pass, but there are some points that are subjective. It comes back to what you will choose. So please, choose well."

"What about the good ones?" Tristan asked his own question.

"Good ones?" Artemis asked, and then dawning relaxed his features. "Ah, like I said the copy you had been told of did not have all the real facts. You were even initially under the impression your brother was running the show, but you now know it was Jeremiah. He kept too much hidden. Though I suppose you could call all the innocent witches and humans 'good ones' and Jeremiah and his followers as the 'dark ones' as they were referenced in the version you had been told."

I looked around at my friends, and most of them were looking at Artemis. Lexi and Fay were looking at me.

"I need some air." I stood and went to the back yard, hoping to clear my head. I slammed the door behind me and paced the yard. Why was I so mad? Artemis was right; I didn't want to have to lead anyone anywhere. I should be happy that the guessing game was over, that I could be sure the prophecy was about me, but I just couldn't see the bigger picture.

What was with all the choices? So I had darkness in me, great. Apparently some other girl does too. Who could that be? Which one of us will choose the light? My mind reeled as I took in all the details of the prophecy. There was so much, and yet I felt like it said nothing at all.

I sat at the patio table and contemplated this new information. I heard the door open and close behind me, and didn't even bother turning to see who it was.

"You okay?" Lexi asked. I ignored the disappointment that it wasn't Tristan.

"Yeah, just confused."

"I know, especially about that whole guy thing," she said coming to sit beside me on the patio table.

"What guy thing?" I asked, searching her face for the answer. Her eye brows pulled together.

"You were there, right? You did hear the prophecy with the rest of us, didn't you?"

I didn't appreciate her sarcasm. I clenched my jaw to stop myself from saying anything rude. She let out a sigh and smiled a small smile.

"The guy thing is the whole Tristan vs. Darien drama," she finally answered. I got more confused.

"What?"

"Sometimes I wonder about you," she said, eyeing me with concern. "The Gemini, the twins, Tristan and Darien. They both want you, and depending what you choose, whether it's the dark side or the light side, will determine who you will end up with.

One will die for you though, so I'm not sure how that will work out," she said dramatically.

"Die for me," I whispered. "Since when has there ever been a competition between Tristan and Darien? I know who I want," I answered.

"Do you?" Lexi retorted, studying me. I wondered what she knew. I peeked in her head – I know I told myself to mind my own business but, this was my business - and I knew Lexi wouldn't be able to sense my presence in her thoughts.

"You talked to Tristan." It wasn't a question.

"Yup," she answered, nodding her head slowly, but she averted her gaze.

"I don't know what to say. It was just a dream. I can't control those, you know?" I said through clenched teeth.

"I know, but it just seems a little weird that you are longing for him. Like, if you didn't have any feelings for him at all, when you woke up you might be like, 'whoa, where did that come from?' but you wouldn't want more. Maybe the time you spent with him at the camp had more of an affect than you thought."

I hadn't realized how much Tristan had seen in my thoughts. I thought he just knew what I dreamed, not what I felt. I thought about my time with Darien to see if there was any truth to Lexi's words.

"No way." I shook my head. But I couldn't ignore the possibility. Could that be true? Oh God, I really hope not. My heart sank at the thought and that wouldn't be a rational reaction if you loved someone – would it?

"Listen, it's up to you. If you want Tristan, then choose him." Lexi smiled.

"I do want Tristan. This is all just some mind game. I'm just not sure Tristan will choose me, though." I let my head hit the table and let out a groan. That actually hurt. "I hate my life," I whined. Lexi chuckled.

"Don't. Tristan will come around, and I have faith in you and I know you will do the right thing. Besides, if you choose the dark side," she said it like a bad actor in *Star Wars*. "Then you will get us all killed. So I'm pretty sure I know what you'll decide."

"I know what side I'll pick too! It's just that when Artemis was saying things like choices and stuff, it just makes me wonder why. What exactly does he know?"

"You'll be fine, I promise." Lexi squeezed my shoulder and then stood to leave. "Uh, speaking of Tristan; when were you planning on talking to him?" She asked.

"Ugh!" I grunted. "Leave me alone, Lexi. I have to sort things out with the dark side."

She laughed, but did as I asked. I sat in the sun and thought about one of the brothers dying for me. I was pretty sure I knew who that was, and my stomach flipped. The thought of losing Tristan was unbearable. A lump rose in my throat, was there no other way? Artemis said it was up to me. So things could change – it wasn't all set in stone, right?

If I went to the dark side, would that save Tristan or officially doom him? My thoughts were poisoning my brain. I had hoped that with Artemis here all our questions would be answered, but really I just had more.

I knew in my heart that I wasn't capable of hurting my friends, or choosing to help Jeremiah, at least not without being under a spell. So I was confident what I would choose. I don't think there was ever any real chance I would do otherwise. I just wish Artemis didn't mess with my head. I would do the right thing. I knew in my gut what I would do and what I wanted, and that made me feel much better.

As for Tristan dying for me, I refused to believe that would happen. There was no way I would let it. I was feeling more positive and felt that I could rejoin my friends and try to discuss things rationally.

Everyone was scattered throughout the house. Only Tristan sat with Artemis in the living room. Lexi and John were talking at the kitchen table, Fay stood watching them from the doorway. I wasn't sure where Genevieve and Lachlan were.

"They went to get food for tonight," Artemis answered my silent question. I spun to see him staring at me with his all-too-knowing gaze. I chanced a glance at Tristan, sitting across from Artemis, leaning in intently. His eyes met mine for only a second before I looked away. I was such a coward.

"Artemis," I started, keeping eye contact with him. "The prophecy says that the answer is in Jeremiah's spell book. What is it?"

"The ritual that he needs the two of you for," he answered vaguely.

"Can you give me any more information on that?" I pressed, sarcasm seeped into my tone.

"Jeremiah needs you and the other whose power is close, but not equal to yours. He will need the two of you, along with the Herkimer diamond, and he has to time it just right. Get you in the right place."

"Gah! Just spell it out for me!" I yelled. I saw Tristan flinch, but I tried to ignore him. Lexi and John, who had been talking quietly in the kitchen, came into the living room to see what was going on.

"Alright, I promised you answers, so I will give them to you," Artemis said. "Jeremiah has a spell in his book of shadows that can raise dead witches. If he gets you and the other one along with the Herkimer diamond in the right moon phase, he will be able to channel your power and raise an army of the dead. This is what he has wanted, the infinite power. He will be unstoppable and he will rain hell on the Hidden City and then he will move to the humans. He wants to kill them all, and his followers want to be a part of that. Is that detailed enough for you?"

I swallowed hard. Okay I now knew why he hadn't wanted to tell me the whole thing. I caught my breath.

"The Herkimer diamond? The rose one? Is that the same one I needed to break my binding spell?" I asked.

"Why do you think he bound your powers to begin with?"

"What do you mean?"

"Jeremiah bound your powers, and then gloated to the Elders that he was an expert on bindings, to force you to go to him, so he could tell you the riddle of where to find the Diamond. He didn't need it for the unbinding, but he did need it to control you. He also needed it for this spell, and he knew he wouldn't be able to get it himself."

"Why not?" I asked, trying to keep all this information in order.

"When I told him the riddle of where to find it, I also told him that he wouldn't be able to obtain it alone because of the shadow men. He didn't trust anyone else to get it for him, and didn't want to risk depleting his army by needlessly sending them to their deaths. Besides, he had you. If you retrieved the stone, great, if you got killed, he wouldn't have to deal with you anymore."

"Then he wouldn't be able to perform the ritual," I said.

"Not that one, no. But there are others that without your existence, would be sufficiently powerful."

"You told him the riddle?" Tristan interjected.

"Yes. He asked where he could find that ingredient. My visions often come in riddles or rhymes, I'm not sure why. Nevertheless, he knew he or his followers would be killed trying to get the stone. He knew you would be desperate enough to get him anything he asked for, so he used that against you."

"That just makes way too much sense," I whispered, finding the nearest seat and taking it. What a mess this all was.

"So wait, let me get this straight," Lexi spoke up. "Jeremiah has been waiting for twenty-five years for Selena's powers to bloom so he could use them and some other girl's, to raise dead witches to get vengeance over everyone?" Lexi asked exasperated.

"Yes. Now if he has Selena on his side, he will be unstoppable, truly. Selena alone is practically unstoppable. That is why he will never bind her powers again. He can't risk her being weakened if there is even the slightest chance she will work with him." I wondered if Artemis said that because he knew I had been worried about that happening again. "But if Selena chooses against him, her power will be stronger than his," Artemis explained.

This was all too much. Way too much in such a short period of time - Jeremiah's story, the prophecy, Jeremiah's plan for universal domination. It was all just too much. I closed my eyes to try and stop my head from spinning.

I pressed my fingers to my temples and focused on my breathing. Was I ready for this? Could I handle what was coming?

I heard Artemis laugh softly and I sprang my eyes open.

"What?" I asked.

"It would seem that Jeremiah has just discovered that I have been taken." He laughed out of satisfaction. "Yes, his precious gift taken from him."

I smiled in spite of myself. That would be something I wouldn't mind seeing.

"He must be pissed," John said cheerily.

"Yes. To think, this won't even matter by next week."

"What do you mean?" I asked, scared of the answer.

"The moon, and planetary alignment will be just right then. That is when he will cast his spell, assuming he can get everything in place in time. If not, then he'll have to wait for the next correct moon phase, which will be in a year. I'm sure he won't like that at all," Artemis answered, almost as if he were talking to himself.

"Wait. Moon phases? Two girls?" Lexi pondered silently, and then her eyes lit up. "That's what we saw!" She turned to face me.

"What did we see?" I asked confused.

"Remember when I got the truth from Jeremiah and it

showed his plan? We saw moon phases and ingredients and… Stefania."

Tristan sucked in a breath.

"She's the other one?" I asked.

"Yes! It makes sense, I mean you guys look alike and are similar in some ways. Tristan would know more about that though." Lexi shot a glance at him. He averted his gaze.

"Jeremiah won't be able to convince her to help him though," Tristan mumbled.

"He might," Artemis said.

"No," Tristan shook his head.

"I mean, it kind of makes sense," Genevieve said. "I don't think the reference is of *her* choosing the light."

"True," Lexi added. "Think about it, she has always been competing with Selena, and not only for your attention." She looked at Tristan. "Not to mention that anyone would want to have Selena's abilities, I mean, they're pretty bad ass. She's grown up looking like her, having great potential, maybe she thought she was the one. But it was never enough because she is *not* Selena."

"That's deep," John said.

"So, what?" Tristan asked. "You think she would jump at the opportunity to achieve greatness, no matter the cost?"

Lexi shrugged.

"How do we know she's not the one and I'm second best?" I asked.

"Like I said, I know," Artemis answered.

"But she's engaged," Tristan said.

"Actually," Lexi said, "I heard they broke it off."

"That doesn't mean she'll agree to help Jeremiah," Tristan said.

"True," Lexi said. "But I wouldn't be surprised."

"Can you tell what the outcome will be?" I asked Artemis.

"I cannot, not for this, but it depends on you, remember?" He said kindly. He stood and tapped my knee comfortingly as he passed. "I will be outside if anyone needs me," he said as he walked out the front door.

"Well this should be interesting. At least we know when it will be over, one way or another," Lexi said.

"I think it'll all work out well," John said, gazing at Lexi. For the first time ever, I saw her blush. There was a loud shattering noise and I jerked up reflexively.

I rushed to the kitchen, vaguely aware that Tristan was right behind me. Right inside the doorway, Fay was bent down, picking up large shards of glass. I recognized the pattern – it was one of Genevieve's fruit bowls.

I mentally imagined the pieces coming together and they did as I willed, repairing itself into its original state.

"Are you okay?" I asked, noticing that Fay's hands were bleeding. I took the bowl from her and placed it on the table.

"Fine," she snapped.

"What happened?" Tristan asked Fay.

"It was an accident," she said. Suspicion swept through me, and I searched her thoughts. (I know, I know.) Then I understood; Fay had seen John and Lexi getting close. She was holding the bowl in her hands, and her anger made it shatter between her shaking fingers.

I needed to talk to Lexi, and even John. This was really

hurting Fay, and I felt bad for her.

"Here, give me your hands, I can fix that," I offered. Fay seemed to consider it for a minute.

"No, I'm fine. Just leave me." She grabbed a towel and pressed it to her palms as she stormed past me. I turned and saw her head upstairs.

I walked to John and Lexi and grabbed each of their wrists.

"What the—?" Lexi started, but I was pulling her before she could finish her question. I yanked them both outside to the back yard and closed the door behind us.

"Um...problem?" John asked sarcastically as he pulled his arm from my grasp.

"Yes, there's a problem. I don't know what your history is with Fay, but you're killing her right now," I said.

"Selena! Why would you say that?" Lexi asked shocked. I knew she was thinking I wanted John to be with Fay rather than her.

"Don't get all pissy, Lexi. Look I know you guys like each other and that's fine, but can you," I glared at John, "please talk to Fay? Let her know there is nothing between you and her and never will be, assuming that's the case?"

John's jaw dropped, flabbergasted for a moment.

"Oh, come on! Please, please don't tell me that you didn't know she is in love with you. Please?" I pleaded. There was no way this guy was that oblivious.

"No I...I figured she had a crush or something, but she never said anything, and I never felt that way about her, so I never brought it up. She's like my little sister. I love her but not in a romantic way."

"I'm sorry about this," Lexi said and she grabbed John's arm. A flash of confusion crossed his face before he realized what was happening. He didn't pull away. Lexi refocused.

"He's telling the truth," she said to me, but she looked at John guiltily.

"See how tempting that is?" I asked Lexi.

"Shit," she whispered.

"I'm sorry, John. I swear I won't do that again."

"You're lucky I like you," he said, "Otherwise we'd have a problem." I thought he was kind of upset, but then he beamed a smile at Lexi. His smile faltered after a moment, and he turned to look at me. "You're right. I will go talk to Fay now."

"You sure you'll be okay doing that?" Lexi asked.

John flashed another smile. "I can handle it." He turned back into the house, and Lexi almost melted.

"He's so cute!" she gushed. I laughed and rolled my eyes.

"Yes cute, but I told you; he comes with way too much drama. Please try to be careful. Fay seems unbalanced right now."

Lexi nodded slowly.

We headed back into the house where Tristan was laying across the couch, staring at the ceiling. I wished I could know what he was thinking, and it took all my restraint to stop myself from finding out.

He hadn't spoken to me since we got back from Artemis' house or well, Jeremiah's house. I figured he could talk to me when he was ready - if he would ever be ready to forgive me. Tristan turned his head and faced me then. This time I didn't look away, but he did.

My heart sank, and I went to sit in the kitchen. I heard heavy footsteps thudding quickly down the stairs. Then Fay was right in front of me.

"Why can't you keep your damn mouth shut?" She snarled.

"What? I-"

"Mind your own business! You can't even fix your own relationship, why the hell would you get involved in mine?" She yelled right in my face.

"What relationship? All you have is some stupid crush on a guy who doesn't even know you exist. Excuse me for wanting to help you so you wouldn't have a freaking aneurysm every time you saw John talk to Lexi!" I yelled back.

"You don't know anything!"

I stood up and got in her face.

"No? How about I know that you love John, but he only looks at you like a sister? I know it kills you to see him interested in someone other than you. I know you never had the courage to tell him how you really felt, because deep down inside you know he doesn't feel the same way. Isn't it better to know for sure so you can try to move on? Isn't that better than watching them and breaking glass and trying to hide your rage induced fist shaking? Tell me how much I *don't know*!"

"You ruined everything," she said to me in a quieter tone.

"How?" I asked angrily.

"By being so weak and needing help! Why couldn't you do this alone? Why did you have to get everyone involved? You're supposed to be the *chosen* one," she said exaggerating the word. "Why did you have to drag everyone else into your fight?"

"My fight?" I yelled. "This affects all witches. You all

brought me into *your* fight!" I knew that wasn't exactly true, yes I got dragged into this, but I was a witch too and faced the same risks as everyone else.

"You're a terrible person."

"And you're delusional, do you know that? John never thought of you romantically, and you're right, he never will, but it's not because of me," I said bringing the subject back to the matter at hand.

"All you do is cause pain. You are good for nothing except that. Look at Tristan – he looks like hell and it's all your fault. Everything is your fault!" Fay stormed out of the kitchen and slammed the front door shut behind her.

I shook with anger, and my lip trembled with the effort to hold back my tears. Maybe Fay was right. Maybe I was weak. All I did was destroy everything I touched, like Tristan. I was a horrible person. I try to make things right, but I ruin them instead.

I heard someone clear their throat, and I saw John standing in the doorway of the kitchen.

"Sorry about that. I guess it didn't go as well as I thought it would. I mentioned your name and I shouldn't have. I had no idea..."

"It's okay. She's just redirecting her anger. She'll come around." I looked down, hoping my face didn't show just how much she hurt me.

John nodded and left the kitchen. I sank back into my chair and placed my head in my hands. I wanted to go home. I missed Arizona and the normal life I had there. I missed the too hot sun. I missed my apartment. I missed my car, and I missed being alone. There were too many people here and I was tired of it.

Jeremiah couldn't do his stupid ritual if I wasn't there, so maybe I could go home, and he would leave me alone till next year. If there's no ritual, there's nothing to protect the people from. This idea was getting better and better. I got to my feet and ran up the stairs, trying unsuccessfully not to look at Tristan, who was now standing, with a torn expression on his face. He probably heard what Fay said about me destroying him, and he probably agreed with her. I closed the door behind me and grabbed my small luggage from the closet. I threw it on the bed and opened it.

I threw all of my clothes and toiletries in and zipped it closed. I ran down the stairs, luggage in hand, and headed straight out the front door.

Peace out, witch people.

I got to the small road leading away from the cottage when I stopped short. How did I get out of here? Could I teleport back to Arizona? Or did I have to leave through the door to Vegas?

Damn. Damn. Damn.

I threw my luggage at the ground and let out a frustrated growl.

"Leaving without saying good-bye?"

My heart skipped a beat. I turned around and saw Tristan standing there. And he was talking to me this time.

"I...I want to go home." My voice cracked over a sob.

Tristan's jaw clenched. He took two long strides and wrapped his arms around me, pulling me into his chest. I let a few tears fall, feeling the security he provided.

"I know. We'll go home soon. Just a little while longer."

I shook my head. "No, I want to go now. No one wants me here, I ruin everything and if I'm not here, Jeremiah can't use me to get super powers and kill the whole damn town."

"I want you here," Tristan whispered. My heart fluttered.

"No, I hurt you worst of all. You should just let Jeremiah take me."

"Right, so we can all die. Great," he answered sarcastically. I looked up into his green eyes and felt even worse.

"I'm sorry. I swear I never meant to make you worry about my reckless behavior or hurt you with thoughts of...him. I can't explain it but I am sorry," I cried.

"Shh, it's okay. We're okay." He kissed the top of my head and held me closer.

"I'll be better. I swear," I said. Tristan stepped back and lifted my chin. He ran his finger along my bottom lip, and my pulse quickened. He leaned down and pressed his lips softly against mine. A low moan escaped his lips.

"I don't ever again want to feel like I can't kiss you anytime I want," he said, chuckling slightly. I kissed him back to make him feel better.

"Wow, I missed that glow. I haven't seen it in a while."

"Well I haven't had much to be happy about," I said.

"Come on, let's go inside."

"No please. I really just want to go home. I'll come back next week if I have to, but I can't stand it here anymore!" I pleaded.

"Selena, you know what you have to do," Tristan said. I clenched my teeth with frustration. I knew he was right, but damn it. I nodded, picked up my luggage and headed back inside.

Genevieve and Lachlan had returned with their groceries, but Fay was still out.

"Anyone hear from Fay?" I asked the group. She had been gone for a while, but they all shook their heads.

"Try contacting her telepathically," Tristan said.

I nodded once. *Fay, are you okay?* I could feel her presence, like she could hear me but was blocking me out.

"She's not answering me. She's probably still too mad." I sighed.

"It's best to leave her alone for now," Artemis, who had been silently observing us, spoke up.

Though I didn't know for sure that Fay was alright, I felt a small sense of ease at his words, I wondered again what it would be like to be him, or at least to have his ability.

Artemis snapped his head in my direction and stared at me intently. I swallowed hard. Had I thought something bad? Why was he staring at me like that?

"Again, I say I know much, but not all. There are some questions that, even if I know the answer, I will not reveal to you. Some things you will have to wait to find out. In due time, everything will be discovered, but like I said before, sometimes fate cannot be thwarted. Sometimes there's no benefit in knowing the future when you can't do anything to change it." Artemis stood then and went upstairs.

"What the hell was that?" Lexi asked curiously.

I shrugged.

"I was thinking what it would be like to have his abilities."

"Oh. I guess you got your answer." When she saw the baffled look on my face she huffed and continued. "Basically he was saying that although he can see things, sometimes if it's meant to be it will be. It must suck when he sees something bad happening, but can't do anything to stop it." Lexi shivered.

"Okay, either you're really smart lately or my binding fried way too many brain cells. I can't seem to keep up with the poems and cryptic messages."

Lexi beamed, "You may be all powerful, but I have super special gifts of my own that you wish you could have," she teased.

John smiled at Lexi. The way they were gazing at each other was making me queasy. Were Tristan and I ever that mushy?

I turned to look at Tristan. He raised his eyebrow and shook his head.

I burst out laughing, and I couldn't stop.

"What's so funny?" Lexi asked coming out of her John-induced trance. My laughter just became more consuming. My stomach muscles ached with the motion, and tears streamed down my face. I tried to speak, but every time I thought I had gotten control, the giggles would reappear.

Tristan smiled beside me and handed me a tissue, which for some reason, just made me laugh even harder. But oh man did it feel good! I hadn't laughed like that in so long, I couldn't even remember the last time. I pressed the tissue to my face to catch my tears and continued laughing.

"Lexi, go get her some water, would you?" Tristan asked, starting to chuckle at my hysteria. I took in a deep breath, trying to calm my insides, but they felt like Jell-O. Lexi came back a moment later, water in hand, and gave it to me, studying me skeptically.

"You're blinding me! Tone down your aura, would you?" Lexi teased. I reeled it in instinctively.

I took a few gulps of water and felt myself regain control.

"Oh man, that was awesome," I gasped. "Sorry, I'm not even sure why I'm laughing so hard, it's just-" I remembered Tristan's face expression and suppressed another bout of giggles. I took another gulp of water just in case.

"You okay there?" Lexi asked sarcastically cautious.

"Yeah, I'm good. Thanks," I answered. My face was flushed and I fanned it with my hand to calm my blood down.

"Dinner's ready," Genevieve called from the kitchen. Lexi and John stood and headed toward an aroma that smelled like spaghetti. My stomach growled.

"Come on, you should put something in your stomach," Tristan said in response to my stomach's auditory complaint. He smiled, and standing, held his hand out to me.

I took his hand, and he squeezed mine gently as I stood. In the kitchen John and Lexi were already sitting side by side, and Lachlan was sitting across from them, piling the spaghetti onto his plate.

Genevieve placed the garlic bread and parmesan cheese on the table, then sat down beside Lachlan. Tristan took the seat at the head of the table and I took the other, feeling awfully exposed.

Artemis came down then, and I jumped at the opportunity to ease my discomfort.

"Here, you can take my seat," I offered, getting to my feet. I put some food in a plate and went to the living room to eat.

After dinner we cleaned up the kitchen. The front door opened and slammed shut. Lexi and John flinched, as they realized who it was.

I guess Fay was done with her alone time. She spoke quietly with Genevieve, but I couldn't make out the words.

John, who had been closer to them, let out a low groan. A few seconds later Fay stormed into the kitchen, pushing Lexi and John apart in the process. Lexi's eyes blazed with hell fire.

Fay grabbed a plate and angrily threw the spaghetti and sauce on it. I was still pissed as all hell at her, so I didn't want to talk to her. When she finished, she spun on her heel and pushed past Lexi and John again.

"If Fay pushes me one more time," Lexi stormed. "I will shove my foot so far up her ass, she'll be giving me a foot-rub with her tongue." I don't think I had ever seen her so angry.

The rest of the night passed uneventfully, and as I was lying in bed I began to feel restless. We had this information about Jeremiah, knew his plan, so shouldn't we do something about it? I decided I would ask Artemis about it in the morning, and eventually fell into a dreamless sleep.

15. KILLING TIME

I was sitting at the patio table in the back yard the next morning when Lexi came out to sit with me.

"Hey," I said as she sat down.

"Are you okay?" She asked, taking in my pensive state.

"Yeah, I'm just trying to figure out what to do now," I answered.

"Why don't you ask Artemis?" She suggested.

"I will, as soon as he wakes up. I just don't know if he'll even have the answer to this one."

"Well he promised answers in exchange for his freedom. He'll tell us what he can to keep his end of the deal I'm sure."

"He better." I smiled. "Hey how is everything with John?"

Lexi beamed. "Good." She bit her lip and I could tell she wanted to say more. I raised my eyebrows encouraging her to go on. "We kissed!" She blurted in a whisper, and her face flushed.

I laughed, "That's a good thing. I'm happy for you."

"Thanks! I just wish things weren't so weird with Fay though."

"Yeah I hear ya." I thought back to my confrontation with Fay. I hadn't spoken to her since. A motion in the house caught my eye and I saw Artemis walking around in the kitchen. "Okay, let's go." I stood and headed inside, Lexi trailing behind me.

"You going to talk to Artemis?" She asked as we entered the house.

"Yeah. What have I got to lose?" I answered, but when I reached the kitchen, he wasn't there.

Everyone had finished breakfast and the kitchen was cleaned. John, Lachlan and Tristan were talking in the living room, while Fay and Genevieve spoke in the kitchen.

"Where's Artemis?" Lexi asked, finding a seat next to John.

"He's outside in the front," John answered, putting his arm around Lexi. I was glad Fay wasn't in the room to see this.

I headed out the front door, and thankfully, no one followed. Artemis was outside pacing slowly, taking in the scenery. He stopped, took a deep breath, and released it slowly.

I felt bad interrupting; it seemed he was enjoying the day as much as I had been.

"What can I do for you, Selena?" He asked kindly, without even turning to see that it was me. I shifted uncomfortably, but moved forward.

"I was just wondering what to do now? We have Jeremiah's plan so...should we...what?" I asked cryptically.

"Yes, what indeed." He chuckled softly and turned to face me. "This is one of those questions I cannot answer. It will happen how it is meant to, and I unfortunately cannot change the course. All I can tell you is to enjoy your time. Rest, relax and appreciate your friends. The time goes by so quickly." His face fell sadly, and it took all my restraint not to hug the man.

"So we just wait then? That's all we can do?" I asked,

bringing his attention back to that part of the conversation.

"Yes. I know it seems frustrating, but it will happen on its own, and you must stay hidden from the Wayward. I can tell you that you will have a nice amount of time to rest and rejuvenate before anything happens."

"Great," I mumbled.

Artemis smiled, "Why do you want to rush everything? Life is too precious to fast-forward." He turned his attention back to the woods, "So short, life is short." He admired the view, not waiting for an answer.

"Thanks," I said. I think.

I found out later that "a nice amount of time" wasn't very long at all...

DAY 1

After I came inside, knowing that the pressure was off for just a little while, I found myself even more at peace. I mean, I was nervous with not knowing what was coming or when, but also knowing that whatever was happening was not in my power was somewhat liberating.

I told the others the news so that they could feel at ease too, or maybe they would become tense.

It was a split of reactions; Lexi and John were more relaxed, Fay, Genevieve and Tristan became tense, and Lachlan seemed undecided, sort of calm but on alert. All we could do was heed Artemis's advice and enjoy the time - if we could get over our anxieties to do so.

I knew one of the reasons why Fay was anxious. I knew she

wanted to leave and take John, alone, with her. Genevieve was tense I'm sure because she had had enough ambushes and attacks on her home and she was no doubt wondering what would happen next.

Lexi and John were relaxed, because if there was nothing to do, they could enjoy each other's company without feeling like they were neglecting any duties.

But what I worried about was what this time would do to us. All of us under one roof for, who knew how long – oh yeah, Artemis knew – well, it could prove detrimental.

As if to validate my concerns, Lexi and John walked through the living room toward the back of the house holding hands. Fay glared at them and then shot an angry look at me.

"Oh, come on," I whispered so only Fay would hear me. She didn't respond, she just glowered.

Yeah, this was going to be just peachy. Tristan came and stood by my side, and finally Fay averted her gaze and left in the opposite direction of John and Lexi.

"So, what shall we do with our temporary freedom?" Tristan tried to joke, but I could sense his tension.

"Do we have to stay under house arrest or can we go out and do things?" I asked, turning to face Artemis who stood just inside the front door.

"Do what makes you happy," he said and went upstairs.

"Dude is starting to act weird," I mumbled to Tristan who chuckled.

"Starting? He's been mumbling and repeating things," Tristan said. "Although, I'd have to say he's been acting relatively normal for someone who was locked up for twenty-six years."

"Yeah, I guess." The thought saddened me."Twenty-six years. That's longer than I've been alive."

Tristan contemplated that for a moment and then shook the thought off.

"So…what makes you happy?" Tristan asked, gazing at me.

"I could think of a few things," I whispered, gazing knowingly back at him. He smiled and grabbed my hand, leading me upstairs.

We hurried into our room before anyone could interrupt us. Once the door was closed another sense of calm overcame me. It was just the ability to shut everyone out, and have a private place for Tristan and I that made me feel better.

Tristan sat on the bed and motioned for me to sit next to him. I did. Instead of going straight for the kissing like I thought he would, he brushed a strand of my hair behind my ear, and just looked at me.

After a few moments, I began to feel self-conscious.

"What are you looking at?" I asked with curiosity rather than hostility.

"You are the most beautiful woman I have ever seen. I could stare at you for days and still find something I hadn't noticed before," he whispered, holding my face.

My breath caught. "Where is this coming from?" I had never seen Tristan so open and mushy. I wasn't sure what to do with it.

"I'm just tired of holding back. I know you may not have noticed, with me behaving so recklessly, but I have been holding back. I can't do it anymore. I just feel too much for you and I don't know what to do," he said.

"Just be yourself. Don't over think it," I offered as soothingly as possible. Tristan's intensity was overpowering all my senses.

"No one makes me feel the way you do. I would kill for you and I would die for you." He pressed his lips against mine and his passion and raw emotion engulfed me.

He was right, he *had* been holding back. He never kissed me like this before, and my mind spun with the feeling. He ran his hands though my hair and pressed my face to his.

I was almost completely sucked into the moment, but something Tristan had said was nagging at me. I gently pushed him back and caught my breath.

He chuckled quietly at my frenzied state.

"No," I whispered. Tristan's face fell. "I didn't mean no, I don't want you, I meant no, you can't die for me. Ever since Artemis told us the prophecy I have been worrying about that. I won't let you die for me. You can't do it, do you understand?" I pushed.

"I can't promise you that. Selena, I love you. I have spent most of my life watching you and protecting you. If my death will mean saving your life, then I will gladly do it. I wouldn't be able to live if you were dead anyway."

"How do you think I would feel? I would be a mess. I can't even fathom my life without you in it. If you died for me, I…I just wouldn't be able to forgive myself," I finished in a whisper, lowering my gaze to my fingers.

Tristan lifted my chin. "Let's not talk about death. Artemis told us to enjoy our time, and I for one am going to take his advice." He kissed me softly then, and I allowed my dreary thoughts to be pushed aside.

How could I argue against him when his lips were moving like that on mine? He trailed his kisses down my neck and across my collar bone. I let out a jagged breath, and I could feel the heat of his breath tickle my skin as he laughed.

"Glow, Selena," Tristan warned. I reeled in my aura. I'd been losing control of it lately. Tristan chuckled. "We don't want people knocking on the door asking about it," he teased.

I lifted his face back up to mine and kissed his mouth, so he'd stop talking. His lips were soft but firm. One hand remained in my hair, and the other pulled my body close to him and held it tight. I wrapped my arms around his neck, and then I did become completely sucked into the moment.

I had no sense of time, no sense of where I was or that there were other people nearby, and I was even beginning to lose sense of *who* I was. I became completely oblivious to the world around me. All I could see was Tristan, all I could feel was the touch of his hands as they roamed my body, the feel of his lips moving with mine, the feel of his muscular body under my fingers. All I could smell was his aftershave, all I could taste was his kiss, and all I could hear was his heartbeat beating in time with mine. He was my smell, sight, taste, touch, and sound.

At that very moment, he was my everything.

DAY 2

"You are being completely irrational do you know that?" I woke to someone yelling downstairs.

"Oh really? And you would know, right? Miss perfect! Miss

I get whatever I want!"

I rolled over and let out a groan.

"Who...? Why...?" I asked incoherently. Tristan was awake before me again. His fingers trailed up and down my arm.

"It would seem that Fay couldn't hold her peace anymore. She's yelling at Lexi," Tristan explained.

"Why? Just cause John likes Lexi and not her?" I asked.

"I don't get whatever I want!" Lexi was yelling.

"As Artemis would say, 'hatred is illogical,'" Tristan said. "But I would say that love is the most illogical of all. She won't get mad at John, she loves him too much."

I lifted my head and placed it on Tristan's chest, listening to his steady heartbeat. I could still hear Lexi and Fay arguing, but I couldn't make out what they were saying. Memories from the day before fluttered back to me and I let out a sigh. "You okay?" Tristan asked.

"Mmm, better than okay. I feel great." I curled even closer to Tristan. "You?"

"Better than great, firefly." He kissed the top of my head.

"I give up hiding my aura."

"You say that now, but when people start staring, you'll want to reel it in," Tristan advised.

"You know," Fay yelled loud enough for me to hear. "Everything was fine before you came along. You and damn Selena!"

"Hey," I moaned quietly, my eyebrows furrowing. Well if they're going to drop my name in their fight, I might as well drop myself in it too. I reluctantly stood up, threw on some clothes and headed out the door.

"Where are you going?" Tristan asked with a hint of disappointment in his voice.

"I'll be back. I need to defend my honor." I laughed. I blew Tristan a kiss and bounded down the stairs. My body was feeling much better today. I must have un-kinked some muscles yesterday.

Lexi and Fay were toe-to-toe in the kitchen. I wondered where everyone else was, until I saw the time on the stove and realized it was way too early for anyone to be up, never mind arguing.

"Speak of the Devil and *she* appears." Fay sneered as I came into the kitchen.

"Oh, get a grip. You are so dramatic." I wanted to yell, but I was so aware of the early hour and everyone sleeping, it came out as a hiss.

"Who do you think you are?" Fay yelled, obviously not taking my hint to lower her voice. "Oh right, you're not even sure *you* know the answer to that. What'll it be Selena, light meat or dark meat?" She coaxed.

That was a low blow. I chuckled disappointedly. "Oh Fay, at least I have a choice of men who actually *want me*," I said. I knew it was harsh, and I regretted saying it immediately, but she was just being so... insufferable.

Fay's lips flattened into a hard line.

"Listen," Lexi started, trying to defuse the situation. "I like John, and I'm pretty sure he likes me. I know that's not what you want to hear, or what you want to see, but it is what it is. Can't you just take comfort knowing that John might be happy?"

"What kind of bull shit talk is that? This isn't some cheesy movie, Lexi. No. I can't take comfort unless John is happy with *me*!" Fay boomed.

"Fay, I understand why you're upset, I really do," I said, "but now is not the time to be fighting over men. We don't know what's coming or when and we need to have each other's back."

"Well maybe you should tell your lackey to back off and focus on what's coming, instead of trying to get a boyfriend," Fay snapped.

"You're one to talk!" Lexi snapped back.

"This is ridiculous," I yelled. "You are both being completely immature, and you need to get over it."

"There's nothing for me to get over," Lexi said, "I got the guy."It was the wrong thing to say. It was the final straw.

Fay's face flushed red, her hands shook and suddenly a huge gust of wind slammed into me and Lexi. I flew backward and landed in the living room. I regained my composure quickly and saw that Lexi did the same.

I didn't want to fight Fay, I really didn't, especially not in Genevieve's home.

Lexi sent an electrical current toward Fay and it zapped her, but I could tell it wasn't very strong. Lexi must have set it to stun. I don't think she wanted to fight either.

Fay tensed and the air pressure started to change. If she released the boom it would demolish the whole house.

"Enough!" I yelled. Fay faltered releasing her spell. Lexi let out a sigh of relief. "You have no right to get mad at Lexi – she didn't do anything wrong," I added.

"How can you say that?" Fay yelled, "She did everything wrong!"

Fay's face contorted into a snarl and her rage bubbled over.

Suddenly in front of Lexi's face was a sphere of water that grew from a drop, larger and larger until it became larger than her upper body. I instinctively jumped in front of Lexi, becoming completely consumed by the water. I barely had a chance to take a breath before the mass was enveloping me. I moved reflexively but the water moved with me.

"Stop!" Lexi yelled, rushing to Fay. I dropped to the floor, trying to roll out of the bubble, but every which way I moved, the water stayed wrapped around me, suffocating me.

Lexi's voice sounded muffled from the water around my head. "You'll kill her!" She shook Fay violently.

"You're right," Fay said angrily, releasing me from the water bubble. I gasped for air as the water splashed on the floor around me. "It's you I want to kill!" She flicked her wrists, sending Lexi flying again, and stood there, staring at her with the hatred of a thousand hells.

"Fay, you need to calm down," I ordered. She turned her hate stare at me and the air in the room began to blow fiercely, taking on so much force I flew into the window. The glass shattered around me, biting into my skin as I fell to the floor. The wind continued to blow, keeping me pressed against the wall.

I saw Tristan and John run into the room, and they both tried to snap Fay out of her trance.

Where was all her strength coming from? Lexi was shooting spells at Fay, but it was no use. I watched in confusion; what was going on here? There was no way I was getting taken out by some love-struck teenager!

I stood, pushing against the wind and swung my arms open in front of me sending water exploding onto Fay. The wind died down.

"Selena, what happened?" Tristan asked, moving my wet hair away from my face and assessing my injuries.

"Fay is a psycho-bitch, that's what happened!" Lexi yelled.

"Why did you do this?" John asked Fay. Her face fell with shame, her wet hair was matted down and sticking to her cheeks.

"What do you care?" Fay snapped. "Do you love her too?"

"Fay, why are you doing this? I...I know you care about me, and you know I care about you too just...just not in the way you want," John said quietly.

"Yeah. I know. Selena made sure of that!" Fay shook with anger. Huh? How did I always get dragged into this? I decided to tap into Fay's thoughts and see why she hated me so much. After a few moments I had my answer.

John shook his head slowly and sadly. Fay stormed past him and out the front door.

Well this was going to be a great start to the new day. We needed to get out of this house or we would all burst and be no better than Fay.

I stood and headed for the stairs.

"Selena?" Lexi called from behind me.

"Yeah, hon?" I turned to face her.

"Thanks for sticking up for me." She smiled and went to stand next to John.

"Anytime." I smiled back and then headed upstairs to dry off.

"Here," Tristan gave me a towel once we got back into our

bedroom. I dried my hair and pulled my drenched shirt and pants off.

"You know, we could pass the time here like we did yesterday," Tristan teased as he took in my lack of clothing.

"Ha-ha. But no thanks. I want more sleep. It is way too early to be elemental battling and fighting over boys and...ugh!" I looked over my scrapes and found that my arms got the brunt of the injuries. I healed the ones I could see and left the rest since they didn't seem to be bleeding.

I threw myself under the covers, and was surprised when I actually started to drift off. Tristan crawled into bed beside me, only wearing sweat pants.

He gathered me up in his arms and I savored the feel of his safety and warmth. Before I knew it, I was fast asleep.

Selena, did you miss me? I heard a voice in my head. I was in between dreams, I think.

"No," I replied. Obviously my subconscious was more aware of who I was speaking to than the rest of me. It took my conscious a few more moments to realize it was Darien.

Well, I missed you. He chuckled in my mind.

"Go away," I cried.

You know I can't do that.

"Yes, you can. It's easy, really, just go!" I yelled.

Suddenly Darien was there, in my dream, standing tall and confident. He wore a black suit and a black dress shirt with the top buttons undone. His hair was brushed neatly, his brown eyes piercing.

"You don't really mean that. You know deep down inside

that you want me here," he whispered.

"No, you're delusional," I answered, but suddenly I wasn't so sure.

"Are you sure it's me who's delusional? I think you need to reevaluate what you want out of life before it's too late. I've been waiting for you. I'll keep waiting, as long as it takes for you to be honest with yourself."

He stepped toward me, and I instinctively took a step back. He clucked his tongue under his breath, as he reached out his hand and caressed my cheek. Before I knew what I was doing, my face had pressed into his warm palm, savoring his touch.

My eyes snapped open. Not again!

I roamed the room with my eyes only, utterly grateful when I realized that I was alone. I didn't want to have to hide this from Tristan. What was going on? Why was I dreaming about Darien and enjoying it?

At least I knew for a fact that the dream itself wasn't my fault. Darien sent it to me, but the reaction...could he have controlled that too? Or was that all on me?

I flung the covers off me and jumped out of bed, heading straight for the shower to wash off the remnants of my dream. Why was Darien doing this to me? My mind replayed the dream over and over as I washed quickly but vigorously.

I didn't get out of the shower until the dream had diminished to a memory that I was able to push aside. It was just a dream.

I ran a brush through my hair and got dressed before heading down to the kitchen. There was no one there, but Genevieve had left a plate of pastries on the counter. I took one and nibbled on it as I walked through the rest of the house.

Where was everyone? The entire bottom floor was empty, so I headed back upstairs to see if I missed anyone there. All the room doors were open, but no one was inside. My stomach dropped. The last time something like this happened, Tristan and Lexi had been taken.

I ran back down the stairs and outside the back door, but the yard was empty. I ran around the house to the front, but again, no one was there. My blood pumped fiercely with fear and confusion. Could everyone have been taken? Why leave me? My mind raced as my eyes searched the woods in front of me.

16. FIRST STEP

It was the sound of an engine that snapped me back to reality. Genevieve's car came up the drive, and I let out a long sigh of relief, as she pulled up with Lachlan, Lexi and John.

"Good morning, sleepy head," Genevieve called from the window. "I see you found the pastries," she teased, motioning to the half-eaten apple turnover in my hand. I hadn't realized I was still holding it.

"Where were you guys?" I asked as they climbed out of the car with some bags. "I was worried."

"Just did some shopping. Some of us bought more important things than others," Genevieve said pointing with her head in Lexi and John's direction.

"Hey, what I bought is important. It will keep us busy and entertained," John said, smiling at Lexi. "Besides, Artemis gave me the idea so it couldn't be that bad."

"Do I even want to know?" I asked as the group headed toward the front of the house.

"Of course you do. I'll show you inside," John said. Lexi laughed beside him.

"Do you know where Tristan went?" I asked following

everyone inside.

"Yeah, he took Fay for a drive, figured he could help her clear her head," Lexi said, keeping her eyes on the ground.

"He did what?" I yelled. "She tried to kill me, and he's trying to help her?"

"I think he's hoping to help so she won't try to kill you again," John said.

"So stupid," I mumbled under my breath. "Did Artemis go with them?" I asked as an afterthought.

"No, he left before we did, probably getting some fresh air or something," Lexi said placing the bags on the table. "Don't worry, I'm sure he'll be back soon." I helped Genevieve put the groceries away and then went to see what John had bought.

Genevieve rolled her eyes as she passed us to head upstairs. Lachlan followed her out of the room.

"Alright, what is this great thing you bought?" I asked sarcastically.

"Hey, don't knock it," Lexi started to say as she pulled the box out of the bag, "until you try it." I looked down at the box and almost laughed.

"A Ouija board? Really?" I asked, guffawing.

"Yes, really," John answered. "It would be fun for us to try. Give us something to do, so we don't lose our minds from boredom."

"Genevieve was right; her purchases were much more important," I teased.

"Oh come on, Selena," Lexi said. "It could be fun! We can try to contact a ghost, get some guidance from the spirit world." Lexi tried to make her voice sound creepy and mysterious. I laughed. "Maybe we should try it tonight, with everyone here."

"Unless we can warn those dead witches whose powers Jeremiah wants to channel, I don't think there's much use for this," I joked, but then I thought about it. "Wait a minute! Can we do that?" I asked, deep in thought.

"I'm not sure," Lexi answered. "But even if we could, it's not like they could do anything to stop him. They're dead and he has a spell that will be able to control them and their powers."

"Well then I don't see what use this could be." I slumped into the chair.

"Like I said, it's just for fun." John smiled. "There doesn't have to be a magical and super purpose for everything, you know."

"Yeah, yeah," I mumbled.

The front door opened and I heard whispering. I stood and popped my head out of the kitchen to see Tristan and Fay coming in. I clenched my jaw to prevent myself from saying something rude, and went back to sit at the table.

I drummed my fingers on the table top, impatiently waiting for Tristan to finish with the she-devil. After a few minutes, I couldn't sit still anymore. I headed into the living room where Tristan and Fay sat, talking quietly.

I cleared my throat and they both looked up.

"Can I talk to you for a minute?" I asked Tristan, keeping my eyes away from Fay.

"Now you know how I feel when Lexi talks to John," Fay said.

"I'm not jealous of you, Fay," I spat. "I just want to talk to him for a minute. I'm setting aside the fact that you're totally unstable and I don't know who you'll try to kill next." Fay's eyes blazed but she said nothing.

"Yeah, I'll be done in a minute," Tristan said calmly.

"Sure, I'll be upstairs. For the record, you're wasting your time. I think Fay needs a lot more psychological help than you can provide." I turned and went upstairs without waiting for a response.

I sat on the edge of my bed slightly miffed. I couldn't believe Tristan was trying to help Fay. She was such a bitch!

"What's your problem?" Tristan asked as he came into the room.

My eyes narrowed, "My problem? You're spending time with the woman who tried to kill me a couple of hours ago! What's *your* problem?" I retorted.

Tristan ran a hand through his hair. "She didn't try to kill you, she just lost control. I'm trying to resolve this. We need to stick together and be on the same side when we face Jeremiah. We can't have petty jealousies compromising our futures. Is that so bad? Am I evil for trying to keep the peace?"

I let out a sigh and lowered my gaze. "I guess not," I mumbled, but I knew Tristan was right. "I'm just so pissed off at her right now. I can't fathom the idea of you helping her."

"I know, and you have every right to be mad. Just try to keep it in check, okay? Hopefully we will be able to get through this smoothly," he said.

"Sure, just let me try to kill her and we'll be even." I smiled

"Selena, please. Be the better person," Tristan pleaded.

"Fine," I sighed. Tristan chuckled. "Did you see what John and Lexi bought?" I asked, changing the subject.

"No, I didn't know they bought anything." He looked out the door as if he could see the object from there.

"Come on, you'll get a kick out of this." I stood and took his hand, leading him downstairs and into the kitchen. Lexi and John were leaning against the counter talking.

"Where is it?" I asked, searching the empty table.

"Oh I put it on top of the fridge," John said as he pulled the box down. "Figured I'd keep it out of the way until we want to use it."

I watched Tristan's reaction as he read the name on the lid. His eyes squinted as he took in the gothic scrawl.

"Cool!" He said as a smile crossed his face.

"What? You think this is cool?" I asked incredulously.

"Sure. I have an appreciation for spirits. They have a lot of information to share sometimes. When did you want to do this?"

"Tonight," Lexi and John said in unison at the same time that I said, "I don't."

Tristan laughed and put his arm around my shoulder. "Don't worry, I'll keep you safe," he teased.

"I'm not scared. I just think it's silly and won't really help us."

"It's. Just. For. Fun!" John almost yelled repeating his original statement.

I rolled my eyes. "Whatever. Let's leave it for tomorrow though, okay?"

John shrugged and then entwined his fingers with Lexi's. Fay chose that exact moment to walk into the kitchen.

Oh joy.

Her eyes locked on John and Lexi's hands and her eyes

narrowed. I could see her chest rising with each breath she took and it seemed to be increasing in speed.

"Fay, remember what we talked about," Tristan tried to soothe.

"Shut up. You don't know anything! Just go on loving Satan," she glared at me, "and her spawn." She shot a glance at Lexi before turning and storming out of the house. She'd been doing that a lot lately. I wondered where she goes to cool down.

"I told you she needs professional help," I mumbled. Tristan sighed defeated.

"I still don't get why she's as mad at you as me," Lexi said to me.

"I still don't get why she's not mad at John at all," I added. John's face fell, and he averted his gaze to the floor, trying to find something interesting to stare at there. "I told you this was too much drama," I said to Lexi.

John's head shot up. "Too much drama? To be with me? Come on," he said, but he seemed uncertain, almost nervous.

"Don't listen to Selena. I think it's worth it," Lexi said, shooting a glance at me. I shrugged my shoulders indifferently. John relaxed with Lexi's words.

"Sorry you wasted your time," I said to Tristan who had been standing quietly, eyes gazing to where Fay stormed off.

"At least I tried," he said and sat at the table.

"You really believe Ouija boards work?" I asked, sitting beside Tristan, hoping to distract him.

"Absolutely," he started. "I saw a voodoo priestess once who was able to contact spirits and ask them questions about the future."

"Huh," Lexi said. I fingered the Ouija board box, new curiosity weaseling its way into my mind. Maybe this could be fun.

"Ha!" John burst a laugh. "*Someone's* intrigued," he said, taking in my curious gaze.

"Shut up," I said, but there wasn't much gusto. He was right.

"Still want to wait until tomorrow? We could do this now if you want," John pushed.

"Nah, tomorrow will be just fine," I said defiantly. I stood and headed outside to the back of the house. I closed the door behind me and stopped short. Artemis was sitting at the patio table, legs outstretched in front of him, hands behind his head supporting it. His eyes were closed and he took in a deep breath. I hadn't realized he had returned from…wherever he had been.

He looked completely at peace. I backtracked, wanting to get back inside before he noticed me. How did I always manage to bother him when he was enjoying a moment? I took two steps backward and reached behind me for the handle of the door.

"No need to rush inside, Selena. Come and enjoy this beautiful day with me," Artemis said, eyes still closed, never shifting an inch from his position.

"I thought you might enjoy the solitude," I answered as I turned to the house.

"Nonsense. Company is underrated. I have a new appreciation for people since being without them for twenty-six years."

I cringed. I went to the table and pulled out the other chair to sit next to Artemis.

"Don't worry about Fay," he said after a moment of silence.

"I don't want to sound mean, but I've kind of given up on

her," I said, easing back in my chair and allowing the sun to beam down on my face. I took in an appreciative breath.

"Is that so?" Artemis shifted then to look at my face. He didn't believe me. "Well, that's good then. One less thing for you to worry about."

I knew he was just humoring me. He knew my thoughts. Why did I bother trying to lie? Well, it wasn't a complete lie. I was starting to give up, but my mind kept coming back to her.

Okay so I still cared.

Whatever.

We sat for a few more minutes in silence. Artemis let out a satisfied sigh, and then stood up.

"Are you going inside?" I asked, feeling guilty that I wasn't better company.

"Yes, I think I will get some food. I have a craving for Thai. I was going to order in. Would you like some?" He asked. It was such a normal thing to say I was caught off guard. Artemis was going to order in? Okay…

"No, I'm fine, thank you," I answered more out of reflex than lack of want. Artemis nodded once and then went inside. What was with him lately? That confinement must have really gotten to him, though I couldn't blame him. I would have lost my mind if I was trapped for twenty-six years with no one knowing where to find me, and not knowing if any of my loved ones were alright. Then I stopped mid-thought. Did Artemis have a family? What exactly did he lose when he was taken captive? Who did he lose? My heart ached for the man. Maybe there was someone we should have been trying to contact for him? I placed my head in my hands and felt horrible. I was so wrapped up in my problems, I didn't even stop to think about Artemis.

"Selena? Are you okay?" My head snapped up. Tristan walked toward me, a glass of iced tea in his hand. He placed the sweating glass on the table and knelt in front of me to keep his piercing green eyes level with mine.

"Yeah, I'm fine, I just feel so bad," I answered.

"Why? What happened?"

"I was just thinking about Artemis. Does he have any family? What if he had a wife waiting for him and he disappeared. She never knew what happened or where he went."

"Yeah, I've thought about that myself," Tristan said, taking my hands in his. "We could ask him, set your mind at ease."

"I don't want to pry. What if it brings back bad memories or something?" I asked.

"Well, I'm sure if there was someone waiting for him, Artemis would have gone to her, or at least told us where to find her." He moved to the seat that Artemis had just vacated, and pushed the cold iced tea over to me.

I smiled and took a sip, savoring the sweet and refreshing taste. The day really was beautiful; I could see what Artemis was sitting out here for.

"Do you think he has kids?" My brain was unwilling to drop the subject.

"Selena, you are going to drive yourself crazy worrying about all of this. He may not have anyone. It's sad, but it happens. Or if he does, who knows, maybe he sent them a message telepathically like he did with you. Maybe they know he's fine now, but that he can't go see them just yet. Or maybe

Jeremiah will be watching his family to make sure Artemis doesn't go back there."

"I hadn't thought about all that," I answered honestly.

"Well, until you want to ask Artemis outright, you should stop torturing yourself with it."

"Do you really think I was the only one who could have gotten him out of there?" I had been mulling over this question for the past few days. It was hard for me to believe that there wasn't a single witch out there who could have helped him instead throughout the last twenty-six years.

"Do you really think he would have stayed in there knowing there was another way out?" Tristan countered.

"I don't know. I mean, maybe he could have gotten out before but he wouldn't have been protected afterwards like he is now?" I couldn't help but analyze the situation. It was bothering me that this poor man had to wait so long just for me.

"I believe Artemis knew what he was doing, and you should trust that too before you lose your mind."

I took the iced tea and sipped at it, realizing Tristan was right. I would drive myself crazy thinking about all these details. And Artemis was a psychic, so he had to have known what was coming. I nodded my head in agreement and Tristan and I sat in silence for a while longer.

"I think John needs to man up," Tristan said suddenly, breaking the silence.

"Where did that come from?" I asked.

"I was just thinking about Fay and how she has been reacting to John and Lexi, and I can't help but wonder if John talked to her alone and just explained his feelings, maybe she would be better."

"But he did. I told him to tell her as soon as he started show-ing interest in Lexi. That's why Fay hates me. Remember when she yelled at me in the kitchen?"

Tristan nodded, "Yeah, but why would she hate you for that?"

"Because," I started, and decided to tell him what I had seen in Fay's thoughts. "So Fay and John had gone to the festival last year, and while John was busy looking at a trinket stand, Fay was looking at him. Apparently a psychic saw Fay, and felt the need to tell her about John. I swear I could see it as if I'd been there," I said, seeing the memory in my mind.

"So, you read her thoughts?" Tristan asked, a frown forming on his beautiful lips.

"I-er-yeah, but I had to know what her deal was and she never would have told me."

"Selena." Tristan shook his head, but said nothing more.

"I know, I know." I smiled sheepishly at him and his frown twitched, smoothing out into a reluctant smile. "So anyways," I started again, hoping his curiosity would override his disap-pointment. "This psychic looked like she fell out of a movie. She had thinning grey hair, standing up around her head, and these cold, blue eyes. She called Fay over and said 'You might have had a chance with your love, but you have a calling, a larger role in all this. You will be asked to help fulfill the prophecy and in doing so, will lose him.' Fay asked the psychic for details, but the woman only walked away.

"So now Fay resents me for needing her, for being too weak to do this without them. John would never have even met Lexi if it weren't for me and the whole witching world being in grave danger thing. Plus, I got involved and told John to let Fay down. Really she has a list of complaints."

"That's just crazy," Tristan shook his head.

"Yeah, kind of, but I can understand that she loves him so much it's killing her to see him with someone else, especially since she's been around him so much longer than Lexi has."

"I don't think that justifies her trying to kill you though."

"I don't either."

"He still needs to take care of this situation. He needs to get Fay to calm down, at least until this is all over."

"Yeah, I know."

"Hey," Tristan said, his green eyes piercing. "You are not weak. You know that, right?"

I shrugged.

"Look, I heard Fay say it before, and you say it now, and I need you to know that asking for help doesn't make you weak. It makes you smart, and strong."

"Okay," I said, though I wasn't entirely convinced.

"Hey," Genevieve strode toward us. "I hate to interrupt, but we should talk." The sun gleaming off her platinum hair gave her the look of an angel.

"Everything okay?" I asked tentatively.

"Yes. Artemis came inside and told us it was time to put some things in motion," Genevieve started. "He can't tell us what's coming, but he told us to proceed with our plan."

"Really?" Tristan asked. A spark of excitement shone in his eyes.

"We decided to go to the Elders and fill them in on what's

been happening. We will tell them all about Jeremiah's camp, his planned ritual, everything. That way whatever happens we will all be prepared."

"Good," I said, "I have wanted to get them involved for a while, but I was worried about trying to convince them without all the details. Now that we know what we know, I guess it would be a good time, not much else we can do anyway. But you have to be careful. Jeremiah is an Elder, so who knows who else has been compromised."

Genevieve nodded, "We were also thinking about taking Lexi with us. We can ask the Elders if they are involved with Jeremiah, and she will be able to tell if any of them are lying."

I didn't like the idea of Lexi getting involved, but she was trained to protect herself and others, so I couldn't stand in her way.

"If she wants to go, that would give us a great advantage," I answered.

"I'll talk to her now and let you know what she says." Genevieve smiled and headed back inside.

"This is good," Tristan said after she left.

"Hmm?" I asked, deep in thought.

"We need to be productive. We can't just sit around waiting for something to happen. We need to be prepared."

"Yeah," I sounded distant even to my own ears.

"What's up, Selena?" Tristan asked, noticing my distracted state.

I shook my head to clear it. "It's so easy to just not care, to push aside any worries and just let whatever's going to happen, happen. But it's stupid to just coast when such a big threat is coming. I'm just being a coward."

"You are not a coward. You are one of the bravest people I know. You are entitled to a break, and I think Artemis knew that, which is why he told you to just wait. I'm sure he also knew that you wouldn't be able to sit still for long, but at least you would try."

"Yeah," I repeated and stood to face Tristan. He looked at me quizzically. "Will you train with me?"

His face lit up with a smile. "Absolutely."

Tristan and I started out sparring. We threw punches, kicks and jabs and worked on blocking. Since I regained my full powers, my speed and strength had increased, and I was starting to appreciate my own potential. It's weird, there were moments when I doubted myself to the point of insanity and other times when I accepted that maybe I was special. Since Artemis confirmed it, it had been easier, but still, I couldn't help but question it sometimes.

One of the more recent times I trained with Tristan, I made myself believe that I was tough, and so we had an excellent training session. I needed to make sure I did that today, and force myself to be even better. The more I believed in myself, the greater I could be. And I had no more room for doubt, not with Jeremiah and Darien to face.

Darien...

I had been trying not to think about him, or the dream he sent me. My mind had been pre-occupied with other things this morning, and was grateful for the distraction to train now, to keep it that way.

I knew I could beat Jeremiah if I got the opportunity to use my fighting skills on him. The chances of that happening were slim though. He knew my strength, and he would do what it took to keep me far away, so I had no doubt he would use his magic against me. I also knew that although he had been practicing magic over a hundred and fifty years longer than me, I was supposed to be stronger than him magically as well, but if he somehow succeeded in his ritual, I may not stand a chance. I needed to practice my combative spells.

I had been so deep in thought I didn't see Tristan until it was too late. He plowed into me, throwing us both onto the ground. His full weight landed on top of me, knocking me breathless.

"Focus, Selena," Tristan warned.

"Sorry," I wheezed. Tristan stood up allowing me to catch my breath.

"Jeez, how much do you weigh?" I teased, clambering back up.

"It's not how much I weigh, it's how *little* you weigh." He poked at my ribs. "It's not my fault you're such a light weight."

"Light weight?" I scoffed. "You know size doesn't matter, it's all about skill." I flicked my fingers and Tristan fell backwards. He was back on his feet in no time and waved his hand sending a whirlwind towards me. I blocked it and Tristan looked impressed.

"I don't remember teaching you that," Tristan said.

"You didn't. That was all me. Though I would think that would be one of the first things you'd teach, don't you?"

"Not when I know you would be able to reflexively do it. You are 'the one' after all," he mimicked. "Greatness is inside you."

"Yeah, yeah Confucius says…" I sent out another spell and we began blocking and dodging, using defensive and offensive spells. I tackled Tristan and we grappled on the ground.

"Aye, take it easy on the lass, will ya?" Lachlan sauntered out, taking in the image of us wrestling.

"Take it easy on her?" Tristan laughed, "She's kicking my ass!"

"As she should," Lachlan retorted. "Just wanted to let ya know that Lexi has decided to come with us, so we're going to the courts now."

"It's just the three of you?" I asked, freeing myself from Tristan's hold and getting to my feet.

"Nah, her lad is coming as well. Can't let her out of his sight that one."

"We should go too. Show a united front," I said.

Lachlan shook his head, "There are other things to do here. Not to mention that all of us going will raise suspicion and could get back to Jeremiah sooner rather than later."

"Wouldn't our information be more credible if I was with you since…you know…the prophecy and all that?" I think I asked, incoherently.

"Yes, but we have Lexi who can show them the truth, same way she can show it to us. Don't worry." He smiled, "Besides, we don't want you near the courthouse right now, in case Jeremiah has people scouting the area for you."

I nodded. "Alright, but please be careful," I pleaded. The desperation in my voice scared me. I was too vulnerable; there were too many ways to hurt me, just by hurting my friends.

"Aye, don't worry." Lachlan threw me a smile and headed back inside just as Lexi came jumping out.

"Guys, did you hear?" She asked excited. I nodded smiling. "I get to be the lie detector. That's so cool! It's amazing to have a gift that the others don't have. One that's actually useful."

I laughed, "Just be careful," I warned again.

"I will!" She hugged us and ran off inside.

I shook my head. "Are we sure this is a good idea? What if they get hurt?"

"They won't. They're going to be in the courthouse, talking to some of the Elders. No war is going to break out. Worst case scenario they alert one of Jeremiah's minions of their plan and Jeremiah finds out. By then they will probably be back here anyway. Don't worry." Tristan kissed my forehead.

"Alright. Break time's over." I lunged at him resuming our training. So long as I was distracted, I wouldn't be able to think about what may or may not be happening at the courthouse.

17. LEAVE THE DEAD ALONE

"Selena, can you please stop pacing? They will be fine," Tristan pleaded. He sat at the edge of the bed, his hair a rumpled mess from tensely running his fingers through it.

"I just can't stand waiting anymore. What if something went wrong? It's been hours." I stopped my pacing long enough to look out the window at the night sky. Tristan and I had sparred for a while after the others left, trying to keep our minds occupied. After we were dripping with sweat, we found other distractions, but that only lasted for so long.

I checked in with them telepathically, but they blocked me after the tenth time. Now all I had was time to think.

I hadn't seen Fay since she left that morning and Artemis left after he ate his Thai food – of which he ordered me a plate. He not only knew that I had wanted Thai food but he also knew my favorite dish was Pad Thai. Creepy talent he had there. I would love to put it to use to ask how my friends were, if I only knew where he was. Unless…

Tristan stood and wrapped his arms around me to keep me still.

"I have to go to Artemis," I said, pulling away from Tristan.

"You don't know where he is."

"You know I don't need to, but..." I started. *Artemis*, I called. *Where are you?*

Selena, by all means join me. He responded. *I could use a lift back.*

I ran out the bedroom door and down the stairs. Tristan was right on my heels.

"Where are you going?"

"To Artemis."

"At least let me come with you," he called after me. I slowed infinitesimally as I headed outside. Tristan stood next to me and held my hand as I envisioned being wherever Artemis was, picturing his aura and allowing it to pull me toward him. In a flash Tristan and I were standing at the outskirts of one of the Cemeteries in the Hidden City. This one was familiar.

Not far ahead of us, I saw a lone figure, sitting in front of a head stone. The darkness of the night enveloped him but I could still see him under the bare sliver of the growing moon.

"Hello Selena, Tristan," Artemis said. Again I felt like I was invading his privacy, ruining a quiet peaceful moment. "Not alone, no, not alone," Artemis whispered. I shifted uncomfortably. Maybe I was being rash, bothering this poor man who had been through so much just to ease my mind.

"Sorry to bother you," Tristan started.

"But you wanted to know if your friends are alright," Artemis finished the sentence. "They will be at the cottage by the time you get back."

Again I felt the guilt of bothering this man. If we had just waited a few more minutes, we would have seen them for ourselves.

"Don't worry so much," Artemis said, reading my thoughts. "I was just finishing anyways."Then under his breath he added, "Nothing left for me, no, nothing here at all."

I stepped closer to the headstone and clenched my jaw so I wouldn't reveal my sadness. Though I'm sure Artemis would know anyway. There were two names side by side, similar to the headstone my parents shared.

The first name was Angelica Siff, born in 1943. The other name was Amanda Siff, who was born in 1975. Both died in 1988.

"My wife and daughter," Artemis explained.

"I'm so sorry. How…?" Tristan asked, letting the sentence hang.

"How did they die? Well once I told Jeremiah the prophecy, he was very willing to keep me happy, to make sure I was always there to help him. As soon as the prophecy got out though, he was scared and angry. He didn't want anyone to use me for their gain, and he didn't want me validating the prophecy. He locked me away and killed my family so that no one would come looking for me. He framed me for my family's murder," he whispered and shook his head before continuing. "Everyone just assumed I fled. No one would have suspected that Jeremiah would have kept me as a pet!" He spat the last words out angrily. "Yes his own personal trained monkey. Monkeys, no parrots."

My heart broke for Artemis and I wished I could help him. If anyone deserved vengeance, it was him. Artemis's shoulders slumped in defeat as he let out a sad sigh. He gazed longingly at his family's resting place.

"I'm sorry," I said, placing my hand on his shoulder. He turned away from the headstones. "So you're like...seventy?" I asked trying to lighten the tension. A small smile played on his lips.

"Yes, seventy-nine to be exact."

"You look good for an old guy," I teased.

"Yes well, I have been on a special diet for a while," he joked. "Would you be so kind as to teleport me back with you? I would hate to walk all that way again - me being so old and frail."

"You walked here?" Tristan asked.

Artemis smiled.

"Well, of course I wouldn't let you walk back," I said, taking his hand. I took Tristan's hand as well and we teleported back to the yard in front of the cottage, just in time to see the front door close behind Lachlan.

"Told you," Artemis said confidently. I laughed.

"Wait 'til we tell you the news!" Genevieve said as we walked into the house. Relief swept through me as I saw all four of them there safe and sound.

Artemis studied Genevieve, staring at her face for a minute. She stepped back reflexively.

"I now know this story. I believe I will go to bed," Artemis said heading upstairs without waiting for a response.

I shook my head, "Why doesn't he get in trouble for reading thoughts?" I asked.

Tristan looked after the man to make sure he was out of ear shot.

"He's crazy, it doesn't count," he whispered.

I huffed.

"Okay, sit down, sit down!" Lexi chirped excitedly. We all gathered in the living room and got comfortable.

"Where's Fay?" John asked.

"Don't know. She's been gone since before you left," I answered. John shrugged sadly.

"So what happened?" Tristan encouraged.

"Okay, so we went to the courthouse and found Victoria," Lexi started, talking animatedly, her hands moving to act out each scene. "We told her everything after I made sure we could trust her," she boasted. "Then Victoria led us to the other Elders and we repeated the process a bunch of times. The best part was that Jeremiah was there!"

"What?" I asked startled. I'm not sure why, but I had expected him to be at the camp or somewhere far away from my friends.

"I know!" Lexi said. "And he tried to sneak out, but Victoria confronted him and you should have seen his face! He was as scared as a mouse in a cat's paw. It was excellent. Well until he teleported." Lexi deflated.

"Jeremiah can teleport?" I asked.

"I guess so," Lexi continued. "The Elders were just as shocked. It's like he was there one minute, and then gone the next. So anyways, after he was gone, we all got to talking. The Elders found a personal item of Jeremiah's in his office; it was some old letter or something. They were able to cast the locator spell. It was so cool! Anyway, they found out where the camp was, so they planned to scope the area out. They sent the Charge there to get information. While they were gone, the Elders decided to get the militia prepared."

"Like soldiers?" I asked.

"Yeah, we do have an army. They were sent straight to the camp only..." Lexi trailed off.

"Only what?" Tristan pressed impatiently.

"They're gone," Genevieve finished.

"What do you mean?" I asked.

"The camp wasn't there," Genevieve said. "No one was there, it was completely empty. We shouldn't be surprised really. Jeremiah knew he was caught, so he must have teleported to the new camp and cleared everyone out. The problem is," Genevieve stopped.

"We can't go after them if we don't know where they are," I finished.

"Can't they cast the locator spell again?" I asked.

"They tried," Lexi said, sighing. "It didn't work. They must have some other kind of security in place."

"So back to Artemis's plan – we have to wait for them to make the first move. Unless I teleported to them," I said as an after-thought.

"I'm not sure if that would work with the new security either. Regardless we should run that by the Elders," Lexi said. "We shouldn't go there alone, especially since they know they are being hunted. They will have a lot more security and even more people guarding their new camp. We need to wait a bit longer 'til the Elders can provide the back up."

"Artemis told us, no matter what he saw coming, we wouldn't really be able to do anything to change it," Tristan said. I nodded defeated. How frustrating.

"Maybe we should ask him just so we know anyway. Even if we can't do anything, at least we can be mentally prepared," I offered.

"Well it will have to wait until tomorrow. Artemis is in bed, and he needs his rest," Genevieve said.

"We can take comfort in knowing that the Elders are informed now and there is an army prepared, so we aren't alone," Lachlan said. "Things are set in motion."

"Maybe we should make a few calls of our own," John said. "Call the Fideles; get them ready."

Lachlan nodded.

"The who?"

"The believers," Tristan said. "Those who believe in you and the prophecy."

"Oh." That was unsettling. There was a group of people who believed in me? I felt a little nauseated.

"Come on," Genevieve said to John and Lachlan.

The three of them left the room, and I had no idea how I could help. I didn't know anyone.

"I have a person or two I could call," Lexi said. "Tristan?"

"Yeah, I'm on it."

They left me as well and I sat alone feeling useless. I paced for a few minutes and then I came across one of the magazines Lexi had sifted through and started reading it. Almost an hour past before Tristan came back, followed by Lexi. Slowly, the others joined one at a time.

"All good?" I asked when they had all returned.

"Everyone who needs to know, knows," Genevieve said. The others nodded.

"We just have to keep them posted," Tristan added.

"So what do we do now?" I asked.

"I have an idea," John spoke up.

"No!" Genevieve and I said in unison.

"Why not?" Jon asked, almost pouting.

"It's creepy," I continued. "I don't like the idea."

"I knew you were scared!" John teased.

"I'm not," I answered too quickly.

He smiled. "Oh, come on, we have time to kill, and there's nothing to do! We need to occupy ourselves."

"I'm going to bed," I said, standing up.

"It's only nine," John said. "You don't have the excuse of being ancient to sleep this early. And I know you're intrigued."

I let out a sigh and turned to Genevieve who seemed to be the only other person who didn't care for John's idea. She merely shrugged.

"Why can't you just leave the dead alone?" I asked.

"It's just for fun," John repeated for the umpteenth time.

"Fine," I hissed. I felt guilty doing this, knowing that much more important things needed to be taken care of, but John was right – we needed a distraction until we could make ourselves useful. There was nothing else we could do today anyway.

John beamed and ran to the kitchen. "Lexi!" He called. She rose and went to see what he needed.

A moment later they came back into the living room and I groaned when I saw what they were holding.

Tristan chuckled and then went to clear off the coffee table. John set the Ouija board down and Lexi placed two white candles on either end. The board was designed to look like it was created on ancient parchment – yellowed and shriveled-looking – and then glued to a board to give it stability. A picture of a sun sat on the top left corner beside the word 'Yes' and a moon on the top right corner beside the word 'No', and the word 'Hello' in between.

Sitting in the center of the board were two rows of gothic letters, which had the full alphabet, a row of numbers below that and finally the words 'Good Bye.' I liked that part. The plastic tear-drop shaped cursor that the 'spirits' would use to point to whatever letter, number or word they wanted to tell us, completed the experience.

"Do we really need the candles?" I asked.

"It sets the ambience," Lexi retorted. I rolled my eyes and sat cross-legged in front of the table. The others did the same, making a circle around the ridiculous board.

"We have to move the candles then, or my hair will catch fire," I said staring at the candle that was placed in front of me. I swept my hair dramatically back to show how much I valued it.

It was Lexi's turn to roll her eyes. "It's not even lit yet," she said as she moved the candles to the end tables outside our circle and then lit them. They didn't provide enough light, so she swept her hand and the ceiling lights flickered to a dim glow.

"Ooh, the lights sure make this feel spooky," I said sarcastically. Lexi and John both shot me a look. I raised my hands in surrender. "Okay, okay, calm down."

"Who are we going to try and contact anyway?" Tristan asked. Everyone looked at the other.

"Can't we just see who shows up?" John asked.

"I don't think so!" I yelled. "Haven't you seen *The Exorcist*?

That girl got messed up because she talked to some random spirit…who happened to be the Devil!"

"Gosh Selena, you are so dramatic," Lexi said. "That was just a movie."

"Yeah, based on *actual events!*" I crossed my arms over my chest.

"Is she always such a buzz-kill?" John asked Lexi in a mock whisper.

"Wha-?" I asked shocked. My mouth hung opened with the unfinished question.

"She's just being careful," Tristan said defending me.

"Listen," I snapped. "I am not trying to be a buzz-kill, this just seems so silly. I think it would make me feel better if we found a way to get some usefulness out of this thing." I tapped the board. "So… should we try to warn the witches then?" I asked.

"Fine," John agreed.

I took a deep breath and tried to focus. Genevieve and Lachlan watched from the sidelines as Tristan, John, Lexi and I squeezed one finger on the planchette, and John started to speak.

"We call upon the spirit of…" And then he stopped. "How do I know which witch—ha-ha." When we didn't laugh he carried on. "I mean how do I know who I'm calling. We don't have a name, and we don't know which cemetery Jeremiah will go after. So who do we call?"

"Ghostbusters?" I offered lamely.

"Ugh!" Lexi let out.

I thought it was funny.

"Alright! Let me think," I said, seriously contemplating this situation. There really was no way of knowing who to contact. I thought about suggesting we contact my mom, but I was scared. What if she didn't come? Or what if she did – that might break my heart, wanting to talk to her so badly, no small amount of time would be enough. She would know what to do, but I couldn't risk hurting myself, and maybe I would hurt her too. I went a different direction. "Is there like a famous head witch that we can tell and have her relay the message to all the witches in the spirit world?"

Everyone thought about this silently.

"Sible Hamilton," Lachlan said.

"Who's that?" Lexi asked.

"She was a very respected Elder years ago," Lachlan answered. "They said she was the kindest, and fairest Elder we've seen in many generations."

"She also prevented the binding of an innocent witch a few years ago," Genevieve added. "When she died, the entire city mourned for her. I'm sure she would have known Jeremiah too."

"Oh yeah, I remember her," John said. "Sweet old lady. That sounds good." He cleared his throat. "We call upon the spirit of Sible Hamilton, with respect, that you may aid us in our task."

That sounded nice enough. I just hoped that Sible wouldn't be pissed that we were pulling her out of…wherever she was, to send a message. We waited with bated breath.

The house seemed eerily quiet, as if it was holding its breath with us.

The cursor twitched, and I let out a quiet gasp.

"Sible, is that you?" John asked. The cursor slid slowly, so slowly, to the word 'Yes.'

"Are you guys doing that?" I asked, not quite convinced it was Sible.

The group shook their heads.

"Thank you for taking the time to help us. We have a message we were wondering if you could deliver," John continued.

The cursor moved back and then forward toward 'Yes' again.

"I believe you knew Jeremiah Lacour as an Elder. He is planning to perform a ritual to control the power of dead witches. We don't know which cemetery he will use, or whose powers, so could you please pass along the message to everyone on your side? Maybe they can do something to prevent this from happening."

Again the cursor moved back and forward toward 'Yes.' John thanked her, and then the cursor moved faster. It went in circles around the letters, faster and faster, we were all moving with it. It stopped and pointed to the letter Y and then O. We were saying the letters as they were being pointed out until the cursor started going in circles again.

I was mesmerized by the spinning cursor, the jumbled letters, but then suddenly the cursor stopped.

"This is taking too long," I heard myself say, but it wasn't my voice. It wasn't even what I was thinking. I tried to clear my throat, but I couldn't. I tried to shake my head or move, but I was stuck. Everyone turned to look at me suspiciously. I knew they could tell something was off.

"What?" John asked.

"You reading each individual letter until I spell out a word is ridiculous. This method is much faster," the voice said.

"You were moving it the whole time?" Lexi asked incredulously.

"Yes, that's the point, isn't it? You ask a spirit questions and they answer you through that," the voice said, eyeing the cursor.

"Sible?" John squinted his eyes as if he could see her inside me. Lexi looked confused.

"Yes," Sible said through me. "Now listen carefully. I will pass this message along, but if he succeeds in conducting the ritual, no spirit will be able to disobey him. We will try to find a way around that though."

What I was feeling was one of my worst fears. I was present, completely aware, and yet I had no control over my body, no control over anything. I was trapped inside my head and I felt suffocated.

"Calm down, child," Sible said. Everyone looked confused. "This one whose body I took. She is panicking inside her head. I was trying to calm her. I won't be here long, don't waste time by worrying. Listen to what I need to tell you," she pressed. I tried to relax and do as she said. I listened to her words, trying to keep it all in perspective.

"Jeremiah will be able to conduct the spell in a week, I think, that's when the moon phase will be right," Tristan said. "Is there anything we can do to stop him?"

"He is waiting for the right moon phase? But he doesn't need that. So long as he has everything else, he can perform the ritual on any day of the waxing moon. It is so now. He could successfully cast it tomorrow if he wanted," Sible answered.

"I don't think he knows that," Lexi said.

"The brother does." My head turned of its own accord to face Tristan. "No doubt he will tell Jeremiah soon enough."

"Darien knows? How do you know that?" He asked.

"The spirits have been watching him since the prophecy. I joined them after I died. It's amazing what things you can see from the other side. Anyways, we have been watching you and this girl as well." Sible motioned to my body. "We were curious to see how it would all pan out. We didn't know Jeremiah was planning this, so we weren't watching him. The only way to stop Jeremiah now, is to make sure he doesn't get the girl."

"Thank you for your help," John said.

"I'm sorry I didn't listen," Sible said abruptly, and she turned to face Tristan. "I'm so sorry." And in a flash I was blinking and gasping for air.

"Selena? Is that you?" Lexi asked. I nodded once.

"Are you okay?" Tristan asked. We moved the cursor to 'Good Bye' just in case and then let go. I stood quickly and moved my arms and legs just to know I could. A shiver ran through me and I shook off the sensation of paralysis.

"Yeah, that was really weird. I could live a thousand years and never want that experience again."

"Well, she was helpful," John said. "At least we know the deadline is non-existent. If Jeremiah doesn't get you this week, he can get another shot next month."

"Great," Tristan mumbled.

"Why did Artemis tell us differently? He knows everything – why not this?" I asked, sitting on the couch away from the creepy board.

"Well he said himself that he knows much, but not all,

remember?" Tristan answered. "Or maybe he knew we would never be able to enjoy ourselves if we knew the real deadline." Tristan's eyebrows knitted in contemplation and he looked away.

"So what now?" I asked.

"Now nothing," Tristan said. "Jeremiah doesn't know yet so as far as we're concerned, he thinks he has to wait until next week sometime."

Lexi sighed and stood, picking up the board and cursor.

"I told you this would be fun," John smiled.

"Fun? I just got possessed. I was not in control of my body! That's not my idea of fun," I snapped. "I told you this would be like *The Exorcist*! I swear if I got possessed by the Devil, I'd come after you first," I threatened.

"Well we got information out of it at least." John sulked, shying away from my outburst.

"Yeah only because I suggested it! Who knows what you would have conjured up?" I stood and blew out the candles and turned on the lights.

The brightness washed away the eeriness left behind from Sible. Lexi placed the Ouija box back on top of the fridge and then came back into the living room.

"And to think, Artemis suggested you buy this." I shook my head.

"Yeah, he said it would come in handy," John answered.

"Are you okay?" Lexi asked me.

I nodded, "I think I'm going to go to bed." I walked toward the stairs, still creeped out. I didn't want to go alone; I almost asked Tristan to come with me but didn't want to look like a wimp.

After closing my bedroom door behind me, I quickly undressed and threw myself under the covers. I sank in the bed and savored the comfort. Tristan walked in a moment later.

"You sure you're okay?" He asked as he undressed.

"Yes, fine. I will feel better when you get in bed to protect me from the boogeyman," I joked.

"Is it bad that I automatically assume I will be sleeping beside you?" Tristan crawled under the covers and pulled me close.

"Yes, but it's okay. I like it." I tucked my head under Tristan's chin and let him hold me. "Have you ever heard of Sible Hamilton?" I asked changing the subject.

"The name sounds familiar, but I didn't know her personally," Tristan answered.

"I feel useless," I admitted. "I want to do something now."

"I know. Try to get some rest and I promise we will do something about it tomorrow."

"Okay," I said around a big yawn, and fell instantly asleep.

18. ALMOST PARADISE

DAY 3

"What do you mean Fay never came back?" I heard John ask as I entered the kitchen the next morning. Everyone but Fay sat around the table. Apple turnovers, doughnuts and scones were laid out. The group gave me a collective nod as I walked in.

"I mean her room is empty, and no one has seen her since yesterday," Genevieve explained calmly.

"Where could she have gone?" John asked. "What if she's in trouble? She's been gone a whole day – who knows what could have happened to her?" He stood and started to pace. "How did I not notice she was gone so long?" He asked under his breath.

Lexi studied his behavior, and I didn't need to read her mind to know that she was wondering just how much John did care for Fay.

John reached into his pocket and took out his cell phone. He pressed a few buttons and held the phone to his ear. "She's not answering," he huffed after a few silent moments, jamming his cell back into his pocket.

"We'll find her. We can even ask the old man." Lachlan was

relaxed, eating a muffin.

"No, let's not bother Artemis with that," I said. "I have a lot more questions I need to ask him. I will teleport to her and get her back here."

"No," Tristan said with such finality I was startled. "I hate to say it, but if John's right, if Fay is in trouble, you'll wind up in trouble with her."

"Then I won't go alone," I suggested. "I'll even take my gun."

"That's not the point," Tristan argued. "The point is that Sible said as long as Jeremiah doesn't get you, he can't do the spell. We need to keep you as far away from him as possible. You are offering to fall right into his lap."

"That's assuming Fay is in trouble. Maybe she just went to a hotel to get away from us," I retorted. Tristan sighed and ran a hand through his hair.

"You are impossible, you know that?" He asked.

I smiled, "I have my moments."

"I got it!" Lexi jumped up suddenly. "We can do a locator spell and see where she is. If it's in some kind of... creepy wooded area... then maybe she's in trouble, but if she's someplace public like Selena said, we'll be able to just teleport there and back." She beamed with pride at her idea.

"Fine," Tristan and I said in unison.

"Can you get something personal of Fay's?" Lexi asked John. He nodded and went upstairs.

Lexi left as well and came back with candles, a pendulum, and a map. As she unfolded it, I saw all the circled marks of the cemeteries.

"You kept that?" I asked surprised.

"Yeah," Tristan said. "When I packed up at the hotel I figured I should bring that just in case."

John came back holding a soft pink shirt. "It's her favorite," he explained, and handed it to Lexi.

We all sat quietly while Lexi conducted the spell. I had never seen it done before, though I knew they used it to find me when I was with Darien. I swallowed hard. I had been doing a good job of avoiding thinking about Darien, but every now and then he would creep into my mind.

I felt an inexplicable longing for him. I...missed him, but why? What does that mean? I have Tristan here who is the most wonderful man I have ever met, and yet I keep thinking of his brother. What was wrong with me?

I noticed Tristan shifting uncomfortably and he avoided my gaze. Had I thought Tristan's name? Had he heard my thoughts? Damn it.

"She's at the courthouse," Lexi said, breaking my reverie.

"What would she be doing there?" John asked, concerned.

"I'll find out," I said. "The courthouse is public, so I'm sure she's not in trouble there."

"No, I'll go," Tristan offered. "We only needed you to go because you could teleport directly to her, but since we know where she is, I can go get her. She probably won't want to see you anyway." Tristan's voice had an edge to it that I didn't like. Damn my thoughts and the stupid connection he had to them!

Tristan pushed his chair back from the table and stood abruptly. I could tell he didn't want to see me just then either.

"Outside!" Lexi yelled. And we all jerked.

"Don't teleport in here, remember?" She amended. Tristan nodded with understanding and rushed outside. John hurried after him. By the time I reached the front door, they were gone.

"That was interesting," Genevieve said. She had been so quiet I forgot she was there. Lexi and I looked at each other.

"I need to talk to you," we both said in unison.

I closed my bedroom door and Lexi sat on my bed, wringing her fingers nervously.

"You first," I insisted.

"I know I'm probably overreacting, but it looked like John might have stronger feelings for Fay than he realized."

I thought about that for a moment, and then said, "I can see how you would think that, but you have to remember that he has known her for a long time. He said himself she's like his sister and he no doubt feels guilty for her absence."

"Yeah, but think about how her potential danger could make him realize his feelings if he had any," Lexi said.

"Just trust that he is trying to do the right thing by going with Tristan to get her back. You can always talk to him when he returns too, just to ease your worries."

"No, I can't. He'll think I'm being paranoid, and he has enough problems with Fay." She let out a sigh. I sat beside her and put my arm around her.

"It'll be okay. He's just being brotherly," I reassured. She nodded, and I knew it wasn't because she agreed with me, but rather that she had nothing else to say.

"What's your issue?" She asked after a quiet moment. I wasn't sure how to answer her. I felt so guilty talking about this, but I had to talk to someone, and I definitely couldn't talk to Tristan.

"Darien sent me another dream and I think... I have... feelings for him. But I don't know why!" I blurted.

"Darien can be sneaky - and charming - in his own way. What was the dream he sent you this time?"

I told her, and I included how I felt longing for him afterwards.

"I've been thinking about this. I think he cares about you. I mean you guys bonded at the camp; I saw that. Maybe he misses you too."

"It's hard for me to think that Darien could have sincere feelings for me. And I don't understand how I could have feelings for Darien when he tormented me so much. Not to mention Tristan is so amazing! And the worst part is that Tristan knows because my stupid ass was thinking about it while you were doing the locator spell."

"I think as much as Tristan is probably hurt, he understands how hard this is for you too."

"I don't know about that, but I know he doesn't want me thinking of his brother that way. How do I know if my feelings are even real? How do I know they're not remnants from Jeremiah's spell like you said before?"

Lexi nodded again. "I think I might be able to help you find out."

"Really? How?"

"Well I can sense the truth right? So maybe I can bypass your guards and see how you really feel."

"Okay, what have we got to lose?" I agreed and held out my

arm.

"How do you really feel about Darien?" She asked and then grabbed my arm. Her eyes lost focus as she saw the images inside my head and sensed the emotions that went with them.

I read her thoughts to see too, and I gasped as I saw what she was seeing. It was a montage of images and memories. It started with the first time I met Darien, how I felt during that initial meeting. Then it rushed through the dates I had, and through the bats, bugs and other disturbing things he sent me. It slowed at a memory I had with him at the camp; Darien using magic to bring me to him and then kissing me. The feel and memory of it made my heart ache, which only made me angry.

Then there were flashes of my dreams, which reignited how I felt. Then I saw images or memories - I'm not sure which because I didn't remember them. I was lying beside Darien, his arm wrapped around me, and he gazed at me, as I lay there resting. Darien reached over and brushed a strand of hair behind my ear. We looked at each other, not needing any words, knowing we cared for each other.

My heart beat fast, and then a rush of emotion threatened to engulf me.

"Oh my God," Lexi whispered, letting go.

"What was that?" I asked, panic cracking my voice.

"I—I'm not sure. That last image, did that happen at the camp?" She asked.

"I don't remember that. Could it have been a dream?"

"I don't think so. It's weird, usually I know what I'm seeing, but I couldn't tell if that was a memory or where that happened."

"Me neither," I admitted, feeling confused.

"Your feelings run a lot deeper than you realize. There is some underlying emotion you have for Darien, and I think that's why when you dream about him, you feel for him."

"So, my feelings are real then? It's not Jeremiah?" My stomach dropped.

"As far as I can tell, it's all you," Lexi confirmed. I flung myself face down on the bed.

"Tristan doesn't deserve me. I'm a terrible, confused woman, who has an amazing man but thinks of someone else. I hate myself."

"Oh come on, you're being way too hard on yourself. You've been through some crazy things the past few months. Give yourself a break. You'll figure it out."

"I hope so," I sighed.

The front door slammed, followed by arguing voices.

"Guess the she-devil is back," Lexi mumbled.

I let out a groan. "I want to go home. I want to leave this crazy place and its crazy people and go back to my boring existence."

"I know, I know," Lexi started. "I'm going to go downstairs and see how John is doing with Fay and find out what happened."

"You can't be this reckless, Fay!" John yelled. I had never seen him so angry.

"Reckless? I was trying to help. I want this nightmare over with just like everyone else," Fay retorted. They stood in the living room, toe-to-toe, while Tristan leaned against the wall and Genevieve and Lachlan sat on the couch. Lexi and I had just reached the room.

"What exactly were you planning to do?" John seethed.

"Well I figured we should get the Elders in on this, maybe let them take over," Fay said.

"We already did that," John roared. "If you had bothered to come back yesterday, you would have known. And who do you think you are to make that kind of decision on your own, without discussing it with the rest of us?"

Fay's face paled, the anger draining from her body.

"I didn't know," she whispered.

"Well how could you? You left! Don't you realize how worried we were? Don't you realize how much trouble you could have gotten yourself into?" John pulled Fay into a tight hug. Lexi averted her gaze to the back door.

"Uh, can we start from the beginning please? I missed some stuff," I asked, hoping I could deflect the awkward moment. John pulled away almost reluctantly, and I couldn't help but wonder if Lexi might be right about his feelings for Fay.

"You didn't really miss anything," Tristan started. At least he wasn't ignoring me. "We went to the courthouse. John talked to her and told her we were taking her back, and I teleported her before she could argue. Though she was waiting for a fight when I teleported back with John." A small smile played on his lips.

I tried to meet his eyes, to see if he was alright, but he wasn't looking at me. I deserved that. I would have to talk to him about it later though and try to explain. Maybe we could both gain a little perspective.

"Breakfast is ready in the kitchen whenever you are all done here," Genevieve announced. I felt guilty that I hadn't been helping her. I just couldn't seem to think about food during this madness, but I supposed that was how she kept herself distracted and sane.

Everyone headed quietly to the kitchen, but I stayed in the living room, not really having an appetite, and needing some space from the others. I watched as they gathered around the table and filled all the seats. But where was Artemis? I walked to the backyard, but he wasn't there, so I walked all around the outside of the house. It too was unoccupied. So where had he gone this time, back to the cemetery?

Artemis, I sent telepathically. *I just wanted to check in and see if you were alright.*

Never better he responded.

Would you mind if I joined you? I asked, needing any excuse to get away from the claustrophobia that was settling in.

By all means.

I closed my eyes and teleported to Artemis. I gasped when I opened them. Before me was the most beautiful beach I had ever seen. The water was crystal clear and the sand so white, the sun made it glimmer like diamonds. The small waves lapped the shore, and I didn't see a single jagged rock, or any seaweed. It was absolutely perfect.

Along the shore was a line of shops and restaurants. As I turned to face them, I saw Artemis sitting at a table on a balcony overlooking the beach. He looked so ordinary in swim shorts and a t-shirt that I had to look twice to make sure it was him. His hair was combed neatly, but the rings under his eyes told me he hadn't been sleeping much. He sat smiling at me as he enjoyed his meal-it looked like a hamburger with a side of pizza.

"Couldn't decide what to eat today?" I teased.

"These are my two favorite meals. I couldn't resist the indulgence," he answered, squinting into the sun as he took a bite of pepperoni pizza. "Care to join me?" he added. He seemed rather lucid, maybe from the peace of the beautiful beach.

I nodded and climbed the steps to the wooden balcony attached to the restaurant. Pulling up a seat, I sat next to Artemis, enjoying the gorgeous view.

"Where are we?" I asked. Witches in bathing suits lay on the sand, tanning, while others swam and some read or ate below the shade of their umbrellas.

"This is Paradise Beach – one of many in The Hidden City. You will never find a beach like this anywhere in the world. The water is the perfect temperature for each witch. For me it's cool enough to tame the sun's sting, yet warm enough that you could stay in there all day without a shiver," Artemis explained.

I looked longingly at the water, wishing I could swim and forget all my worries and troubles, but I couldn't even stop thinking of how I should have told the others I was leaving. After they chewed Fay out for doing the same thing, I should know better.

"Just tell them," Artemis offered.

"Hmm?" I asked, not following his train of thought.

"You are worried your friends will panic when they discover you are no longer there, so tell them." He tapped his temple

"Oh," Was all I said – really how do I keep forgetting I can do things like that? I decided to send the message to Lexi; I wasn't sure Tristan would want me in his head in any way just now.

After a few silent moments I received, *You're where?*

Paradise Beach, I sent back. The thought crossed my mind to invite them, maybe we could all use a nice break, but the truth was that I needed the time away – from all of them. I wondered if this was how Artemis felt, if this was why he kept leaving.

I reassured Lexi that I was with Artemis and that I was safe and would be back soon. She promised to relay the message to the others, and I sighed in relief.

"I was going to test out the water, would you like to come?" Artemis asked. I looked at his now empty plate.

"Don't you have to wait an hour after you eat before you swim?" I asked.

He laughed quietly. "I can assure you I will not drown." His face fell slightly and then brightened before I could register what that meant. He pointed to a small shop with palm trees painted on the front. "Front of the rack on the left side, you will find a nice black bikini to your liking." He smiled and stood, heading down the steps toward the water.

I laughed in spite of myself and headed to the shop. A little black bikini sat on the front of the rack waiting for me to wear it. I tried it on and it fit perfectly. Imagine how much of a fortune Artemis could make if he became a personal shopper. Maybe I would suggest the idea to him when this was all over.

I searched my pockets for my credit cards-did they take credit cards here?-but found a few twenties instead and paid for the bikini. I walked out of the store wearing my new purchase.

Artemis stood in the water, facing the horizon. He still wore his shirt, and I wondered how uncomfortable that might be.

I cautiously put my foot in the water but needn't have

worried. It was perfect, just as Artemis said. I waded into the water and stood next to Artemis.

"Do you really want a t-shirt tan?" I teased, taking in his soaking shirt.

"I don't think anyone would want to see me without a shirt on." He smiled sadly.

"Oh, come on, no one cares," I assured him.

He just shook his head.

I lowered my body into the soothing water and then went in, head first, into a breast stroke. I swam a short distance and came back up. I expected the water to sting my eyes or the salty taste to fill my mouth, but it was tasteless. I dipped my head under and dared open my eyes. Nothing happened. I was able to see pain free.

A few feet ahead of me a school of fish swam. The experience was better than snorkeling. I thought to tell Artemis, sure he would enjoy this, but just as I was about to lift my head, I saw him next to me. He too peered down into the water, and I saw a smile light up his face as he saw the fish.

I went up for air, and Artemis did the same, sputtering a laugh as he came up.

"It really is beautiful! I had forgotten such beauty existed." The excitement on his face made him look years younger, and I caught a glimpse of how he must have looked as a young man.

I had planned to push him into telling me what to expect, what was coming so we could be prepared, but I couldn't do it, wouldn't do it. I would wait until we got back to the house.

We spent hours at the beach, going back and forth between the water and beach chairs. The sand never stuck to our bodies, making drying off completely enjoyable. If humans ever found this place, tourists would be swarming around, packing their umbrellas so close they were bumping, and would never leave.

We watched the sun set in silence, taking in the beautiful pinks and oranges that swept the sky. It was the perfect place, and the perfect day.

By the time we decided to leave, it was evening, and that was only because Lexi kept bombarding me about when I was coming back.

Reluctantly we teleported back to the house, and I think we both felt the same disappointment when we saw the dark structure looming in front of us. Back to the house meant back to reality. I think our hearts broke a little in unison.

Artemis patted my shoulder reassuringly and headed for the front door. Inside, the house was oddly quiet. What time was it exactly? Could everyone be asleep?

"Thank God! I was starting to freak out!" Lexi rushed toward us and gave us each a hug.

"Where is everyone?" I asked, taking in the empty living room.

"They're out in the back. We decided to hang out and enjoy the night. Took the idea to relax from you." She smiled.

"I will be out in a minute," Artemis said. "Will you make sure there's a seat for me?"

"Of course," I said, and I followed Lexi out to the back. "Did you talk to John?" I asked her before she could open the patio door.

"No. It's not the time. I figure it'll all pan out how it's supposed to, and if I have any doubts after this is over, I will talk to him then." Lexi sounded so mature, so unlike the rambunctious, outspoken girl I had grown up with.

She opened the door then and I saw everyone sitting in a circle around a fire that seemed to have no source. Lachlan and Genevieve sat on the patio chairs, but everyone else had a chair from the kitchen table. They were talking quietly, and they did indeed look like they were enjoying the night.

It was beautiful to see that, in the face of all that was happening, we were all able to take some time to enjoy the moment. I waved and was greeted by smiles and scattered waves.

"Took you long enough," John said. "Did you have a nice day?" His spirits seemed to be better.

"Sure did." I noticed I needed a seat for myself and Artemis. "Hang on and I'll tell you all about it."There were two chairs left at the kitchen table. I lifted one and was wondering if I could pick the second up as well – it wasn't heavy, just bulky - to save myself a trip when Tristan walked through the door.

"I was worried about you," he said quietly. "I don't like you being where I can't protect you." I dropped the chair and flung my arms around him. He hugged me back gently.

"I'm so sorry. I'm so sorry that my brain is messed up, but I will figure it out so you won't have to worry, okay?" I wasn't sure if I was talking about Darien or being away from him – probably both.

"I know." He kissed the top of my head and then released me.

"Can you grab the other chair?" I asked as I lifted the one I had just dropped. Tristan picked up the second chair without a word and we walked to the backyard.

Lexi shifted over, and Tristan and I sat in the two chairs we brought, leaving the seat Tristan had been in for Artemis. Lachlan and Genevieve were sitting side by side, Fay sat next to Lachlan, and John sat between her and Lexi. I sat between Lexi and Tristan and stared at the odd fire. The base was blue, and blended into purple, then pink, then red, and the tips of the flames were orange. The fire sat a few inches off the ground with nothing feeding it or sustaining it.

"John did that," Lexi said, answering my unasked question. I nodded in understanding; why get a fire pit when you can create a fire and make sure it didn't burn anything around it?

Artemis took the vacant seat between Genevieve and Tristan a few moments later. It was nice having him hang out with us for a change.

I told the group about our day at the beach and made them promise that we would all go there when this was over. It was too beautiful a place not to share.

"I have a story of my own that you should all hear," Artemis said. "I know I have given you a lot of information already, but this is the last story I will tell you. I think it will help you all understand the story surrounding the prophecy, and what some people are willing to do to protect the ones they love." Artemis turned to face Tristan. "You especially will want to pay attention. It is after all, about your family."

19. BEDTIME STORIES

The story was told the same as Jeremiah's. I could hear Artemis speaking, but really I just saw it like a movie as he projected his vision into our minds.

THE HIDDEN CITY 1988

It was a dark night; only the moon shining through the stained glass window of the tomb gave off any light. Marcus Gabriel stood at the small table, sealing in the spell.

"Are you sure no one will find it?" Jordana asked in a whisper. Her green eyes darted around her anxiously. She pulled her long black hair over her shoulder and tried not to touch anything around her.

"I am pretty sure. I chose the tomb at random. No one would think to associate this place or this person to us. I've also placed my shadow men as guards." Marcus ran a hand through his short, brown, curly hair. His brown eyes roamed the tomb.

"Marcus, he has a psychic, don't you think he will just tell him where it is?"

"Maybe, but I can't just do nothing."

"Are you sure there is no other way?" Jordana looked out the door, making sure no one was approaching. Marcus stood behind her and wrapped his arms around her waist. He placed his chin on her shoulder.

"We've been over this, Jordana. I know what the psychic saw. I was there, and in the prophecy he makes mention of a ritual in Jeremiah's book of shadows. You know what will happen if he gets those girls. You know what will happen if he uses all that power for himself."

"I know, but what does this have to do with us?" Jordana asked, knowing she was being selfish.

"We may not be able to stop him from getting the girls, but we can stop him from getting this crystal," Marcus whispered. "The spell is in place, it's out of our hands." He released Jordana and reached over her shoulder to open the crypt door so they could leave.

"I wish you never created that crystal," Jordana said as they walked across the cemetery and back to the car.

"You say that now, but you weren't complaining when we used it in Manhattan," Marcus teased.

"I guess." Jordana's lips curled up at the ends. "So, what do we do now?" She asked as she climbed into the car. Marcus walked around the driver's side and climbed in.

"Now I will do what I have to. I know where Jeremiah keeps the prophecy. If I make it public, he won't be able to get away with his crazy plan. I still can't believe I didn't see this coming."

"You looked up to him. You saw only what you wanted to see," Jordana answered.

Marcus nodded. "Well, tonight I will correct that oversight."

"You're going tonight? To what, steal the prophecy?"

"Yes."

"What if you get caught?" Jordana almost yelled. "What if something happens to you? Do you have any idea how that would affect me, and your boys? I won't be able to go on without you."

Marcus caressed Jordana's face. "I know. I will be careful I promise. Jeremiah still thinks of me as a friend. He let me sit in when the prophecy was revealed, and he won't suspect that I've hidden the crystal. He definitely won't suspect that I would steal from him. Just trust me on this."

Jordana crossed her arms over her chest and looked out the window. She knew, in her gut, that this was all going to end very badly.

By the next morning, Jordana was a wreck. She'd spent the night pacing, and talking herself out of going after Marcus. Had he been caught? What would happen if he were? Would Jeremiah actually hurt his friend? The sound of a child crying snapped Jordana out of her thoughts.

She hurried to the boys' room. She would have to thank Mrs. Laurel again for watching the boys while she was at the cemetery.

"Darien, stop kicking your brother," she said, pulling the two-year-old away from his twin brother.

She gave a yellow toy bird to Darien, who watched the bird flying in circles before coming to rest on his hand, and a blue one to Tristan. Immediately Darien started fussing, wanting Tristan's toy. Tristan just sat quietly and allowed his brother to rant and rave and take the toy away. Jordana shook her head.

The front door slammed shut, startling her, and she rushed out of the bedroom and down the stairs.

"Told you it would be fine," Marcus said, throwing his jacket over the back of the kitchen chair. Jordana ran and hugged him fiercely.

"I was so worried! What took you so long?" She pressed.

"Well I had to hang out for a while, so Jeremiah wouldn't be suspicious, and gradually performed the sleeping spell until he fell asleep. I had to make sure he wouldn't wake before I had the guts to steal it. Then I went straight to the Prophetic Journal head office and donated the information." Marcus suppressed a smile.

"Do you think they'd publish an un-verified prophecy?"

"Why not? Artemis has been known for his abilities. They'd have to publish the prophecy and make it available for anyone who wants to see it. By the time Jeremiah figures out where it is, it'll be too late, and once they talk to the Artemis to confirm, Jeremiah won't be able to do a thing about it. Anyways I stayed there until I saw an employee open up and find the parchment. I wanted to make sure it was in her hands before I left," Marcus explained.

"So this is over then?" Jordana asked, afraid to believe it could be that simple.

Marcus worked his jaw, deep in thought.

"What aren't you telling me, Marcus?" Jordana asked as fear crept through her.

"The prophecy mentions the Gemini – twin brothers," Marcus reluctantly answered. "I'm worried Tristan and Darien may have a part in this."

"What? Why didn't you tell me this before? What exactly did the prophecy say?"

"I don't remember it word for word, but they will both love the one who will save us. One will gain strength from the darkness and one will sacrifice himself for her."

Jordana swallowed hard. "Do you think…I mean…are there no other twins this could be speaking of?" she stammered.

"Of course, anything is possible, which is why I didn't want to worry you unnecessarily. It's just that this is all supposed to happen in twenty-six years. Our boys will be almost thirty by then."

"I'm not sure I'm convinced."

"I know it's hard to think of now, because they are so young, but I just have a feeling in my gut that our boys will be involved, that's all." Marcus went to the fridge and opened the door looking for food. One of the boys was yelling again, and Jordana ran up the stairs to see what was going on now.

"Tristan don't…"

"Where is it?" Jeremiah yelled at Marcus.

"Where is what?" Marcus asked, feigning concern.

"The prophecy! I had it when you came over and then it was gone. What did you do with it?" Jeremiah grabbed Marcus by the collar and pulled him close. "Tell me or I will rip your tongue out."

"I didn't do anything with it. Why would I?" Marcus said calmly.

"Really? Prove it."

"How?"

"Show trust; give me the crystal," Jeremiah spat.

"I have it in a safe place. Don't worry about that," Marcus assured.

"I don't want it in a safe place. I want it with me. Give it to me now!"

"Jeremiah! Stop!" Jordana yelled as she rushed into the kitchen. "You are a guest in our house and you will respect my husband, let him go."

"I will let him go when he tells me what he did with my belongings," Jeremiah said.

"What belongings?" Jordana asked, as she gently placed her hand on Jeremiah's so he would loosen his grip. He did, and then he started pacing.

"Never mind," he said, and then he turned and faced Marcus. "If I find out you had anything to do with its disappearance, I will come for you." Jeremiah slammed the door behind him.

"Are you alright?" Jordana asked, checking Marcus for any injuries.

"I'm fine, really."

"This is a mistake. We should leave here, go somewhere safe."

"We can't. Our lives are here; we can't uproot the whole family just to run away from Jeremiah. He's all talk. We'll be fine." He kissed his wife on the cheek.

It took three weeks for the prophecy to become published in the Prophetic Journal, three weeks for Jeremiah to find out where his prophecy had gone, and three weeks for him to officially lose his mind.

Everyone knew about the prophecy now. He had to get it back, take back what was rightfully his before it was too late. He rushed to the library and checked out the journal and cast his spell, erasing the page from that book and every other one in print. Next he had to cast the memory spell, but he had to make sure no one could ever get the prophecy again. He had to make sure they couldn't get hold of Artemis.

As for who donated the prophecy, he knew the answer. He would have to take care of that loose end as well.

Three years. That's how long Jeremiah's memory charm took to start to slowly fade, for Jeremiah to graciously donate the copy on behalf of his friend. But three years was a long time, long enough for those who didn't forget its existence to forget the details.

Five years. That's how long it took Jordana to get hold of the second edition. She wished she had the foresight to write what her husband told her of the prophecy, since Jeremiah saw to it that no one would be able to talk to him again. Five years she had been raising her twin boys alone. Now she sat in bed reading the prophecy – well the second edition. She guessed there weren't enough witches who remembered about the first, but she did, and she had to make sure her boys knew. She wasn't sure if they were the twins in the prophecy, but she had to be sure that they ended up on the right side of the fight just in case. Every night she would tell them what she could remember of the prophecy. She even added what was in the copy just for details.

Every night she would tell her boys of the woman who would save the Hidden City, and how they might have to protect her one day. And every moment without them, she plotted her revenge against Jeremiah. She knew he killed her husband. She knew it wasn't an accident like the Charge believed; Marcus would never have gone to the beach at night, and he was an excellent swimmer. Someone had drowned him. She just couldn't prove it. If she kept poking around though, it would only be a matter of time before Jeremiah came after her.

She couldn't risk that. She had to take care of her boys. She kept her head down and her thoughts to herself. Another five years passed without any conflict, and her boys were now almost teenagers growing into young men. Marcus's words about the Gemini always sat gnawing in the back of Jordana's mind. She took extra steps to encourage them to be good and kind and considerate, so that neither of them would ever turn to darkness.

Deep in thought, Jordana was washing the dishes when she heard the screams. It wasn't their usual arguing banter, but actual terror. Her blood froze in her veins as she rushed up the stairs.

"What is it?" She cried as she ran into the room. Darien and Tristan sat in a circle with their friends, John and Lachlan. Their mouths hanging open as their glazed eyes sharpened into focus.

"We... we were playing and then... I saw something," Tristan said.

"I saw it too," Darien said and the others nodded.

"What did you see? On the T.V.?" Jordana turned to see that the television was off.

"No," Tristan said, "in my head." Again the other boys nodded.

The hair on the back of Jordana's neck stood on end.

"What did you see?" She asked. The boys all looked at one

another, none of them wanting to say.

Finally Tristan spoke, "We saw a girl get...hurt and then killed."

Jordana gasped. Why? Why would anyone do that to these poor children?

"Alright, I can fix this," she said and she held Tristan's face for a moment and willed his memory to erase what he had just seen. Then she did the same for Darien and John, leaving all three boys in a haze. Jordana knelt to help Lachlan when there was a knock on the door. Jordana hesitated, unsure if she should leave the boys even for a brief moment. Then a heavier knock sounded, booming throughout the house.

"Elder council," a voice boomed. Jordana cursed under her breath. The three boys had been in a frozen state for too long. She quickly snapped the boys out of the trance, and they looked dazedly at each other.

"Stay here," Jordana hissed, and closed the bedroom door as she ran down the stairs.

Jordana opened the door where three witches stood.

"We received an anonymous tip that you had tampered with mind control," Sible Hamilton said, flanked by Jeremiah and Edmond.

"Well you were misinformed," Jordana said, chin up. She went to close the door.

"I'm afraid we have a court order to search your house," Jeremiah said, a glint in his eye.

"How did you manage to get a court order so fast?" Jordana asked, and bit her tongue.

Sible looked at her quizzically. "We received the tip an hour ago. Plenty of time to get the documents we need."

"An hour ago?" Jordana whispered to herself. "How is that even possible?" Jordana took the paper and studied it a moment before opening the door to allow the elders in.

Sible took a deep breath, and fanned her hands out. "I'm sensing something upstairs," she said, and the others followed her steps. She opened the bedroom door where the boys sat, still not completely focused, but not obviously enchanted either. Sible furrowed her brow, and sighed.

"I hoped it wasn't true," she said.

"What are you talking about?" Jordana asked, unsure if the woman could really tell what had happened.

"Jeremiah received the tip that you had tampered with these boys' minds, but I didn't want to believe it," Sible said. "The spell I cast proves it's true though."

Jordana couldn't deny it. "No wait!" Jordana pleaded, terrified of what Sible would do. "They were sent a vision of a girl being murdered!"

Sible paused, studying the boys.

"Never the less, it is illegal to conduct spells on the minds of children," Jeremiah snapped.

"Really? Well, maybe we should tell them what you have been up to and see if any of that is legal," Jordana threatened.

"Please, Mrs. Gabriel, that will only make it harder on you," Sible said kindly.

"It's not untrue, but I suppose nothing I tell you will change your mind," Jordana said through clenched teeth. She chanced a glance at Jeremiah whose lips twitched almost in a smile.

"You did this!" she lunged at Jeremiah, who held his hand

279

out, freezing Jordana in place. Sible gasped.

"Jordana Gabriel, we have proof of you mind molding and charge you with such. We will now deliberate your sentence," Sible said and turned to her colleagues in a silent conversation.

Before the silent conversation ended, Jeremiah turned to Jordana. With a flourish of his hands, Jeremiah performed a spell that was hauntingly familiar to her.

"Jeremiah!" Sible said stunned. "We hadn't officially decided on that sentence."

"My apologies, Sible. I misunderstood," Jeremiah said avoiding Sible's glare.

"What was my sentence?" Jordana asked, already assuming the answer.

After a few agonizing moments, the silence was broken. "Your sentence is binding for one year," Sible said with finality.

"Wait, you can't, I-"Jordana started, but before she could finish, Jeremiah interrupted.

"It has begun. It will set in fully in a few hours," he said smugly.

Jordana buckled over, on the verge of fainting. "Please, I have been bound before, when I was a teenager. I can't go through that again," she pleaded.

"What were you bound for?" Sible asked curiously.

"I was experimenting for a school paper, and used illegal magic to study the effects of compulsion on others, but I didn't harm anyone. It was so stupid, but they bound my powers for a month anyway. A month was agonizing, I can't bear a year!" Jordana found the floor and sat down. Her attention vaguely drawn to the boys sitting nearby, watching but not fully aware yet.

"Is that so?" Jeremiah asked. "I had no idea." His faked innocence fooled the others, but not Jordana.

"It is difficult to go through, but it *is* only one year," Sible said softly. Edmond quietly cleared his throat. Sible turned and looked at him starting a silent conversation. A moment later Sible gasped. Stunned, she turned to Jeremiah and asked out loud, "Can it be undone?" The sadness in her voice alerted Jordana.

"It cannot. Only once it expires will the spell be broken," Jeremiah said. Sible spun on her heel and faced Jordana.

"I am so sorry, my dear. I had no idea." Tears welled up in her eyes as she took in Jordana's confused expression.

"No idea of what? That Jeremiah is scum?" She spat. Sible flinched as if she had been slapped.

"That this being your second binding will-" She swallowed but couldn't continue. She gave Jordana one final sad glance, and then teleported. Jeremiah smiled at her and tapped his head before Edmond took his hand and they too teleported.

With that motion, she knew what she had only suspected. Jeremiah was responsible for the vision these boys saw. He made sure it was traumatizing enough for her to alter their memories and get caught. She knew then that her boys were the ones in the prophecy and that Jeremiah was after them. What better way to get them than to get rid of their last living parent? Jordana seethed with anger, but she was too weak to move.

"Mrs. Gabriel?" Lachlan asked quietly. He was the only one who would remember this, and she didn't have her powers to alter his memory. The poor boy would have these memories burned in his mind forever.

"Yes, Lachlan," Jordana answered weakly.

"Are you alright?"

"No, I don't think I am," Jordana started, and then she looked right into Lachlan's eyes. "Lachlan, I need a favor." The boy nodded. "I'm sorry I can't make you forget what you saw, but please, please, promise me that you will never tell Tristan or Darien what you saw today. Nothing at all, can you promise me that?" She tried to hold the boys arms to show him how important this request was, but she was too weak. He nodded again urgently. "Thank you," she sighed, and then dragged herself so she sat in front of the three boys and grabbed their attention, officially snapping them out of the haze they'd been in. When they came around, they looked at each other, but said nothing.

"Come on," Lachlan said, pulling John by the hand. "We need to leave Mrs. Gabriel; she's not feeling well." Lachlan and a confused John left quickly, leaving the bound witch with her sons.

"Who was that?" Tristan asked, watching the boys' shadows recede.

"Who? Lachlan?" Darien answered. He seemed to have his mind straight.

"No, the boy with him," Tristan said. Jordana sighed. So he had forgotten one of his friends, but he still remembered Lachlan. Hopefully he wouldn't have lost much more than that. She waited for Darien to answer but he seemed as confused as Tristan.

"That was John, Lachlan's friend," she answered. She gained

enough strength to attempt to stand.

"Mom, are you sick?" Darien asked. Jordana nodded sadly. She had a feeling, with the way Sible reacted, that she was much more than sick. Jeremiah knew she had been bound before. He must have known that this time it would be different. She hugged her boys tightly and vowed to teach them as much as she could. She needed them to know how to protect themselves, and she needed to make sure they always chose the light.

20. FATE HAS ITS OWN PLANS

"You all know what happened next," Artemis spoke as we all snapped out of the vision.

"Yeah, Darien followed Jeremiah while Tristan protected Selena," Lexi answered softly, deliberately omitting the part where their mother died.

"Why did Darien follow Jeremiah?" I asked.

"Darien has his own way of doing things," Artemis answered in his usual cryptic way. The circle grew quiet as we all pondered the story.

"If the second edition isn't much like the original, why would anyone want to steal it?" I asked.

"It was just another one of Jeremiah's mind games," Artemis said. "He thought if you didn't have any reference you would doubt yourself, as you doubted the prophecy's existence. It would seem he was correct," he added snidely. I shot him a grimace.

"That's the thing I don't get," Genevieve said. "How did Jeremiah steal the second edition when the library has spells to automatically return books?

"Yes, well as we have been learning, spells can be broken,"

Artemis answered vaguely.

"You knew? All this time and you never said anything?" Tristan asked Lachlan, though his tone was more of awe than accusation. I could tell he didn't care a damn about the prophecy just then. I could only imagine what he must be feeling with all this information.

"Aye. I promised never to tell," Lachlan said.

"Are you okay?" I reached over and took one of Tristan's hands in my own. He nodded and swallowed hard. I could tell he was holding back tears.

"I need a minute." He stood and left the circle. I thought about following him inside, but figured he would prefer to be alone. I know I would.

"Will he be okay?" I asked Artemis.

He smiled kindly at me. "Things are set in motion now. He will be as he was intended to be," Artemis said cryptically. I repressed the urge to roll my eyes. I looked at Lexi who studied me speculatively before nodding her head in the direction Tristan went in.

I shook my head, and waited in silence. I wanted to give him his space.

The minutes stretched on and after about ten I felt restless.

I excused myself and went inside. Tristan sat in the armchair, elbows on knees, head in hands.

He looked up as I approached, and I sat on the arm of his seat. He wrapped his arm around my waist.

"Jeremiah killed my parents," Tristan said in a raspy voice.

"Join the club," I murmured.

"How would you like to kill him? Shall we torture him like

Crystal and Yuri? Or burn him from the inside out like you did with our intruders?" Tristan's voice was filled with icy hate. I shuddered at the memories of murder that Tristan spoke so lightly of.

"Tristan, you are understandably upset, but don't make plans to kill anyone. Take some time to process this – it was a lot of information," I said. Tristan clenched his jaw and nodded.

"Why wouldn't my mom tell me who my father was?"

"Probably to protect you. Maybe she thought it would be easier if you just thought he was never there rather than miss how great a father he was," I said.

"We killed my father's shadow men, stole his crystal, and gave it right to Jeremiah! I undid everything that he put in place to protect us. Maybe if she had told me about him and his plans, I would have done things differently." Tristan fumed.

"Well, she didn't, and you couldn't have known," I started, "and I needed the crystal to remove my binding spell or I would have died."

"No, Jeremiah needed it to control you. He lied to us, remember?" Tristan seethed.

"Right, but if you knew about your father's spell, and Jeremiah told you we needed the crystal to get my powers unbound, would that have stopped you from getting it?"

Tristan pondered the question a moment. "No, I guess not. I'd do anything for you." We gazed at each other and I gave him a sad smile before kissing him softly.

We sat silently for a short while before I decided to give Tristan some more time alone. I kissed the top of his head as I stood.

"I'll be outside if you need me," I said.

"Thanks," he whispered. The circle was quiet when I joined them, and stayed that way for what seemed like ages, until finally John spoke up.

"Do you remember the vision Jeremiah sent?" He asked Lachlan.

"I do. It haunts me to this day," Lachlan answered and Genevieve squeezed his hand reassuringly.

Artemis cleared his throat. "I sent you that vision, under Jeremiah's persuasion of course. And for that I am deeply sorry."

Lachlan nodded.

Tristan finally came outside, but didn't sit. He leaned quietly against the door frame, arms crossed over his chest.

I walked up to him and whispered, "You feeling any better?"

He nodded, but his expression showed his frustration. "All this time I thought my mom had done something bad, that she had been selfish to do something that would get her powers bound, but she didn't. She was innocent."

"I know, it's hard when you find out everything you believed was a lie," I said, remembering how it felt when I found out Jeremiah had killed my parents too. I ran my hand down his arm reassuringly and went back to my seat.

"So when you told me I knew Tristan from before, that's what you meant?" John asked.

"I couldn't tell you how you two knew each other without telling you everything else that happened that day," Lachlan answered. "I suppose I just should have said you'd never met, but I didn't think it through."

"How is it we went through the last sixteen years without

meeting again?" John asked Tristan.

Tristan shrugged, "Well, after my mother died, I went to protect Selena. That was about a year from the time my mother was bound."

"Right after that day is when John moved, and didn't come back until five years later," Lachlan said.

"Oh, that's right," John said.

"I was glad you came back too, even though it reminded me of that day. Tristan had already been assigned to Selena by that time, and I needed my old friend back. I guess you two never crossed paths until now."

"Huh," John said. "I didn't see Darien either. I didn't even know we used to be friends."

"Wait," I said suddenly, a thought dawning on me. "Darien doesn't know Jeremiah killed your parents, does he?"

Tristan shrugged, "I didn't know, so how would he know? I doubt Jeremiah recruited him by telling him he killed our mother and father. Then again, Darien doesn't talk to me so…"

"Well, I'm only asking because if Darien doesn't know, and we tell him, or have Artemis send him this memory, maybe we can get him to turn on Jeremiah and come join our side," I said excitedly.

"You'd like that wouldn't you?" Tristan said quietly, but I could hear the anger in his voice.

"What? No, I only meant-"

"I know what you meant."

I felt like he slapped me across the face. That wasn't fair to assume I had some ulterior motive for wanting Darien to know. I couldn't control my feelings, but I wasn't acting on them. I clamped my jaw shut and went inside, deliberately bumping Tristan on my way through the door.

"You know she only meant we would have one less bad guy to worry about," I heard Lexi snap, but I didn't stop to hear the rest. I stormed up to my room and locked the door. No way in hell Tristan was sleeping beside me tonight.

Hey beautiful, I heard the familiar voice bouncing around in my head. I had been dreaming of the lake by the cottage. I was staring into its crystal clear waters, staring at my reflection which kept changing. Every time I thought I knew who I was, it would change again.

This voice interrupted my dream and made it change. I was standing in the courthouse lobby, only it was deserted; not the busy, people packed place it usually was.

"Go away, Darien," I snapped as he appeared right in front of me.

"You know you keep saying that, but obviously you don't mean it." He took a step closer to me. "Interesting place you've got here," he said looking around the marble room.

"You actually have good timing for once. I found out some information today that I thought you might be interested in knowing," I said, dismissing his comments.

"Really, and what's that?" He asked smiling. I thought about blurting it, but as much as I hated Darien sometimes, I couldn't bear hurting him with this information. I had to be cautious with how I told him. I didn't want him to think I was making it up so he would turn on Jeremiah.

"I know…about your parents," I said. His smile faltered for

a moment.

"I don't have any parents." He replaced his smile with a pained grimace.

"No, but you did, and I know all about them."

"I see, and how do you know this?" Darien asked. I hadn't thought about Artemis or how I would explain where I got this knowledge from. I knew Jeremiah was aware that Artemis was gone, but I wasn't sure if he knew we took him, or if he thought he escaped some other way, and I didn't want Darien knowing the truth.

"Let's just say I have been discovering that I have a wide variety of gifts," I answered somewhat honestly.

"Alright, spill the beans, princess."

I told him the condensed version of what I learned, making sure I emphasized Jeremiah's involvement in his parents death.

Darien was quiet for such a long time, I wondered if it was time to wake up.

"Selena," he said softly, and my heart ached at the pain in his voice. He looked up at me with so much sadness I couldn't help it – I threw my arms around him and hugged him. He wrapped his arms around my waist and rested his head on my chest, and I held him.

DAY 4

"Selena!" My eyes snapped open and I saw Lexi hovering over me.

"What?" I groaned, still feeling tired.

"We're going to talk to Artemis and have him tell us what's

going on. We thought you would like to be there," she said smiling.

"Why haven't we done this yet?" I asked, agitated from what felt like no sleep.

"Oh, I don't know. I guess between your beach day and him talking his throat raw about Tristan's family, we just didn't get the chance," she responded sarcastically.

"Fine, yes, I'm coming." I threw the covers off and almost whimpered when I got out of bed. "What time is it?" There was no way I got more than a few hours of sleep. I was exhausted.

"It's ten," Lexi answered walking to my door.

"What? I slept for nine hours and I feel this bad? Oh," I said, the answer suddenly dawning on me.

"What? What's wrong?" Lexi asked, coming to stand next to me.

"Darien sent me another dream last night, so I told him about his parents. I guess when he visits I'm not really resting."

"What did he say to the news?" She asked.

"Nothing, he just took it. He didn't deny it, and he didn't accuse me of lying. I think on some level he already knew. I just confirmed it."

"Well I'm glad you told him. He has good timing, popping in your dreams right after you get some juicy gossip." Lexi smiled. It was weird, but he had been visiting me randomly so I guess it was just coincidence.

Lexi wasn't kidding. Everyone was in the living room, and I would have missed it all if she hadn't woken me.

"I know what you all brought me here for, but I will not

change my answer," Artemis said, leaning back into his chair. "You can't whip it out of me, I won't let you."

"No one's going to hurt you," Tristan said, his voice gentle. "We just need to be prepared. We need to know what's coming."

"I understand that, but you need to understand that telling you what is coming will not change the outcome! How many times must I tell you this, Jeremiah?"

We all exchanged glances.

"Artemis," I said, "Are you okay?"

"Of course." His eyes flickered in and out of focus. "I'm just fine."

Tristan cleared his throat.

"Why won't it change the outcome?" John asked as politely as possible. "If you said the light fixture above my head was going to fall, I would move out of the way."

"Yes," Artemis stood. "But then a shard from the debris will ricochet off here," he pointed to the table, "and still hurt you anyway by hitting you here." He pointed to John's thigh. "But because you moved, the fixture would shatter in a different angle." He flourished his hands, demonstrating the pattern the glass would shatter in. "And now Lexi would be hurt as well, because the glass will hit her here." Artemis motioned to Lexi's face and right arm. "It's not changing anything, only making it worse. I have told you everything you need to know to defeat Jeremiah. I have not held anything back that would help you. The only information I have now I cannot tell you, because when you change your course of action, in each different scenario I see, someone gets hurt."

"What do we do then?" Fay asked with frustration in her

tone.

"Keep preparing for the fight you know is coming, and speak with the Elders to make sure you are well coordinated," Artemis said.

"Fine, I will go to the courthouse and speak with the Elders," Genevieve said. "Tristan, would you mind teleporting me?"

"Sure," Tristan answered.

"I'll go with ya," Lachlan said getting to his feet.

"Why don't I teleport you? I can take you both at the same time," I offered.

Tristan looked down at his feet and then looked back up at Genevieve.

"No, no, it'll only be a second longer, no need to put you out," she answered. Tristan seemed to relax a little. Was he that worried about me that he wouldn't want me to teleport but wouldn't tell me 'no'? Or did he want Genevieve to speak for him because he wasn't talking to me?

"Thanks for the offer though," Lachlan said, and Genevieve smiled appreciatively.

"Sure," I said, and the three of them left the house to teleport.

I headed upstairs, showered and dressed, instantly feeling better. When I came back down, John, Fay and Lexi were nowhere to be found.

I went to the kitchen for breakfast and saw that Genevieve hadn't prepared anything for once. I was glad she took the day off – well that or she was too preoccupied with Artemis and the Elders to remember.

I ate a muffin and went outside to find Artemis sitting at the patio table again.

"I talked to Darien last night," I informed him as I took a seat at the patio table.

"I know." He smiled. "So how did it feel?"

"How did what feel?" I asked, panicking at the prospect of Artemis discussing my emotions for Darien.

"How did it feel to be the one who sent the dream?"

"What? I didn't. Darien just came to me like usual," I stammered.

"I'm afraid not. This time it was you. You wanted to talk to him, wanted to tell him of his parents, so you subconsciously called out to him and created the dream," Artemis said. "It also explains why you are so tired this morning. Dream visits take a lot out of a person."

I sat in silence, thinking this through. Then some of Darien's words came back to me, *'You know you keep saying that, but obviously you don't mean it.'* Yes, obviously I didn't want him to go away, if I were the one who called him. And then, *'interesting place you've got here.'* I heard his words repeated in my head. So I must have chosen the venue. But how?

"I didn't think I was capable of doing that," I said, still thinking it all through.

"You have abilities that you are still developing."

"Wait. Lachlan told me something when we were planning on saving you..."

"Yes, that a strong psychic could create and send a dream," Artemis finished my sentence.

"Yeah, so does that mean I'm psychic? And Darien too?"

"You both have the potential for the gift, though neither of you have actually received visions or premonitions yet. Dream manifestation is only the beginning, but it doesn't guarantee either of you will become psychic."

"But you could tell me, right?" I teased. "You can see into my future and tell me if I will get that gift."

"Yes, I could," he said.

"Ugh. Fine, be that way," I joked. I would figure it out sooner or later anyways. Artemis looked at me, and something flashed in his eyes and was gone just as quickly, like he wanted to tell me something but thought better of it. He turned and took in the view of the back yard again.

It was over an hour before Tristan, Genevieve and Lachlan came back.

"Anything new?" I asked the group as they walked into the living room.

"Not really, just plans finalized," Genevieve answered. "They are going to go after Jeremiah and his army as soon as they find the location of the new camp. They will call us as soon as they know so we can call the Fideles and join them."

"Good," I said. "Finally this may just come to an end." I dared imagine being able to stop Jeremiah before he even tried to perform the ritual. I could be home in a day or two – back to my job hunting life in Arizona.

Genevieve and Lachlan headed to the kitchen where they prepared a meal for themselves.

"Um," Tristan started. I hadn't expected him to speak with me, especially since I had chosen to ignore him after his rude remarks last night. "How are you?" He asked lamely.

I just glowered at him. I didn't want to give him the satis-faction of letting him off the hook so easily.

Thankfully John, Lexi, and Fay chose that moment to walk through the front door.

"Where've you been?" I asked.

"Just went to get some food," John answered. I studied Fay and Lexi who seemed to be getting along for some reason.

I squinted at Lexi and she met my gaze, shrugging in response to my unasked question.

We took your advice. You were right; it's not worth fighting right now. We have more important things to worry about, so we called a truce. Lexi sent me telepathically. I smiled and nodded. A truce was a good idea right now.

Everyone headed toward the kitchen to make lunch, but I didn't follow.

"Selena," Tristan said coming up to me. "Look, I was an ass last night."

I chortled in response.

"I'm really sorry, I was just so mad about what happened to my parents, and I didn't handle any of it very well. I'm sorry; I should never have said what I said. It wasn't fair to you, but I can't help but feel like an idiot for loving a girl who is thinking about my brother. You can understand that, can't you?" He asked, brushing a stray hair behind my ear.

"Of course. I hate that I'm hurting you, that I can't understand my emotions. Do you think I want to be feeling anything for him? He tried to hurt me so many times. Do you think I want to be thinking about anyone else when I have someone as wonderful as you in my life? I even asked Lexi if she could figure out the truth."

"You did?"

I nodded, "Yeah and all she could say was that there was some underlying emotions I have for him. I think it's from the camp, but I'm not sure."

Tristan nodded sadly.

"I talked to him last night," I continued.

Tristan looked up sharply, "What do you mean? How?"

"I...I accidentally sent him a dream," I admitted. Tristan clenched his jaw. "Anyways, I told him about your parents, so he knows everything now. Maybe he will rethink his alliance."

"Maybe," Tristan said distantly.

I reached out and grabbed his arm. "Please don't freak out. It's not a big deal. We need everyone on our side right now, and I just felt like he had the right to know the truth. They were his parents too."

Tristan sighed in defeat. "You drive me crazy, do you know that?" His tone was soft, not angry, and I felt that familiar longing. I looked up and saw that he was staring at me.

Before I could respond Tristan cupped my face with one warm hand and lifted my chin as he pressed his lips against mine.

My breath caught. It was as if I were kissing him for the first time. There was so much tenderness and love in that one kiss, I was overwhelmed. I felt that whatever feelings I had for Darien paled in comparison.

He broke the kiss first and leaned his forehead against mine.

"Hey, where's Artemis?" Lexi asked walking into the living room. She was completely oblivious that she was interrupting a moment.

"He was out back last time I saw him," I said. Lexi headed out the back door and came back in a moment later shaking her head.

"I'll try the front," she said and headed out the other way. I looked back at Tristan and saw that he was smiling at me.

"What?" I asked, pushing him away teasingly.

"You forgive me," he stated as a fact.

"Do I have a choice?" I retorted. "I'm a sucker, I'm hooked," I admitted, only part of me feeling stupid for the truth of the statement.

Tristan laughed.

"I have no idea where he is this time," Lexi said coming back in the house. "If you see him, tell him lunch is almost ready."

"Will do," I said, "though he's probably just having his alone time. If he's not back in a few hours, I'll go get him."

A few hours passed, and Artemis hadn't returned. I waited another hour before getting completely restless. I tried calling him telepathically and he didn't respond. Normally I didn't panic when Artemis went out, but it wasn't like him to ignore my call. I felt like we had been getting closer lately, and I wanted to make sure he was alright.

"I'm going to find Artemis," I said, as I headed outside.

"You going to teleport?" Tristan asked concerned.

"Yeah, same thing I did yesterday. He can't teleport, so he couldn't have gone far. Then again, we found him at one of the farthest Cemeteries the other day so, who knows?" I furrowed my brows and shrugged.

"Let me come with you," Tristan said, standing so close to me I could feel his body heat. The front yard was deserted, the darkness quickly descending.

"Don't worry, I'll be fine. I will be back before you blink." I kissed Tristan's cheek and teleported.

I found myself in a dark room with no light whatsoever, and I almost hyperventilated until I heard him.

"Selena," Artemis said, his voice sounded weak.

"Artemis, are you okay?" I asked rushing toward the sound.

"No, go," he said.

"What? Why--?" I was blinded by a bright light. It took a minute for my eyes to adjust, but when they did, I saw Artemis tied up on the concrete floor. The walls were white and bare, the exposed bulb hung from a wire in the ceiling. The room was empty except for Jeremiah smiling over Artemis.

"How nice of you to join us, Selena! I must admit it took you longer than I thought," he said smugly. I clenched my jaw. I had to get out of here and go back to Tristan. We could come up with a plan to save Artemis again. I was about to teleport when I saw that Jeremiah was holding a knife to Artemis' throat.

"You're not leaving so soon, are you?" He said as he pressed the blade into Artemis's flesh.

"Run, Selena. You can't save me!" Artemis gasped. I knew he was probably right, but I also knew that I would never forgive myself if I didn't at least try.

"Don't hurt him," I said uneasily. "I'll stay. We can...chat."

Jeremiah barked a laugh. "I don't want to chat. I want you to pay for stealing my psychic!"

"So how will killing your psychic make me pay exactly?" I asked sarcastically.

"I know how much you would enjoy another death on your conscience," Jeremiah snarled.

I looked at Artemis and saw no fear in his eyes, only frustration that I was still there. I swallowed back a sob and started to teleport.

"No! Run," Artemis said as I started the process, but it was too late. I slammed into that unfortunately familiar barrier and completely lost my bearings. I groaned as my eyes opened and I found myself on my back.

Jeremiah stood next to Artemis laughing. My head spun and I felt disoriented.

"So tell me, old friend, what will happen now?" Jeremiah asked.

"Now you will try to get information out of me, but I will not tell you anything, and you will kill me," Artemis said matter-of-factly. I gasped at the possibility.

"Perhaps you are right. Though you are worth more to me alive than dead, I feel I have no more need for you. I have what I want, and once I conduct the ritual tonight, I will be unstoppable. Isn't that right?" He asked Artemis.

Artemis looked straight at me, and said nothing. Jeremiah growled in frustration and moved the blade from Jeremiah's throat to his back.

"I can stab you; cause you a lot of pain without killing you. It will give you plenty of time to tell me that I will be victorious!" Jeremiah gloated.

"Believe what you want, but only I know what will happen,"

Artemis said. I could see Jeremiah's patience wearing thin and knew that Artemis could be right; he could die today. I willed the knife to fly away from Jeremiah's grasp but nothing happened.

Artemis shook his head sadly. I tried again, and still nothing. I tried calling the elements, doing anything, but nothing worked. It was like the holding room where Crystal and Yuri tortured me. My powers were blocked here. How was I able to even begin teleporting? I looked around and realized I had been close to the door when I tried to leave. It mustn't be blocked outside this room. Maybe if I inched back I could feed off the area outside. I took a step back, then another. Reaching behind me I tried to turn the knob but it was locked. Hoping I was close enough to the outer room I tried to cast again, but still nothing worked. I wished I had my gun, I knew exactly where it was; on my night stand where I left it last night.

"I will give you one more chance. Tell me that I will succeed!" Jeremiah stormed.

"I could tell you that, but you wouldn't know if it was the truth or not," Artemis said calmly. I wondered why he wouldn't just tell Jeremiah what he wanted, so he wouldn't get hurt. "You are losing your mind, aren't you? I knew this would happen eventually," Artemis taunted. "Soon you will be as crazy as me." He laughed.

"Tell me!" Jeremiah boomed.

"No," Artemis said quietly, all humor gone. Jeremiah drove the blade into Artemis's back, and the man gasped in pain as he fell forward.

"No!" I screamed. I was frozen in place by shock.

"Have it your way," Jeremiah said, wiping his blade on

Artemis's shirt. "Selena, take note of what happens when you don't cooperate." I couldn't let him get away with that. I wouldn't. I snapped out of my panicked state and charged him. Jeremiah's shock was evident as he went down. I was about to pummel him when arms pulled me up and off of Jeremiah.

"Let me go!" I screamed, trying to squirm out of the confining grasp.

Jeremiah stood and dusted his suit jacket. He shook his head, and gave me a half smile as he strode past me and through the door. The guard released me and left, closing and locking the door behind him.

Oh God, not again.

I rushed to Artemis and rolled him onto his side making sure he was still alive.

"Selena," he whispered. "I'm sorry I couldn't tell you."

"Shh, don't worry about that now. I understand my friends could have died if you did." I brushed the matted hair back from his forehead. When I pulled his shirt up to assess the damage, I gasped.

Scars overlapped across the entirety of his back, some vertical, some horizontal.

"I...told you...no one would want...to see me with...my shirt off," Artemis joked weakly.

"What is this from?" I asked.

"Jeremiah was very...persuasive with... his whip," Artemis wheezed. I shook my head and tried to hold back the tears that threatened to fall. I looked at his fresh wound.

"It's only...a matter of...time...now," Artemis said.

"No, no, don't talk like that. Tristan was waiting for me

when I left. He'll know something went wrong, and he'll come for us. He'll save us."

"Yes, he will save…you. But I will be gone long…before then," Artemis said. I ripped a piece of my shirt and held it over his wound, knowing that it wouldn't really help, but I needed to feel like I was doing something.

"Please, help me onto…my back."

I did as he asked and held his head in my lap.

"Selena, you are…everything that I thought…you would be. You can…beat him if you just…believe in yourself." Artemis coughed and blood sputtered from his mouth. I wiped it away. "Know you will succeed…and know that…whatever you choose will be…the right…choice." He coughed more, spattering the light concrete floor with red.

"I'm sorry I didn't save you," I said, allowing the tears to flow now.

"You…did." Artemis closed his eyes and released his final breath. I held him sobbing over his still form. No one came in. No one bothered me. I was left alone with only my grief for company.

21. GONE

-TRISTAN-

What the hell was I thinking letting Selena go alone? She had only been gone for ten minutes, but it made me worry since she was so sure she would come back right away.

What was worse was when I tried telepathically comm.-unicating with her, she didn't respond. I tried her cell too, but found that she had left it in her room, along with her gun. How the hell was I supposed to find her? I should tell the others, but maybe I was overreacting. I walked back and forth between the house and the front yard waiting for her. After another two minutes I ran my hand roughly through my hair and went inside.

"Did you find him?" Lexi asked.

"No and Selena's been gone a while. I'm worried something bad happened," I admitted. The others looked up from their dinner, no one daring to say anything.

"Did you try calling her?" Genevieve asked.

"Yes, her cell is upstairs and she's not answering me telepathically. She said she would be right back; why isn't she back yet?" I yelled.

Lexi placed her hand on my arm, "Don't worry. I'm sure she's fine. Remember yesterday she spent the whole day at the beach with Artemis? She's probably found him in some beautiful place and got caught up in it."

I nodded my head, "Yeah, maybe, but she said she would be right back. She knew I was waiting for her. Yesterday she told you where she was. Why wouldn't she do that now?" I paced the small kitchen.

Suddenly the Ouija box on top of the fridge flew onto the floor, popped open and spilled its contents. The board fell face up and the cursor fell directly in the middle of it. The cursor began moving on its own, spinning and pointing at the letters so fast I couldn't form the words in my head.

"Someone get a pen and paper, quick!" I ordered. Seconds later, the objects were thrust into my hands. I wrote down each letter as it appeared, not bothering to try and figure out what each word was. The letters I wrote down connected into a long line, and then a few lines. Finally the cursor stopped.

We waited for a few minutes to make sure there was nothing else I had to write and then I looked at the pad with my messy scrawl on it.

DEADJEREMIAHTOOKMESELENATRAPPEDNEWCA
MPINFRONTIERFORESTSELENATHEREIMSORRY

I decrypted the message and almost dropped the pad.

"What did it say?" Lexi asked quietly.

"Someone's dead. Jeremiah took me? I'm not sure and Selena is trapped. The new camp is in Frontier Forest, and that's where Selena is. Then they said, 'I'm sorry.'"

"Who's dead? Who's sorry?" Fay asked panicked.

The cursor on the board moved quickly again, and I jotted down the letters. There were only seven. The seven letters I missed in the beginning.

ARTEMIS

"Artemis is dead," I whispered, 'Jeremiah took me. I'm sorry.' Sorry he couldn't tell us probably. I saw the sadness on the faces of my friends, and only then let the full realization hit me. Artemis had been caught and killed, and Selena could be next.

"We need to tell the Elders right now," Lexi stammered. "We need to go after Jeremiah, and we need to get Selena back before he performs the ritual."

"He could do it tonight," John said. "We may not get there in time."

"Then we have to go now!" Lexi stood abruptly. "Lachlan, call the Fideles. Tristan, teleport to the courthouse and tell the Elders. Then come back here and teleport us one by one to Frontier Forest." When I just stood there staring, trying to grasp what was happening, Lexi yelled, "GO!"

I snapped into action and did what she ordered. I ran outside the cottage and teleported as soon as I thought it was safe. I landed smack in the middle of the courthouse lobby. It was still early evening, plenty of people around, so there was no need for the security systems to be on yet thankfully.

I ran to the first clerk I saw, "Elder Victoria. Call Elder Victoria right now!" I yelled. The clerk stared wide-eyed at me, unmoving. "Now!" I yelled again. The clerk blinked and hustled to the phone, dialing numbers so fast his fingers were a blur.

"Y-yes, hello, um there is a man here demanding I call-" I took the phone from his hand.

"Victoria. It's Tristan. They have her and we know where the camp is," I said sternly. She didn't speak, and I didn't hear the phone click. I suddenly saw her before my eyes.

"We have to move fast," she said, and I nodded in agreement.

"Go to Frontier Forest," I said. "I am going back to my friends, and I will teleport them there."

"No. Teleport everyone here and we will go together," Victoria instructed.

My temper rose, but before I could say anything she continued. "I know you care for Selena, but you can't act rashly. Wait for us, and we will figure out a way to get her out."

"What about the Fideles? They can't all converge here."

"Keep them on stand-by."

"Fine." I teleported back to the cottage and stormed through the front door.

"What happened?" Lexi asked.

"The Elders know, and they will send their militia there. I have to teleport you all to the courthouse, and then we have to wait for Victoria to tell us what to do next," I rambled.

"Good, let's go," Lexi said. I knew she was just as worried about Selena as I was. We all were. I teleported her first, knowing she would feel better being there.

Then, one by one, I took Genevieve, Lachlan, John and Fay. We stood huddled in the courthouse lobby, trying to figure out what to do next. How long would we have to wait for Victoria and the others? What would they do to help Selena? We didn't have time to wait, we had to act now! I was too worried about Selena to think straight, and I mentally chided myself for my stupidity. I had been trained to protect Selena, to deal with stressful and intense situations, and in a moment of worry over the girl I loved, I forgot everything.

I had to tell myself to be smart. There was nothing we could do now but wait for the Elders. That was the smart thing to do. I just hoped I wouldn't lose my mind in the process.

22. VISITORS
-SELENA-

"Selena." When I looked up, I saw Darien closing the door behind him as he walked into the room. He rushed toward me and knelt in front of me, holding my face in his hands. "Are you okay?"

I jerked my head away. "Just fantastic," I mumbled.

"I'm sorry about this, all of this."

"Yeah, I'm sure you are."

"I am, really. I never meant for him to get this far."

"What are you talking about?"

"I've been..." Darien paused, chewing over the words. "I decided a short while ago that I didn't want to help Jeremiah anymore. I know you won't believe me, but I've had a change of heart. I suppose that would be the best way to describe it."

"Right. Yeah, I believe that. That's why you set Yuri and Crystal on us and allowed them to tear me up. I'm sure you were trying hard not to help Jeremiah," I seethed.

Darien flinched at my words. "I did send them, but only so they could get you to us, to me. They weren't supposed to hurt you."

"Right, just torture me, kill my best friend and your brother. That's what their plan was, right? They could play with them as long as they shipped me back to you guys."

"They weren't supposed to hurt you. As for the rest, yes," he confirmed. I shook my head in disgust. "I was there that day. I came to stop them, but I was too late."

"What is this? You're...what? Trying to show me you're a good guy? You sent me bats, and bugs. You tormented me, tried to make me jump off a roof. I'm not buying."

"I'm not proud of what I've done. Jeremiah told me to do certain things and I blindly followed. Most of it before I spent time with you at the camp. After I got to know you more and especially with the information you gave me last night, I've thought twice about my alliance with Jeremiah.

"Look, I'm not evil, but I am selfish, and I did want you all for myself. I tried the best way I knew how, but I guess I went about it all wrong. I just didn't want to lose you."

"You never had me," I whispered.

Darien nodded and stood. "Yeah, I guess Tristan wins again."

"Wins? I'm not a prize! Tristan is good and kind and takes care of me. All you ever did was hurt me. You don't deserve me."

"You're right," Darien said and dropped his gaze to the floor. "What can I do?"

I glared at him, "How about you get me out of here? All of your talk about being changed, well, prove it."

"There are a lot of people out there," he said. "It's not as easy as you think."

"That's what I thought." I looked back down to the man on my lap.

"Maybe I should…" Darien started as he made his way toward me and Artemis again. He bent to move the body.

"Don't you touch him," I snarled. Darien stepped back reflexively, hands raised in surrender.

He left without another word. I sat staring at the lifeless body of my friend, trusting his words that Tristan would save me and that it would be sooner rather than later.

The door opened again, and my head snapped up.

"Darien go-" I started, but it wasn't Darien at the door. A woman stood just inside the doorway, her black hair hung straight to her collar bone, her blue eyes slightly lighter than mine, but she had a gleam in them I didn't like. Her full lips turned up into a half smile. I had seen her before, in Lexi's vision.

Stefania.

"I guess you're not all that powerful after all. Or maybe it's not your weakness, just your stupidity that landed you in here," she said, eyes darting around the room. I gently moved Artemis off my lap and stood to face her. She looked down at the old man and faked a pout. "Aw, poor psychic didn't see his death coming?" She let out a laugh.

"Why are you like this? It can't be all about jealousy," I analyzed.

"Jealousy? You don't even know who I am!" She boomed.

"I know who you are, Stefania," I said. Her eyes flashed with anger, probably mad that she didn't have the element of surprise.

"What the hell do I have to be jealous of?"

"Me," I said confidently.

"Ha! You're nothing, not even powerful enough to foresee getting trapped here."

"Okay," I said, knowing my lack of response would taunt her.

"You are weak! You don't even defend yourself. How could I ever be jealous of you?" She continued.

"I don't know. You tell me."

She scoffed, but said nothing.

I smiled, but spoke very calmly. "Here, let me help you out. You're jealous because I got Tristan, because my powers are so bad ass and the only reason you're still alive is because this room has prevented me from using them on you. You're jealous because all your life you thought you were the one, wanted to be, but knew deep down inside you weren't good enough."

Stefania's face reddened, her hands clenched into fists and unclenched, shaking with rage. I took a step closer to her, knowing it wasn't the wisest choice; if she was this angry she could easily lash out. But I knew I could take her, and was very tempted to right then.

I stepped forward, just a few steps away from the door and pondered running past her instead. As I took another step though, I hit an invisible barrier that wasn't there before. It didn't hurt, but it forced me to step back. I reeled in my frustration.

Stefania cocked a half-smile at me.

Oh, so it was going to be like that.

"What's the matter?" I asked. "Scared you just might be wrong and that I am strong enough to take you down, even without my powers?"

"Hardly." She eyed me up and down.

"Figured you'd be too scared to try." I looked at my nails, feigning indifference. I started to turn away from her, to let her think I had my guard down.

She lashed out then, crying out in anger and crossing the barrier that separated us. She threw a punch at me, but I turned and blocked it and countered with my own, landing it on her jaw with such force her head jerked sideways. Unfortunately it didn't break her neck.

Even more unfortunate were the guards that came into the room right after she screamed. She kicked and yelled at them and I tried to escape again, but the barrier was still firmly in place, hindering only me as the others moved freely through it. Jeremiah strode through the door and placed his hand on Stefania's shoulder.

"Now is not the time," he whispered and she relaxed instantly, allowing him and the guards to escort her out of the room and close the door behind them.

Great, so she was under Jeremiah's spell. I suppose that would explain her instant hatred towards me. Then again that spell can also enhance what was already in place.

I sat cross-legged on the floor beside Artemis, and Stefania's words came back to me. '*Poor psychic didn't see his death coming?*' But he had. He was always admiring the view, nature, that gorgeous beach. He told me life was too short, that I shouldn't rush things. He ate whatever he craved - a morbid last supper maybe. He told me to appreciate my friends, enjoy their company while I could. He knew. All those times I saw sadness flash across his face for a moment. He knew he was going to die.

I placed my head in my hands and cried. Was there nothing I could have done to save him? Was there really no scenario he could have seen that would have gotten us all out of this alive? A vision flashed before my eyes and I gasped. What had I just seen? I tried to focus on remembering the quick vision, and it was as if a flood gate had been opened.

I suddenly saw a slew of images, and it took me a minute to realize what I was seeing.

Then I understood: I was seeing all the scenarios Artemis had talked about. If he had told me what was going to happen to him, we would have tried to prevent him from getting taken in the first place. Like Artemis said, had we done that, Lachlan would have been killed trying to fight off one of the witches who came after him. The next scenario was if I had brought Tristan with me to save him; Tristan would have been killed when Jeremiah called his guards. Tristan would have rushed into the fight before I had a chance to, and would have been out-numbered.

It went on this way, every idea that I could come up with to prevent Artemis' death resulted in one of my friends dying, and Artemis always died in the end anyway. There was nothing I could have done. Artemis was right, as usual. But how was I able to know that, to see that? Clearly the room blocked powers but Jeremiah had Artemis here, wanting the use of his visions so maybe there was some alteration to the spell to allow that.

I needed to counteract the spell. I remembered Tristan defiling the spell in the last Eter room we were in with a pen, but I found nothing in this confined space to use. I searched my pockets for anything with a point or sharp edge, but I had nothing on me. I couldn't even see where the spell was hidden in these walls.

The door clanked open again snapping me out of my thoughts and my blood boiled. What now? They already had me, did they have to keep bothering me?

Two guards came in and reached for Artemis.

"No!" I yelled. "Leave him alone!" I threw myself over his body.

The guards carried on as if they hadn't heard me, easily moving me out of the way. I beat against their arms, to release my friend, but they didn't stop. I rushed forward and punched one of the guards as hard as I could. He dropped Artemis's legs and reached for his bloody nose as he cursed. The other guard dropped Artemis and came after me. He tackled me to the ground, my head smacking against the hard concrete floor. They regained their composure quickly and took Artemis out of the room. My head swam as I stood to follow, but another guard came and pushed me back in the room, knowing I would hit the barrier before he closed and locked the door again.

I was completely alone now. Even though Artemis was dead, I had a morbid sense of company. Now I didn't even have that.

"The time has come, Selena," Jeremiah said as he came into the room sometime later.

"The time for what exactly?" I sounded as tired as I felt. I was emotionally exhausted.

"The ritual. I'm sure Artemis told you all about it, but I found out recently that I don't have to wait any longer. I can do it tonight, right now!" His eyes gleamed with anticipation.

"What do you need me for?"

"I need your presence in the circle, so your power can be leeched, and then I will need your blood."

"So you're going to sacrifice me then?" I asked. I was amazed at how calmly I spoke of my own death.

"No, no death involved, just a little blood. Your life depends on what you do after the ritual. Fight with me and we will be unstoppable. We will take over the Hidden City and then move on to the world. But fight against me, and I will kill you."

"You will try," I said with confidence.

"Sure, sure," Jeremiah said, not really taking in my words, or what they could mean. "I see you've already met Stefania. Seems you didn't hit it off." He smiled.

I stayed quiet, not really sure what he wanted me to say.

"I know you don't want to die today, but she will try to kill you after the ritual. It would be a shame to lose your abilities, especially when they could benefit me so."

Did he really think that by warning me against Stefania he would gain my trust? This man was delusional.

"What if I decide not to participate?" I asked.

Anger flashed in Jeremiah's eyes. All signs of the kind ally gone. "You don't have a choice. You will either join the ritual on your own, or I will force you."

"Force me how?" I dared ask.

"You saw Artemis's scars, I know you did." He pointed to a small, black globe hovering in the corner of the room. I clenched my jaw in anger. How had I not seen the camera? He had watched my reactions to my visitors, watched me cry over

Artemis. But could he hear me? Darien spoke freely with me – did he not know there was a camera? Or did he know he couldn't be heard? Maybe it was all just an act, set up by Jeremiah, starring Darien and the weak victim…me.

"So you're going to whip me into submission then?" My mind whirred with the possibility of torture and wondered how much I could take before I broke. Would I actually have to agree to go or would he incapacitate me and just put me in place like a pawn?

"Not necessarily, but I do have means of persuasion. You met Crystal and Yuri," Jeremiah said smugly. Was he actually going to imply that they were here? Use them as a threat?

"You can't threaten me with them."

"Oh?" Jeremiah asked, still smiling.

"I killed them. I turned them into ash. Incinerated them from the inside out." My voice sounded strange to me; half boasting I killed his minions, half sadistic joy.

"Crystal and Yuri had methods of torture I'm sure you remember," he said finally, neither denying nor admitting to my claim. Though I'm sure he knew the truth. Knew his pet psychopaths were dead. "Regardless of who is administering the pain, you will still feel it."

The question was whether I should endure the torture. I could participate or he could make me. Was it worth the fight?

Absolutely.

"Well, let's test that theory then. I believe that the torturer does make a difference. Who do you have in mind? We can compare notes." Sarcasm seeped from my voice, but that was better than fear.

Jeremiah's lip twitched in irritation. "Have it your way. I do need your blood; the means by which I gain it is irrelevant." He snarled and left the room.

I remained cross-legged on the floor, and decided I should try to meditate. Now that I knew Jeremiah was watching me, I needed him to see that I was perfectly calm. If I meditated, hopefully I could keep myself relaxed and try to clear my head from the thoughts of torture that were trying to haunt me.

I needed to center myself the way Tristan had taught me, to mentally prepare in hopes that when I got hurt, I wouldn't show it. I wouldn't give them the satisfaction.

I had maybe ten minutes of mental clarity before they came for me. Jeremiah wasn't wasting any time. Three of his guards came in, and I just stared at them, waiting for them to make the first move.

It was fast and swift. Two of the guards walked slowly toward me from the front while the third came at me from the side. I didn't have a chance to do anything before I was knocked unconscious.

23. UNBREAKABLE

When I came to, I was tied to a wooden plank outside in the middle of camp. The plank was set up so that I was somewhat upright, on a makeshift stage, visible to the growing crowd around me.

There were straps across my shoulders, waist and ankles. I couldn't move really, except my head. I turned it side to side to gain my bearings. I was outside though, so I could use my powers. I tried a small command, something that would go unnoticed; I tried to snap a small branch from a nearby tree but nothing happened. I strained again, but I was unable to do what I willed.

"You seem to be concentrating awfully hard." Jeremiah stepped beside me. "You wouldn't be trying to use magic, would you?"

I stared straight ahead, completely ignoring him. "You can't see it, but trust me when I say there are binding markings on this fine piece of wood you are on. It prevents you from using your magic, like the room did. Once you have agreed to participate, I will release you from it and put you directly in the ritual circle where you can do no harm," Jeremiah whispered.

No harm. Wait till he sees how much *harm* I can do. I continued to stare straight ahead and act as though he hadn't said anything.

Jeremiah moved to stand in front of me, facing the crowd.

"I thought you all might enjoy seeing this. Selena has chosen not to help in our mission, so we will have to change her mind." He gestured for one of the witches to come forward. At seeing this very large man walk onto the makeshift stage, the crowd cheered. So he had a reputation.

Fantastic.

He wielded a very odd looking dagger. The tip sprouted into a split-pronged end, reminding me of a snake tongue.

There is no pain, there is no pain, there is no pain! I mentally chided to myself.

"Theodore, show this crowd that Selena isn't as strong as she thinks she is," Jeremiah commanded. Theodore chuckled. Had he not been about to dismember me, I might have thought he was handsome. He was well over six feet tall, tan complexion, built body and his brown hair hung just above his shoulders.

However, seeing as he was walking toward me with this macabre knife, I could only think of him as an ogre.

I closed my eyes and held them shut, not wanting to know how close Theodore was getting to me. For that moment, I was able to pretend I was somewhere else, somewhere far away. I reveled in a memory of the beautiful water of Paradise Beach.

I tried to hold onto that memory, but when I felt the cold metal slice through the flesh of my arm, I was thrown into another memory, a nightmare of Crystal and Yuri. I guess Jeremiah was right; the pain is the same even if the tormentor is not. Still I tried to block it out.

"Make sure you don't waste the blood," Jeremiah instructed. "I need it for the ritual. I'm sure the more we have, the better it will work. Also, make sure you don't kill her. She needs to be alive and conscious when I cast the spell."

I kept my eyes shut and was glad that Theodore was slicing the meaty part of my arm. He seemed to be more intent on drawing blood than causing me pain.

It was the shuffling going on that made me open my eyes. Theodore was holding the blade above me, but his attention was on the crowd.

To my shocked surprise, Darien was fighting to get through the onlookers. He pushed his way onto the stage and stood toe-to-toe with Theodore.

"What are you doing?" Darien yelled.

"Persuading her," Theodore explained.

"You don't have to torture her! All you need is her blood and her presence. Tie her up in the circle and perform the ritual," Darien argued.

"Darien, are you having a change of heart?" Jeremiah sneered.

"I don't see the necessity."

"We need her to cooperate, so she won't use her magic or do anything to affect the results of the ritual."

"Again, you could just tie her up. Once she's part of the ritual she won't be able to do anything to ruin it." Darien looked pensive. "You're just making an example of her, aren't you? Trying to show that you can hurt her just because." The disgust on Darien's face was unmistakable, and I was caught off guard by his action to defend me.

"Darien, this doesn't concern you. Theodore, carry on," Jeremiah ordered. Then he waved his hand and a group of men restrained Darien. He struggled against them, but didn't get far. Darien created a whirlwind that blew viciously, but a witch tackled him and the other men ganged up on him.

I closed my eyes again wanting to block this whole thing out. Theodore continued, and although I was screaming and crying in my head I didn't break. I didn't give in to Jeremiah, I didn't scream, I didn't make a sound.

"Why isn't it working?" Jeremiah said in hushed tones to Theodore.

"I don't know, she's just not normal," Theodore said almost in awe. By this point, both my arms had been sliced, the warm blood dripping down my sides, and Theodore was starting on my legs.

"Do something more extreme," Jeremiah hissed.

"What do you suggest?"

"Fingernails."

Oh. My. God.

Theodore followed the order and I felt the tip of pliers grasp the top of my nail. It took every ounce of restraint not to scream, whimper or pass out. I held my breath so I wouldn't be tempted to make any noise and show how much I was hurting. And I was really hurting. The pain was excruciating as he peeled the nail off my pinky. I think I did pass out at one point, but it didn't last longer than a moment.

The crowd started to boo and I opened my eyes - which were wet from the tears I was trying desperately not to shed - to see that many of them began to disperse. Darien was nowhere to be seen. Jeremiah's plan had backfired. Instead of showing that I was weak and would break, it showed them how strong I was.

I looked at Jeremiah and smiled. I could tell he was stopping himself from attacking me; he couldn't kill me or his precious ritual wouldn't work.

"Take her to the circle," he hissed to some nearby witches. I prayed they would untie me and let me off this board, so I could unleash my full power on them.

Instead they wheeled me, board attached, to a clearing in the forest. I felt like Hannibal Lector, only missing the mask that would prevent me from eating everyone.

As we neared the clearing, I saw that there was a pentacle burned into the dried grass. About thirty feet away was a small cemetery – headstones shot up from the ground sporadically. I rummaged through my memory to figure out which cemetery this was, but I came up blank. It must have been the last one, the one we didn't search.

Standing at one point of the pentacle was Stefania. She took in my bloodied appearance and snarled; clearly she was as disappointed as Jeremiah that I didn't show my pain. In the center of the pentacle was a black, satin cloth with a jar of dried herbs and a jar of liquid on it. Jeremiah walked there and placed a half full jar with the other items. It didn't take me long to realize it was full of blood. My blood.

Darien had been right; Jeremiah didn't need my permission to be in the ritual, he just needed my presence, willing or not. He had been trying to make me look weak, and I was proud as all hell that I made him fail.

I was set up at the point of the pentacle across from Stefania. Jeremiah stood between us and started his incantation. A circle of fire burst forth and surrounded the pentacle. The onlookers had come back and were watching the spectacle. Jeremiah lifted the vial of dried herbs and started sprinkling it within the star, and as he chanted words I didn't understand, I felt a strong wind sweep through the circle of fire.

"Untie her!" Jeremiah called. Within seconds a pair of hands had unfastened the straps holding me to the board and I fell to the ground. I threw out my hands to protect myself from the fall but they buckled under me, too injured to keep me up. I crawled onto all fours, but the pain in my limbs was becoming unbearable.

I wanted to use my magic, stop this ritual from happening, but the strong wind drained me and I wasn't able to. I now understood my purpose for the ritual; the sweeping wind was using my energy, my power to fuel the spell.

Darien was right again; once I was part of the ritual I couldn't do anything. Jeremiah had me tortured for show and that pissed me off. I just couldn't do anything about it. Jeremiah raised his arms above his head as he yelled more foreign words. I looked at Stefania and saw the reflection of the fire in her eyes as she smiled. Stupid bitch. She dropped to her knees shortly after as the circle started to take her power too.

I sat on my haunches and almost yelped as the change in position stretched the sliced flesh on my thighs. I moved again and sat cross-legged on the ground. I hated that I was so useless, that all I could do was watch as Jeremiah stole power from the dead.

The flames flickered as I looked out at the crowd, and I shook my head, not believing my eyes. I closed them for a moment and then opened them as I tried to see past the hot flames. Tristan stood, half concealed behind a large oak. My heart raced at the sight of him. He was here to save me.

I saw him motion to the surrounding trees and knew that there were others hiding behind them as well. I would have smiled if I had the energy.

Tristan crouched and inched closer toward the pentacle. Still out of sight, he raised his hands, sparks flying from them and hitting the wind barrier, but it did nothing to phase the ritual.

I'm fine, I sent mentally to Tristan, but I had no idea if it went through with the ritual draining my powers.

The wind continued to gust, whirling around my hair and taking my powers with it. On the other side of the pentacle I saw the ground of the Cemetery shake.

The tombstones shattered and toppled and the grounds rose and shifted. Through the cracks in the earth a purple mist emerged and made its way slowly toward us. Jeremiah opened another vial, this one containing a purple liquid. He spattered it on the ground around Stefania and then around me. Then he took the jar of my blood. He sprinkled some on the ground on each of the points of the pentacle, and then, to my astonishment and disgust, Jeremiah drank the remainder of my blood, leaving the jar empty, only the smear of my blood around its insides.

Jeremiah took the Herkimer diamond out of his pocket and stood in the center of the pentacle, arms outstretched towards the heavens as he yelled his enchantment. The purple mist crawled toward the pentacle and extinguished the flames as it entered the circle. Smoke surrounded us, and the purple mist hung above the ground at Jeremiah's ankles.

Jeremiah said the final words and then grew quiet as the mist was absorbed into his skin, starting at his feet and moving its way up until it was completely consumed. Jeremiah let out a sigh of utter satisfaction and opened his eyes.

The gusting wind settled, and I was able to feel my powers returning. While everyone was distracted by the ritual's success, I sat quietly, healing my wounds. The blood was still smeared on my skin, so no one would notice I was healed without getting a really good look. Finally easing away my pain, I thought of how to dismember Jeremiah.

I wanted to attack, but I had to be smart. There was no way to know how strong he was now. He could kill me with a flick of his wrist for all I knew. He reveled in his power, and I struggled to crawl away undetected, hoping to get to Tristan and come up with a plan. Unfortunately Stefania was watching me and wasn't about to let me get away – not after I humiliated her.

Her eyes blazed as she stood and barely moved her fingers, but the spell hit me square in the chest. I hadn't even seen it coming really. Jeremiah lowered his arms and looked from Stefania to me. The look in his eyes was 'I told you so.' So now I either fought Stefania and Jeremiah or with them?

Well that was easy. I stood, showing that I was no longer injured and sent a miniature version of a sphere-shield spell at her, throwing her backwards. The crowd looked around anxiously; were they supposed to help one over the other or just watch? They faced Jeremiah for guidance but since he just stood there watching, they watched as well. No doubt Jeremiah wanted to see who would be the victor.

In my peripheral vision I saw Tristan gather the others. I took a longer glance and saw how many of them there were closing in around the crowd. Tristan stood with Lexi, Genevieve, Lachlan, John and Fay. Victoria came out with ten of the Elders and Lexi's parents; Angela and Mark stood close to their daughter. With them was an older woman with a tight, gray bun on her head, and glasses hanging on a chain around her neck, and...my Sensei? He was a witch too? I looked at this group of people with awe and pride. Even the old woman was going to fight. Then I took in the army. All together I would guess there were over a hundred witches there - enough to match Jeremiah's army.

I refocused on Stefania, who had regained her composure and was preparing her own attack. I focused my powers onto the sky and smiled in satisfaction when I saw the lightning crackle through it, and then I heard the familiar rumble of thunder and felt it through my bones. Stefania stood there, mouth agape as she took in the sight.

As if a cue for the Elders, when the thunder struck, so did they. They surrounded the crowd and began to fight. A surprised Jeremiah stood motionless for a moment as he took in the scene before him.

The Elders, along with my friends and their army and what I assumed were the Fideles, ambushed Jeremiah's pawns. Jeremiah's men were caught off guard and scrambled un-organized, trying to figure out what to do. Stefania refocused first and cast a spell that pushed me back. I held my ground and needed to decide right away if I was going to kill her or not. I could end this quickly if I chose to kill her. She wasn't a very nice person, but she was under Jeremiah's control, so did that mean she deserved to die?

I threw a whirlwind at her and it caught her off balance, throwing her onto the ground, buying me some time to decide her fate.

Stefania bounced back and raised the dirt, pelting rocks at me, but I blocked them all. I looked to where Jeremiah had been standing, but he was no longer there. Did he run away from the army? I found that hard to believe if his spell worked. If he took the powers of all the dead witches, he was as strong as his army combined. He could end this very quickly. I had to stop wasting time with Stefania and get my friends to safety.

"Stefania, stop this. You don't have to fight me. We could work together!" I yelled across the pentacle as I blocked one of her shock spells.

Stefania laughed, "Oh yeah, sure, savior Selena come to convert the evil Stefania! I don't think so. I don't want anything to do with you, and once I kill you, it will be easy to forget you ever existed." She threw a fireball at me and I dodged it, but barely. It singed part of my shirt.

So she was definitely trying to kill me then. Well that made my decision easier.

"You won't kill me," I yelled. "You can keep trying, but you'll fail. So it's up to you. Die now, or fight with me and save the city from Jeremiah."

"Oh my God, you are so predictable." Stefania rolled her eyes. "I would rather die than fight on your side." She threw another fireball at me, and again I dodged.

I wanted to say, "Done." And send a spell that would throw her backwards and block out her screams as she burned from the inside out, but I couldn't. I knew what it was like to be under Jeremiah's control, and I couldn't blame her entirely for her behavior. I lifted my hands, and Stefania levitated in the air with the motion. Her eyes widened in surprise as she kicked her feet trying to find ground. I resisted the urge to laugh. I flicked my wrists and she went flying, her head cracked on the ground as she landed, rendering her unconscious.

I ran from the pentacle toward where Tristan had been. The crowd was thick, everyone was fighting, and some took cover behind the trees as they shot off spells at each other. Sparks, elements and bodies flew in a whirlwind of color and chaos. There were already a few bodies strewn about lifelessly. It was such a waste. All these people were fighting for what, for Jeremiah and his quest for power? Stupid.

I pushed my way through until I saw Tristan fighting another witch. I ran forward, elbowed the witch in the face, knocked him unconscious and threw my arms around a stunned Tristan.

He wrapped his arms tightly around me and kissed me quickly but fiercely. He pulled me away and took in my bloody appearance, his eyes widening in worry.

"What happened?" He asked observing the damage and then furrowing his eyebrows when he found none.

"I healed myself. Jeremiah thought it would make a nice show to torture me in front of everyone."

"That son of a bitch!" Tristan yelled. He threw a whirl wind spell at an attacking witch who dodged it. Another witch came for me.

"I know, but listen, I'm fine; I didn't give him the satisfaction of knowing he hurt me. Well, Theodore was the one who hurt me," I said, fighting off my attacker. I threw a fire ball at him and he fell to the ground writhing in pain. Before I could take a breath, another witch was in front of me. Tristan knocked his attacker unconscious. I called the winds and flung them at my newest attacker, sending him flying several yards away.

"Theodore?" He asked, scanning the crowd. It wasn't hard to spot him since he stood a good half foot taller than everyone else. I pointed Theodore out and felt a sense of morbid satisfaction when I saw Tristan smile wickedly at him.

Three more witches cast fireballs at us. I nudged Tristan, redirecting his attention to the fight in time to defend ourselves.

I sent an electric current into two of the attackers, watching them shake as they fell.

"How did you find me?" I asked.

"Artemis told us where you were," he said, making the earth open below his opponent, sucking him in. Tristan's words confused me. Oh, he didn't know yet. I swallowed a sob and lifted my head.

"Artemis is dead. Jeremiah killed him," I said sadly.

"I know. He gave us the message through the Ouija board," Tristan explained.

"The Ouija…?" I processed this and then couldn't help but laugh. That stupid game I hadn't wanted to play with, indirectly saved my life. Artemis really did plan everything.

Tristan kissed my forehead quickly, and I saw Darien standing a few yards away watching our embrace. There was a pained look on his face that I never wanted to see on any other human being. But why? He couldn't possibly care that much for me to be hurt by this. I shook my head to clear my thoughts. There was no time for this.

"You need to go someplace safe," Tristan said.

I laughed, "Give me a break. You know I can handle myself, and everyone needs me. This is my purpose after all."

I saw Theodore in the midst of battle and felt revenge rear its ugly head. I headed toward him. When Tristan realized what I was doing, he grabbed my arm and took the lead.

Tristan smiled and ran toward the crowd. I was curious to see how Theodore would handle pain. Tristan reached him and threw him away from the Elder he was fighting. He caused the earth to shake beneath Theodore, but then found that unsatisfying. Tristan tackled him and punched him in the face.

Theodore shook his head vehemently.

"Did you enjoy it? Huh?" Tristan asked as he continued to pummel the giant man. Theodore retaliated, trying to punch Tristan, then grabbed his arm. Tristan yelled out in pain, a blue mark scarred on his forearm from Theodore's touch. Tristan was forced to back away from his foe. Theodore took advantage of his freedom, stood and shot icicles at Tristan, who kept blocking.

I wasn't sure if I should get involved just yet. It seemed Tristan had a personal vendetta against Theodore that had nothing to do with me.

Tristan made the earth shake again, and a gaping hole spread beneath Theodore's feet. He jumped out of the way before he could fall in.

Tristan's frustration erupted. He grabbed a knife that had been sheathed in a holster at his waist, and flung it at Theodore.

It spun, end over end, the light glinting off its metal surface like a shooting star, and landed squarely in Theodore's chest.

Tristan ran to where Theodore landed, blood oozed from his chest as he tried to gasp for air. Tristan lifted his head from the ground and spun it quickly, and I heard the snap of his neck through the fighting. It was oddly satisfying having Tristan avenge my torture. I hate to say that his violence was attractive to me now, but it was. He was my protector.

Tristan pulled the knife out of Theodore, wiping the blade on his jeans and re-sheathed it. He then turned to fight another witch. I turned and saw Victoria with thorny vines erupting from her hands to wrap around the two men she was fighting and the sight was disconcerting. She seemed so frail and old, and yet she tightened the vines, and severed them within seconds. I needed to do my part. I needed to find Jeremiah.

The earth shook again and I looked to see if Tristan had something to do with that, but he had been trying to keep his balance. I heard a loud groaning and I spun to find the source. I saw movement from the gaping hole among the tombstones. I ran in that direction to get a better look and skidded to a stop once I was close enough.

Grey, rotting hands reached for the edge of the crevice as the bodies of the dead tried to climb out. I froze as they emerged from their resting places. Their clothes were tattered, and some bodies were fresh while others were in a deeper state of decomposition. Some were only bones; their clothes nearly falling off their shoulders. The smell of death permeated the air as these ghoulish beings crawled forward, dragging their limbs.

The groaning I heard was coming from them as they spewed

from the hole in a herd toward the battle. The image in and of itself was horrific, but it was the ones with eyes that froze my insides and raised the hairs on the back of my neck. They were aware. They knew what they were doing, but it didn't look like they could control it. Anger and rage seeped from them all as they made their way to fight for the enemy.

I ran away and through the crowd. Lexi and John fought side by side, Lexi casting her electric current and John shooting fireballs while Fay was in the process of drowning someone nearby.

"Lookout!" I heard Fay yell, and I turned to see her jump in front of Lexi and deflect a fire spell that was coming her way.

"Thanks!" Lexi beamed at Fay, who, surprisingly, smiled back.

Genevieve and Lachlan were fighting together against a group of witches, and I contemplated helping them until I saw Genevieve send a wind spell that blew three of them away, landing on top of each other.

There are zombie witches! I mentally yelled to all my friends, now that I could see where they were.

"What?" Tristan yelled.

I pointed to the area I had just come from, and my friends turned to see the reanimated corpses approaching us.

Lachlan cursed, saying what we were all thinking.

"Mrs. Ledsmith!" Tristan called. I turned and saw a witch converging on an older woman. The old woman cast a lightning bolt, just missing her attacker, but the effort took its toll on her as she bent over to regain her strength. I ran toward her in an attempt to help, but before I could reach her, the witch she was fighting cast a spell I couldn't see, and the old woman fell to the ground, her eyes staring unseeing.

My stomach fell, and I stopped in my tracks. Tristan ran toward her and fell to his knees when he confirmed she was dead. He hung his head sadly.

"Selena!" I heard someone call me, and I turned in time to see a rogue witch moving her hands to cast a spell at me. Iran toward her and punched her as she came within reach and then I levitated a large rock to hit her across the face, sending her to the ground unconscious.

"I see you're still fighting." My head whipped around, and I saw my Sensei standing behind me smiling.

"You're a witch too? Why didn't you say anything?" I asked as I gave him a brief hug.

"Didn't get the chance. Once you found out what you were, you stopped coming to class." He sent me a disapproving look and I averted my gaze guiltily.

"Yeah, sorry about that," I said.

We couldn't talk anymore because witches were attacking from all sides. We all fought together, as dead and living witches came at us.

"We meet again," I heard a low voice, practically in my ear. I spun to see a tall, lanky man standing before me. His hair thinning down the middle, his thin lips turned up in a half smile, but his eyes were cold. Angry. A part of my brain told me I had seen this man before, but I couldn't place it.

He started moving his hands in an elaborate gesture, his body glowing with the motion and the pieces fell into place. I had seen these movements before, at Jeremiah's house. This was the man that we almost didn't escape from.

A grey light shot toward me, and I instinctively moved to block it, but I was too slow. The light surrounded me, cocooning me, and wrapping me tight as it surrounded my body and up to my head. As soon as the pressure began, it was released. I opened my eyes, and had no idea where I was.

24. MISPLACED

I found myself in a clearing, dead grass around me, blue sky above me, and no one around for miles. What the hell? Where the frack did that guy send me? It didn't take me long to realize I was nowhere near the fight. I imagined being back in the battle and teleported.

I materialized right in front of the thin man.

"Ah," he said, as if expecting me. "Now I know what you can do."

I cast a fire spell, flames pouring from my hands in a wave of inferno. He easily deflected my spell and cast another of his own. I tried again to block it, and again I couldn't.

I stood alone in a circular room; solid white walls; white floors, no door. I felt around the walls, but found no seam to indicate I was missing a door.

I growled. I didn't have time for this. I closed my eyes and took a deep breath before teleporting. I felt the familiar pull, and the sadly even more familiar feeling of smacking into a brick wall.

I found myself lying on my back on the white floor.

Oh my God.

How was I going to get out of this? I regained my bearings and sat up. I tested my magic; I was able to cast so this wasn't an Eter room, just one that wouldn't let me out. I slammed against the walls, swept my hands over every inch in case there was a hidden door, but there was nothing.

"Hello!" I called, hoping somehow, someone would hear me. "Hello!" I cried again, even louder.

Laughter filled the room. I spun around but no one was there. "Let me out you son of a bitch!"

The laughter echoed around me a moment more before completely vanishing. I sat in silence.

A low rumbling sounded around me, then grew louder as the room began to shake.

Shit.

I jumped to my feet, on guard but unknowing what for. What was happening? The room contracted and then expanded like an over inflated lung. I braced myself in the middle of the room as it started to constrict.

Tristan! I mentally called. *Can anyone hear me?* Oh please, someone hear me.

The walls slowly pulled in, the space around me shrinking as my fear rose. I couldn't handle small spaces, the word claustrophobia absolutely applied to me and I found myself prematurely hyperventilating.

Selena, where are you? Tristan called back.

Thank God!

I... I don't know. You have to find that guy, the one we saw with Jeremiah at his house. He cast a spell and I ended up here. I sent a visual image of the man along with where I was to

Tristan. *Beat the living shit out of him to find out where he sent me! And hurry! I don't have much time!*

I threw my hands out in front of me, willing the walls to move back.

I sensed a moment of confusion, and then anger coming from Tristan before he said, *You bet your ass I will.* I could sense his frustration and anxiety as he searched, and then, *Found the piece of shit.* I couldn't sense Tristan anymore. I was alone in my mind. Waiting.

Beads of sweat formed on my forehead as the force of my magic pulsed stronger toward the walls. They only moved away marginally, but at least they weren't coming closer. "Come on, Tristan," I said, and pushed harder, grunting with the effort. Would he get the guy to talk? Was there even a way to get me out? How is this even possible? My anger at the man slowly turned into awe. How can I learn to teleport someone else? My strength wavered and the walls started to pull in again, sliding toward me faster as if making up for the inches I had regained. Suddenly the pressure of my spell released and I fell backwards. I screamed, throwing my hands over my head as the walls crashed toward me.

I no longer saw the room, only darkness. I felt I was floating in black oblivion. I couldn't feel my limbs, couldn't see an inch in front of me, I couldn't even hear myself breathing. I was lost, I was nothing, I was no one.

It took less than a second for me to feel terrified of my new surroundings, and then another second before my feet landed on the ground. The loud sound of fighting resumed around me; I was back in the same spot I had been in, Genevieve and Lachlan fighting around me, Li next to me, Tristan holding the thin man a foot off the ground by his neck before me. Tristan choked the man, blood streaming down the man's nose, his eyes rolling as he gasped for air.

Tristan turned at the sound of my landing, saw that I was alright and then turned back to the man. He simply moved his thumb, cracking the man's neck.

"Are you alright?" Tristan asked, dropping the man.

I nodded. "Thanks to you. I don't ever want to be in that situation again."

"Agreed." He ran his thumb along my jaw and then turned back to the fighting.

A zombie inched toward me, its jaw hanging off its face, teeth yellowed, eyes sunken in. It made a wailing noise as it cast a shock spell at me that I deflected. I was surprised it would still have magical abilities.

I cast an icicle spell, pelting the shards of ice at the creature. The skin fell off the bones as the icicles sliced through it, but it kept coming.

"How do I kill it?" I asked.

"I don't know!" Genevieve yelled, fending off her attacker with a wind spell, as another one shot metal spikes at her. She screamed as the spikes hit her arm and side.

"Geni!" Lachlan yelled, trying to escape his attacker.

I created another icicle, but I held it as a knife and rammed it into the dead witch's eye. It stumbled backwards and fell to the ground motionless. I hoped it was dead... again.

I ran toward Genevieve and shot a beam of light at the witch who attacked her, killing him. I crouched next to her, pulling the spikes out, and she clenched her teeth as I did. I placed my hands on her and the holes in her skin sealed themselves. Genevieve took a deep breath and stammered a thank you before allowing me to help her stand.

Lexi and Fay were throwing high-voltage shock spells, killing the witches they fought, and Tristan blocked pelted rocks from his attacker, before getting hit with one across his jaw. Tristan spun, losing his footing and falling to the ground. I rushed toward him, but he was up and fighting before I reached him.

Standing next to Tristan, another zombie witch inched toward me, a spell shooting from its bony fingers. I dodged it, spun around Tristan, took his knife from its sheath on his jeans, and stabbed the corpse in the eye in one swift motion. It too fell to the ground motionless.

"I think stabbing them in the head kills them," I said, pulling Tristan's knife out of the eye socket, and sheathing it.

I heard a grunt from my right and I turned to see Sensei Li drop to his knees.

He gasped and fell over, a pool of blood oozing from his chest. I rushed to him to try and heal him, but he was already dead.

My rage flared and I swept the group of attackers before me, sending them flying a few feet away from my friends. I made the earth shake, and the trees bend until it created a makeshift cell, keeping the attackers blocked from me and my friends. Then I created an inverted sphere shield that contained all the witches and their spells within.

I had to stop this before any more people died. I had to find

Jeremiah. I ran through the forest, leaving the others to finish up where they were.

Searching the area, I heard whispers coming from behind the trees. I crept forward slowly, unsure what I would find. A group of witches sat together, others lying on the ground injured while one tried to help with their wounds. They saw me and straightened. I tensed, unsure if these witches were with me or against me.

A young woman, leaning against a tree gasped as she saw me.

"It's her," she said, eyes widening as a smile crossed her face.

Excited murmurs ran through the group, some stood and took a step closer to me. I hesitated a moment and then smiled. These must be the Fideles.

"Maybe I can help?" I asked, approaching one of the more severely injured witches. The man who had been tending to him nodded vehemently and stepped aside. I knelt down, healing the wounds I could see and sense. The main one a gaping hole in the man's side. The man gasped in relief and sat up.

"Thank you," he whispered. I nodded, and then tended to the others. I worked as quickly as I could, knowing I still had to find Jeremiah. After a few minutes I left the group who seemed eager to return to the fight.

I grew restless of searching soon after and teleported to Jeremiah.

25. SORROW

I found Jeremiah and Darien talking... or arguing. I took cover to eavesdrop on their conversation. Witches fought around them, but the two men somehow ignored it, deep in conversation.

"What are you doing?" Jeremiah asked Darien. "You have been part of this from the beginning. Why aren't you out there fighting for what you believe?"

"Because I don't believe in killing to gain power," Darien argued.

"Is that so? And when did this born-again behavior start? As of last week, you were willing to kill anyone who got in your way. Or was that only when Selena was involved."

"You leave her out of this."

"How can I? This entire situation we're in revolves around that girl! I need her powers to exact our revenge; she got her powers to stop me from destroying the world. You and your brother are in love with her. How exactly am I supposed to leave her out of it?" Jeremiah yelled.

"This is all your fault," Darien shouted.

"Oh, please don't throw a tantrum. This will all be over

soon, and maybe if you're lucky, she will choose you. But right now, you need to follow the path you already chose."

"I changed my mind," Darien said quietly.

"Really? Will your loyalties remain when she chooses your brother?"

"She already has."

I knew Darien was right. There really was no choice of who I wanted to be with. Tristan had my heart from the beginning.

Selena, where are you? Tristan asked, hearing my thoughts.

About to kill Jeremiah, I said back.

Tell me where? Tristan asked urgently. I ignored him and stood up.

"Jeremiah!" I called, stepping into his view. "Come and fight, you coward!" He spun and looked at me. "What are you scared of? Don't you want to try your new powers out?"

"So foolish, Selena. Why must you wake the sleeping dragon?" Jeremiah said suddenly standing right in front of me.

"Give me a break; you're more of an iguana than a dragon."

"You say that now, but you haven't seen what I can do." He snarled.

"How could I? You took off. What did you do? Run away and hide to play with your powers?"

"Why would I hide? As you say, I have unlimited power now."

"Because it's not your power. You stole it and you know you won't be able to keep it."

"Oh Selena, you do have a big mouth." Jeremiah merely looked at me, and a blue bolt sprang forth. I barely had time to deflect it, but the wind was knocked out of me, my chest feeling like it was on fire. I folded over, feeling like a deflated balloon. I gasped for air, but none came.

I focused my energy on thinking of a counter-attack. I was standing close enough to him, still buckled over trying to catch my breath, so I did what came naturally; I punched him in the groin. Now he buckled over too.

I guess I was still learning to rely on my magic first. Now that he was in pain, I was able to breathe again. I took in a few lungs-full and then swept my arm, throwing him backwards against the trunk of a nearby tree. He landed on his feet, brushing the dirt off his pants.

He sent a gust of wind that lifted me a few feet off the ground and threw me backwards into the crowd. I rebounded quickly and charged at him. The sight of me running headlong toward him distracted him from seeing the lightning bolt I sent. He tried to dodge it, but was a hair slow; the bolt struck Jeremiah in the shoulder. His eyes blazed as he stared at me, unfazed by my spell.

He pushed his arms out, twisting his wrists and a ring of fire sprang to life around me. The heat engulfed me, smoke seeping into my lungs. I coughed reflexively, and tried to move, but the flames were so close, if I moved even an inch I'd get burned. I raised my arm straight up, careful to keep away from the fire. Clouds roiled above, colliding, lightning streaking across the sky as water fell heavily, slowly, but eventually, putting out the flames. Standing, soaking in the rain, I began to cast another spell, just as Jeremiah flicked his wrist, sending me flying, and knocking me breathless again as I hit the ground hard.

I curled in on myself, my entire body aching, coughing out

smoke.

A movement to my right made me raise my head instinctively. There stood Darien, just watching. He wasn't fighting with anyone and he wasn't jumping in to defend Jeremiah. The ground suddenly started to shake and everyone still fighting stopped and widened their stances, throwing their arms out to regain their balance.

I saw Tristan run toward me then, and helped me to my feet. His spell bought me the time I needed to catch my breath and regain my strength. I stood tall and faced Jeremiah.

"This ends now," I said.

Jeremiah barked a laugh, "My, Selena you are quite dramatic. This will end when I say so."

I threw a miniature shield-sphere spell at him, but he deflected it.

Jeremiah sent an electric current at me, I blocked it, but the remnant voltage jolted through my body, throwing me onto my back. I lay there jerking while Jeremiah laughed.

Tristan shot fireballs at Jeremiah who blocked them easily and cast a paralysis spell on Tristan that froze him in place.

Tristan was able to move his head, but his body was immobile as if restrained by straps from shoulders to toes. He struggled to break free.

I managed to get to my feet and I sent a gale toward Jeremiah, and Darien standing next to him, was swept of his feet as well. I wasn't sure what spell was on Tristan but I waved my hand and willed him to be free and, to my amazement, it worked.

Tristan and I stood side by side alternating in casting spells at Jeremiah, but he was so strong now. He easily blocked our attacks and was able to cast offensive magic attacks just as quickly.

I crossed my arms over my chest and spread them open, sending a lightning bolt at Jeremiah. He leaped out of the way.

"Die!" He jerked his arms outward in an odd motion.

"No!" Darien yelled as he threw himself in front of me, receiving the full brunt of Jeremiah's attack.

Darien fell to the ground limp.

"Fool!" Jeremiah yelled.

In Jeremiah's moment of distraction, Tristan threw a whirlwind spell that hit his chest. Jeremiah fell backward. Tristan moved toward his fallen enemy. I knelt by Darien.

Darien lay on his back, eyes closed, skin pale as snow. I tried to shake him, but he wouldn't wake.

"Darien, get up!" I chided. But he was lifeless. Darien had died saving me. Although I had chosen Tristan for all intents and purposes, there was still a part of me that remembered wanting Darien. I knew he had done bad things, but he was right, he wasn't all evil. He was just misunderstood.

Suddenly I saw it; the image Lexi had seen of me and Darien lying together, caring for each other. I now knew what it was. It was a vision, a premonition of what I could have had with Darien if I chose him. So I guess my psychic abilities were progressing. Lexi saw it because I had subconsciously known it could happen. If I had chosen Darien and we walked away from all this, we could have had a good life together. That's why I kept feeling so strongly for him, because an alternate me-one in the future who made different choices - did.

He sacrificed himself for me, but I had thought all this time that Tristan would die for me while Darien took strength from darkness. Clearly Jeremiah had too, which is why he invested so much of his time in Darien. But maybe their mother had gotten through to them after all, making sure they always chose light.

But if one sacrificed himself for me and the other took strength from darkness, that meant...

I looked up to see Tristan hovering over Jeremiah, sparks shooting from his hands repeatedly like fireworks, Jeremiah twitching on the ground.

"Tristan," I said softly. He looked over for a second, long enough to read my facial expression, long enough to know his brother was dead.

Tristan's face contorted in rage. "You killed my entire family!" The shadows pulled from the trees and forest around us and sucked into Tristan. He unleashed a black ball of inky shadows, and it engulfed Jeremiah, causing him to scream in anguish.

I wasn't sure what to do. We needed to stop Jeremiah, stop him, kill him, whatever, so I wasn't sure I should stop Tristan just yet, but what was he doing to Jeremiah exactly?

"I'm making him pay for all the pain he caused us," Tristan said, hearing my thoughts.

"Jeremiah, it's over," I said. "You have a choice to make. We can release you-"

"What are you doing? You know we can't trust him!" Tristan sneered.

"You can either stop fighting, or die by Tristan's hand."

Through the anguished cries, I heard sporadic laughing. "No."

"No, what?" I asked confused.

"I will not stop, and I will not die!" The blackness engulfing Jeremiah started to recede.

"You can't let him get away. He will kill everyone," Tristan said through clenched teeth as he tried to hold his ball of blackness around Jeremiah.

Before I could think of what to do, Tristan lost his hold on the black prison, and Jeremiah barreled toward us. He knocked Tristan away and onto the ground.

"Die!" He screamed again and aimed his spell at me. This time Darien wasn't around to jump in front of me, and Tristan was still on his back.

The spell hit me and my chest felt like it was engulfed in flames. I landed on my side, unable to stand, the feeling of burning spread across my skin, across my entire body, and I screamed out with the pain.

"Selena!" Tristan yelled as he came toward me.

"Don't bother," Jeremiah sneered. "She's dying."

My body convulsed as it was encompassed by the heat.

"You're lying!" Tristan yelled.

"Whatever makes you sleep at night," Jeremiah retorted and then he buckled over and gasped in pain.

Tristan charged at Jeremiah and kicked him down.

I'm still alive. Still alive. How can that be? The burning pain receded, and I felt my skin for the burn scars I was sure would be there, only there was nothing. I still felt the heat in my chest and I reached up to touch the sensitive spot. I was expecting to find my scorching hot skin, only my hand closed around a searing stone.

I jerked my hand back reflexively and then looked down. There on my chest, sat the amethyst necklace Tristan had given me for protection. The stone which was usually purple was, at this moment, a bright red. I slowly got to my feet and saw that a green light shot from Tristan's hands, engulfing Jeremiah who was deflecting as much of it as he could. Jeremiah stood straight, sending blue light from his hands trying to dominate Tristan's spell.

"She's dead, just accept it!" Jeremiah yelled, but he sounded like he was drained.

"Soon you will join her!" Tristan yelled attacking Jeremiah.

"I'm not dead," I said loudly. Tristan stopped his attack and looked at me.

"It's not possible," Jeremiah yelled and cast a spell at Tristan who flew backward. Jeremiah turned to run like the coward he was, but then he gasped again in pain.

"No…" he said.

I looked at Jeremiah and saw that he looked pale, like all his energy and power was drained from him.

I looked behind me and could just make out some of the undead standing completely still. A white mist seeped out of their bodies and they collapsed.

"They took it back, didn't they?" I said.

"What?" Tristan asked.

"The witches, they're taking a stand. They figured out a way to take their powers back."

"It's not possible," Jeremiah said through clenched teeth.

I smiled. Jeremiah grimaced in pain and anger.

"Selena, whether or not he has power, he must be stopped,"

Tristan yelled.

"You can't stop me. It was foreseen!" Jeremiah yelled.

"If you recall, it was foretold that there cannot be darkness without the light. Did you forget that part?" I snapped.

Jeremiah stood tall, "You are too weak! You are nothing, and you will die as nothing. Just like your parents."

My blood rushed in my ears. My hands shook, and the entire forest shook with me. Clouds swept across the skies, and lightning and thunder erupted. Strong winds whipped around us and knocked Jeremiah off balance. My hair whipped around me, and Jeremiah's eyes widened in astonishment.

For a split second, I saw myself in Jeremiah's eyes. The wind blew my hair, my arms were outstretched, my eyes were wild and blazing with fury, and I glowed with the brightness of the sun.

I thought about the pride I felt for the spirit witches who heeded our warning and prepared themselves to get their power back. How could I doubt myself now, how could I not be strong enough to follow through and do my part? I couldn't. There was no more room in my life for self-doubt, only belief; belief in myself and what I was capable of.

"*You* are nothing," I said and I clenched my hands into fists and then flicked my fingers open. Jeremiah was lifted off the ground and I turned him so his body was facing me. He stayed still, arms and legs outstretched like a star.

"What are you going to do?" Jeremiah asked angrily. But I sensed the fear in his voice.

"Like I said, this ends now. You lose." I clenched my fists together again, releasing every emotion and bit of power I had in the motion. Jeremiah's body crumpled and he let out one long agonizing scream before falling dead to the ground. The storm died down, and I lowered my arms.

"Selena. Selena, are you hurt?" Tristan stumbled toward me, eyes wide with astonishment as he stared at my glow.

"I'm fine, thanks to you," I reassured him.

"To me? I was too far away to help, too slow to protect you."

"You did protect me though."

"How? What did he do to you?"

"The necklace you gave me blocked the spell. It absorbed the worst of it, but it hurt like hell," I explained.

"Absorbed…" Tristan lifted the now warm stone.

I nodded. "Thank you." I threw my arms around him and hugged him tightly.

"Stop thanking me," he mumbled, but he couldn't hold back a soft laugh.

"Are you okay?" I asked, looking him over.

"Yeah, fine." He nodded. But held his arm, where blood was streaking his skin.

"Here," I said, touching his wound and taking away his pain. "What about… the darkness?" I asked.

"What do you mean?"

"Darien died for me, and you got power from the shadows to engulf Jeremiah. Are you… I mean do you feel…"

"Evil?" Tristan asked.

"Yeah, I guess, for lack of a better word."

"No. I mean, I did feel great with that power, but it's like it was all directed at Jeremiah. Now that he's gone, I don't have a need for it, it's like it served its purpose," Tristan explained. He walked slowly toward Darien and knelt by him.

"Is it possible that your mom really did get you both to choose the light? That although you used the darkness, you only used it to defeat darkness, not to become it?"

"I think that's exactly it."

"I think Jeremiah was hoping Darien would use that power for his own benefit. He was shocked as hell to see that you were the one he should have been sucking up to," I managed to smile.

Tristan smiled, but then his face saddened.

They were still brothers, and I could see the loss Tristan felt. I stepped away to give him some privacy.

He knelt by his brother, whispering to him, and then kissed the back of his hand. He stood and faced me.

"Let's go," he said after a last longing look at his brother.

We rejoined the others in the forest who had been fighting their own battle.

"Jeremiah's dead," I said loudly so all my friends could hear. The Wayward who were nearby stopped fighting, unsure of what their path was now. After a moment, they ran away.

"Thank God you're alright!" Genevieve said.

"Thank God *you're* alright." I threw my arms around her and hugged her.

Lachlan, John, Fay, and Lexi were all there. They were all hurt one way or another, all scuffed and dirty, but none seemed injured beyond repair. They all stopped and stared at me. I decided to reel in my aura now.

Victoria came then with the remainder of her army, and ordered those who were well enough to detain the witches I had held captive in the sphere. I lowered the shield to allow them to do their job. I walked around the injured soldiers that stayed behind, healing them. I was exhausted, the adrenaline coursing through my body had vanished.

"The rest of the Elders are gathering the rest of Jeremiah's people," Victoria said. "They will be taken to the courthouse for trial."

"How many did we lose?" I dared ask.

"Well," Victoria started sadly. "We lost four Elders, and fifty-seven of the army."

"Plus Mrs. Ledsmith, Li and a few of our other friends," Lachlan added.

"So many," I said sadly. My friends nodded in agreement.

"I can't believe it's over," Genevieve said, as she walked to me.

"Me neither," I allowed myself to smile. Genevieve helped heal a few soldiers before she felt drained. She went to lean on Lachlan.

"Lexi!" A yell pierced the calm that had finally settled around us and my blood ran cold. I turned to see a witch wave her arms, sparks flying toward Lexi. "Get down!" John cried, throwing a fireball. Time seemed to slow as his arms flew out in front of him, the flames shooting from his fingers toward the witch. I met Lexi's gaze as the spell the witch cast hit her a split second before John's landed, engulfing the witch in flames.

Lexi fell to the ground and lay motionless. I ran towards her, my feet feeling as if they were encased in concrete. The witch's screams were muffled in my ears as I fell next to Lexi and rolled her over. She took shallow breaths and tried to open her eyes.

"Lexi. Oh my God, are you okay?" I asked automatically. A

tear rolled out of the side of her eye and she slowly shook her head no. "It's okay. I'll make you better." Tears blurred my vision as I took in the sight of my best friend dying. John huddled over her as I tried to heal her wounds. I didn't know what spell was used on her, so I wasn't sure how to heal it.

"Where does it hurt, hon?" I asked soothingly.

Lexi whimpered in response, and then she managed to point. I nodded and focused my healing energy above her belly, but it didn't feel like I was doing any good.

"Is it feeling any better?" I asked. Lexi shook her head. "Why isn't it working?" I yelled.

"She's too hurt," Tristan said stepping behind me.

"But I'm supposed to have super powers!" I yelled. "I have to fix her!"

"Selena," Lexi whispered. I looked at her, my hands fluttering everywhere trying to find something to heal. "Selena, stop."

"No. I won't stop! I can fix this," I said with determination. I placed my hands on her stomach again and tried to focus on it healing itself. "Genevieve!" I called, and I turned to see her push off of Lachlan in her haste to reach me. She stumbled, unable to hold up her weight, and Lachlan caught her around the waist before she fell. She looked at me, her eyebrows pulling together in sadness. She couldn't help me.

"John," Lexi started.

"I'm here, babe," he said, lifting her head and placing it into his lap.

"I hope you find what you're looking for," she whispered. "I hope you realize what makes you happy." A tear trailed down John's face.

"Don't talk like that," John said. "You'll be okay."

Lexi shook her head. "I won't."

"I'm so sorry, Lexi," he said. "I'm sorry I wasn't fast enough. I'm sorry I couldn't block the spell from hitting you."

"'Sokay," Lexi tried to smile, but let out a pained sob.

"I'm sorry. Did I hurt you?" I stammered.

"You can't fix this," Lexi said. "It's okay to let me go."

"No! I won't! I can't!" I yelled, my head swimming as dizziness hit me. I took a deep breath to regain my focus, ready to try again.

"You have been the best friend anyone could ask for," Lexi whispered, and started to cough. "Seeing what you have become, how your abilities are growing makes me happier than you know." Her shallow breaths quickening as she tried to speak. "I love you, you know that? You're my sister." She spoke so softly I had to strain to hear her. "Selena…" She said, but that was her last word. Her eyes stared unseeing at the dark night sky. John pulled her closer to him and held her.

"Lexi?" I cried. "Lexi!" Tristan pulled me into his arms, and I sobbed against his chest. Lexi was my sister, my best friend, my mother, everything and everyone I needed. She couldn't be dead, she couldn't!

I wrenched myself free from Tristan and threw myself at Lexi, placing my hands on her stomach, on her shoulders, everywhere, and I imagined her being whole and healthy. My brows pulled together in concentration and sweat beaded on my forehead as another wave of dizziness hit me.

"Selena, she's gone," Tristan said softly, touching my arm.

"No!" I yelled and continued to try and heal her.

"Selena, stop." Tristan's voice was soft. He pulled me back again and I let him.

"Why couldn't I save her? Why couldn't my powers be enough to heal her?" I asked through sobs.

"You're exhausted, Selena," Genevieve said. "You have nothing left."

"I never had a limit before!" I cried.

"You never used enough power to know. Your limit is much more than anyone else's, but she was hurt too badly. There was nothing anyone could do."

Tristan wiped away my tears. I listened to Genevieve's words, but all I heard was that I failed. I wasn't good enough, strong enough to save my best friend. I took one last look at Lexi in John's arms and felt my heart shrivel; I was on the verge of a meltdown, and maybe, when I felt like this was all over, I would allow myself to properly grieve. Not just for Lexi, but Artemis too, and all the other good, innocent people who died here today. I looked around at my fallen comrades – there were so many. The initial violence and rage dwindled with the fighters. Such a senseless battle.

"Selena," a faint voice said. Turning, I saw a faded image of a woman, hovering in the air and smiling at me.

"Sible?" I asked, astonished.

She nodded.

"Thank you for taking your powers back," I said.

"Thank you for warning us. Is there any way I can repay you?"

I thought for a moment, "Yes. Can I borrow the witches' powers to bring Lexi back?"

Her face fell, "I'm afraid it doesn't work like that. You can't bring someone back from the dead. I'm so sorry." She gave me a sad smile. "Is there anything else I can do?"

I shook my head, tears rolling down my face.

Sible cast her eyes down and vanished.

I let out an anguished moan, and laid my head on Lexi's chest.

"Oh, Selena," Tristan said.

I let out another frustrated growl before allowing Tristan to help me up. I let him hold me for a few minutes. I couldn't accept she was gone. Not Lexi.

I stood in silence, shock threatening to take over all my senses and felt sorrow and death around me.

"What do we do now?" I asked over a sob.

"Let's go home." Tristan wrapped his arm around my shoulder.

"Home."

The next morning Tristan and I had our luggage packed, ready to head back to Arizona. I hadn't slept much, but the prospect of finally going home gave me the energy I needed to get through the morning.

"You know they will be having a festival in your honor for what you've done," Genevieve said.

"What *we've* done," I corrected.

"Yes, we all worked together," Genevieve said. "But you need to understand that seeing you heal and fight encouraged the Elder's army and the Fideles. We succeeded not only because you were the only one who could defeat Jeremiah, but because your power and determination strengthened the army."

"I think you're giving me way too much credit," I said. "And anyways, I don't think anyone should be celebrating anything just yet. We need to have time now to grieve. Maybe in a while they can have a festival, in Lexi's name the way she wanted, and I'm sure Tristan and I will attend."

I looked at John's red-rimmed eyes. Fay stood behind him, rubbing his back comfortingly. I knew Fay hated Lexi being with John, but I had no doubt that she hated seeing him like this even more. I wondered if the psychic was wrong. Maybe Fay just needed to fight for it, like Artemis always had a plan, maybe this psychic did too. Only telling Fay what she needed to hear. I had a feeling that after John healed from this loss, he would see Fay for who she was – a woman who truly and unconditionally loved him.

I hadn't allowed myself to cry over Lexi yet. Not since her final moments. I would reserve that pain for a time I could be alone and could actually think it through. Everything was happening so fast, I couldn't stop to think about it now.

Tristan and I went upstairs to gather our belongings.

I packed the few items I had and then I went into Lexi's room.

"What do we do with her stuff?" I asked as Tristan moved behind me. I almost started bawling right there, but I forced myself to keep it together.

"Leave it," Genevieve said startling me. I didn't know she had come upstairs.

"You don't need any more to deal with," I said.

"No, I won't deal with anything. I like it here. I know that sounds weird, but it feels like Lexi's still here and might come back for her stuff."

"Won't that make it harder for you? To see her stuff here every day will taint your house even more, won't it?" I asked.

"Maybe, but if that happens I'll get Lexi's parents to pick it up. They may want it later." Genevieve closed the door to Lexi's room and we headed downstairs.

"Uh, with Lexi... gone... will that security spell stay in place?" I asked curiously.

"It should," Tristan answered.

"That's good," Genevieve said. "Lachlan and I can't teleport, so it doesn't hinder us, and it's a comfort. Just make sure the next time you visit you don't teleport in." She smiled.

"No offense, but I don't think I will want to see this cottage again for a while," I said.

Genevieve smiled, "I kind of feel the same way." She sadly looked around her now tainted home.

"Thank you all so much for your help. We couldn't have done any of this without you," I said taking in the sad, but relieved faces of my friends.

We all hugged each other and said our goodbyes. As we left Genevieve's cottage I looked at Tristan.

"Ready?" He asked.

"Actually, there's something I need to do first." I looked down at my hands as my fear spiked. I tried to rein in my emotions and do this one last thing before I could finally leave the Hidden City.

26. PROMISES

I couldn't go home yet, as much as I desperately wanted to. I had to do this before I lost the nerve, knowing it could be a while before I would get the chance again. I didn't plan to visit the Hidden City again for some time. Not that I didn't like it; it was just too painful to be there. The events were too raw to be able to appreciate the beauty and tranquility the city was finally able to obtain. As stories do, they were already spreading like wild fire. Overnight I had become somewhat of a celebrity, a savior, and that made me uncomfortable, because I still didn't think I was worthy. It was a reminder of my failures, the many people I couldn't save.

But there was one thing I could do, one wrong to try to right, a long over-due promise I had yet to fulfill.

I looked up at the quaint house before me; red brick, black roof, white door. I lifted my hand to knock when the sunlight glinted off an oddly shaped metal plaque.

"What is this?" I asked Tristan as my fingers traced the crossed arrows.

"It's an honorette; it means someone died in the line of

duty," Tristan answered in a soft whisper. He squeezed my hand, giving me the comfort I so desperately needed just then. I took a deep breath in an attempt to calm my nerves. "Are you sure you want to do this now?" Tristan asked. "We could come back another time, after you've had time to deal with everything."

"I'm sure," I whispered, though my voice wavered. I knew I had to do this, I just didn't know if I could. A lump formed in the pit of my stomach. I knocked on the door before I lost the nerve and a moment later I heard running footsteps from inside the house.

Just then the door opened and a young boy stood before me. His brown hair was rumpled and his sweet smile revealed his two front teeth were missing. He had his father's eyes and kind face, and for a moment I lost the courage to speak.

"Is your mother home?" Tristan asked kindly.

"I know you," the boy said softly, studying my face, and my insides turned to ice. "You're Selena."

"How--?" The question died on my lips as I saw images from the battle playing on an invisible screen in the middle of the living room. Witch news. Guilt and shame forced my eyes to the welcome mat I stood on.

"Who is it, Josh?" A female voice called from another room within the house.

"Mom, it's her!" Josh yelled back. "The one who saved us." I swallowed back a sob. Unworthy of the title. I couldn't understand how he could be excited to see me, when I was the reason his father was no longer in his life.

A moment later a middle-aged woman came to stand behind her son. A smile spread across her face, her ash-brown hair fell loosely to her shoulders and she wiped her hands on a towel.

"So it is." She beamed. "I'm Rebecca, and this," she ran her hand through the boy's hair, "is Josh. Please, come in." She ushered us inside her home. I looked around at the simple furnishings, the toys along the floor, the pictures hung up on the walls. I found myself staring at one picture with Hal smiling a large grin beneath his mustache, one arm wrapped around his wife, his other hand resting on his son's head. I looked away quickly.

Tristan and I sat on the couch, Josh bouncing on the seat across from us.

"Can I get you something to drink?"

"No, thank you," I answered, wringing my hands in my lap.

"To what do I owe this pleasure?" Rebecca asked, sitting on the other chair across from us. I licked my lips, unsure of how to start. Tristan clasped one of my hands in his own reassuringly.

"As you know," I started, "I spent a brief time with your husband, but it was one that saved my life…" I proceeded to tell them of that night, how Hal let us into the prison when the brakti were attacking, and how he so bravely gave his life for me, leaving out the gruesome details. By the time I finished the story, I was crying and so were they. The pride I saw in their eyes gave me little relief from my guilt. Rebecca had moved to the chair Josh was occupying, and she sat on the armrest, wrapping an arm around her son.

"I know this must have been very difficult for you," Rebecca said. "I am grateful you came and that my son was able to hear of his father's heroism, and from you, no less." She smiled sadly.

"I am so sorry," I whispered. "He was a good man." I blinked back the remnant of my tears and averted my gaze. Rebecca came and knelt in front of me, her hand on my knee.

"You have nothing to apologize for," she said, trying to catch my gaze. When I looked up I saw the sincerity of her words in her eyes. "He died, so you could save us all. It's what he would have wanted, and what we can now hold our heads high and honor him for. He will always be remembered as a savior in his own right. Please, know that this is not your fault." She smiled again and my stomach turned.

I couldn't find the words to respond, so I nodded instead. This was too much; how could she sit there, telling me that it was all right? My emotions threatened to engulf me and I felt the urge to run out of the house, away from the kindness and for-giveness I couldn't even bring to give myself. I stood, Tristan by my side.

"Thank you," I managed to whisper, and I gave her a hug. "If there is ever anything you need, ever," I emphasized, "please, call me."

She smiled, "I will."

I gave Josh a hug as well before we left. As we stepped out into the daylight I took a deep breath of the fresh air. I hoped I had done right by Hal. Although that was one of the hardest things I had to do, it was a step towards healing, and I knew I'd be able to come back here soon, with positivity and hope in my heart.

Tristan smiled down at me, his eyes shone with pride. He kissed the top of my head and wrapped a warm arm around my waist, pulling me toward him.

"So, daddy really was a hero," I heard Josh say as the door closed behind us.

The emotions that I had been bottling up finally bubbled to the surface. As soon as I sat in the car a sob escaped my throat and I placed my head in my hands and cried. Tristan held me until it passed.

Seeing how proud Hal's family was put things in a different perspective for me. One that I could understand, but still couldn't accept. At least not yet.

Tristan wiped my tears and held my face in his hands, gazing at me until I met his eyes. He placed a soft kiss on my lips and sighed as he got into the driver's seat.

As Tristan drove away from the small house, he placed his hand on my knee and an overwhelming sense of relief overcame me.

"You going to be okay?" He asked softly.

I surprised myself by nodding.

It was time to try and put my life back together.

THREE MONTHS LATER

Fall in Arizona is really a beautiful time of year. It's warm but not unbearable like the summer. I was finishing packing up some boxes, getting ready for my move, when I saw the book.

It was hard to believe that it had been just five months since I was only human. Five months since Lexi had been here in my apartment showing me our memory book. I ran my hand over the laminate surface and carefully opened the book. I read through our jokes and comments and allowed myself to cry.

We had a service in the Hidden City for our fallen friends and Lexi's parents came back to Arizona to clear out her apartment and get her affairs in order. They were understandably heartbroken, but they were strong. They knew, with their daughter protecting me, there was a chance she could get hurt, or killed. They all seemed to accept that risk, and the consequences. Still, I made myself promise to visit them often. I didn't want them to think they lost me too.

After we came home, I stayed in bed for a few days just to let myself cry over Artemis, Lexi, and even Darien.

I pressed the book to my chest and let the tears fall. I should be all cried out by now, but this wasn't the ugly, angry cry I had when I first came home. These were tears, silently shed over the loss of my best friend.

I returned to the task at hand, taking my belongings and locking the apartment door behind me for the last time. I placed the few remaining boxes in the small backseat of my Mustang, Lexi's book on the front seat next to me and I drove.

I thought a lot about what Artemis said: that whatever choice I made would be the right one. I knew that when the prophecy said I would have to choose darkness or light, it had two meanings.

The first was obvious; if I fought with Jeremiah I would have chosen darkness, but to fight against him, I chose the light. I chose to do the right thing, to follow the right path. Darkness wasn't even an option. I couldn't hurt those innocent people, or anyone I loved. Artemis knew that.

The other meaning wasn't so literal.

For Tristan and Darien, it wasn't about choosing good or

evil. I truly believe that Jordana had done right by her boys. I believe her telling them the bedtime story and teaching them to choose light allowed them to be inherently good even if the choices they made were sometimes bad.

In choosing Tristan, I indirectly chose darkness, not because Tristan was dark, but because he could wield the power from the shadows. Artemis told me that he was becoming who he was destined to be. Tristan used the sadness and anger of losing his parents and his brother to become stronger. Through that strength he was able to wield darkness, and in controlling it, he gained strength from it. Darien was light, not because he was so very good, obviously, but because he couldn't use or control the darkness the way Tristan could.

I do think about him from time to time, but not in the longing way I used to. I understand now that I longed for the possibility of what we could have been, but the reality was much different. Darien and I were never really meant to be together.

So occasionally when I think of him, I send him a thank-you for sacrificing his life for me.

I allowed myself to grieve for a month, and then decided to get myself together, pick myself up and get my life back on track. I was hired to work as a receptionist at the hospital, and when I would occasionally visit patients, they would miraculously heal. What a wonder?

No one knows I have magic, and I plan to keep it that way. I help those in need, and it makes me happy. The paycheck doesn't hurt either, even though it's not much.

"I thought you got lost," Tristan teased, opening my car door for me after I parked in the driveway. He had been great during the last few months. He stayed over at night to make sure I was alright, held me when I cried, gave me food when I forgot to eat because I was so consumed by sadness. He was my rock.

"Ha-ha." I got out and pulled the last boxes from the car.

"Is that everything?"

"Yup, my apartment's as bare as a bone." I looked at the fountain in front of Tristan's house... well my house now too, I guess. That would take some getting used to. Since Tristan's place was almost empty, we decided to use all my things and furniture to fill it up. That would hopefully make it easier for me to adjust.

We also decided that eventually we would settle in the Hidden City.

My eyes trailed along the red roof and over the garage, then stopped, and then bugged out of my head. "What the hell is that?" I stared at the green sports car sitting in Tristan's driveway next to his Camaro. Then I saw the Nevada plates.

"It's a Ferrari 599 Hy-Ker. Do you like it?" Tristan said smugly.

"It's freaking awesome! How can you afford that? Where did you get it from? When...?"

"Easy, detective. I'll tell you the story some time."

"You know I could just read your mind, right? Or I could tune into my newly heightened psychic senses and figure it out."

"Yeah, you could, but where's the fun in that?" Tristan reached down and pulled me toward him. I looked up into his yellow-specked green eyes, and he pressed his lips against mine. My head spun with the intensity of his kiss. He lifted me off my feet and carried me inside, my last few boxes forgotten.

Carol Rayyan is an avid reader of Fantasy and Paranormal Romance who decided to write her own trilogy, and create her own magical world. She grew up in Brampton, Ontario Canada but now lives with her husband Isa, and dog Chewbacca in Scottsdale, Arizona, where she is currently working on her next novel.

Questions or comments? Find her author page on Facebook.com or follow her on twitter @CarolRayyan

www.ingramcontent.com/pod-product-compliance
Lightning Source LLC
Chambersburg PA
CBHW030400180626
46812CB00005B/1871